Marta's Promise

A Novel

Marta's Promise

*Jeanne Dennis and
Sheila Seifert*

Publications

Marta's Promise: A Novel

© 2006 by Jeanne Dennis and Sheila Seifert

Published by Kregel Publications, a division of Kregel, Inc., P.O. Box 2607, Grand Rapids, MI 49501.

Library of Congress Cataloging-in-Publication Data
Dennis, Jeanne Gowen.
   Marta's promise: a novel / by Jeanne Dennis and Sheila Seifert.
      p. cm.
1. World War, 1939–1945—Refugees—Fiction. I. Seifert, Sheila. II. Title.
PS3604.E5864M37   2006
813'.6—dc22   2006021946

ISBN 0-8254-2489-5

Printed in the United States of America

06 07 08 09 10 / 5 4 3 2 1

To Axel and Beverly Johnson,
who taught me the importance of
family and history.
—Sheila Seifert

To my husband, Steve,
the hero of my heart.
—Jeanne Dennis

Historical Note

In 1765, the German emperor held no tangible power. The German state comprised more than three hundred individual regions, kingdoms, estates, and provinces, each governed by its own prince. Peasant men and boys were forced to fight their prince's battles in the Hundred Years War, and then the First (1740–1742), Second (1744–1745), and Third Silesian (1756–1763) Wars. By 1765, so many men and boys had been killed that the German princes found themselves running short of able-bodied peasants.

Also during this time period, the animosity between Papist Catholics and Lutheran Reformers sparked intense violence. Many governing princes tried to put an end to the bloodshed by ordering their subjects to convert to their own religious beliefs. Those who did not convert were either persecuted or forced to leave the region. More Papists lived in the south and more Reformers lived in the north; therefore, Reformers were more often persecuted in the south and Papists in the north.

In the midst of this upheaval, Czarina Catherine, a German woman who sat on Russia's throne and was known later as Catherine the Great, decided to invite her Germanic people to settle the vast steppes of Russia's Volga frontier. The settlers would not only provide crops for the country but also form a barrier between the Russian people and the fierce nomadic tribes that threatened their borders. In the German states, Russia advertised exemption from military service, free land, free houses, and travel expenses to all who would emigrate, even single women.

However, by 1766, the German nobility desperately needed peasants to work their land, so the emperor made emigration a criminal offense. Some German princes enforced his edict and others did not. In spite of the law, and the possibility of being killed for disregarding it, approximately thirty thousand men, women, and children (about eight thousand families) relocated to Russia from 1765 to 1768.

German immigration to Russia was handled by Russian commissioners, who hired recruiting agents (mostly French) to gather groups of families together to travel by means of the Baltic Sea to Kronstadt, a Russian island in the Gulf of Finland. To receive their land and houses, immigrants had to register at Kronstadt, no matter where they eventually settled. Some had to wait for months in makeshift twig shelters before they were allowed to enter Russia.

Unfortunately, after registration, many of the travelers did not receive their promised houses, tools, and livestock. Also, single women learned that they would not be given anything if they were not married. By this time, however, they were so far from home that most did not have the means or spirit to return. Soldiers were sent to guard this new human cargo—not to protect the settlers from nomadic tribes, but to keep them from returning to the German states. The immigrants often found themselves prisoners of the harsh climate, enforced poverty, and a primitive culture that treated them with contempt.

Although the following story is a fictional account about fictional characters, it commemorates the courage and determination of the German pioneers who forged a new life on the frontier of Russia's southern Volga region.

Russian names, words, and locations vary in their spelling, depending on the translation source. (For example, Kronstadt may also be spelled Cronstadt or Krohnstadt.) We have simply chosen the ones we prefer.

Chapter One

1766

The chill April wind whipped a strand of fine brown hair across Marta Ebel's cheek, as if punishing her for betraying her homeland. Though she looked like the other German women standing on Lübeck's splintered pier—homespun brown raiment, white apron, white cap, and wool cloak—Marta had no relatives to help her cart her goods to Russia. She fingered the document tucked in the waistband of her skirt and raised her chin. She might not be able to decipher the letters on this paper that promised her a new life, but she understood Russia's offer of a respectable future for unmarried women. The German states offered only a slow death of servitude or a life of shame for women without the protection of family.

Why is it treason to want a better life?

She smiled down at Hans Binz as his pudgy fingers slid over the top of her hand. His blond hair played in the breeze, reminding her of a younger Wilhelm, before the prince of her state had kidnapped him to fight in one of his many battles. She had never seen her youngest brother again. Hans beamed at her, completely unconscious of the smudge of dirt on his cheek or the perils of the journey ahead.

"*Guten morgen*, Fräulein Ebel," the five-year-old said. The excitement in his light blue eyes mirrored the hope in her heart. He pointed toward the harbor, where the turbulent waves seemed to be fighting battles of their own. "Today we shall sail on that big ship! It is almost my turn to go."

"True," Marta said. They glanced below the pier at the rowboat that would take them to the *Maria Sophia*. It creaked as another passenger settled onto its wooden slats. "You look like your father in your handsome boots and jacket," she said. Hans stifled a smile and brushed a hand over his white cuffs. He took a small step closer to the edge.

Too much was at stake to wait on the pier like sheep as the other emigrants climbed down into the rowboat one by one. Marta glanced behind her, searching the shoreline and Lübeck's wakening streets. She felt a growing tension with every passing moment.

"Make haste!" she wanted to cry as a man slowly lowered himself into the rocking boat, but she kept silent.

At last Herr Binz, whose sand-hued hair was tucked behind his ears and beneath his worn black hat, tossed a bundle into the boat and made room for his wife to step onto the ladder. "Mother first, and then you, Hans."

Frau Binz began the climb down, but then paused in her descent as if realizing that this was her last contact with German soil. She was a plain woman, whose large, compassionate eyes seemed to see only the best in people. When her lips formed a smile, which they often did, her joy was infectious. She smiled now, and her blue eyes scanned Lübeck one last time before coming to rest on her son and husband.

"Make haste, Mutter," cried Hans. Frau Binz laughed nervously and placed one foot and then the other into the boat.

The lead sailor bellowed, "Strike oars!" A wooden oar pushed against the pier, and the small boat jerked away. Frau Binz lost her balance and fell onto a woman's lap. Marta looked down and then quickly glanced behind her at the others on the pier. The sailors' actions seemed irregular.

"To the ship!" yelled the lead sailor.

As Frau Binz regained her balance, she called, "Don't abandon my husband and son. Turn back!" Yet the oars dipped in and out of the water in synchronized splashes. Perhaps seeing that they would not listen, Frau Binz leaned forward and appeared as if she were about to dive in and swim to shore.

Herr Binz yelled, "No! Abide there, Gretta. We shall come to you."

"Mother!" called Hans. A man with ale-numbed eyes and gray hair shoved Marta aside and dove into the frigid water after the boat. Hans turned to his father. "May we swim to Mother, also?" His father held him back.

"It is too cold," Marta explained. "You would not reach the ship."

The moment she finished speaking, she heard the first whispers. "Soldiers. The soldiers are come."

They heard a splash as Frau Binz plunged out of the boat and into the water.

Herr Binz pushed Hans toward Marta. "Take Hans. I shall return for him." Before she could agree, he dove into the water after his wife.

"Vater!" yelled Hans. "Mutter!"

Their fellow travelers, those closest to the cobblestone streets of Lübeck, grabbed their possessions and scattered. Marta's mind was wild with thoughts. Hans yelling. Footsteps pounding over the creaking wooden pier. People drowning. It was as if Marta could hear her mother's shrieks of fear—or worse, her father's silent acceptance of injustice all over again. She flattened her hand against the document in her waist, her guarantee of free land. She would not give up on life as her mother and father had. She could not.

"Mother is safe," said Hans. The sailors had disentangled Frau Binz's skirt from the oarlock and pulled her back into the boat. Herr Binz stopped swimming once he saw that his wife was safe, and turned to rescue the intoxicated man, who was now calling for help.

Herr Binz's voice, garbled by water, yelled, "Marta! Flee! Hide!"

Marta snatched up their goods, looping her canvas bags over her arms and clutching the rest with one hand as she grabbed Hans's arm with the other. "Make haste."

Hans clutched his bundle. "But Father—"

There was no time for explanations. They raced over the splintered wood, lugging everything they owned. At the edge of the pier, Marta caught her first glimpse of the advancing red jackets and black triangular hats.

Hans gasped. "Soldiers!" The company was moving toward them along the river's edge. Marta fumbled and then released her bundles, her last tie to the past and the evidence that she was an emigrant. The bags slid to the ground with a thump. She yanked Hans's belongings from him, and hand in hand they raced into Lübeck's narrow streets.

—⸙—

Carl Mueller stood outside the blacksmith shop savoring a warm bite of brötchen. Emigrants were fleeing past him into the city through the arched entranceway of the docks. Carl brushed a hand through his dark hair and chewed contemplatively. Herr Schmidt gave recruiting agents a bad name. Once Schmidt got his emigrants to sign their contracts, he did not look out for them. Carl took another bite of his roll and brushed the crumbs from his brown silk vest. He could do nothing for any of them now. Besides, he had problems of his own.

"We shall all die," a woman shrieked as she trundled past.

"No," said Carl under his breath, "you shall not die; but you may wish you had." Rotting in a prince's prison was a horrible way to live. From the folds of his shirt he withdrew a small gold box, won the previous night in a wager with an officer. The soldier had seemed to dote on the trinket with the ornate *S* engraved on it. Perhaps Carl could change his last name again to something starting with an *S*. He had been Hernandez in Spain, Moore in England, and was now Mueller in the German states. His true surname was French, but he had not used it since he was a child. *S*. He would need to think of a Russian surname that began with *S*. The scent of fish drifted from the fishmonger's doorway next to the blacksmith's shop and seemed to attract a white stork on a nearby roof.

A young woman with flushed cheeks turned the corner and stopped in the middle of the red-cobbled street. Carl slid the gold box into his shirt and raised his eyebrows. Her hair was a soft brown and of a texture that begged a man to run his hands through it. Except for a few loose strands, it was pulled back severely, hidden beneath a white cap. Her dress was plain, covered by an apron and a wool cloak, in the style of an emigrant who had traveled from the southern German states. She held tightly to her child's hand but stood only a few handbreadths taller than the lad.

With a quick look around, she stepped forward and asked Carl in a soft, unhurried voice, "I would have your barrel. What price do you ask for it?"

Carl glanced behind him. "The one beside the crate?" Lengths and coils of discarded rope hung over the edge of the barrel and tilted it at a slightly precarious angle.

"Yes."

"The rope is of no value," he said.

"It matters not," she replied. "I require only the barrel."

Carl thought her request odd, until he realized what she was asking. He threw his brötchen to the ground and grabbed an armload of rope from the barrel. While others were whining of their own demise and running haphazardly into dead-end lanes, this woman had come up with a scheme. He grabbed another armful of twine and tossed it on top of the refuse. Without asking permission, he clasped his hands around the woman's waist—such a small girth—and lifted her into the barrel. She gave him a ghost of a smile before sinking into the oversized bin.

Quickly, Carl lifted the child onto his mother's lap and said, "Set your faces by the knotholes to breathe." He tossed a weathered piece of canvas over them and returned some of the ropes to their previous positions.

"What are you doing there?" demanded the blacksmith, looking out of his open side window.

"I'm waiting for my horse to be shod," said Carl.

"That you, Mueller?" The blacksmith poked his head farther out the small hole. "Thought it was one of those traitorous emigrants. Cannot have 'em here. Won't let soldiers take my shop for the likes of them."

"It's a bad business," said Carl. Down the road, the doors to houses and stores slammed shut, seeming to echo "You are abandoned" to the fleeing emigrants. Carl continued, "Is my horse ready?" The blacksmith muttered an unintelligible reply and left the window.

Carl leaned against the barrel. Although it appeared to be teetering at a precarious tilt, it was firmly lodged between a crate filled with scrap metal and a pile of hay. The hiding place was ingenious. A woman who could think quickly under pressure might be of value to him, and a boy who was old enough to keep from crying but young enough not to ask too many questions could serve him well. Besides, the woman was . . . well, she was beautiful. Her large blue eyes, almost violet, had caught his attention even before she had demonstrated her ingenuity. He had been looking for a way to smuggle himself back into Russia, and now a ready-made family had found him. He smiled.

The clipped march of the soldiers echoed between the buildings, causing the exhilaration of risk to heighten his senses. Carl stood alone on the abandoned street. Although he knew he should leave, he could not. The fishmonger finally closed his door. Clearly, he would make no more sales until the emigrants had been removed.

In the distance, Carl heard a woman yell, "My babies! God save my babies!"

"Filthy traitors," yelled a voice from an upstairs window. "You shall be fodder for the birds."

Soldiers poured into the narrow road. For a while, Carl watched them roughly hauling emigrants toward wooden carts meant to carry animals. His lips tightened. Russia would pay Herr Schmidt for the few poor souls he delivered from this botched affair, but they would not pay Carl for all the immigrants he had safely transported. He wrinkled his nose. The air still smelled of fish.

"You there," demanded a young soldier, moving closer. "Depart this street now." Carl straightened his long frame so that the brocade and fine wool of his outfit would not be lost on the youth as he towered over him. "Wait!" The soldier looked around him. "How can I be certain you're not an emigrant?" Although the soldier's expression did not change, he now stood taller. "I arrest you in the name of the prince!"

"Arrest me? Lübeck is governed by a league, not by a prince." Carl dusted a speck of imaginary dirt from the sleeve of his jacket and let his eyes slide down the youth's slender frame as if he were of no consequence. With a condescending sigh, he removed the small gold box from the folds of his shirt. "Take me to an officer in your regiment immediately."

"Lübeck gave my prince leave to—" The soldier's eyes focused on the trinket in Carl's hand. "Where did you get that?"

Carl gave the youth a condescending glance and waved a hand in the air to show his impatience. "I am a Lübeck resident, and a close friend of your superior officer. I wish to see him immediately." The boy licked his lips as if deciding his next course of action. Carl almost felt sorry for the lad, but he looked well fed and too full of his own importance to garner much sympathy. Because of the many years that Carl had had to fend for himself without family or friends, he had learned how to read people's faces. He could see that even though the young soldier wore a uniform, an emblem of power, his eyes were uncertain.

Carl looked away. A stocky woman with a large scar on her left cheek was pulled past him toward the wooden wagons. She did not go with the soldiers meekly, like many of the others had. She fought, spit, and called them names the entire way. She was a stubborn one, a survivor.

"Arrest me now, and take me before your captain," said Carl as he shifted his gaze to the dark clouds stirring overhead, "or go about your business."

The boy neither moved nor lowered his weapon. "I mistook you for an emigrant."

"Do I flee?"

"No."

"Do I bear the raiment of an emigrant?" Carl held out his arms so that the youth would not miss the gold watch fob or his exquisite, embroidered cuffs.

"No, sir."

"Well then." Carl closed the gold box and placed it back within the folds of his clothing. "The time is come for you to be off. There are emigrants to catch, and I wish to finish my transaction with the blacksmith."

With a quick nod that could have been mistaken for a bow, the soldier hurried away. Carl tried to hide his smile. The lad was probably relieved that he'd gotten off so easily.

When everyone was out of earshot, Carl said softly, "Abide here. Do not move until I return. I shall draw attention to the barrel should I remain."

He thought he heard a soft, "I thank you," but was not certain if it was the woman's voice or just the movement of a breeze.

He called through the window, "Blacksmith, I shall return for my horse as soon as the streets are cleared of traitors." Then he thought, *Perhaps now that I have a means to enter Russia, I can sell the horse for a good price.*

Marta's rescuer whistled as he walked away. Perhaps he did not whistle to reassure her, but somehow she thought he had. His commanding presence reminded her of a prince from a fairy tale her mother had once told her. Maybe that was why she had trusted him. She leaned her head against the barrel. But what if she were mistaken about his character? Would he turn them in for a reward? How could she trust a complete stranger? Her head tilted forward. It was his face—the square, determined jaw and compassionate brown eyes. That's why she trusted him.

"Are we going to die?" whispered Hans.

"No," she whispered back. "Hold your tongue, or they shall hear us." Was she wise to trust the only person in Lübeck who seemed to care whether she lived or died? No, she decided, trusting a stranger with their lives was too great a risk. They would need to leave their hiding place immediately, before he returned. She would find Herr Binz. He would know what to do.

Marta heard the muffled screams of other emigrants as they were caught and thrown into wagons. Their wails echoed through the streets, conjuring pictures in her imagination of writhing bodies being cast into hell. She shivered. She glanced out her knothole at the bedlam. Perhaps she and Hans could wait a bit longer before finding a new place to hide.

Townspeople watching from upper story windows began jeering with such intensity that their taunts were only occasionally drowned out by the harsh cries of the soldiers. Marta and Hans, confined within the wooden walls of the foul-smelling barrel, were faring better than those in the open. Turning slightly, Marta was able to get a better view through the knothole. It appeared that at least half of the two hundred people she had wintered with in the barracks outside of Lübeck had been captured.

The air inside the barrel was putrid; it smelled of manure and mold. If only she could breathe fresh air again. Her legs tingled. She inhaled deeply through the knothole, almost sucking in a fly that buzzed nearby.

Despite the horror, she could not keep herself from watching her fellow emigrants being herded into the wagons. At the sight of their fearful faces—men, women, and children whose hopes had turned to despair—compassion gripped Marta's heart. A noisy clatter drew the attention of the soldiers to the far side of the square. At the same moment, Marta saw a scramble of movement underneath one of the carts, and a figure emerged from the shadows. As light fell on his face, she recognized Herr Binz. He untied the prisoners nearest him and motioned for them to run. Marta recognized one of the women, the stocky one with the scar, as Frau Doenhof. She ran faster than Marta had ever seen her move as the escapees darted into the side streets.

With renewed vigor, the officers shouted commands to the soldiers, but as the regiment prepared to move the wagons forward, another noise, along with a scream, drew their attention away. For a second time, Marta saw Herr Binz emerge from the shadows.

He was sneaking back toward the wagons when a rough voice from an upstairs window yelled, "There's one. Another dirty emigrant!" The prisoners in the carts began to yell as if to drown out the warning, but it was too late. A soldier leveled his musket and ordered Herr Binz to halt. Instead of obeying, he darted out of Marta's view.

The captain called, "Volker! Ericks! Fetch him." The two men hurried away. The captain continued, "Forward." The carts started rolling away, probably toward a prince's dungeon.

"What is happening?" asked Hans.

"Shush!" said Marta sharply. "Do not speak another word."

Once the carts had disappeared, the street grew quiet, except for the occasional scream or shout when a stray emigrant was found. Hans's body felt like deadweight, his head sweating against Marta's neck. He had fallen asleep. Sweat trickled down her chest.

As she tried to readjust her position in the barrel, she heard footsteps nearby. Had she been discovered? Was the stranger coming back for her? The ropes above her began to move as if someone was frantically pushing the lengths aside.

Fear gripped Marta's heart. This was the end. There was nowhere to run. She pulled her arm from Hans and positioned it near her face. She would scratch her assailant's eyes out if she had to. Her attacker might win the battle, but she would make sure he never forgot the day he captured Marta Ebel. The moment the canvas was removed, her hand shot out.

Herr Binz came into view, and he moved his face aside to avoid her attack. Her hand froze in midair. He glanced at Hans, gave her a quick smile, and immediately pushed the canvas back in place and piled on the ropes. She watched him through the knothole as he sprinted to the other side of the street.

"There he is!" a deep voice shouted.

Booted feet rushed past the barrel. All Marta's muscles tensed. Herr Binz had almost reached the corner. He was almost safe. The sound of a shot echoed through the street, and Herr Binz's body lurched forward, landing facedown on the cobblestones. Marta stifled a cry that almost suffocated her in the stale air of the barrel. This could not be happening. She closed her eyes. In her mind, she saw Herr Binz's kind blue eyes and his strong hand reaching out to hold her father's wrinkled hand. The thought of his merry smile was almost too much for Marta. She wanted to do something to help him but knew she could not move without endangering his son and herself.

By the time she opened her eyes, Herr Binz's body lay unmoving on the ground. She could feel tears welling up from deep within her heart, forming a lump in her throat, but she did not cry. She had not cried when her brothers had been taken away, one by one, to fight. She had not cried when her mother died of a broken heart in the Rheinland. She had not cried at her father's funeral outside of Lübeck. She would not cry now.

Marta could not tell how late in the afternoon it was when the boots of Lübeck's residents again clipped down the cobbled street. She watched a soldier grab Herr Binz's collar and drag his lifeless form in the direction of the docks. Her arms instinctively enfolded Hans. They were truly alone, and the boy needed her now just as she had needed his parents when her father was dying. She recalled how tenderly Frau Binz had nursed her father during his illness, even when no one else would draw near to him for fear of catching his disease. The compassion of the Binzes had meant so much to her. It was Herr Binz who had said the final prayers over her father's cold body. She shivered.

And now, Herr Binz was dead, killed while protecting her as well as his son. She wished she could say the same prayers for him now, but she didn't know how. Herr Binz prayed differently from the other Reformers she knew. Marta could almost feel God's love in his words.

Grieved as she was, questions had plagued Marta. She had always been a good Reformer, helping her mother tend local widows and orphans, but Herr and Frau Binz seemed to have something more. She had planned to ask them about their faith on the ship, but now it was too late. Her chest heaved as she again fought off the urge to cry.

Under her breath, Marta whispered, "I shall do all in my power to take you to your mother, Hans. All. I promise." She leaned her face against his silky hair. By sheer strength of will, she pushed the horror of Herr Binz's death from her mind. She had to think clearly. She had to concentrate on getting Hans and herself to Russia. That is what Herr Binz would have wanted. Marta set her jaw. Nothing would stop her.

Gradually, new noises invaded the silence. Vendors returned, rolling their wheeled carts down the bumpy streets. Voices called. Merchants answered questions. Even the blackbirds and sparrows overhead chirped and trilled. Marta was thankful that the blacksmith and others ignored the trash heap where the barrel stood, especially when Hans began to move. He was waking up.

She covered his mouth and said, "Lie still. We're still hiding in the barrel." She felt him relax. No sound escaped his lips.

The rest of the day passed slowly. Marta could no longer feel her legs. She was not even certain that she would be able to move her body from the confines of the barrel when the time came. She wondered whether the stranger would really come back for them and listened for his approaching footsteps. Her mouth tightened. She was ashamed of herself. Whether he returned for them or not, she must depend only on her own resources. Whatever was to be accomplished would be up to her.

At dusk, Marta heard the first sounds of thunder. She readied herself. The storm rumbled closer, and the darkness outside grew deeper. Through the knothole, she saw heavy raindrops splattering on the cobblestones. It was time.

"Hans, I shall stand now." She forced her legs to work. She stood up with Hans in her arms, scattering ropes over the junk heap. People running for cover in the growing darkness paid them no heed. Marta leaned over the top edge of the barrel and held Hans until he was able to set his feet down on a neighboring crate. Marta pointed, and Hans scampered down the crate to the cobblestones below. He gulped at the rain.

She looked around her at the raindrops skittering and sliding across the indifferent city as feeling gradually returned to her legs and feet. She hoisted herself up to the barrel's edge and then threw a leg over it, causing the barrel to tilt farther. Not wanting to knock the barrel completely over, she quickly threw her other leg and skirt over the opening and hopped out. Only when her feet were firmly on the street did she brush the hay and rope fragments from their hair and clothing, and let the water slide into her mouth.

"We shall seek shelter." Marta ducked her head to shield her eyes from the rain. The steady patter turned into a downpour. The water was cold, but it felt good after their long stay in the barrel. Before long, though, it had soaked their clothes. Fortunately, it also hid them from evening onlookers. The rain would also wash away the barrel's smell, Marta thought.

She took Hans's hand and said to herself as much as to him, "We shall be safe if we can find shelter in a Reformed church tonight."

Hans nodded. "I see one." He pointed to a majestic spire towering over the buildings around them.

Marta did not mention the many other ornate churches silhouetted against the angry sky. By their spires alone, Marta could not tell which belonged to the Reformed Church of Martin Luther and which housed the Catholic Papists. She supposed that Hans's guess was as good as any.

"We must depart with haste." As they ran toward the church he had spotted, Marta whispered, "Please, may this building be for Reformers." With dread filling her heart, she prayed as if their lives depended on the outcome of Hans's choice. Deep inside, she knew they did.

Chapter Two

M arta stood at the bottom of stone steps and visually traced the lines of the cathedral with her eyes. Papist hands had surely built this structure. Yet German churches changed the services they housed as often as the ruling prince changed his faith. She picked up a section of her skirt so that she could climb the steep steps to the enormous church. The rain pelting the rough, wooden doors in front of her suddenly metamorphosed into soldiers ramming into her parents' home, swords in hand. She stopped, afraid she would see the same vindictive bishop standing before her with the flaming torch he had used to burn her family's home and vineyard.

"My mind deceives me," she muttered. She let go of the handful of homespun material she held, causing her skirt to drop back limply to her ankles. Rain stung her face, a thousand icy slaps, as water ran down her neck in rivulets and slid beneath her clothes. Simultaneously, lightning streaked the sky and thunder echoed off the stone edifice. She caught her breath, inhaling a mixture of fresh air and moisture so thick she felt she could drown.

"Fräulein Ebel?" Hans yelled. "What ails you?" Only the expression in Hans's eyes gave Marta a hint of the terror he was feeling.

She turned her face away from him. Lübeck was part of the Hanseatic League, she told herself. A prince did not rule it. Both Reformers and Papists lived here. Still, deep inside, a slow-rising panic urged her to flee.

"Fräulein Ebel?" repeated Hans. A couple soaked by the storm hastened past them and entered the church. Hans glanced nervously around the darkened street.

"Are not the doors beautifully carved, Hans?" No matter what she feared, she would not subject Hans to the same torment she felt. With a determined step, Marta pulled open one of the heavy doors.

The pungent smell of burning candles assaulted her in the entryway, a vestibule larger than most of Lübeck's piers. Deep shadows flickered against the rough-cut, stone walls.

From the dim interior, she heard a woman in a dark red cape with twisted gold cording say, "But Könburg is yet a day's ride hence. The roads shall be filled with mud."

A gentleman with a bored expression reassured the well-dressed woman, "Fret not. I have seen worse storms. It shall pass."

Marta noticed that some of the other people were drenched like Hans and her. Others looked as if they had sought shelter at the first signs of the storm.

Marta hoped the foreboding she felt was nothing more than her stomach craving food or her heart aching with loss. She caught Hans's arm so they would not be separated and pulled him toward the second set of doors that led from the vestibule into the sanctuary.

A man's harsh voice rose above the others, "The number of dirty traitors caught exceeds one hundred—"

Marta took an involuntary step away from him. Thunder obscured the rest of the man's words. When the rumble subsided, the many conversations around them blended into one intangible dialogue. Marta hoped that she and Hans looked like other drenched peasants. As she moved forward, she searched for familiar faces but was disappointed. She recognized no one from her emigrant group.

Hans whispered, "I do not like this place."

She gave his shoulder a squeeze and pushed open the sanctuary doors, guiding him inside. Candles lit the lower portion of the cavernous room, small islands of light in an enormous sea of darkness that shrouded the upper walls and ceiling. Marta could feel the tomblike staleness permeating her senses. She shivered and wrapped her cloak tighter. Hans's icy fingers found her hand as he pressed his body against her soaked skirt, causing a chill to run up to her neck.

Slowly her eyes adjusted, and she surveyed the dark interior. The stone floor was barren of benches, allowing people to rest wherever they wanted. Even their winter barracks seemed small in comparison to the enormous sanctuary. Alcoves on either side of the main room, each large enough to contain all the Reformed believers in Marta's hometown, lined the walls. The echo of muffled voices rose and fell with the fury of the storm. Somewhere in the darkness, a child giggled.

Marta walked toward a shadowed area on the empty side of an alcove, pulling Hans behind her. With each step, she had to carefully push her legs past the weight of her dripping skirt so as not to slip on the damp floor. At least the walls thwarted the storm's effort to siphon all remaining heat from her body.

"Those candles rest behind bars," whispered Hans, pointing to the front of the church.

"To prevent thievery," Marta said.

Hans drew closer. "Is this a prison?"

Marta shivered at how close he might be to the truth, should this prove to be a Papist church. Keeping her voice calm, she said, "In the city of my birth, travelers may lodge all the night in the church. Everything of value stands behind the iron grate." In a lower voice that she hoped would not bounce off the stone walls, she added, "We shall not go to prison, Hans. I shall find a way to take you again to your mother."

"And to my father?"

She put her finger to her lips and led him to a spot at the base of an enormous pillar. "We shall rest here." The pillar would muffle their words.

Marta sank to the ground. The stones on the floor, red like those of every other building in Lübeck, were cold but dry, except where their clothing had wet them. Hans sat down and shivered against her.

"Fräulein Ebel," he whispered. "Will my father be able to find us here?" His thin voice carried and then hung in the air between them. "Fräulein, shall we not look for Father when the rain stops?"

When Marta still remained silent, Hans was insistent. His voice rose above the storm's fury. "We must find Father!"

As the child's last words echoed, the sound wrenched Marta's heart. Slowly she wrapped her arms around the boy's shivering form. How could she tell him the truth? If ever she needed wisdom from above, it was now. Marta tried to remember how Herr Binz had prayed the times when she could almost feel God's love reaching down to her. How she wished she had asked him the secret of his faith.

She took a deep breath and lowered her voice so she would not be overheard. "Hans, I shall answer you, but you must hold your peace, else we shall be in grave danger. Do you understand?"

He turned his head to look up at her and nodded. His eyes were filled with so much trust, so much innocence, that she had to look away. He was only five. Five short years that would now stretch into a lifetime without his father's love and protection.

"Do you remember when we hid in the barrel?"

He nodded again.

"Your father found us in the barrel while you slept. He said nothing, but I know that he was pleased to see you safe."

"Where did he go?"

"The soldiers came."

"No! Did they arrest him?"

Marta choked on her next words. "No, I fear not." The boy looked confused, and she continued. "Hans, I once heard your father say that if a person has put his faith in Jesus, he shall never die." His look of confusion suddenly turned to horror. He pulled away. Marta placed her finger to her lips to remind him of his promise. When she did not deny the question in his brimming eyes, he buried his face in her homespun skirt, his whole body shaking with silent sobs.

She drew him closer and gently rocked his small form the way she had held her mother after their eviction, the way she had held her dying father. She could no longer ignore the pain. Once again, she felt the unrelenting grief of bereavement crushing her chest. How she had longed for release from it after each parent's death.

How could Hans bear it? He was so young! His mother was on her way to Russia, and his father—good Herr Binz—was dead. Hans had no one but Marta now. The two orphans clung to each other on the stone floor, Hans's tears mingling with the wetness that already soaked their clothing.

When his silent tremors subsided, he fell asleep, spent, in Marta's arms. His small form on her lap comforted her. She felt ashamed of the new feeling rising within her. Heaven forgive her, but a small part of her rejoiced who she was not alone anymore. She had another human being who needed her and cared whether she lived or died—even if it was only a five-year-old boy.

Suddenly, a huge flash of lightning forced its terrifying brilliance through the stained glass windows and lit the sanctuary. From their elevated lairs, the holy smiles of elaborate icons mocked her. Terror filled her heart as the light confirmed her worst fears. They were in a Papist church.

Marta peered into the gloom, willing herself to summon the courage to flee. But where could they go? If only the pounding in her head would subside. Her panic crescendoed when she heard the grating noise of iron twisting against iron from the front of the sanctuary.

A priest, candle in hand, entered from behind the grillwork. Marta had heard enough sermons about Papist priests being the devil's servants. She knew she had to flee at that moment, but with Hans resting on her, she could not move without drawing the cleric's attention. She tried to squeeze her body against the pillar as she watched the religious leader's black gown move from one set of people to the next.

She could not see his face, but she heard his clear voice ask each person, "Son, how do your children fare?" or "Daughter, are you well?" The light from his candle danced eerily closer and closer as the priest meticulously greeted each lodger. Then his candle shone on Marta.

"Good evening, Daughter." Red freckles peppered the white-haired man's face.

"Good evening," she answered. Under burgundy-feathered brows, his pale eyes seemed to peer into Marta's soul. She averted her gaze and stared at Hans's sleeping form. Marta heard the rain, a slave to the wind's fury, pelting the church. The commotion outside seemed tame compared to the cacophony of her pounding heart and racing mind.

The priest bent closer, and she forced herself to face him. "I have seen you not before this night. I am Father Dominick." His eyes drifted to Hans as Marta's stomach growled audibly. She searched for something Papist to say that would keep him from suspecting who they were.

The priest smiled. "It would be a blessing to sleep like a child again."

"Yes," Marta agreed in a faint voice. Perhaps it was best to say as little as possible.

"He is a handsome boy, Daughter," Father Dominick continued. Hans sighed with the ragged breath that follows only the bitterest tears. Marta placed her hand protectively over him and nodded.

Father Dominick smiled again, turned from Marta, and moved away. After a few more greetings, he went back through the door in the grillwork. Relief washed over her.

"Hans," she whispered. The howling wind and booming thunder drowned her voice. "Hans," she said more urgently. The boy opened one eye and then closed it. "Hans, there is danger. We must get away." Of course she had not recognized other emigrants here. Papists and Reformers may live side by side in Lübeck, but no Reformer would willingly enter a Papist church, escaping possible imprisonment for certain death. They needed to leave before the priest reported them, or worse.

Hans did not move. Marta tried to pick him up but could not. He was too heavy. She was too tired. Her body would no longer obey her commands. In order to escape, she would have to leave without Hans, and that she would not do. She leaned against the pillar and closed her eyes. She did not have enough strength to resist what would surely come next. She wondered if this was how her mother had felt before she succumbed to a broken heart after the prince stole her last boy from her and she knew she would never see him again.

No! Marta would not allow it to end like this. She refused to allow one tear to flow past her eyelids. She put her hands beneath Hans's armpits to lift him, and then heard the priest's door creak open again. She removed her hands and leaned back as if she were asleep. His measured steps moved directly toward her. What could she do? She pulled Hans closer.

"Daughter," the priest said. Marta gritted her teeth, grasping for a final measure of strength to stare death in the face. Purposefully, she looked up. The priest held a loaf of bread, a cup of water, and a wool blanket. "Take these."

Marta's mouth opened to respond and then closed. His actions confounded her. Tears rose to her eyes.

The priest continued, "I can forgo one night's bread; you and your child should not."

Not trusting her voice, Marta nodded her thanks. She tucked the blanket around Hans and herself and then took the loaf and cup from him. Perhaps her mother would have scolded her for taking food from a Papist priest, but Marta was too confused to worry about which rule of Scripture she might be breaking, or even if there was such a rule. The bread's fresh aroma silenced her scruples. She set the loaf in her lap.

"You hail not from Lübeck?" the priest asked.

Keeping her voice steady and ignoring her hunger pangs, she said, "We visit from the Rheinland." At least that was true. She hoped he would not ask where they were headed.

"There has been much bloodshed. You are fortunate to live in the south. We are few here in the north."

Marta looked away. He had mistaken her for a Papist. What should she do now? How did a Papist act? She looked back at him. The priest's brow drew together as he continued to study her. She fidgeted under his stare.

In a low voice, he said, "One hundred and fifteen emigrants

of Martin Luther's Reformed Church were imprisoned this day. Others were killed."

Marta stared at the bread. He knew. She was an emigrant. She was a Reformer. And the priest knew it.

Father Dominick continued, "Lodge here this night. This night you are safe."

Her mind frantically raced for words to muddy the truth, but she could not bring herself to lie. "I thank you. The church will shield us from the storm."

Father Dominick gave her a slow smile. "You have weathered many storms this day. I shall guard the doors to keep safe all who seek refuge in my church."

After Father Dominick bade her good rest and positioned himself in front of the distant sanctuary doors, Marta stared at the place where he had stood. With every taste of the warm, coarse bread, her confusion increased. A priest had fed and warmed her. A Papist priest! He had been kind to her, but could she trust him? Was he guarding the doors to keep soldiers out or to prevent her escape?

Nothing made sense. Her brain hurt with strange and possibly heretical thoughts. Could the priest be truly good and not evil? She shook her head. He had to be a wolf in sheep's clothing. Marta covered the remaining loaf in a fold of the blanket and closed her eyes. She did not fight sleep as it seduced her into its numbing blackness.

She felt herself running, searching for something or someone. Around every corner, a soldier lay in wait, ready to pounce on her. A staccato thunderclap. Herr Binz fell to the pavement. Suddenly, she held her father's cold form. A scream caught in her throat. A child's hand reached for hers, and then it was gone. *Hans! Where was Hans?*

Marta's eyes startled open. It was still dark. A bony hand was clasped over her mouth. She tried to jerk her head away as she recognized Father Dominick, but he held her in place. What would he do to her? The occasional muffled snores of others met her ears.

"Daughter," Father Dominick whispered. "The authorities shall

search for stray emigrants now that the storm has passed. You are
in danger." The priest released his hold and rolled back onto his
knees. Marta leaned forward and felt the chill of her damp clothes
rub against her skin. In a low voice, Father Dominick asked the
person beside him, "Are these your wife and child?"

Marta looked up into a candlelit face and recognized the man
who had helped her hide in the barrel.

"Yes," he said. "This is my family."

Fear, more than cold, sent shivers through Marta. She must still
be dreaming.

"Come," the stranger said, "We must make haste."

How had the stranger and the priest found a way into her dream?
The stranger lifted Hans effortlessly to his chest and started moving away from her. Nothing in Marta's world made sense to her except that she could no longer feel Hans's weight or warmth. Dream
or not, she had to keep Hans near her. She stood up quickly, and the
priest's tin cup bounced on the floor with a loud clank. It echoed
through the alcove before the vastness of the church swallowed the
tinny sound.

In the shattered quiet, both men stopped, motionless, as if holding their breaths. Marta's mind cleared. This was no dream. The
snoring of sleepers around them continued in a steady rhythm. The
priest picked up the cup and fallen loaf, placed the loaf in her hands,
and beckoned her to follow. She wished there were time to ask why
he was helping a Reformer at the risk of his own life, but he hurried
ahead of them. She tied the loaf into her apron and followed. The
cleric's shoulders were hunched under his priestly black garb. In
contrast, the stranger's shoulders appeared strong and straight.

The priest led them to a side door hidden in a dark alcove. He
unlocked it, made the sign of the cross with his hand, and in a low
voice said, "May God bless and protect you on your journey."

The stranger checked the lane for soldiers while Marta searched
the priest's face. Like the stranger, the priest seemed to see past her
appearance to her need. He offered her a tired smile. She wrapped
his withered hand in hers.

"All clear," said the stranger. They had to leave. She would not endanger this kind soul any longer. She released his hand and stepped into the cold aftermath of the storm. The lock clicked in the door behind them. As it did, Marta felt her panic rising.

Where could they hide? Could they put Lübeck behind them before morning light? How far would she and Hans be able to travel? Would they ever make it to Russia? Marta shook her head. She would not let her uncertainties overwhelm her.

The scent of rain hung in the air as a chill wind whipped her skirt around her legs. Marta took a deep breath. She and Hans had made it this far. They would find passage to Russia by some means—by any means possible.

She turned to the stranger and reached for Hans. "You have been my angel of kindness this day. I thank you."

Instead of handing the child to her, the man held tightly to him and dashed into a darkened street. Marta gasped, and hastened after him, two quick steps for each of his long strides. She was behind him and then beside him. He held tightly to the sleeping boy. She grabbed the man's arm and pulled. He appeared not to notice. Latching on to Hans's leg, she made the child stir but not awaken. The stranger stopped, and she almost bumped into him. He blocked her path.

Quickly, he faced her. "Allow the child to rest." In the distance, the familiar tread of soldiers drew near. The wind slid cold fingers across her neck. She shivered. The man bent toward her, his breath warm on her face. In a pool of dim moonlight, dark eyes stared into hers.

He whispered, "Trust me. I mean you no harm."

She felt suspended, unmoving, as if waiting for something to happen. Then without warning, he sprinted into the darkness with Hans securely in his arms.

Chapter Three

Marta tried to yell, "Halt!" but the word came out as a stran-
gled gurgle, and she had no time to say more as she hurried
after the stranger and Hans. As they traversed one narrow street
after another, she berated herself for her foolishness in trusting a
man full of deceit. He turned down another street. She followed
him, slipped on the wet cobbles, and turned again to keep him in
sight. Her side ached, but she tried to ignore it and pushed herself to
move faster, desperate to keep up with the man's long strides.

Where is he taking Hans? she wondered. *And why would he want
to kidnap a child?* Whatever the reason, she knew kidnapping meant
no good. She hoped Hans would continue sleeping so he would
never understand the danger he faced.

The rush of footsteps stopped suddenly. All Marta could hear
was the swish of her skirt, and then silence. She stopped. *Where
did they go?* She heard no movement in any direction, only more
silence. *Where are they?* She turned back the way she had come,
gritting her teeth to keep them from chattering. The cold from the
early morning air seemed to seep directly into her bones. Her eyes
darted from side to side, desperate to detect any movement in the
shadows. Then her heart dropped into her stomach as she heard the
clipped march of boots on cobblestones.

Soldiers!

Carl glanced behind him. Again, the woman was nowhere in sight.
He retraced his steps, muttering under his breath. Soldiers were
approaching on the next street over. Furtively, he leaned around
a dark corner. There she stood, in the middle of the lane, looking
lost. His heart constricted at the naïve innocence he saw on her

face. He hissed under his breath, and when she turned he caught her eye, motioning silently as the marching grew closer. She hurried toward him, and they rounded the corner together. Treading carefully to muffle their footsteps, they turned sharply to the right and threaded their way through another dark lane and then onto a wide street, with Carl leading the way. When he could no longer hear the marching soldiers, he relaxed his pace.

Suddenly, the woman grabbed his arm. "The child is my burden. I pray you, hand him to me at once."

"That isn't necessary." Keeping in the shadows, he continued to the edge of the street, and her petite hand brushed from his arm.

He heard her inhale deeply. "I know not what sort of man you are, nor even your name—"

"Carl Mueller."

"—or what you mean to do—"

"I mean to save your life." He intentionally kept his voice low and gentle. He moved the sleeping form of the young boy to his other shoulder. "The boy fares well. You must hold your peace, unless you insist on drawing the soldiers' attention." He regretted the words as soon as they left his mouth.

Her voice grew louder. "Pass Hans to me this moment, and I shall bear him alone. I did not seek your help." Her words echoed off the unending row of narrow, two-story houses.

"Hush." They were in danger now. He strained to hear, trying to determine the direction of the unwelcome hunters he knew were coming. Instinctively, he pulled the woman toward deeper shadows and placed his arm over her with the child between them. He heard her stifle a cry just before two soldiers appeared from around the corner. Through her tensed back, he felt her rapidly beating heart. She was afraid. He wished he had time to comfort her fears.

The soldiers passed, but her heartbeat did not slow. He wondered why. Then an unwanted thought pushed to the forefront of his mind. Could she be more frightened of him than of the soldiers?

Perhaps he was not handling this situation well. He was used to working alone, but she must realize the importance of their haste.

He chided himself. *How could she possibly know?* She probably thought the soldiers were still after her. What could he say to reassure her without offering a long explanation?

When the soldiers had passed, he whispered, "You must trust me."

He released his grip on her and distinctly heard her say, "I shall not." Against the rough brick wall, they rose as one, both refusing to release the boy.

Carl's arm ached from the child's deadweight. He wished the woman were able to bear the lad and travel quickly, but she was much too small. Besides, she might flee from him, which would most certainly result in her arrest. "I am able to transport you and your boy to Russia."

She had been breathing heavily, as if winded, and now he heard nothing. She was holding her breath. Had he been mistaken in his assessment of her intelligence and courage? Could she really hold up under the pressure? She released the air in a soft sigh.

"Very well." She placed a protective hand on Hans's back and bent in close to Carl, within a breath from his ear. "Betray not my trust." Her words sounded like a warning. Good. She still had strength of will. She would need it.

He winked at her, though he was certain it went unnoticed in the darkness. "Abide near me."

With clouds now masking the moonlight, the night grew darker. Marta concentrated on keeping up with Herr Mueller. Once again, she wished that Frau and Herr Binz were near to help her send up two prayers—one of thanksgiving for sending this man to her, and the second a plea for their protection from him.

After so many turns up and down the streets of Lübeck, she was confounded about which direction they were traveling. A sudden, chill breeze on her face carried odors of wet wood and dead fish. Almost immediately, the hollow sound of Herr Mueller's steps confirmed her suspicion. They had reached a pier. The night was so dark that she could not tell where the land ended and the pier began. She reached out to touch Herr Mueller, but he was not there.

What if she fell off? What if he dropped Hans into the river? She shivered.

A dim light flickered below her. Someone was beneath the pier. She could not tell whether he held a candle or a lantern, but the light defined Herr Mueller's form and soothed her frayed composure. She moved toward him at the edge of the pier and saw that another man awaited them in a small boat, which held the light. The faint glow silhouetted Hans's body as Herr Mueller descended a rope ladder and lowered the boy into the craft.

"You're next," he whispered when he was back on the pier. Taking her hand, he steadied her as she dropped one foot over the edge and felt for the top rung. Grabbing the ladder with a firm hand, she climbed down, feeling the breath of recently thawed ice rise up her skirts until her foot reached the wood beneath her and the vessel rocked under her weight. She sank onto a narrow bench and realized how tired she was.

The boatman touched her arm. "Over there." She saw Hans's still form and made her way to his side. Just as she reached Hans, Marta heard the wooden hull creak as Herr Mueller dropped nimbly into the boat. Marta curled into a ball around Hans, and the boatman extinguished his light. The air grew stagnant as he pulled a dark canvas tarp over them. She could hardly breathe. Then she heard the muffled clip of soldiers' boots approaching.

A hoarse voice said, "Hold your tongue. One more to search afore you owe me the largest pint of ale in Lübeck." A set of boots clomped onto the wooden pier. Beneath the canvas, Marta could see nothing. The footsteps stopped.

"See ye signs of 'im?" another voice whispered loudly.

"It's too dark."

"Venture farther."

"And drown? The scoundrel's purse has too small a value for that. See to it yourself."

"My thirst's for ale, not water. Is it not the cap'n's golden box? Where is he? It does not have so much worth for all this trouble."

"It is worth a great deal."

"Not to me."

"To the tavern then. We are done here."

Marta heard their footsteps fade as water lapped against the small craft. What did a golden box have to do with capturing emigrants? Everything in her world now confounded her. Marta derived comfort from Hans's warm breath on her skin. At least he was able to sleep through the night's terror. When the boatman lifted the tarp, the cold slapped her with its frosty hand, and she had to take several shallow breaths. Hans roused. The boatman's lantern did not reappear.

Mueller settled himself in the boat's stern. Immediately, the boatman slid the oars into the water and pulled the craft toward the open river that circled Lübeck, away from the pier's pungent odor of decay. The old boat's rhythmic wooden creaks seemed lost amid the endless swish of the flowing river.

Hans rubbed his eyes. "Where are we?"

"Hold thy peace!" the boatman whispered.

Marta enveloped the child in her arms. Even in the darkness, she knew that fear haunted his eyes, in the same manner that worry gripped her heart. He leaned his head against her chest.

After a few hundred oar strokes, he whispered, "I am hungry." Marta untied the loaf she had saved and gave it to him. As he chewed slowly, she heard the river rushing by in the blackness as they traveled farther and farther from the safety of land. The cold crept beneath her damp clothes and seemed to flow directly into her tired body.

The boatman suddenly spoke. "They almost caught ye this time."

Mueller laughed. "Almost, Stoltz."

"You should 'ave giv'n the cap'n leave to keep 'is trinket."

"I won it fairly. Besides, I was able to raise your payment because I can trade it to the captain for passage. You wouldn't have risked your life or given me your papers for my thanks alone."

"'Tis true," said Stoltz. The boatman's laugh sounded more like a guffaw. The men said no more. Marta did not understand their discourse, but she knew she already owed this Mueller more than she could ever repay. For the hundredth time that day, she wished she were home along the Rhein, safe in her father's house, living a life of simplicity. Whether from cold, grief, or fear, she knew not, but her body began to shake. The only warmth, the only comfort she had, came from Hans.

As the night dragged on, her arm around the young boy's shoulders grew numb. She shifted his weight to her other side. Did the man intend to row all the way to the Baltic?

Oars out. Oars in. Oars out. Oars in. The constant motion lulled her into a half sleep. Only when the rhythm varied did she waken. The rowboat was being maneuvered into a dark inlet.

"What is this place?" she asked.

"You have no supplies or change of raiment, but Russia shall provide them for you." Herr Mueller's words were said too smoothly, which made Marta wonder if he was telling the whole truth. He continued, "The next ship sails in two days."

Marta swallowed hard, trying not to show her fear. It was almost dawn. How she hoped that this man was worthy of the trust she had placed in him. Herr Mueller stepped out of the boat and pulled it in to shore. He secured the rope to a large rock on the beach and then reached over the gunwales to carry Hans to land. When he returned, Marta assumed he would take her hand, but instead he slid his arms around her and effortlessly carried her up to where the sand was dry.

Carl smiled to himself. The task had been almost too easy. When he had lifted the woman, he had taken the document from her waistband without her noticing. She would not miss it until it was too late. He led her and the boy toward the small, one-room cabin hidden in the brush. As long as she did what he told her for the next two days, his transactions would be completed in time, and they would have all the necessary provisions for travel. Once they reached Russia, he would make use of his old connections—the dishonest ones, of course. He smiled to himself.

As the early rays of morning sliced through the darkness, Marta looked around the inlet. The area near the water was about the same size as the vaulted church where they had spent part of the night. The clearing was bounded by trees so thick that she could see nothing beyond them. Herr Mueller led the way along a thin, winding trail that ventured into the woods. They stopped when they reached a rustic cabin partially hidden inside a particularly thick stand of trees.

Mueller swung open the door. "You shall tarry here until bidden to leave. And make no noise, if you value your lives." His face was stern, the way her father's had been when the Papist bishop told them to leave their vineyard and then gave the order to burn all their vines and their few possessions.

"The reason?" she asked.

"Soon traders, smugglers, and others who are not as trustworthy as I shall join me. If they see you, I cannot be responsible for their actions." He gave her a bow that acknowledged her worth as a woman.

Marta blushed. "We shall abide inside."

With a laugh, he tossed a canvas sack on the dirt floor. "You'll find food and water in the sack. Bolt the door behind me."

The moment his stalwart frame turned away, Marta slid inside the cabin with Hans and fastened the door. Before long, she heard other voices outside. She supposed Herr Stoltz was still there, but she had not heard him talk enough to recognize his voice among the others.

Dim shafts of light penetrated the wooden structure, revealing a dirt floor and a single log bench. "Do you understand what Herr Mueller requires of us?" she asked Hans. It looked as if his eyes had grown even larger beneath his blond hair. She touched his shoulder. His clothes were still damp, like hers. They would be fortunate if they both did not die of the cold. "Hans, do you understand why we have come to this lodging?"

He nodded. Marta breathed a sigh of relief. Hans was truly Frau and Herr Binz's son. They walked quietly around the small cabin together to stretch out their legs. It was three steps across and five steps long. The dirt floor smelled musty and dank. Marta could tell that mice had been living there.

Throughout the day, they heard more men arriving. Hans grew tired of walking, so they looked in the canvas bag for food. When they had eaten, they sat on the wooden bench, and Hans dozed. The voices outside the cabin, a mixture of German and foreign tongues, grew louder, until by evening the din was boisterous and full. Marta and Hans ate more hardtack from the bag, and they relieved themselves when necessary in one of the corners of their voluntary prison.

"Will he ever release us?" whispered Hans.

"He protects us," said Marta, hoping her words were true and that he was not selling them as slaves to the highest bidder. She did not know why she trusted him, but she did. She felt for the reassuring document in her waistband. It was gone! Had she lost it on the streets of Lübeck? Had it fallen into the river? She tried to recall all the sights and sounds of her flight. Would Russia let her in without it?

As the evening progressed, she occasionally recognized Herr Mueller's voice among the others, although he seemed to be speaking another language—possibly French—as if he were a native. Then he would use another tongue she did not recognize. Marta shivered beside Hans as they tried to sleep side by side on the narrow bench.

It was not until the early morning hours that Marta was able to drift off into an uneasy slumber, and by the time she awoke, the daylight looked to be half gone. Complete silence now surrounded them. They ate another meal of hardtack and water. There was no sound in any direction. Once their meal was complete, Marta went to the cabin's door and slowly opened the bolt to peer into the trees beyond. The entire inlet was deserted. No one, not even Herr Mueller, was within sight, and there was no sign that anyone had been in the area. If Marta had not heard the voices the previous night, she would never have believed that a large group of men had held their bawdy ritual there.

As Marta and Hans ventured out of the shack and headed toward the water, a large dog, a mutt with ferocious looking teeth, jumped in front of them, barking between its growls.

"Flee!" said Marta. Hans did not need another warning. They hastened inside and bolted the door behind them. Marta was breathing heavily as she continued, "That did not go well."

Hans shook his head. "No."

To keep Hans's mind off the dog and other dangers, Marta told him stories about her brothers and her life as a youth. She rather enjoyed spinning tales for someone who enjoyed hearing how her oldest brother had hidden in the vineyard to keep from being punished for throwing an egg at her; and how the brother closest to her age had taken her on adventures to find invisible creatures when she did his chores for him. It felt too long since she had had time to enjoy the good, common laughter of her father's house.

Occasionally Marta and Hans tried to peek out the door. Whenever they did, the dog barked at them as if they were his sole entertainment. The day seemed endless, and sleep did not come easily to either of them that night. Every time Marta began to drift off, she was awakened by the scratching of mice or knocking of branches flailing in the wind against the cabin. But when she awoke on the second morning, everything was still once again. A knock on the door startled them both.

"We're ready to leave," said Herr Mueller.

Marta took a deep breath. When she left the cabin, she would begin a new life, as a slave or a free woman, she did not know. She and Hans unlatched the bar and followed Herr Mueller through the thick foliage of the German forest into the open. As Marta breathed in the fresh air and looked around, she saw a rowboat on the shore and an English ship waiting in the river. Herr Mueller was already striding toward the water.

"A ship," said Hans. "Mama's ship!"

Marta shook her head. "I think not. Her ship sailed three days ago. But this ship shall bear us to Russia, where your mother awaits us."

Herr Mueller helped them into the rowboat without ceremony or words. Marta thought it best to remain quiet also. The oars clunked against the side of the boat as Mueller picked them up and began rowing. His companion of two nights ago was nowhere in view and neither was the dog. Marta tried not to stare at the muscles swelling under Herr Mueller's sleeves as he rowed them toward the waiting ship. The only other item in the rowboat was a large sack that looked as if it were filled with grain.

"Seed for your new life in Russia," Herr Mueller said casually.

Marta turned her attention to the ship. It looked even more worn than the one that Hans's mother had sailed on. "Did it come from Lübeck?" she asked.

"From the vicinity," he said, maneuvering their boat closer. "The route it took was a bit more circuitous than the one from the other day. This captain is more particular about seeing his passengers safely aboard."

Once the rowboat reached the ship, Herr Mueller told Marta, "You shall climb first." She gave Hans's arm a squeeze and moved to the rope ladder. Her heart beat quickly. How she hoped that this was what it seemed. Herr Mueller held the boat steady.

"Leave me not!" Hans cried. Marta stopped.

"Climb up," said Herr Mueller. In a soothing voice, he added, "You'll be next, lad."

Marta's heart ached for the child, who had seen this scenario once before with his mother, but she obeyed. The rope sagged and swung with each step, but she forced her mind away from the frigid water below, concentrating on taking one step at a time. Only when she had climbed safely over the rail did she let out a breath of relief.

Marta could not force herself to watch Hans climbing with Herr Mueller behind him, so she scanned the deck instead. English sailors moved quickly about their business, working with ropes, mopping the deck, and yelling, as if that would be the rhythm of the voyage. Marta's lips turned up slightly.

Although she could not understand their language, a sailor responded to her smile with a toothy grin. She looked away. The sound of metal clanking against wood told her that they were weighing anchor.

As soon as Herr Mueller reached the deck, he guided Hans toward Marta. She held him in her arms, and he clung to her. "We shall be safe," she said, comforting him. "We sail to Russia now." Herr Mueller climbed down once more to retrieve his bag of grain. Marta averted her eyes from the sailors and watched until Mueller was safely back on board and their rowboat, without guidance, had drifted away.

"You said we would have all manner of supplies," said Marta.

Herr Mueller nodded. "They are even now stowed below."

A man hurried past her as if some task needed his immediate attention, but then he stopped beside Herr Mueller and spoke in a foreign tongue. He seemed impatient. He also seemed to be the one in charge.

Herr Mueller extended his hand, and the man took from him a small golden box. "Better be worth a g'd deal," he said switching to German.

"Pardon me, Captain," said Marta, "is this ship bound for Russia?"

The man stopped and deliberately turned with a leer. He scanned her form from head to toe before sauntering closer to her with raised eyebrows. When he leaned close, he smelled like sweat and garlic.

"Ask thine husband, Woman."

Marta took an involuntary step closer to Herr Mueller, meeting him with her back. The officer laughed at her discomfort and swaggered away.

Father Dominick's words flooded her mind, "Are these your wife and child?"

And Herr Mueller's answer, "Yes. This is my family." Marta set Hans down beside her. If only she could relieve the pressure constricting her throat.

Hans leaned into her and gripped her hand tightly. "Do we leave for Russia now?" She squeezed Hans's hand and used him as an excuse to move away from Herr Mueller. Without looking directly at Mueller, she asked, "I beseech you to tell me where you plan to take us."

"To Russia, as I have promised, Frau."

"Frau? Whose Frau am I understood to be?" Marta caught an amused look on Herr Mueller's face.

"Mine," he said easily. "Know it or know it not, in the absence of your husband, you have need of me."

"I have need of no one." Almost involuntarily she flinched. "Especially not you."

"With what instrument shall you pay for your passage?" He watched as she started to reach for her document, but then stopped, remembering that it was gone. He continued, "I have troubled myself much to obtain passage for you on this ship. Everything is arranged. We sail with family papers."

"I shall not comport myself as your wife!"

He smiled. "Rest easy. It is for your protection. Without me . . ." He shrugged and motioned toward the sailors.

Marta stood as tall as her five-foot-three inch frame would allow, but a feeling of helplessness tugged at her bravado. "And who is to protect me from you?"

Mueller chuckled and steadied Hans as the boat listed starboard. His voice gentled. "I shall not harm you. Your husband, is he dead?" When she refused to respond, he continued, "What are your plans, once you reach Russia?"

"I shall lay claim to my land."

He shrugged. "Russia will not give you land without papers."

The ship righted, and Marta almost lost her footing. "Then I shall sign a new contract. Russia welcomes women, even those who travel alone."

A sailor's voice bellowed at them, but Marta could not understand his words.

"Come Hans, we shall find a place to rest." Marta sidestepped a coil of rope and looked for a way to go below. She had never been on a vessel of this size. A sailor ran past. She could tell by his odor that he had a craving for ale and a loathing for lye soap. Hans grabbed her hand. "I fear this place, Fräulein Ebel."

"Fräulein?" Herr Mueller said. "But I thought . . . You have no husband then?"

"I am not married."

"But the boy—"

"The child of friends." She hurried toward the center of the ship.

"I see." Mueller picked up the bag of seed with one arm and grabbed Hans's hand with the other. "You are mistaken, Son. This is not Fräulein Ebel, but Frau Ebel." He paused meaningfully as Marta faced him. "I am her husband."

Hans shifted his questioning gaze between the two of them.

A different voice bellowed something, but Marta could not understand the language. Another sailor pushed past her.

"We must go below," Carl said, nudging Marta and Hans in the direction opposite the one Marta was taking. "Aboard ship, you must present yourself as my wife, as *Frau* Ebel, or the captain will set you off his ship immediately. He has already broken laws to take us on. He will give neither food nor drink to those without papers."

Marta's words came out with vehemence. "To say I am your wife would be a lie."

"You must know that Russia welcomes unmarried women only as far as Kronstadt. Once there, you shall be permitted to journey to the settlements and claim your land only if you have wed." Carl pushed them along, wondering again if choosing this woman and child had been a mistake.

Even though she did not want to believe him, Marta felt certain that Herr Mueller was telling her the truth. Why would Russia allow women more freedom than the German states? Unmarried, she had a right to nothing. Would that she had been her father's fourth son instead of his only daughter.

"I'm afraid the position of my sister has already been taken by another, but I promise that if you pose as my Frau, it shall be in name alone. If not . . . well I can't promise you a happy voyage. If not for your own sake, think of the child."

What a predicament! Why had she so wholly believed Russia's promises? Why had she trusted this stranger? Marta could blame no one but herself. She took another step toward the hold. Just as she was about to go down, the ship listed again. She would have fallen except that Herr Mueller steadied her at the waist and then quickly removed his hands as if he knew how short her breath had suddenly become.

"Truth has value to me," Marta said, "yet a truthful person is hard to find. I will not become a liar, even though the law forbidding emigration makes me a criminal. We shall travel as husband and wife only if we *are* husband and wife." She turned to help Hans down the ladder. "Which we are not."

Descending into the hold made Marta feel as if she were being swallowed by a putrid darkness. She pulled herself up to inhale one more breath of fresh air and then descended into the blackness. How was she ever going to provide food and water for Hans and herself without papers?

Carl had miscalculated. He had not bargained for the honesty of the woman now in his care. The set of her jaw told him that she would not change her mind. To retrieve the money that was his, he must enter Russia with a family . . . and a new name. Could he hope to be successful with only a sister and not a wife? He doubted it. He would need both for his entrance to go undetected.

The hold was packed tight with sleeping emigrants. Carl led the way to the space he had secured for them—one small berth and the floor space beside it. He clenched his teeth against the stench of vomit and urine that permeated the air. As they approached the berth, he nodded to Frau Doenhof, another emigrant he had rescued, and turned to address Marta.

"Fräulein Ebel, I want you to meet my sister, Frau Doenhof." He put emphasis on the word *sister*, hoping she would understand his meaning.

Marta recognized the woman by the prominent scar on her

cheek. Of all the emigrants Marta had met, this woman was the last one she wanted as a traveling companion. Not that she wasn't respectable, but she seemed to see only unpleasantness in everyone and everything. She was not Herr Mueller's sister any more than Marta was his wife.

Marta forced her words. "Frau Doenhof." The woman nodded recognition but the line of her mouth was tight. She went back to scrubbing the berth. Marta turned to face Herr Mueller, but he had already retreated from them and was climbing back up to the deck.

Marta busied herself by sifting through the meager possessions that Herr Mueller had been able to procure. She found places for everything along with the burlap sack of grain. Frau Doenhof continued with her scrubbing and spoke not a word to Marta. Her strokes were harsh and unrelenting on the wood.

To remove Hans from the woman's presence, Marta took him to explore the hold. The space under the low ceiling was filled with other emigrants, and a cluster of women had gathered around the lone cooking stove. Marta noticed that the people she passed still had hope in their eyes, even though the ship was overcrowded. Entire families were jammed into the tiny berths, and there was barely room to step past in some areas. Marta took a deep breath and reminded herself, *Eleven days. It's only for eleven days. We may be packed in here like human cargo, but we can survive it.* The hope of the future would carry them through all manner of pain and inconvenience. At least, she hoped so.

Carl returned by evening and remained by Marta's side, trying to be as helpful as he could to show her his good intentions. Still, by nightfall, he knew that kindness would not be enough to change her mind. If asked, she would deny that they were husband and wife. Hans gave a loud yawn.

"Weary?" Carl asked.

Hans nodded.

Carl unrolled his mother's old patchwork quilt and spread it on the small, freshly cleaned berth. "You may sleep here." He guided

Hans to the back of the wooden shelf, where he could curl up next to Frau Doenhof, who was already sleeping. He instructed Marta to squeeze in next to the boy. She looked too exhausted to argue. The children in the berth above were snoring. The wooden vessel creaked, shuddered, and groaned.

"You made an interesting proposition," Carl said as Marta pressed in next to Hans. "One that might be of benefit to us both."

"Proposition?" Marta said, yawning. "What do you mean?"

Her eyes drooped as she spoke. Carl pulled out a woolen blanket from their belongings and covered her.

"We have each one blanket." Carl slipped his blanket under her head as she lay down.

He smiled. She was already asleep. He sat next to the lower berth and leaned his head against the mildewed wood. The floor was wet, but he chose to ignore it. Several men snored, and a child mumbled in her sleep.

Throughout the night, Carl wrestled with his conscience. If he married Fräulein Ebel, she might be able to own land in his name, even though it was an alias. But by staying unmarried, she would be free to find a real husband, a German like herself, instead of a displaced Frenchman. He concluded that it was better for Marta not to marry him. But he did not see any reasonable means to convince her. He had nothing to lose. If she insisted on marrying, he would not fight her. He had to gain admittance to Russia. The means to obtain his goal were of no consequence to him.

Marta awoke early the next morning. Carl watched her eyes scan the shadows and then settle on his face.

"I accept," he said in a low voice.

Her brow drew together. "Accept what?"

"The course you propose." He smiled. "The captain shall perform our marriage ceremony this day."

Chapter Four

The sun was bright, but it had not yet warmed the air as the ship cut through the water on its northeastern journey. Marta squeezed the ship's rail and let the breeze tingle her senses. Joy had seldom entered her life since her mother's death, but today she could laugh. She had escaped the German states, and now she would be married. It would be a marriage in name only, but the thought of it filled her with a sense of security. As a married woman, she would have the right to own land of her own in Russia. She refused to heed her doubts about marrying a man with whom she barely had an acquaintance, but still they came. His last words echoed in her mind.

"I'll abide in Russia only as long as it takes to make arrangements for you to lay claim to your land."

Unbidden, the questions came. "What shall become of me once Herr Mueller departs? Is my honor of such import? Do I condemn myself to early 'widowhood,' with no chance to ever wed another or have a child of my own?" Her stomach suddenly felt unsettled, almost pukish. She shuddered, resisting the urge to gag. No matter what her future held, she had to do what was right at the moment. If Herr Mueller wished her to travel with him, he must marry her. Besides that, if she wanted to receive land in Russia, she must have a husband. She grasped the rail tighter as an angry wave rocked the ship.

"Where's Hans?" Herr Mueller asked from behind her. Marta startled, causing her hip to ram into the rail as she turned. "I didn't intend to give you a fright," Herr Mueller said. "Where's Hans?"

Marta rubbed her hip through the layers of her thick skirt. "He still sleeps." She stepped away from Herr Mueller and backed into the rail again.

"Nervous?"

She nodded but did not look up. Instead, she stared at the deck, her stomach churning from the boat's rocking motion. She had heard that the Baltic could be treacherous. She wondered how she would be able to bear a storm at sea should one develop.

"Women aren't allowed above decks alone," Herr Mueller said. He was not dressed in the fashionable manner he had been on the streets of Lübeck. His simple peasant clothes—dark pants and jacket with a white shirt—fit in with the others, but the way he stood tall and surveyed the area as if the world itself belonged to him suggested that he was from a different class.

"I shall not abide in the hold for the entire voyage." Her stomach began to sway out of rhythm with the boat's movements. "I have need of fresh air."

"The rule is for your own protection," he said sternly. "I don't want to unnerve you, but there are good reasons. Sailors are only men. I shall escort you above deck whenever you like, but never come up here again without me." He paused. "Are you unwell?"

"I . . . yes. I feel ill."

"You've a green pallor."

"I must go to bed." She started for the hold.

"That shall make it worse." He pulled her back to the rail. "Lean here. Breathe deeply." She did what he said, closing her eyes to try to regain her equilibrium.

"Do not close your eyes. Watch the horizon." His fingers, calloused but gentle, tilted her chin up. Although all her instincts told her to keep her eyes shut, she forced them open and concentrated on the line where the unending water met the low-hanging gray-blue of the sky. Her stomach rolled in opposition to the waves, but before too long, her distress subsided.

He must have noticed her expression, for he said, "Are you recovered enough to go through the ceremony, even though it's unnecessary?"

"It is of great necessity." She gulped in a breath of the moist air. The taste reminded her of springtime and her home in the

Rheinland. She was alive, and she had a future in Russia. She must remember that and never let her circumstances overwhelm her.

Herr Mueller leaned on the rail. "To live under the pretense of marriage until we reach Kronstadt would be more desirable for us both. Think of me as your protector. As a former recruiting agent, I have protected many on their way to Russia." His voice dropped to a pleasant pitch. He sounded convincing as he said, "The journey is not overlong. Would you not rather wait and wed a good German man who'd remain true to you in Russia?"

"Herr Mueller, we must marry." She faced him, setting her chin so that he would not mistake her resolve. "I shall not travel with you as your wife unless we are wed."

His hands rose in the air in mock consternation. "Such a stubborn young woman! But come now. If we are to be man and wife, you must call me by my given name."

"That is not necessary."

"My name is Carl. And your name is . . . ?"

Marta felt her stomach roll. She turned to stare at the horizon again. The rail dug into her side as she took another deep breath. "Marta. My name is Marta."

"Marta," he repeated. In spite of her resolve, she enjoyed hearing him say her name. Neither of them spoke. To Marta, the atmosphere seemed charged with promise, and yet she knew that she must remain clearheaded. She shivered.

"Are you cold, or frightened?"

"Perhaps a bit of both." She was surprised at how near Carl was standing. He took a step back. "Herr . . . Carl, shall you keep your word and leave me untouched?" She could not hide the blush that rose with involuntary briskness.

"Most women enjoy my company." He stooped slightly to bring his face even with hers. "Even so, you have naught to fear. We shall be a couple only so that I can reenter Russia, and you can make claim to your land. You have my word on that."

"And is your word true, I wonder?"

He turned and leaned back on the rail, supporting his weight with both elbows. "In this case it is. The ceremony is not necessary. I shall even pay Frau Doenhof to protect me from you."

"Protect you from me?"

His smile was slow and teasing—relaxed, almost convincing. Marta shook her head. Why Frau Doenhof, of all people? Still, the idea offered her a sense of security. "We must be wed, but I wish you to hire Frau Doenhof."

He turned his face into the breeze and stretched his limbs as if he had no care in the world. Marta wished she felt as unconcerned as he appeared. "Very well," he said, "your wishes prevail. You understand that I shall desert you in Russia?"

"Your actions are your own concern. My actions are mine. I will not say we are wed unless we truly are."

"I knew you were a determined woman when you forced me to help you into the barrel," he said.

"I forced you to do noth—" Marta stopped. Carl's face was serious, but his eyes were sparkling with mischief. "Again, you tease me."

He gave her another slow smile. "If I can't make you waver in your decision, then the captain awaits us below, my lady." He bowed with a flourish and spread out a hand to direct her toward the hold. Her stomach clenched again, but this time she looked at neither the horizon nor Carl. She focused her attention on keeping her legs from collapsing beneath her.

The boat groaned. She shivered again. *That was not an omen*, she assured herself. Yet even the breeze's voice sounded like it was moaning for her by the time she reached the hold's ladder. The next time she returned above decks, her future would be sealed.

Marta looked at a billowing canvas sail above her. "Oh that I might be as free as a sail in the wind!" she said, not realizing that she had spoken aloud until Carl answered.

"Even sails are secured to the masts."

She searched Carl's eyes as she took her first step down. Once again, she would place her trust in this stranger. Although she knew what she had to do, she pondered whether she could actually do it.

The ship listed to starboard. Her foot slipped, and she struck her head against a beam. She could not tell if she was falling or standing. Had a scream of pain passed her lips, or had she been able to bridle her anguish into an inner groan?

From a distance, she heard Carl say, "Are you hurt?"

"I am well." Her voice was clear, but intermittent spots of blackness grew and receded all around her. She felt numb to everything, as if she were floating in a dream, but she clearly smelled the dankness of the ship's dark passageways. In a moment, she was standing in the officer's eating area before a man in uniform. Perhaps he was the captain.

Frau Doenhof stood by her side, scowling. Her angry expression made the scar on her cheek more pronounced. She stood slightly taller than Marta, hands on her ample hips. Other faces blurred before Marta until the whole room began to spin and then receded in a haze of colors. Carl's face appeared in front of hers. *What did he say?*

"This is my wife." Suddenly, she was chasing him through the streets of Lübeck. Clouds swirled around their feet. A shot rang out. The street turned red with Herr Binz's blood. The stars descended on her, and she could not escape them.

"Hans! I must find Hans!" she yelled. She was shivering in a rowboat.

"Vater! Mutter!" Hans cried. He fell into the tumultuous water. Swirling fog rose from the waves, hiding him beneath its icy cloak.

"No!" Marta dove. She had to save him, to take him to his mother in Russia. Instead of getting wet, she found herself standing in front of the ship's officer.

"Take ye this man as thine husband for all time, for all time, for all time?" Faces. More faces. What was she doing? Marta put her hands to her throat in an attempt to stop the shriek of fear that she felt rising from deep within her.

The scream escaped, but sounded more like a breathless, "I do," than a cry for help.

From far away, she heard Hans saying, "Fraülein Ebel, awake. Please awake."

"Frau Ebel," Carl corrected him.

Marta forced one eyelid open. Her head felt the squeeze and release of pain around her throbbing temples. Carl and Hans bent over her. The worried lines on their faces looked almost identical, which made her smile. Carl might have been Hans's father.

"There you are," said Carl. He leaned back slightly.

"What happened?" asked Marta. The boat creaked. She could tell by the odor of cabbage and the cries of children that she was in the hold with the other emigrants. She forced her other eye open and touched the spot on her head where she had fallen against the beam. A lump had formed. She grimaced and drew her hand away.

"You struck your head with more force than we thought. After the ceremony, you swooned into my arms. You've been deep in slumber for many hours."

"Are we wed?" asked Marta. She tried to sit up. A wave of dizziness spread from her head down to her unresponsive body.

"Do you not remember?" He gently pushed her back down. "Try not to move with such swiftness."

"I do not . . . that is, I cannot . . ."

"Such a fine groom am I," teased Carl. "My bride has forgotten me already." He ran a hand through his thick, black hair.

Marta saw Frau Doenhof standing behind Carl. She shuddered and wished someone else, anyone else, were there to help her, but she needed the truth now, even if it fell on her with the sharpness of a knife slashing into her soul. Marta turned to the woman, trying to concentrate on the severe manner of her light brown hair and not the force of her frown.

"You were present when we were wed?"

Frau Doenhof leaned forward. "Ye cannot deny him now." Marta tried to breathe. She raised herself on one elbow, but pain like blows from a horse's hoof pounded in her forehead, and she could not catch her breath.

Firm but gentle hands met her efforts. "Lie still for another moment," said Carl. Marta was forced to comply. She closed her eyes.

Carl continued, "Frau Doenhof understands our peculiar situation. Her presence shall keep me honorable and—"

"Ye shan't be with child when the scoundrel takes his leave of you," said Frau Doenhof through clenched teeth.

Air. Marta needed air. Could she abide with this harsh woman, whose gruffness she had always tried to avoid in the barracks? Was she yoked for life to a man whose sole purpose was to leave her? She willed herself to relax. A breath finally came. She rested on the stiff, hard boards. The sound of someone snoring hammered at her ears and throbbed in her brain.

"Fräulein Ebel, I am thirsty," said Hans.

"Frau Ebel," corrected Carl. Marta wished she could bring the wedding to remembrance. If only she knew how to read, she would ask to see the marriage lines in the captain's log.

"Frau Ebel?" Marta was suddenly alert. "You mean Frau Mueller."

"Why is everything so muddled? Does not anyone hear me?" Hans threw one of their pots to the floor. "I am thirsty." The clanging made Marta wince. She was uncertain what was happening, but she dearly wished she could clear her mind.

"Halt thy nonsense!" In a single movement, Frau Doenhof was by Hans's side, her arm extended as if to slap him, but Carl's hand caught Frau Doenhof's in midair. She glanced at Carl as if she were about to be struck instead of the child.

"You are not his mother." His voice was soft, yet dangerous. The peril of the moment was not lost on Marta as Frau Doenhof and Carl glared at each other, completely still, each with an arm raised in invisible battle. A shiver ran up Marta's spine.

Carl released his hand from Frau Doenhof's arm and turned to Hans. "You shall make an apology." The pounding increased on Marta's temple. She rubbed her forehead.

"I have had no drink the whole time Frau Ebel slept," said Hans.

"Make an apology," said Carl.

Hans picked up the pot and placed it in their burlap bag. "I am sorry I threw it."

"Forgiven." Carl's natural expression, a mouth ready to smile and eyes prepared to laugh, returned. He addressed Frau Doenhof. "Please take Hans to the barrel for water."

"I am not his mother." The scowl had disappeared from her face as if the emotional wind that kept moving her forward had left her stranded. The hull of the boat rocked.

Carl raised one eyebrow, but his voice was gentle. "And bring a ladleful of water for my wife." To Marta's surprise, Frau Doenhof picked up a large spoon and glanced at Hans as if inviting him to join her, but he was not looking in her direction. In the berth next to theirs, a toddler began to howl.

Frau Doenhof's look immediately changed to her usual scowl as she grabbed Hans's hand. "Keep close watch on thy manners."

"Go on, lad," Carl said. "You have more to fear from my hand than hers."

"I thirst no more," he said, which seemed to infuriate Frau Doenhof. She pulled him along after her.

"It is too late for that. Next time, think hard before ye open thy mouth . . ." Frau Doenhof's voice was drowned by the noises of the emigrants around them.

Carl could feel Marta's eyes boring into him. "I'll help you sit up if you like."

"Yes. I thank you."

He slid his arm gently around her and cupped the back of her head in his hand to protect it from striking the low ceiling of the berth. Then he slowly helped her down to the floor. Marta's eyes were shut as he leaned her against the wooden side.

"Feeling better?"

She looked at him. "Yes."

Carl had his doubts. "I don't look for a brave answer. I seek to know whether you shall swoon again." He removed his hand and arm from her slowly so as not to eliminate all support at once. Marta's eyes glazed over. He continued, "You slide down. Let's try this." He moved behind her and had her lean against his chest. "I'm slightly softer than wood."

She tensed for a moment and then relaxed in his arms. They faced the dark, crowded hold. An older man with a large pot began arguing in a loud voice with a young woman whose child remained firmly around one of her legs.

Carl lowered his voice and spoke with intended urgency. "Marta, you must remember that you are Frau Ebel, and I am your husband, Herr Ebel. Do you understand? If you forget our names, it could cost me my life and you your land."

"Frau Ebel? If we were wed then I should be—"

In a purposely gruff voice, he said, "Ebel is the name we must use to enter Russia. I am Herr Ebel, and you are Frau Ebel. That is all you need to know."

He could feel Marta tense. "Those are the names on our emigration papers?"

"Yes." He softened his voice. He was relieved that she had thought of a reason on her own. "It's the only way."

"Why can we not use your name?" Marta asked. "Have you committed a crime?"

Carl wondered how much he should tell her. The old man and the young woman continued arguing as they tried to cook their meals in the only area available to those in the hold. The young woman had more strength, but the older man would not budge.

"What horrible thing have you done that you fear to use your true name?" Marta insisted.

"I was born—" On sudden impulse, Carl reached for the patchwork stuffed in the corner of the berth. He needed to distract her, and the distraction would work to his advantage. If Marta had the blanket, then it would not incriminate him, ever. "I know we won't abide long together," he said in her ear, "but I desire that you should share this with me while we're together. Here. Care for it as if it were your own." He placed the cover on Marta.

Over her legs lay a blanket of black, blue, and red patches. It was not flat like most patchworks but large and puffy, like oddly shaped pillows sewn together into a blanket. It was heavier than any covering she had ever felt. She wondered why. She noticed that the center square had a more complex design than the others.

"It belonged to my mother." He cleared his throat.

"Is this a wedding gift?"

He let out a breath. "Yes. That's it. A wedding gift for us both to share."

Marta's hand fingered the material as if it were embedded with jewels. At least four layers of cloth were hand stitched together.

Carl looked away. "The seed that I have brought is more valuable than any other possession, even this." Marta imagined herself sowing the seed on her own land in Russia. He continued, "We must guard it with our lives." Marta nodded, but she instinctively felt that he was hiding something from her. Who was this man she had just married? She saw Frau Doenhof and Hans weaving through the crowded passageway as they returned with a ladle of water.

"You must lie down and rest." Carl slid out from behind her and helped her back into the berth. "Our watchdog returns."

Chapter Five

Marta awoke to Hans's steady breathing, warm and moist against her ear. The queasiness had left her. She felt for the bump on her head. It was almost gone. Crammed into the bunk with her, Hans and Frau Doenhof appeared peaceful, without a single line of worry creasing their faces. Her hand traced the lines of one pillowlike square on the heavy patchwork that rested over her. If it had belonged to Carl's mother, then he had come from a noble family. Some of the fabrics sewn into the coverlet were not the kind that common families used. They were smooth, like an infant's skin, and they shone like the gleam of the moon over water. Remaining still so as not to disturb her bunk mates, she peered out of the berth to the floor where her husband of seven days sat chewing on a crust of bread.

Carl smiled, and Marta felt her heart quiver. What was it that she found so appealing in this man she had known for less than a fortnight? Carl put one finger to his lips and then motioned for her to leave the berth. She wondered what he had in store for her as she rolled away from Hans.

The wood creaked. Hans sighed in his sleep. She waited until his breathing was regular and then moved slowly, trying to keep the patchwork tucked firmly around his body.

Once free, she reached for the comb that Carl had included in their provisions. She could sense his eyes watching her but gave her full attention to combing and then pinning her hair in place. Others in the hold were beginning to stir as she placed her once-white cap on her head. Marta could hear the sailors opening the hatch above them. She always rested easier when she knew the emigrants were granted freedom to move around, regardless of how much they were discouraged from doing so.

Carl whispered against her ear, "Let's go above."

She picked up her wool cape and tried not to think about how disheveled her dress looked from wearing it day and night. The cape would hide most of the wrinkles. Among their supplies, she had found a nightdress, but in the company of so many and with Carl always near, she would certainly not change into it.

Marta followed Carl on deck. Even wrinkled clothing looked fine on him. Clouds rolled in the sky, and a damp chill breeze brushed the last remnants of slumber from her mind. They walked together slowly, without a word, without touching. She was glad. Talking would have seemed too much noise right then. The calls of the sailors blended with the swishing of the water as if they were a duet designed for musical harmony.

Marta remembered having to keep pace with her father when he walked the vineyard. Carl's pace was more leisurely. It fit hers well. A piercing birdcall disrupted the calm, but Marta could not spot the fowl. They strolled around the deck twice in silence, as if the groans of the wood answering the sea's insistent call said more than they could ever hope to say. Finally, Marta followed Carl to the rail. He leaned his forearms on it, and they surveyed the unending choppiness of the sea.

"The sea, it's like life, ever changeable, ever wont to beat you apart," he said. "But then, we're survivors, both of us." She liked the resonating bass tone of his voice. He caught her staring at him, and she averted her gaze as he continued, "You haven't told me your history. I desire to know more about the women I marry."

Marta laughed. "Has it been your manner to wed again and again?"

"I would be loath to do so." He rubbed his hands together, as if for warmth. "I liken marriage to the Black Death, a malady to be avoided at all costs—but you overpowered me in a moment of weakness." He was teasing again. Marta pretended to ignore him, but every fiber of her being listened for what he would say next. He grasped part of the rigging and then let it go. "I fear I may be in danger of being tied as tightly to you as that sail is to this rope. The harder it pulls away, the tighter the knot gets."

His words surprised her. What did he mean by them? Might he consider remaining with her, as her husband, once they entered Russia? Even as her heart soared at the hope, she did not allow herself to dwell on the possibility. In the next moment, her heart plummeted in confusion. Perhaps he resented the bond that tied them to each other. Perhaps he wished to be free of her.

"You have such a desire to be rid of me?" she asked and then immediately regretted her words. What unsettled her so with this stranger? She had to stop looking to others, to him, for her comfort. She continued, "I, like you, am eager to begin my new life, with nothing to restrain me." A gull swooped overhead, calling to the open, gray sky. If only she were free to follow her own path, enter her own dreams for her future. She stepped away from Carl.

Carl tried to sidestep a man approaching the rail, but the man jostled Carl's arm as he dumped a bucket of human waste overboard. The odor permeated the air. "Let's move to the other side." Carl took Marta's elbow to lead her, but she hesitated.

"The hour for Hans to rise is at hand. I should see to him." She appeared unconcerned about leaving Carl, as if she did not know the moments they had had together that morning would be the sole highlight of his otherwise dreary day. He searched his mind. What could he say to prolong their time together?

"I wish I did not have to leave you in Russia."

Marta turned toward him. "Verily?"

"Yes, but the future isn't mine to determine. We have only the present. Stay and talk with me. We can't converse privately at any other time. The cacophony below assaults my ears and muddles my mind."

"Hans may have need of me," she said, but her words were soft, as if she hoped to be persuaded.

"Frau Doenhof shall see to him." He was pleased when they resumed walking. "What wakens such devotion in you for the boy?

You told me what troubles befell his parents, but many children have been made fatherless. What is your reward for your trouble?"

"Reward?" She looked out to sea. "There is no reward. I repay a debt. His parents aided me in Lübeck." Marta's words sounded matter-of-fact, but she turned her knuckles white with the tightness of her fists.

"Your debt to them must be great."

"My father's was. Even so is my own."

Carl studied the water that hid so many secrets below the surface. "What became of your father?" If he were not afraid that she would move away from him again, he would have moved closer to her.

She gripped the rail, as if she needed its support. "He slowly froze to death in the barracks while we awaited our ship."

Carl tried to stifle the curse that came freely to his lips. "Your recruiting agent should be burned at the stake."

"Herr and Frau Binz were the only ones kind to him and me at the end. I seek to return their kindness. I shall help Hans find his mother."

"I've wondered what you intended to do . . . after I've gone. Do you plan to remain with them?" His lips moved freely without consulting his thoughts. He should not have asked her about the future.

She let go of the rail and raised her chin, a gesture he was beginning to think was her weapon against adversity. "Russia offers me a respectable future, as long as I can lay claim to my land."

He picked up a feather from the deck and ruffled it, combing his fingers with its softness. "And I'm the key that shall open that door to you."

"No." She backed away from him. "I need only the 'Frau' before my name. Once you are gone, Frau Doenhof and I shall fare well together." Her eyes sparkled with mischief.

"You and the worthy Frau shall take up housekeeping and grow food on the Russian steppes?"

"Most definitely." Marta paused. "In time, I shall learn to sit and complain about all persons and things so that one day people shall know not whether I am Frau Doenhof or myself." Her hand trailed along the railing, following the grains of wood and yet not touching them.

"My ignorance appalls me. I've been under the misapprehension that you didn't favor my eavesdropping sister."

"She is not your sister."

Carl laid his hand over hers, gently forcing it onto the wood. "She feels herself indebted to me for her life just as a sister." Marta quickly withdrew her hand from his and stepped away.

A powerful voice rose from the center of the ship. "Frau Ebel, ye are wanted below." Frau Doenhof hastened toward them.

Carl teased in a low voice, "You're a woman whose presence many seek. Few would be wanted both below and above decks at the same time." Her fair cheeks turned noticeably pinker, which made Carl smile.

Marta took a few of steps toward their intruder. "What do you need of me?" She tried not to let her annoyance, or perhaps relief, show.

"The Hummels' youngest has the same illness that the Pettys' grandfather did. They need you. I'll take you to him."

The woman's eyes looked wild, as if she believed every dire rumor she had heard about women alone on the deck and the evil of sailors. Marta suspected that the woman's scowl was a pretense she adopted to protect herself from her fears. Certainly, Frau Doenhof could have helped the child as easily as she. But perhaps not. The children feared Frau Doenhof's gruffness and the frightful scar on her cheek.

In a low voice that only Marta could hear, Frau Doenhof said, "He shall seduce ye in broad daylight if ye be fool enough to let him." Marta's eyes opened wide. Frau Doenhof continued in a louder voice, "Make haste."

Marta gave Carl a nod good-bye. His return smile warmed her as Frau Doenhof's strong arms pulled her toward the hold. Her touch was cold, as if even her body chose not to give its heat fully to the world around her. Yet she stood with Marta by the child's berth until nothing else could be accomplished. From the moment the child died, one day blurred into the next—so many nights where first the children and elderly, and then others were taken with one ailment or another. Their eleven days at sea turned into more than two fortnights.

Marta had forgotten how many days she had bent over bodies hovering between life and death by the time she gently closed Frau Zweig's eyes. "The fever has taken her."

"No! No!" boomed the woman's husband, a large redheaded man. "This cannot be!" Marta slowly moved back from their berth. He grabbed her small hands with his large ones. "No, no! She has been my wife for twenty years. We would grow old together in Russia. We have no children to comfort us in our old age. She was all I had."

Marta gently pulled her hands from his. "Herr Zweig, I offer you my pity."

He flung himself onto the berth and held his wife's body, wailing at such a pitch that his grief seeped into Marta's very soul. Her back ached from leaning over the woman, and her hands felt raw from the cold rags she had used to cool her fevered brow. Nothing had worked. The smell of decaying flesh, the stench that death left, lingered around her. She had to remove herself from it before it engulfed her. She no longer cared about the rules that kept her confined to the hold. She had to find a place where Herr Zweig's grief could not penetrate.

She stumbled to the ladder and pulled herself on deck. Sitting on a coiled rope, she sucked in gulps of fresh air, determined to feel life coursing through her veins once again. Gulls. Air. Water. Breathe in. Breathe out. The sailors left her alone. The noises around her faded. Life had been reduced to its basics. Breathe in. Breathe out.

Time passed, and her exhausted body once again inhaled and exhaled on its own. In the quiet, she found solace to fill the crevasses that had formed in her soul. Sailors calling to one another and the groaning of the ship as it slid through the sea blended into the quiet, a stillness that was eventually and cruelly broken by the men who carried Frau Zweig's body out of the hold and to the rail. Others followed, accompanying Herr Zweig. The procession was shorter than the first few death processions had been.

Marta forced her legs to obey her as she joined the group for a prayer, but then she turned away, refusing to watch them commend Frau Zweig's body to its cold, wet grave. For two days, Marta had soothed this woman's burning flesh and fought for her life even when Frau Zweig had lost her will to live. Marta would not admit defeat now or ever, not even as she heard the splash behind her and Herr Zweig's renewed wailing.

She blinked quickly to block her tears and pushed away from the group. She found a new place to sit near the bow of the ship, but still Herr Zweig's wails floated to her ears. She pounded her fist against the deck. She would not—she refused—to mourn for people who chose death over life. Her heartbeat increased. Her breathing grew shallow. She tried to capture the cold air that could cleanse her from the anguish that threatened to overwhelm her. She needed to escape her confines. She sprang to her feet and leaned against the bow into the wind.

Her eyes settled on ragged waves ready to claw the ship in their endless appetite for more bodies. She turned her back on them. Above her, the sails billowed and flapped at the mercy of the riotous winds. Marta's heart sank. They were all at the mercy of the wind and the sea—and a captain who she suspected was prolonging their journey deliberately.

The question screamed in her mind. "How many more shall die before this voyage ends?" Having nowhere to go, she resumed her seat and remained on deck until the sun began to soak itself in the sea, staining the large blue monster with hues of magenta and orange, reflecting the blood from the victims already devoured.

Although the sailors had ignored her as they went about their business, Marta did not dare stay alone on deck after the sun went down. With a final look toward the west, she lowered herself into the dark, dank dungeon of her confinement.

At the bottom of the ladder, Marta stopped and surveyed her surroundings. "You shall not conquer me," she murmured. She clenched her fist. "No matter the arrows that fly at me, with God's help, I will survive." In the din of voices around her, Marta's words were inaudible, and she invisible, but she had made her stand. She squared her shoulders and forced her face to resume its natural expression. She would not whine or complain about her lot as her mother had. No one would ever know about her inner battles. She took a step forward.

Carl noticed Marta the moment she entered the hold. Her cheeks were flushed and the serenity of her features had been displaced by a hollow look. He returned his attention to the game he was playing with Hans.

"No. You must catch the rock before it touches the ground. Here, watch this." Carl tossed a stone in the air, picked up two rocks on the ground, and caught his stone with the same hand.

"I cannot. It is too hard."

Frau Doenhof sat behind the boy, not exactly touching him but close enough to show interest. "I've seen thee do much harder tasks than this."

As Marta drew near, Carl spoke in a low voice. "Another death?" She nodded.

"That makes three in two days. We shall all die. I know we shall," cried Frau Doenhof. "Ye pass your days touching them and then bear their illnesses to us by night. Have ye no compassion for the child or us?"

Carl forced his voice to be pleasant. "You look well enough to me, Frau." He took his turn, throwing up his rock and picking up two others. "It does no good to panic. I've escorted some groups where most survive and others where almost a quarter of the passengers die. There is no way to predict who shall travel safe to Russia and who shall not." Carl cleared his throat.

Frau Doenhof crossed her arms. "'Tis this musty air that breeds death. The boy needs fresh air."

"Shall we truly die?" asked Hans with widened eyes.

Frau Doenhof opened her mouth to speak again, but Carl cut her short. "No. I sail to Russia and a future."

Marta nodded. "I too."

Hans's worried face relaxed and then changed to a smile. "I shall not die either."

Frau Doenhof scowled. "Bold words shan't save ye in this grave-yard of the sea."

Carl chuckled. "Our departure from this ship shall not be possible until the captain sails only to Kronstadt and not back toward Lübeck each night."

"Is that what the men tell ye on deck while we remain below in this hole of despair?" Frau Doenhof's mouth looked pinched.

"I suspected the captain of trickery," said Marta.

"Why would he want to sail back again each night?" asked Hans.

Carl grimaced. "The captain intends to sell all his food before we land. Bad weather and dishonest captains prolong journeys."

"Greedy men cause all manner of problems." Frau Doenhof glared at Carl. "All things are about money."

Carl faced her. "Enough." Frau Doenhof's eyes narrowed. Carl knew she owed him her life for getting her out of Lübeck after Herr Binz had released her from the wagon. Keeping his secret was a small price for her to pay. He glanced at Marta. She was biting her lip and wrapping herself with her arms, evidently trying to keep her emotions in check as the sounds of a man's mourning once again permeated the hold.

Marta turned toward the doleful sound. "Not all things are about money." Carl felt relieved. She had not caught Frau Doenhof's slip. For a while, everyone held their peace.

Hans finally broke the silence. "Should we buy all of the captain's food? Then he shall have to hasten the ship. May we buy some food now?"

"Thine hunger never ceases," grumped Frau Doenhof, but she patted his shoulder and helped him pick up the game.

"Let's you and I go buy food," Carl said, taking the patchwork down from their berth. He put the rocks into an opening at the edge of one of the patches.

"It was a curiosity to me as to where you found rocks on the ship," said Marta. "Now I see. How did the patch tear?"

"Herr Ebel pulled it open," said Hans. He turned to Carl. "Should I be very good, would you consent to tear open the other patches? So I may see inside?"

"What do you think you'll find?" Carl asked, amused.

Hans fingered the blanket as if it were a treasure. "More games?"

Marta grimaced. "No wonder it weighs overmuch. I have rocks in my blanket. What else is hidden inside my 'wedding gift'?"

Carl winked at her and turned to Hans. "Now, what do you crave for supper?"

"Zwieback," yelled Hans.

Marta's weariness was obvious, but she joined in their nightly ritual, for Hans's sake. "Pickled meat."

"Wine," said Frau Doenhof in a sour voice that convinced no one.

"I'll purchase it all," Carl said with a laugh.

"All the food on the ship? May I come with you?" begged Hans.

"Can we carry so much?" Carl asked. He scooped Hans into his arms and began to tickle him without mercy. Hans tried to hold in his laughter, but could not.

Carl was surprised at how much he enjoyed his role as father of this makeshift family. He took Hans's hand. "We live a good life. No cooking. No wood to chop. And—"

"No work at all," said Hans. They passed two adults arguing, a family in their berth snoring, and a toddler bawling. Two men near the ladder moved aside to let them pass. One seemed to be comforting the other, a red-haired man.

Carl lifted the boy on deck. "Our lives shall change soon, so we must take our enjoyment while we can." When he reached the deck, he switched to speaking English.

"Hello, Manchester. We'd like our final fare for the day." Carl laid the coins on the table. The wind caught the smallest one, and it skittered across the wood. Hans slapped his hand over it and handed it to the man with one peg leg. The sailor dumped their portion on the table just as distant lightning lit up the darkened, gloomy sky.

Carl peered up at the wildly billowing sails "Another storm approaches," he told Hans, reverting back to German.

"But we shall feast tonight," said Hans. Carl ruffled the boy's blond hair. He had never been around children much, at least not for any length of time.

"Ready?"

Hans shouted, "Let's away."

They picked up the food and headed back to the women. Carl agreed with Frau Doenhof. He hated for Hans to stay in the hold so much of the time. Busying him on deck as often as possible would keep him in the fresh air and protect him from the illnesses that plagued the vessel.

Carl stopped. "I like to stretch my legs every day, so I have decided to inspect every part of this ship and make certain that the sailors do their jobs well. If only I had help, the burden would be lighter."

Carl watched the child's face as he formulated his words. "I might help you."

Carl crossed his arms. "Hmm. Are you a lad who works hard?"

"I am," said Hans. "I can work very hard."

Carl rubbed his chin, pretending to consider the offer. "But you're still quite young." He looked the boy up and down as if weighing his age. He could see that Hans was holding his breath and standing as tall as he could. "I suppose you have had to rise to manhood more quickly than most boys." He slapped his thigh. "I've decided. As the man of your family, you're old enough to be my helper."

The child's face beamed. "I shall work very hard."

"I know you will, lad. And at the end of the voyage, I'll pay you handsomely for your labor. We begin tomorrow."

Carl enjoyed watching Hans's excitement as they made their way back to the women. He stared at the meager fare in his hands. It was time to have a word with the captain. He did not want to wait another fortnight to arrive in Russia.

Watching Carl and Hans weave through the crowd together, Marta felt her lips draw up into a smile. Hans was giggling, and Carl seemed to be enjoying himself. Marta even noticed a ghost of a smile on Frau Doenhof's lips. Carl had enough optimism to infect them all, even amid disease, deprivation, and death. Marta's eyes rested on the child. Hans was adjusting to his life with them. He had had several nightmares, thrashing around between Frau Doenhof and herself, but now his crying came only right before sleep, when he missed his parents the most. Last night, for the first time, he had snuggled next to Marta and had not shed a tear.

Thunder crashed above as Hans and Carl reached them. Hans looked up, as if he could see through the deck to the sky. "Frau Ebel, did you hear about the ship that was wrecked?"

"Do you mean to fill my heart with fear?" Marta gave Hans a stern look.

"'Tis true. The Baltic was so wild that it broke a boat to pieces. All the emigrants fell into the sea."

"Nonsense," said Frau Doenhof. "Next, ye shall tell us that sea monsters ate the people."

"It is the truth." Hans looked to Carl for help.

"The boy's right. A ship was lost."

"What kind of tales do you tell him?" asked Marta. She had enough problems with death stalking her days and did not need Carl giving Hans more reason for nightmares.

Hans placed a hand on Marta's shoulder. "Let not your mind fret, Frau Ebel. All the passengers found rescue and traveled safe to Russia. So even if the storm gives you fright, remember that everyone shall arrive safe."

Marta looked at Carl. He had used a horrendous story to relieve the child's fears. "It fills me with gladness that we shall not become lost at sea." She touched Carl's sleeve to thank him for everything. He winked. She dropped her hand to her side.

They ate quietly, the ship's noises pounding against their ears—seasick people groaning, babies crying, and adults fretting that the captain sailed back again at night. Every once in a while they heard Herr Zweig still weeping for his wife. Marta nibbled on her strip of pickled meat and wondered why each of those on the ship had chosen to give up all they knew and start over on foreign soil. When they signed their contracts, did they have any idea of the sacrifices they would have to make? She studied Carl. What was his reason for going to Russia as an emigrant and not as a recruiting agent? She knew so little about him.

In the middle of the night, Marta woke to overwhelming queasiness. It quickened as the odors from other sickened passengers reached her nostrils. She was thankful that those who slept above them were not seasick like so many others.

A child cried. Adults moaned in their sleep. The boat shifted wildly, causing bodies to slide into one another and across the floor. She heard a few people tumble from their berths. If she had not been so tightly wedged in with Hans and Frau Doenhof, she might have fallen out too. She wondered how Carl fared on the floor. The wooden vessel groaned as if the pounding storm would break it apart. Marta thought about the ship that had been lost and prayed that theirs would stay in one piece.

Chapter Six

L ying in the dark, Carl wished he had his pipe. Forty-two days was too long to live in cramped quarters that smelled like a chamber pot while the Baltic Sea lashed at them with its wildness. He rubbed a sore spot on his leg where a barrel had rolled against him during the night. Although he had not been able to convince the captain to take a direct route—without a bribe, which Carl chose not to offer—the sailors had assured him that they would reach Kronstadt today.

The last half fortnight was permanently etched in his mind by the number of deaths and the eerie wails of mourners, most of them poverty-stricken cases who should have felt relieved at having one less mouth to feed. Their cries seeped into his consciousness, reminding him of how much was lost that could never be recovered.

Some nights as he stood on deck with the other men, he watched the sailors slide corpses into the water. The limp bodies arched in their final descent, as if leaping to freedom from the wooden dungeon that had confined them for too long. As the dead entered the dark recesses of the unknown abyss, Carl had feared the day he would share their lot. He was able to survive all that life threw at him, but death was still a horrifying mystery that he wanted no part of. Whenever memories haunted him, the walls of the hull seemed to close in, and he used anything and anyone as an excuse to leave the close confines.

He shook his head. Only during his early morning strolls with Marta was his calmness restored. He crept quietly to the bunk where the women and Hans were sleeping and placed one hand on Marta's shoulder. Her startled eyes opened, and he tilted his head toward the hatch, his invitation—or perhaps his plea—for her company. She slipped from the berth, and as was their routine, he watched her comb her fine, long, brown hair before pinning it up and covering it with her cap. She gave him a questioning glance. Her cape was caught under Frau Doenhof's sleeping form.

Carl picked up the woolen blanket he had used the night before. She smiled. She was so unassuming and natural. He enjoyed their conversations and appreciated her refusal to dwell on trifling topics, except when she gave in to her penchant for discussing religion. Just like his mother. He supposed no woman was perfect. Of course, who was he to complain? He was probably the least perfect of all men.

Together, they made their way to the ladder, where Marta turned to him and whispered, "It's too early. I don't think the hatch is open yet."

"It's open," he said. He had paid a sailor to unlock the hatch before sunrise. "I have a surprise for you."

She gave him another questioning look. "Truly?"

"Truly."

Once on deck, Carl draped the blanket around Marta's shoulders. She rested her hand in the crook of his arm, and he led her around the deck in silence, a ritual to which they had both grown accustomed. Perhaps it was the quiet and not Marta that calmed him on these early morning walks. Still the pressure of her hand on his arm felt warm, and he enjoyed the way she matched her steps to his. They walked the deck, unseeing, trusting that their feet would know their path from memory, for it was not quite dawn.

On their second tour, Marta said, "It is still so dark. How shall I know your surprise?"

Carl laughed. "Is that a gentle reminder? I'm shocked. I thought I'd married a patient woman."

She joined his laughter. "I have not had a truly good surprise for too long. Do you hide the surprise on your person?"

"No."

"Then you have hid it here on the deck. Must I find it, or shall you show it to me?"

"Neither."

"How shall I know it is mine?"

"You'll know. I give you my word, which I have given to you only once before and to others less than five times in my life. When I give it, I keep my promises and speak the truth. You have trusted me before. Trust me now."

He felt her hand relax. "I do trust you," she said, "but will you not give me a hint of when to expect it?"

He led her to the rail and pointed toward the east. "Look in that direction, and you'll be one of the first on this ship to see the sunrise over Kronstadt." As if on cue, a line of brilliance began to slip above the edge of the dark horizon.

Her hand gripped his arm. "My future."

Perhaps it was the rising sun or the pureness of the hope in her eyes, but he wished they would never reach Kronstadt, wished that pain and disappointment would not be given free rein to tear her dreams from her and fill her eyes with the hopeless expression that haunted so many. But Marta was different. He had to believe that somehow she would prosper where others could not.

He kept his voice low, almost reverent, as he watched her. "The skyline is dim compared to *your* future."

"You tease me mercilessly." Her eyes remained fastened on the changing hues of the sky.

"I tease you not. I gave you a compliment, and here's another. In this light, you're truly the most beautiful woman I've ever seen." He stopped before he made a complete fool of himself. He had no right to enjoy her beauty, to trifle with her affections.

"I wish I could believe you," she said quietly, "but I do not."

"You think I'm a liar? I thought you trusted me."

She turned toward him and smiled, but only halfway. "I know you are a liar. To trust you and believe every word you say are two different things. If you became a Reformer, you would understand the value of truthfulness in both words and deeds."

"I'm beyond reformation. To convert, I must have a conscience, and that would be highly inconvenient." He forced his eyes away from her to stare into the churning water below them.

"It would mean much to Hans." Marta's hand slipped from his arm. She turned fully toward the glory of morning. He stepped behind her so as not to detract from the scene.

"I've given you a sunrise, and instead of thanks, you proselytize me." Carl knew his words had worked when she turned away from her future toward him. He felt a twinge of guilt. The maneuver had been too easy.

"I meant not to.... It is just that ... we might never see each other again." Her skin looked soft in the morning light. He could not help drawing one finger along the side of her face. It had been too long since he had truly felt a woman's touch.

His hand dropped to his side. "I couldn't become a Reformer just for Hans."

She bit her lip. "It would mean much to me, too."

"Why would it mean anything to you?" The ship and the coarse, ruddy sailors disappeared. He saw only Marta gazing up at him against the backdrop of a glorious sunrise. He stepped forward, close enough to feel her breath on his face, to smooth back a strand of her hair. What was he doing? He quickly stepped away.

"Even though you plan to leave me, you shall be my husband still. Naturally, I want you to share my faith." She made a soft noise, as if frustrated with her own efforts. "I wish Herr Binz were here. He would know the words I seek to express."

"Mere words shall never convince me." His heart caught at her look of disappointment, so like his mother's. He turned her around to face the growing light. He had nothing to offer her, no comfort, no hope, no future. "Perhaps when we find Frau Binz, she'll know how to reform my character."

"You mock me."

"No," said Carl. "The truth is that I have too many unanswered questions, and I've heard too many reasons to join one group of believers over another. I've escorted Papists, Mennonites, and Reformers to Russia. I've enjoyed them all. I'm not such a bad man not to believe in any of their gods, am I?"

"You do not fool me," she said. "You are not such a scoundrel as you would like me to think. You have a good heart. One day you shall believe in Jesus Christ."

"No, I won't. I can't." He took a deep breath. "You asked me once what crime I had committed that forced me to use your name and not my own to enter Russia." Carl stiffened. "My crime, and it's a grave one, is that I was born a Jew."

There. He had said it. Now she knew the truth. The distance between them would only grow with time, as it should, as they both needed it to. Their glorious moment had been beautiful, but now it was over.

She looked at him, eyes wide. "You are a Jew?"

"Don't let my heritage bother you. I have no use for any god, Jewish or Christian."

The tone of his voice was light, almost casual, and his words flowed freely as if they meant little to him. Marta was not fooled. She watched his amiable face darken like storm clouds in an otherwise blue sky, and she felt a battle begin to rage within her. In her mind, she heard her mother's voice: "Christ-killers!" She saw her father's furious face: "Scum!"

When she found her voice, she said, "You cannot mean that."

"Hate me if you must, but don't expect me to believe in your Jesus. I've seen too much pain inflicted in His name." His face looked open, vulnerable, as if before her eyes he had transformed into a hurting child, injured and confused by the lies of hatred, prejudice, and arrogance. It lasted for only a moment, and then it passed. The relaxed expression of her rescuer and protector returned, but now she knew his countenance for what it was: a mask.

She tried to ignore the fear rising within her. She had married a Jew! If anyone in their group even suspected the truth, then she, as Carl's wife, would be branded a traitor to Christ along with him and would be expelled from their company. She reached out to Carl, as if to span the gulf that had formed between them. She wished she could remember all her parents' teachings, especially those that would tell her how to deal with a situation like this, but those days seemed a lifetime ago. She felt certain that God held the answers for Carl, but she did not know how to convince him.

The scents of wet wood, misty air, and fish brought her back to the reality of her situation as it slammed into her consciousness. She had married a Jew. She was attracted to Carl, perhaps beginning to love him. Part of her wanted him to stay with her in Russia, not as a friend or protector, but as her husband. Yet, he was a Jew. Their marriage could never develop into a covenant relationship. What a mess she had made of her life by trying to do what was right. Somewhere, demons were laughing at the joke they had played on her good intentions.

In the silence, the sun rose to full circle, shining its brightness on one side of Carl's face and marking the other with deep shadows. Did their marriage and his confession belong to the light or dark side of his soul? She could feel her mother's tendency toward despair creeping forward, grasping at her consciousness, trying to overtake her future. No. She refused it any room in her heart.

"No," she repeated out loud, once again raising her chin. "God is God, and you are my husband."

His eyes blinked rapidly. Then, for the first time in their married life, his arms circled her waist, and he pulled her against him. Her heart beat quickly against his. There had been too many wrongs in their lives, too many unforeseen shadows that had tried to consume them. Yet here they were, with his arms around her, and hers tentatively creeping around his neck.

He would still leave her, no matter the longings that stirred within her. He was not the perfect man that she had thought he was, but heaven help her, she did not want to leave the strength of his arms. She leaned her head against his chest.

Later that day, when the ship finally pulled into the channel that led to Kronstadt, the memory of her time on deck with Carl both warmed and confused her. A commitment of some sort had formed between them, and Marta was at a loss to put that bond into words. For too long, she had been anxious to pull into the harbor. Yet now, the excitement held a distant second to the morning's events. By the time their group stood on the dock with all their belongings wrapped in bundles and in the patchwork, Marta never wanted to board another boat of any kind again, and she never wanted to go anywhere if Carl were not by her side.

The seaport of Kronstadt was bustling. Observing a ship docked not far from theirs, Carl recognized a dark-haired man as Quentin, an English captain who had carried immigrants for him in the past. Quentin must have just delivered a load of immigrants to the Russian port for a different recruiting agent.

Carl pulled his cap lower over his eyes and fingered the forty-day growth of beard that now covered his face. He could not act like a greenhorn. He was here, in the enemy's camp, on business. No one must recognize him.

Marta stood next to Carl on the dock. She longed to change out of her dress, heavy with the stains and odors of their prolonged voyage, and give it a good washing. She knew that that might not happen before they reached their final destination, though, since she had only the one good dress.

Hans laughed. "Watch me." He tried to walk. His legs bowed, and he lost his balance. He giggled as he fell on the dock.

"Take it slowly. You still have your sea legs," said Carl. Hans jumped up. His legs bowed again, and he fell, laughing.

Frau Doenhof, looking smaller and less domineering in all the commotion, pointed to the end of the dock. "Who're they?" She stood rooted near Hans.

Thick-bearded men with large, horse-drawn carts lined the shoreline in front of them. Marta had never seen fur coats or hats like theirs. Instead of being woven from sheep's wool, these garments appeared to have been made from the whole sheepskin. The men's coarse shouting created such a commotion that she was surprised their animals stood still.

Immigrants were climbing over each of the four wheels, then over the sides, into the cart beds. When one cart was filled, another drove up. This bustling was quite different from the secretive manner in which they had left the German states.

"Do we have to go with them?" asked Hans, holding Carl's hand. With his other hand, Carl held the burlap sack of grain.

"Yes," said Carl. "They'll take us to the place where we'll register."

"I suppose we must pay them any money that the captain hasn't already stolen from us," said Frau Doenhof in an uncharacteristically quiet voice.

Carl touched the woman's arm. "They're not as rough as they look. They speak Russian. We speak German. They're frustrated. And no, we don't have to pay. This ride is compliments of the Tsarina of Russia." He steered them toward the rough carts through the crowds of people who had traveled with them on the ship. Herr Zweig stepped aside for them and doffed his cap.

"I thank you," said Marta quietly. Herr Zweig always made her feel as if she had rendered him a service that he could never repay. One of the Russians pointed at Marta and began yelling to her in a loud voice.

"Why does he shout so?" she asked. Carl, Hans, and Frau Doenhof looked at the man blankly. The teamster put his hands on the top of his hat as if in frustration before speaking even louder and faster in his native tongue. Finally, he motioned Marta to his cart with exaggerated swings of his arms.

"He bids us get in," said Hans.

"The boy is right," said Carl.

Frau Doenhof stiffened. "I don't care what he says. I shall not climb into one of those rickety old things. They bring to mind the one that almost bore me to the dungeons."

Marta saw Carl squeeze Frau Doenhof's elbow but could not hear his words in the din until he turned to Marta and said, "Why don't you go first?" As she took a step forward, he spoke again to Frau Doenhof. "See? There's nothing to fear."

The teamster motioned to Marta again as if she were the stupidest creature in Russia. Carl helped her over the sides into the splintered cart before helping Frau Doenhof and Hans. Sitting on the cart's bed, Marta could just see over the vehicle's sides. To Marta's surprise, Hans sat in Frau Doenhof's lap. The woman's eyes blinked quickly, as if warding off tears.

Frau Doenhof turned her head, but Marta was certain she had heard the woman softly say, "Ye be so like your father."

Carl hopped in and sat with them. Hans moved from Frau Doenhof's lap to Carl's. Marta held their belongings tightly to her body. Even the weight of the quilt gave her comfort in the strangeness of this new world. She did not mind having to carry the stones and other mysterious items secreted beneath its patches. They were Carl's secrets. She did not have to know what they were to guard them well.

Though constructed differently, the carts reminded Marta of the ones that had originally taken them to the dock in Lübeck, not the ones that had carted her fellow emigrants away. She shuddered and whispered a prayer for those captured and a word of thanksgiving for the safe arrival of her ship. The driver commanded more and more immigrants into their cart, until they had to overlap one another to fit. Marta's back was pinned against the hard sideboard that smelled of a previous earthy cargo.

She had concentrated all her efforts on reaching Russia. Now she had arrived. She was here. Instead of her dream coming true, instead of completing her travels and finding her home, she realized that her journey was only beginning.

Shouting more unintelligible words, the teamster whipped his horses into action. Marta fell against Frau Doenhof, who was reaching out to regain her balance. Instead of berating her, Frau Doenhof reached for Marta's hand and the two women faced the bumpy road together. Marta felt almost as if she were back in the ship's berth being buffeted by another storm. On the other side of Frau Doenhof, Carl was hunched over Hans.

As the cart pulled away from the teeming docks, Marta noticed stacked crates and barrels. Perhaps if she could read, she would have known what was inside, but even the letters looked ill formed, not like anything she had seen in her own language. The city of Kronstadt, with its large open fields and few buildings near the dock, appeared to be better suited for the military than civilians. Farther inland, the island opened to a flat area with occasional areas of birch thickets and needlelike foliage that hugged the earth. She breathed in the cool air, testing the unfamiliar scents of this new land.

Just as every bone in Marta's body had begun to feel as if it had been jounced out of place, the wagon stopped at a large, open field. Hundreds of German immigrants congregated around official-looking men, while others lounged around crude stick shelters that covered the land for as far as she could see. Carl lifted Hans out and then helped Frau Doenhof down.

"Welcome to Kronstadt," he said in a low voice to Marta as she slid from the cart.

"It looked better from a distance," she said with a saucy smile to keep up her spirits. He gave her a conspirator's wink. The teamster spoke impatiently and pointed to the officials before driving his cart away. Marta suspected that no one but Carl could understand what the man had said. The others from their wagon hurried in the direction the teamster had pointed.

Russian soldiers were stationed throughout the area. Most were shouting garbled commands at people who probably did not know what they were being asked to do. "Stay with me," said Carl, herding his charges away from the others.

"Ye know Russian," said Frau Doenhof loudly with some of her old bluster returning. "What are we to do next?"

Carl gave her a stern look. "What I know and what I want others to know are two different things."

"Tell us what we should do before our arms fall off and our feet grow roots," said Frau Doenhof. Marta was relieved that the woman was directing her ire at Carl instead of her for a change.

"I'll take you through as many steps as I please so that no one else shall guess that I understand Russian. Follow my lead, or go it alone." His threatening tone made Marta nervous, and she could tell that it was scaring Hans. Frau Doenhof's eyes remained angry, but she fell silent. Marta wondered what had caused such animosity between them.

Carl calmed himself and nodded toward a line of immigrants waiting for officials to check their documents. "We'll join that group." He reached into his shirt for the papers that he had prepared for them. In a lower voice that captured only the attention of the women and Hans, he said, "No matter what happens, remain silent. I alone shall talk." Marta's eyes grew big and then narrowed as if she mistrusted his motives. Her expression amused him. He felt himself relax. Everything would work out fine.

They walked into a mob of people who appeared to have no order whatsoever. The crowd milled around the official who seemed to be in charge. As they pushed closer, Carl recognized the agent— one of the men whom Goralski, his former commissioner, had on his payroll. Carl tilted his head down and carefully glanced behind him. The group had grown in size.

He could not let the man recognize him. From where they stood, if the agent looked up from the documents he was processing, he might notice Carl. Then the game would be over even before it had gotten underway. Carl gently pressed Marta and Hans backward. Frau Doenhof followed.

He spoke in a light voice. "There is no hurry. Allow some of our fellow passengers to go first. We have arrived. That's enough for now." Hans looked as if he was about to protest, but thankfully, he obeyed without question. He reached for Carl's hand.

"You there," boomed a voice. Carl looked up into the eyes of a Russian soldier.

Chapter Seven

Carl's hands formed fists around his belongings. He would not give up without a fight if this man turned out to be one of Goralski's men. He wished the soldier had spoken in Russian instead of German. Then Carl could have pretended that he did not understand. The soldier was shorter than Carl, but large and muscular with dark, curly hair. He leaned forward, his chiseled face glaring at Carl in a way that made Carl dislike him immediately.

"Yes, sir?" Carl asked in his most pathetic voice.

"You have not respect for your new home and generous gifts? Your belongings trail you. Pick it all up now!"

"Yes, sir." Carl looked at the items that had fallen from Hans's pack. This soldier was not a threat, and he hoped the exchange had not drawn the attention of others.

Another officer bellowed to the soldier in Russian. "Sergey! Here!" His arms floundered in the air, as if in surrender to the two irate German women before him. Evidently, he was unable to understand them. Carl's shoulders relaxed as Sergey went to the other man's aid.

"Hans," Carl said in a gentle voice, "you have a hole in your pack." Hans did not seem to hear him as his eyes searched the groups of people around him. Marta quickly retrieved a filthy piece of cloth, perhaps Hans's nightdress, and a spoon.

"But there is dirt on them," said Hans as she slid them into his blanket-turned-pack.

Carl immediately tied up the hole. "Good as new." They turned back to the crowd of people they had been waiting behind, and Carl let two more families move ahead of them.

"It is too heavy," Hans complained. Carl patted the child's shoulder. Hans was tired and no doubt anxious to find his mother. Carl knew how he felt. He was anxious to make contact with someone who could help him put his plans into action. But he could do nothing until they reached Oranienbaum, and Hans could do nothing until they had registered.

Cartloads of people continued to arrive. At Carl's insistence, Marta and her companions again dropped behind a group of immigrants pushing forward to be registered. Marta tugged at her clothes, trying to allow an errant breeze access to the space between her heavy cloak and skirt. The cloak was too hot in the spring sun, but she, like so many other women, had opted to wear her garments instead of carrying more items.

Carl had seemed happy to reach Kronstadt, and eager to leave the ship, but now he seemed content to wait. Marta peered ahead to glimpse the heavily bearded official who was processing the documents.

"Is he our problem?" she asked in a low voice that she hoped even Frau Doenhof would not hear.

Carl's eyebrows rose as he gave her a searing look. "He will not process us as the documents are written. See those to the far side of him?" Marta looked. Five people spoke with many hand motions to a bland-faced soldier to the side.

"We don't want to end up with them," he said. "We'll wait."

A family of four bumped into Marta as they pushed past her. "There are other officials over there." She nodded toward the right.

"It's better to be lost in a large crowd than to move from one line to another." Carl looked away from her as if to indicate that their conversation had ended.

Better for whom? thought Marta. She knew that Hans had had little sleep the night before in his excitement to see his mother again. His arms were tired from carrying a heavy pack. It would not be long before he began to lose whatever self-control he had left.

Two official-looking Russians approached the bearded man at the front of their group. Carl bristled and pulled his cap farther over his eyes. After a brief conversation, a new man took over the proceedings. The other two left.

"Now it's our turn," said Carl in a pleasant voice. "We've been generous enough. Hans, lead the way."

Firmly, Carl pushed them forward until they were in front of the new man.

"Carl and Marta Ebel?" he asked with a Russian accent. Carl nodded. He continued, "You travel with your son and widowed sister." Another nod. They stood unmoving as the man continued reading. "Everything seems to be in order." He handed Carl a few coins.

Carl tried not to grimace. The official had cheated them out of the full amount they were promised. No wonder those people on the other side of the soldiers were so upset. If he truly had to feed his family on that amount, he would have been perturbed, too.

"Is something wrong?" asked the official.

"No, sir," said Carl.

The man leaned over to a soldier and spoke in Russian. "*Nyemtzy!* The idiots don't even know they've been cheated. I have no patience for them." In German, he said, "You may pick up sticks and rope to make a shelter over there. On the morrow, you shall be assigned to a group." He handed back their papers.

A village of stick shelters stretched before them. Without asking, Carl knew their wait would be at least a few days.

"It shall give us something to do while we wait," said Marta quietly. They picked up as many tree branches and as much twine as they could carry before moving to an area that was surrounded by other shelters.

The following evening, Marta alternately squeezed and opened her hands, trying to ease the stiffness. They had finished making their shelter, which was barely a lean-to, but it might afford them a small amount of protection from the elements if it rained, especially with their cloaks placed over the top. Fortunately, she felt no chill in the air and saw no sign of clouds. She surveyed the city of twig lean-tos. How would she ever be able to find Frau Binz among so many nondescript dwellings?

Hans said, "Can we find my mother now, Frau Ebel?"

Carl chimed in, "Not tonight." He placed the extra coil of twine on the side of their shelter.

Frau Doenhof harrumphed. "I suppose that means that ye be hungry. I worked as hard as ye, but now I am expected to make a meal appear. Men!" She grabbed their lone pot and left.

"Tomorrow, Hans," continued Carl, "you and Frau Ebel shall search for your mother."

"But it's still daylight," said Hans.

Marta put her arm around Hans. "You know very well that it stays light here far into the night. It is the time of year."

"On the morrow, you shall search all morning, afternoon, and evening," said Carl. "You may do it on the morrow and its morrow and its morrow, until you find her or find out where she abides." Carl laughed as Hans threw his arms around his waist. He continued, "You are a patient lad, Hans. A man must work first before doing what his heart longs to do."

Marta watched Carl's face. She could not help but wonder if the message was meant for her, too. Carl would not leave yet, but he would be going about his business.

Frau Doenhof returned with a pan of vegetables that she had been able to buy from the Russian officials with Carl's money.

"I can return the twine for others to use," said Marta, moving toward the side of their shelter.

"No." Carl cleared his throat. "I have a use for it."

"Very well. I'll help Frau Doenhof make a special meal, since we do not know how many more we shall have together."

Later, as they ate their cabbage and beet soup, Marta watched Carl. He sat in front of her on the ground near their lean-to, but it was as if he were already on his way back across the Baltic. Yet each time a Russian soldier passed, she saw him tense. Then he would look up slightly and stare at the place where the official's boots had passed.

There was so much that she wished she had asked him on the ship instead of just being content to be with him. Now, it was too late. She could do nothing to help him unless he chose to confide in her.

Marta sipped the hot soup, grateful for anything made from fresh food. It helped fill the emptiness she already felt. Once their eating utensils were cleaned and the fire in front of their shelter doused, the noises of the day settled into the lull of late evening, even though the sun still shone as if it were midafternoon. Pots clinked, and people conversed, but the sounds became only an occasional humming noise in the background of Marta's consciousness.

She crawled after the others into their shelter. Hans rolled next to her, and she could feel his excitement. To help ease his tension, she rubbed his back. Slowly he relaxed and fell asleep as the light dimmed.

Listening to the steady rhythm of Frau Doenhof's breathing, Marta's mind wandered. Tomorrow, or the next day, or the next, Hans would leave. Then Carl would go, and she would be left with Frau Doenhof. What would the frontier hold for two unprotected women, one who used all her strength to keep the world at bay and the other who had no worldly knowledge? There was a movement on the other side of Frau Doenhof. Marta could not tell if it was Carl or if a rodent had entered their open shelter. Slowly she reached for their heavy metal spoon. Nothing would be allowed to hurt Hans while he was in her care.

Carl slid from his cover. No one else stirred. He could tell that Marta was awake, but he knew she would not give him away. He paused. A soldier's tread could be heard from the path in front of their shelter. Another soldier would not be patrolling their area for a while. He had noted their pattern during dinner.

When the man was gone, Carl darted into the darkness gained from the shadow of their shelter and picked up the excess rope. He skillfully made a large noose on one end of the rope and then draped the twine around his shoulder and arm. Making certain his way was clear, he crept from the back of one twig dwelling to the next, the embers in front of each having turned to ashes. At the far end of the camp, a league away from the twig shanties, soldiers warmed their hands by a fire. He drew as close as the cover of pale darkness would allow.

The soldier named Sergey stretched out his hands and spoke in his native Russian. "It won't be long until I've tamed another German filly."

The other man chuckled. "You and your women."

Carl skirted the light cast by their fire and moved in the direction of the docks. He ran in the shadows until his side hurt, and then he ran more. The exercise warmed him by the time he reached the dock. He had come back for Goralski, but seeing Quentin, the English captain, on his ship had solidified Carl's resolve. Quentin's boat was recognizable by its carved dragon edifice. It was only two ships away from the boat that had transported Carl.

Carl lowered himself into one of the dinghies tied to the dock and quietly paddled alongside the ship. The crew had kept their rope ladder in place, as was the practice of the sailors in this Russian harbor, for errant sailors to return unnoticed. As he drew close, the ship's name, *Lativia*, came into view.

Carl pulled himself onto the deck opposite the sentry. Stealthily, he made his way to the captain's cabin, slipped inside, and barred the door. Then he lowered the twine noose until it was around the snoring captain's head.

"What? What's this?" said the startled man.

"Good morning, Quentin," Carl said in perfect English.

"You!" the captain growled. He reached for his knife, but Carl tightened the noose. Quentin's hand went instinctively to his throat, now fully aware of his situation. "I 'eard ye lurked in 'ese parts," he muttered. "What want ye?"

"Your right hand," said Carl. When Quentin did not respond immediately, Carl tightened the noose so the rope dug into the man's neck. Quentin extended his right hand toward Carl. The noose loosened.

"That's neighborly." Carl tied the man's hand to the corner of his

bed. "And now your left." The captain's left arm rose. Carl tied it to
the other corner of the bed before moving to the end of the bed.

"Ye'll ne'er get away with it," said Quentin.

Carl muffled a chuckle. "Isn't that what I told you when you used
the same set of knots on me? I merely keep my word. I doubt if
you'll be able to keep yours."

Quentin offered his legs to be tied. "If I call my men, ye'd be at
my mercy."

"I'd be at your men's mercy, not yours," said Carl. "You'd be
dead. Your throat would be slit long before they knocked down the
door." When Quentin's legs were tied, Carl returned to the man's
side. "As long as you don't pull your arms or legs, the loop around
your neck shall remain as it is."

"How'd ye escape this? No one e'er escaped when I tied the
knots," said Quentin, remaining quite still.

"I'm extraordinary," said Carl. "Now, shall we get down to business?" When Quentin grunted, Carl moved to the captain's strongbox. He took the man's keys from his desk and opened it.

"Superb." Carl took out Russian money and gold pieces, and
then tied them into a cloth that he knotted around his waist.

"So ye've become a common thief."

"Is it thievery to take back what rightfully belongs to me?
Goralski's too well guarded to reach and Ivanov has already been
taken care of," Carl lied. "You're all I have." Unbidden, Marta's
disappointed eyes rose in his mind as if perturbed by all his lies.
Fortunately, her image disappeared almost before he had time to
register that it was there.

"Ye've been busy," Quentin growled.

"No," said Carl. "It was assumed that I had left Russia after I
escaped your knots and Ivanov's betrayal."

"Ye've been here the 'ole time?" Quentin's words ended in a garbled sound.

"Don't move, or you'll choke yourself," reprimanded Carl. A
coin fell to the floor with a jingle. He did not bother to retrieve it.

The strongbox held an assortment of jewels, probably stolen

from a Russian princess by Goralski and given to Quentin for safe-keeping. Carl put a few choice stones, those that would look good on Marta, in his pockets.

"What 'arm did ye to Ivanov?" asked Quentin.

"What I did was artful, even brilliant," said Carl. "It was so good, that only he knows what I did. Everyone else shall think it was merely bad luck." Another pause. Carl put a smirk on his face. He hoped Quentin could think of some touch of bad luck that Ivanov had recently had that could be attributed to Carl.

"Not the carriage wheels and sled runners," said Quentin incredulously. "Ye broke 'em?"

Carl laughed. "He lost every penny that he made when he betrayed me. I don't need his Russian money, so long as it isn't his to use either. I much prefer to spend yours. You told Goralski about my heritage. I expected more loyalty from you."

"Ye're nothing but a dirty Jew," said the captain.

"That's quite right." Carl cut a strip from the man's blanket to gag his mouth. "And you should be grateful that I am a Jew and not a rotten Englishman. At least I shall leave you with your clothes, a courtesy you didn't extend to me. Since I shall leave this great country tonight, I bid you farewell and good riddance."

By the time Carl returned to the twig shelter, he was exhausted. He had declared war, and he knew it. Once Quentin was found, which was probably not long after he left, Goralski would be informed. He would order a general search of all areas nearby, most likely concentrating on the harbor. More importantly, Goralski would assume that he was too shrewd for Carl to attempt a personal attack. He would let down his guard. Now, all Carl had to do was wait.

"Carl?" Marta whispered into the gray light of early morning.

He almost answered, but the cloak of predawn gray made her voice sound too sweet, too trusting, too loving. He remained silent. The less she knew, the more protected she would be. Her lovely face and naïve innocence would have to be purged from his mind. Now. He had to start now.

"Carl?" she asked again.

No, Fraülein Ebel, he thought, reverting to her true title in his mind. She must learn to do without him. He would secure her an immigrant group with which to travel. She would be assured of receiving her land, and then he would leave. Fraülein Ebel had her life to live, and he had his.

The camp was quiet except for an occasional infant's cry or the tread and call of a patrolling soldier. Marta heard Hans stirring. She closed her eyes and waited for him to waken fully, trying not to dwell on the pain of Carl's rejection. Soon, it would all be over. Carl was only with them to provide her with her land. No more. No less.

"Frau Ebel," whispered Hans. "'Tis the morn. May we seek my Mutter?"

Marta smiled. "Let us prepare for the day with a meal first." She was going to miss this little one. "We shall set out afterward."

Hans scurried out from under their shelter. "I shall fetch the water." She heard a thump.

"Watch you where you run!" demanded a harsh voice in broken German.

Marta crawled from their shelter. A Russian soldier stood in front of her. He wore black boots almost to his knees, skin-tight pants covered partly by a red regimental jacket, and a black hat that rose high on his head. Others stood behind him. They had their weapons extended. Hans looked disoriented.

The soldier continued in broken German, "Insolent! I should make you whipped."

"What is this?" said Marta in a firm voice. "Is it your duty to attack children?"

The soldier's hard eyes turned to Marta and softened slightly. She recognized him as the soldier who had stopped them the day before. Although she still wore the same dress, having had no occasion to change into her nightdress, she felt less than adequately covered before his eyes. Without thinking, she put a hand to her hair to tidy it.

"Forgive, good Frau," Sergey said in broken German. "My temper is hot and jumps quick."

Marta nodded her acceptance and held out a hand to Hans. The boy charged into her arms for protection.

"What is the problem here?" demanded Frau Doenhof as she threw herself out of the shelter and into the open.

"We must do order to check every person. We speak now with the husband of you," said Sergey in his faulty German.

"I too," said Frau Doenhof. "I would discuss many things with the worthless scoundrel, but he drank himself to death years ago."

"We speak then with the husband of you," said Sergey in his faulty German, turning to Marta.

"That is not possible," said Marta.

"Why not? He is here," said Frau Doenhof. "Herr Ebel, get ye up for these soldiers!"

"Enough," said Marta in a tone that Carl had once used with Frau Doenhof. "While you slept, I was yet awake. He was not himself last night."

"No!" cried Frau Doenhof. "With all thy nursing of sick and destitute, thou hast finally brought the plague to us. How could thou?"

"Your husband is not well?" asked Sergey.

"He needs rest," said Marta. "He is not fit to lift his head. Still, should you require proof, I shall disturb him."

"No disturb this sick man," said Sergey in his fractured German. "Da. Let sleep be with him. We search for man of crime, not illness."

"Water. We need water," cried Frau Doenhof. "Hans. Make haste. We must flee the illness. Come." She grabbed the child's hand and pushed through the group of soldiers, as if she were more fearful of illness than of their weapons.

"Forgive the interrupt," said Sergey. With one last look that lingered across the whole length of Marta's body, he directed the soldiers to the next hovel.

Marta turned from them and busied herself with the fire so as to appear unconcerned with what the soldiers had said. Yet, her mind raced, and she had to force herself not to go in and shake Carl, demanding to know why he had put himself in harm's way.

Once the fire was burning steadily, she crawled back into their shelter to comb her hair. "The soldiers are gone." She pinned her hair in place before setting her cap over it. When he did not answer her, she continued, "You did not sleep here last night."

He opened his eyes. "What I do is naught of your concern."

Marta ignored the pain his remark caused. "It is my concern if it imperils Hans or me." She placed her hand on his forehead, as if checking his fever. There were so many gaps between the twigs that formed their shelter, she thought it best to give the impression that Carl was sick in case anyone watched.

He brushed her hand away. "The less you know, the less danger for you." There was a pause before he said, "You didn't fully tell the truth out there."

"I told the truth," she said. "They misinterpreted."

He gently took her hand in his. "Whatever you did, or did not do, I thank you." He let her hand slide from his.

"Good enough," she said. "Tell me this. How does your being a Jew make you a criminal?"

Carl remained still. "The Tsarina's laws state that no Jew may be paid money or given land. If a Jew is paid wages, then both the Jew and the person who paid him are criminals."

"So as a recruiting agent, you broke the law when you received the money Russia owed you. Now I see," said Marta. After Carl nodded, she touched his hand lightly. "Sleep. You shall be rested before long." She crawled outside and tended to the smoky fire.

If only she could let go of Carl in her heart as quickly as he already seemed to have forgotten her. She told herself, *I feel this way because I want someone to take care of me, not because I love him.* Hers was the struggle for self-sufficiency. She should not, must not, cling to anything or anyone out of fear. She knew she could overcome her emotions, but she also knew that with each day her resolve grew weaker. She longed to reach her new home and set everything right.

A wet-faced Frau Doenhof and dripping Hans returned to warm themselves by the fire. Frau Doenhof started cooking the morning meal. She did it with such calm, that Marta suspected her earlier drama had been a well-played ruse.

Carl was exhausted, but could not fall asleep. Marta's touch had seared his skin. She certainly did not deserve him and all his intrigues. She needed someone solid, stable, and capable of loving her the way she deserved to be loved. She needed a husband who would take care of her and their children and work to keep her smile from fading. Yes, she needed a husband.

That was it! He sat up and hit his head on an extended branch. If convenient, he would do for her what she refused to do for herself. As he lowered his head back to the ground, he formulated a new plan. Today he would remain out of sight and rest, but first thing on the morrow, he would seek out someone for Marta. He would find her a true husband.

Chapter Eight

Marta looked around and pushed back a stray hair, frustrated that the fine strands near her face never stayed in place. She had the oddest feeling that she was being watched. The makeshift village of immigrants was slowly beginning to rouse. She heard a spoon clink against a metal pot, sleepy voices calling greetings, and even a distant bird heralding the new morn.

A wet and disheveled Frau Doenhof scolded Hans. "Ye shall not go to see thy mother like that! Get Frau Ebel's comb." Then comb in hand, she attacked the unruly strands of Hans's hair, not declaring a truce even while he ate.

Hans cleaned his bowl. "It is time to go." He yanked his head from Frau Doenhof. "I know we shall find Mutter today."

Frau Doenhof harrumphed. "I shan't let ye go 'til ye look respectable." She scoured the ground, collecting soft twigs.

Marta shivered. There it was again. The hair on the back of her neck was standing up, giving her the feeling of being observed. She looked around, but saw no one.

Frau Doenhof used the twigs to brush the dust off Hans's clothes. Only then did she stand back to examine her work.

"Do not cry, Frau Doenhof." Hans wiped his nose with his sleeve. "I shall come back to visit."

"See that ye do," she replied in a rough voice.

Marta cleaned off the clumps of grain that encrusted the large spoon, while Hans shifted his weight from one foot to the other. "Frau Ebel, make haste! Mutter awaits me."

"Be off with ye. I'll clean up," said Frau Doenhof. "Ye be sure to take care of our boy."

Marta stood up and brushed the dirt from her skirt. Her mind must have been playing tricks on her. No one was watching. Her thoughts had been filled with too much mystery—wondering about Hans's lost mother and Carl's nocturnal adventures.

Hans bounced impatiently. "May we leave now?"

Marta nodded but took one last look around. The sky was a brilliant blue, and the sun was already warming the day. She hoped its heat would burn away the cobwebs of suspicion that had been growing in her mind.

"Which area would you like to search first?" she asked.

"Hurrah!" Hans skipped around Marta and Frau Doenhof with his arms raised. Marta caught Frau Doenhof's eye and for the first time, they shared a look of amusement.

"Now ye be the one to waste time, Hans," scolded Frau Doenhof. Although tired, Marta felt much better having something to do that was of value to someone, especially to Hans. Frau Doenhof waited for him to settle down and then wet down his last two unruly strands of hair. He wrapped his arms around her skirt. "Thank you." Marta noticed tears forming in Frau Doenhof's eyes.

"Very well, Hans, now where shall we start?" asked Marta.

"Let's start down there," he said, pointing to the other side of the encampment.

"I shall follow, but abide near me. Do not run ahead." Marta stretched her muscles with purpose, ignoring the tightness of her joints and ligaments. "Lead the way."

When Hans reached an area where they did not know the inhabitants, he stopped and yelled in his loudest voice, "Mutter! Mutter!"

"Stop that clamor." Marta hurried to his side.

"More people can hear me if I shout," he said.

"They may hear you, but they shan't listen to your words," she replied.

"My mother shall." Hans's lip stuck out. The air smelled of burned wood from the fires that had been in their glory only moments earlier.

"Let's start with this shelter," she said. Hans's face immediately changed to a smile, and he rushed ahead as if he expected to find his mother waiting.

"Good morn, friend," Marta called.

"A good morn to you." A woman crawled out of a bramble shelter that looked wide enough to sleep two people. Her clothes were dull, similar to Marta's, but the joy in her face immediately caught Marta's attention.

"Forgive this disturbance, good Frau," said Marta. "We seek the boy's mother, Frau Binz. They became separated in Lübeck."

"The poor dearie," said the woman, giving Hans a large hug. He pulled away gently. She tilted her head upward as if paging through the memories of all the people she had ever met. "I am not acquainted with a Frau Binz, though I have heard of a Frau Bender. She resides with her new husband over there. I'm sorry I can't be of more help. I shall pray for you and your search."

By the time Marta turned away from her, Hans was already standing before the next shelter.

A man's voice growled, "Why gape ye, boy? Be gone!"

"I seek my mutter," began Hans in a small, thin voice.

"Are ye blind? Do ye think I'm a woman?"

Marta hurried to where Hans stood unmoving, as if he did not know what to do next. The area around the man's shelter smelled of strong spirits. When he began swearing like a sailor, Hans's face paled.

Marta put her arm around his shoulders and quickly led him to the next hut. "Not all people are kind or willing to help us. That is why we must stay together and speak as politely as we can."

"Maybe you should talk to the grown-ups, and I shall talk to the children." He reached for her hand, and she gave it a squeeze.

"A good idea," she said.

At the next shelter, the man was all friendliness. "No, I do not know a Frau Binz, but my sister-in-law also became separated from a loved one, her husband. I shall tell her your story to fill her heart with hope." The man hurried away.

"I do not know why you tarry and talk overmuch," said Hans

after they had questioned the occupants of the first eight shelters. "The sun is already high, and there are many places to seek her."

"We dare not peer into any shelter without the owner's leave," said Marta. "Do not be discouraged. We shall take all the time we need till we find your mother."

"Please do not talk so much this time." Hans pushed ahead of her.

By midday, Marta's back began to hurt from leaning into shelters in search of Frau Binz. In the back of her mind, she wondered how, even if they found Frau Binz, she would be able to tell her of her husband's death. Closer to her heart, she did not know how she would be able to say good-bye to Hans, who had become like family to her. When they had not found Frau Binz by nightfall, she comforted Hans with the promise to begin the search anew in the morning.

The following day, after a good night's rest, Carl crawled out of the shelter, and then reached back inside for his black hat. He watched a single ray of sunlight caress Marta's sleeping form and envied the morning light.

"Don't look back," he scolded himself. He was feeling guilty, that was all. Once he found her a protector, he could leave without guilt—without guilt, but not without regrets. He grabbed a dry biscuit that Frau Doenhof had made the night before. It caught in his throat, and he had to wash it down with water, although he craved a hot cup of tea. It would be a good morning, he told himself. He strolled through the camp to further his dealings and keep on the lookout for a suitable husband for Marta.

The first single man he engaged in a conversation seemed congenial, but Carl could not abide the man's inordinate obsession with Tartan tribes attacking them once they had settled on their new land. With that kind of fear, he might not survive the first winter on the barren steppes. A second candidate looked sturdy enough. Carl was about to speak to him when the man kicked a cat that was wandering the camp in search of food. Marta was strong, but this man would never tolerate her independent ways. She deserved someone who would treat her with kindness and respect.

A third man reeking of spirits asked, "Care for a swig o' ale?"

Carl shook his head no. It was not even midmorning. He went from one man to the next, mentally crossing each off his list of possibilities. After hours of searching, Carl could only conclude that the morning had been a complete disaster. He had assumed he would find a suitable husband for Marta before the noon meal. Matchmaking was a more difficult job than he had anticipated. It might take several days, and he could not concentrate solely on the task. He had other plans to set in motion.

_ᴄ_

Marta prepared to start her second day of hunting for Frau Binz. After the morning meal, she quickly put away the utensils and tidied up the blankets in the lean-to. Frau Doenhof returned with a supply of water and said, "Ye best be on your way."

"Certainly we shall find her this day," said Hans. "Where did Herr Ebel go?"

"As the man of the family, he has many tasks he needs to accomplish before we continue our journey." Marta hoped her words sounded convincing, but inside, she felt the same doubts that Hans did. Each time she heard Carl leave, she wondered if she would see him again. She turned to Hans. "Where shall we begin our search this day?"

Hans did not respond immediately. He squeezed his eyes closed and folded his hands. "Dear God, You know where my mother abides. Please lead us to her. Amen."

"Amen," Marta said in a soft voice. This child had more faith than she did. She should have admonished him for not addressing the Almighty more formally, but she could tell that his mind had turned from spiritual matters back to finding his mother. Besides, his prayer reminded her of Herr Binz's prayers. She wondered how Hans had known what to say.

"Let's begin over there," Hans said, pointing to a cluster of lean-tos halfway down the next row. When Marta nodded, he led the way. They moved from one poorly constructed structure to the next.

"Let's go over there," Hans said over and over until Marta's feet hurt. The smell of beets and cabbage cooking in pots filled the air. Marta's stomach growled. One family had meat gravy and potatoes boiling in their pot.

As Hans trotted toward an especially crowded section of the camp, Marta said, "This must be the last one, Hans. Frau Doenhof shall not keep our midday meal warm much longer. We shall seek your mother again after we sup." That was all she needed, she told herself, a few bites of food to reinvigorate her sagging spirit. After scouring the area, Hans reluctantly took Marta's hand and started walking back toward their hut. Just as they were turning a corner, he stopped and cocked his head to one side.

"What ails you?" Marta asked.

Without a word, he released her hand and bolted into a crowd, pushing between people and squeezing through a tall man's legs.

"Mutter! Mutter!" he yelled.

"Hans!" Marta could not weave through the crowd like Hans. She lost sight of him almost immediately. Panic rose to her throat. "Hans! Hans!" Looking over and around people, she pushed through the throng. Faces everywhere turned toward her, but they were moving slowly as if in a dream. "Hans!"

She saw him. He was standing all alone, looking around him with a wild, disoriented expression on his face.

As Marta drew near, he said, "Frau Ebel, I heard her."

"Are you sure?" She tried to catch her breath and still her racing heart.

"I heard her voice in song," he said.

They listened. All around them, people jabbered and complained. Two men were in the midst of a heated argument that was only stopped by a woman who crawled out of a shelter and shouted at them. In a moment's lull between so many sounds, Marta began to hear a soft strain, a sweet voice singing a lullaby.

"That is her voice!" Hans turned back in the direction they had already come, weaving in and out of shelters and stopping every few seconds to listen. Marta followed closely.

Growing ever more frustrated, Hans stopped in the middle of an area between a man smoking a pipe and a woman carrying water. He raised his voice and shouted repeatedly, "Mutter, it is Hans! Where are you? It is your son, Hans!"

Marta saw Frau Binz's head appear from inside a small shelter. In a single movement, she pulled herself from the ground and ran toward them, yelling, "Hans! Hans!" Her arms were extended and a look of unmitigated joy lit her face.

Hans flew into her arms and immediately fell into uncontrollable sobbing. "Mutti. Mutti. They killed Vater. They killed him."

Frau Binz's face turned ashen. Her eyes moved to Marta as if to confirm the terrible news. Marta nodded gravely. Frau Binz's legs crumpled under her so that she sat on the ground. She pulled her boy into her lap, where they wept together.

The area was busy. People passed them, some looking concerned and others ignoring them completely. Marta wished she could help them find a place all to themselves, but she knew they could not make it far in their grief.

She put an arm around Frau Binz, who would not let go of her son. She helped them to stand and eased them toward the lean-to Frau Binz had left. Instead of stopping there, though, Frau Binz continued to an ill-made shelter put together with brush and a few twigs. Marta shuddered. She could not imagine how the woman had lived in it for over three fortnights. She doubted if the structure did much to protect her from the weather. It was too small to sit in and almost too narrow for one person to lie down. Frau Binz sat in front of her shelter, and once again held Hans on her lap.

"Glory be!" said a voice from another shelter. Marta turned. An older woman with a cheery smile said, "The prodigals have returned. Where is Herr Bi—?" She stopped short, evidently noticing Frau Binz's red and swollen face.

Marta shook her head. The twinkle in the woman's eyes dimmed.

"Now, now," she said, moving toward Frau Binz and placing her arm around her shoulders. "Now, now." Frau Binz turned toward the woman, as if deriving comfort from her closeness.

Marta looked away. She wished she could help, but she had not cried for so long that she was not even sure what a person did to comfort those who cried.

The older woman said, "God forsakes you not. He yet abides here with you. Offer Him your grief. He knoweth all. He gave His only Son." An infant began to cry in the shelter next to them, and a young voice mimicked Frau Binz's lullaby.

With a quick, "I shall return on the morrow," which she was fairly certain no one heard, Marta turned from the women and hurried away, almost running to escape the emotions that were trying to boil up from deep within her.

By the time Marta arrived back at the shelter, Frau Doenhof was cooking a mixture of vegetables in a large pot. "Ye lost the boy?"

Marta shook her head no. "We found his mother."

"So Hans abides with us no more," said Frau Doenhof, pursing her lips. "One less mouth to feed." She turned toward the fire, and Marta could not tell whether it was emotion or the smoke that made the woman's eyes water. "If ye shut thine heart down now . . ." Her words faltered, and she stirred the pot vehemently, ". . . then it'll 'urt less."

Marta was suddenly overcome with loneliness. It would be like this once Carl was gone, a lonely existence with Frau Doenhof—not sharing, closed from the inside. Marta gave her head a violent shake as if to rid her mind of those thoughts. Rather than offering to help with the meal, Marta walked away from the shelter, not caring where she went, but wanting to move away from the pain that seemed to be engulfing her heart and paralyzing her.

She passed family after family, but her thoughts would not settle. Frau Binz had a kindly neighbor to help her deal with her grief. The woman might even have been there for Frau Binz during the entire time she waited for her family. Marta had only Frau Doenhof.

God took care of others. Why not her? Instead of giving her

someone who understood and cared, God had brought her Frau Doenhof and a man whose mission was to leave her.

Marta took in a quick breath. Frau Doenhof was like her mother, a woman whose lot was fraught with disappointment. The day Frau Doenhof could no longer fight, she would wither quickly, just as her mother had, like a flower whose petals had fallen. Neither woman could hold safe the small portion of her heart left unscarred. Yet her mother had once laughed as loudly as any other. With a sinking heart, Marta realized that Frau Doenhof had also probably laughed at one time. Would it be Marta's lot to watch another woman die of a broken heart? With a quick turn, as if to escape her own thoughts, she headed into an unknown area and came face-to-face with the soldier who had accosted Hans the previous morning.

Sergey's eyes surveyed her from head to toe. "How does the husband today? He lives?" he said in halting German. The man made her feel unclean. She took a quick step back from him.

"Yes, I thank you for your concern." She was glad that there were many people around them.

"The husband must not let wife roam alone." He took a step forward. "I care better for you."

Ducking to the side, she hurried past him, almost running. How dare he speak to her in such a manner! The will to fight once again coursed through her veins, replacing self-pity.

I may be alone, she thought. *The people around me may not be those I would choose, but I am yet responsible for the manner of my life. No one can take that away from me.*

By the time she returned to the shelter, she could even enjoy the vegetable soup and tolerate Frau Doenhof's sulking.

"How do my two favorite women fare?" Carl came upon them as they were cleaning their dishes. He looked around. "Where's Hans?"

Marta ignored his first question. "Hans and I found Frau Binz. They have renewed their affections."

"With tears?" asked Carl.

Marta nodded. "Frau Binz's shelter is little more than twigs leaning against one another."

"She was a lone woman who did not speak the language," said Carl.

Matter-of-factly, Frau Doenhof added, "Her heart remained behind in Lübeck."

"I barely recognized her. She has the look of an older woman. So little flesh covers her bones."

"Nothing that some good food wouldn't cure," said Frau Doenhof. "Ye should've invited them for supper. Of course good food cannot be had here. How can they expect anyone to survive on Russian food—only cabbage soup, millet porridge, and beetroots. We need eggs, cheese, butter, and fresh meat." She turned to Carl. "When shall we depart this place?"

"Soon. When we receive word, we'll pack up our shelter and move to Oranienbaum, and there we'll be placed in groups. There have been so many immigrants arriving that things have gotten a little behind. The earliest immigrants went directly from the ships to Oranienbaum, but unfortunately, that is no longer the procedure." He leaned over the soup. "This smells delicious."

"The scoundrels've cut our coin again. I had but half the amount to buy provisions."

"They don't want you to leave, Frau Doenhof. So few great cooks come to Kronstadt," teased Carl.

"Go on with ye." Although Frau Doenhof did not smile, Marta could see that her eyes were twinkling. She wondered about Frau Doenhof's and Carl's relationship, which changed from animosity to congeniality and back within the length of a single conversation, especially when Carl expressed appreciation for her cooking. Perhaps their lives had given them each a hardness that the other understood and a defense that did not allow others close.

"If they paid you the full amount of promised butter money, you'd run off and marry a Russian count. Then where would I be?" he continued.

"Now stop that nonsense before I refuse to feed ye," she said in a much lighter tone than usual.

Carl appeared almost lighthearted. Could he have accomplished his purpose? Was he about to leave her?

All the better to be rid of him, she told herself. It was hard not knowing if the next moment she spent with him would be the last.

"Shall you have need of these branches here, or should we take them with us?" she asked.

Carl turned and studied her face. "I doubt if things shall work out so quickly. I'd rather have twigs, branches, and brush over our heads as we wait together in Oranienbaum."

In spite of her determination, Marta felt a wave of relief at his words. He would leave her, but not immediately. She would have time to get used to the fact that Hans was no longer with them.

She hesitated and then reached out to touch Carl's arm. "What shall happen to Frau Binz and Hans?"

He shrugged but did not move away from her. "They'll have to abide either here or at Oranienbaum until she finds a husband."

Frau Doenhof snorted, and Marta cried, "No! They would not make her marry. Her heart still bleeds. Why should they not join us?"

Carl opened his eyes wide. "Does this mean I've gained another woman in our family?"

"Of course it does," says Frau Doenhof. "Ye knew that when we started."

Carl threw up his hands in mock consternation. "So now I can read minds. What am I to do amid so many women? I'm glad that at least I'll have Hans."

"What of their papers? Shall they be given leave to travel with us?" asked Marta.

Carl nodded. "I'll arrange it." He would alter their papers after he discussed the plan with Frau Binz.

When they had eaten and cleaned up the meal, Frau Doenhof scolded, "Ye should have made them come eat. Everyone has to eat. We have plenty of food. Would it be too much to ask ye to help another?"

"Frau Binz wanted to be alone with Hans tonight," said Marta. She crawled into their shelter.

"Greetings, my fair wife," said Carl, crawling in beside her. "This is the closest we'll sleep together in our married life."

"No thanks to ye," said Frau Doenhof, squeezing between them. "This is as close to her as thou wilst get."

Carl smiled. Marta would make a good wife for someone. He began to think about a couple of prospects that looked promising. The wait had been long enough. Goralski would assume he had left the country.

Much later, when the women were both sleeping soundly, Carl poked his head out of the lean-to into the quiet of the night. He saw a large black hat peeking from behind a neighboring shelter. It looked like a soldier's hat. There should not have been another soldier in the area for quite a while. Their section had already been patrolled. Then Carl's heart began to beat quickly. His mouth grew dry. He saw the soldier's long black boot step forward as if he were looking in their direction, spying on them.

Carl averted his head in such a way that he could still study the soldier without the soldier knowing that he had been spotted. Perhaps Carl had not escaped Quentin as easily as he had imagined. The soldier peeked out from his hiding place again, and Carl recognized him. His blood ran cold. It was Sergey!

Chapter Nine

The morning sun, mixed with a cooling breeze, shone on Marta. Everything seemed better now that she was rested. As Carl carried a bucket of water back toward their shelter, Marta felt Frau Doenhof touch her arm.

"He acts like there's a ghost behind every bush."

Carl's face did look sterner, devoid of the lightheartedness from the night before. Something was definitely plaguing him. At one shelter not far from theirs, Carl stopped as if he were studying something.

Frau Doenhof continued, "Could be he's in the midst of a relapse." She moved to the side of their shelter.

"He seemed hale yester eve." Marta's brow wrinkled. Had Carl gone out again? She had slept so soundly that she had not heard a thing.

Frau Doenhof faced Marta with her hands on her broad hips. "'Twould be like him to catch a sickness and die on us."

"Then I'll do my best not to," said Carl, coming up behind her, but she did not flinch. "In the meantime," he said turning to Marta, "why don't you lead me to Frau Binz so we can finalize our plans?"

"I shall finish here," said Frau Doenhof. "Be off with ye."

With Carl at her side, Marta retraced her steps to Frau Binz's shelter. They found Hans and his mother sitting on the ground eating crusts of bread.

"Frau Ebel! Herr Ebel!" Hans ran to them, giving Marta an enormous hug and then rushing into Carl's outstretched arms. "Mutter, this is Herr Ebel, the one I told you about. He can do anything. He is taller than Vater, but he is almost as pleasant. He married Fraülein Ebel."

Hans's mother stood up and took Carl's hand. "Thank you for caring for my son." She turned to Marta. "Forgive me. I didn't properly thank you yesterday." With a tilt of her head, she looked back at Carl. "Herr *Ebel?*"

"Yes," said Marta. "We have come to invite you and Hans to travel with us. Carl shall be your protector, as well as mine." Frau Binz looked uncertain. Marta continued, "Tell me you shall come with us. Please."

"You save us. And you say, 'Please'? Of course we shall go with you."

Marta smiled, but something was different about Frau Binz, and it troubled her. Perhaps the time away from her family had been harder than they suspected.

Marta shook her head to rid herself of unpleasant thoughts. Having three women and one child on the Russian frontier would be much better than being alone with Frau Doenhof. She would have a family.

Carl interrupted her thoughts. "We leave for Oranienbaum today. Hans, help your mother dismantle her shelter and meet us at ours in time for the midday meal." Marta looked up at Carl. *What did he say? They were leaving today?*

"Yes, sir," replied Hans.

"I'm off to finish our arrangements," Carl said.

Before Marta could question him, Carl hurried away. She waved to the Binzes and then threaded her way back to the lean-to, wondering at Carl's urgency, Hans's unquestioning obedience, and the timing of their journey.

"We must pack our belongings," Marta said when she reached Frau Doenhof. "We leave for Oranienbaum after our midday meal."

—⟨⟩

Carl stopped under a birch tree to make the final changes on their papers to include Frau Binz. Sergey's spying had made it imperative that they leave immediately. He studied the officials who were clearing people for boat rides to Oranienbaum and chose one who looked especially shiftless.

"It's busy today," Carl said, sidling up to the man.

"It is busy every day. State your business."

"I seek passage today to Oranienbaum for five people."

"Impossible."

Carl surreptitiously showed him a gold piece. "I'm sorry to hear that."

The official looked around. No one appeared to be watching. He grabbed the gold and hid it in his clothing. "Your papers?" Without even looking at them, the official said, "This won't work." Carl set down another gold piece. After sliding it into his clothing, the man wrote down Carl's name. "Much better. Be on the dock before the end of the next watch."

_҉

A lump caught in Marta's throat as she helped pull apart the hut. Tonight she would be another step closer to owning land—and losing Carl forever. After Frau Binz and Hans arrived, they shared a cold meal of biscuits and dried fruit. Even Hans was silent during the meal.

"I trust everything is in readiness," Carl said, as if trying to relieve the tension. Without waiting for an answer, he laid all the branches, even Frau Binz's small collection, across his back. At his direction, the women tied their clothing, blankets, and cooking utensils into their blankets. Hans hauled his own pack, as before, but stayed close to his mother, urging her to walk carefully. They made a slow but steady procession to the dock, with only Frau Binz's occasional coughs to interrupt their otherwise silent party.

"I'll make certain that everything is in readiness." Carl set down their wood. "Wait here."

"May I go with you?" Hans asked. Carl nodded, and they left together. Carl's hand was on the child's shoulder, and Hans was looking up at him, smiling and talking. Marta thought that they appeared more like father and son than ever.

Carl was relieved not to recognize the official organizing the Oranienbaum crossing. "I'm Herr Ebel, and this is my son, Hans," he said in German.

The man checked Carl's papers and answered him in German. "You travel with your wife, your aunt, and your wife's sister."

Carl cleared his throat. "Yes." The official checked the information against his boarding list.

"When you registered, there were only four in your group. Only four may leave for Oranienbaum. One must stay."

Carl's mind quickly sized up the man before him. Should he become irate or feign stupidity? The official looked tired, but more likely to laugh at someone than to be intimidated.

"Nein. Nein. There are four of us." Carl held out his hand as he counted. "Me, my wife, my son, and the aunts." He held up four fingers. "There is no problem." The Russian gave Carl a look of disdain.

Before the man could speak, Hans piped in, "Nein, Vater. We have two aunts, your aunt and mine." He pulled out Carl's thumb. "That makes five, not four." Carl counted his family on his fingers again silently.

The man turned to Hans. "What is the other aunt's name?"

"Frau Binz, sir."

The official wrote Frau Binz's name on the document and handed them to Hans. "Once he ciphers correctly, give him these." The official waved them away.

Carl and Hans walked close together, as quickly as they could and as far away from the man as possible to keep him from hearing Hans's giggles.

"My mother is my aunt," said Hans.

"And Frau Doenhof is mine," said Carl, chuckling.

After the child's amusement had run its course, Carl stooped to Hans's level. "That was quick thinking back there. Let's keep the details to ourselves, man-to-man, so we won't give the women cause for worry." He took a small leather bag of coins out of his waist and handed it to Hans. "I never paid you for the work you did for me on the ship. You're to hide this away and save it for when you need it most."

The boy smiled. "Yes, sir."

Carl untied another small bag from the inside of his vest. "These stones are yours now."

Hans untied the string, looked inside, and grinned up at Carl as he fingered the smooth stones that had been kept in Frau Ebel's patchwork.

"Thank you." Hans threw his arms around Carl, who returned his hug. Then Carl helped Hans tie the two bags to his clothes so no one would suspect the treasures they hid.

"Frau Ebel's quilt shall be light now," said Hans as they continued back to where the women were.

"No," said Carl. "I replaced your rocks with stones that I think she will prefer, but don't ruin my surprise. She doesn't know."

Hans smiled, and Carl knew his secret was safe.

Before long, Marta and the others were climbing aboard the boat that would carry them to Oranienbaum. To Marta, the ketch looked as if it would have been a tight squeeze for twenty people, but it transported more than a hundred with all their belongings. Only by concentrating on the two large sails above her was she able to ignore the creaking of the aged craft. Perhaps, as Carl told her, this boat had been splendid during Peter the Great's reign, but now it looked like a small replica of the worn-out ship that had brought them to Russia.

The Russian sailors looked like counterparts of the teamsters who had taken them to their twig village in Kronstadt—frighteningly large beards and furry hats. At least the water looked calm, with only a few small ripples where it was scurried along by the wind. As the boat pulled away from Kronstadt, Carl's mood lightened noticeably.

"We'll be there soon," he said from directly behind her. "Look." He pointed in the distance. "You can see where we're going."

Marta felt warmth steal over her. She did not know if she needed the reassurance that they were close to land or simply needed it from Carl. He never seemed to be watching her anymore. Yet how could he have known what she was feeling? He shifted his weight away from her, and she stole a glance at his handsome face. If he had been watching her so closely, perhaps he cared more than he showed. Perhaps if he were learning to love her, he would not be so intent on leaving.

Once they arrived at the immigrant site, Marta noticed little difference between their new camp and their old one. White trunks of birch trees, interspersed with pine and an occasional spruce or fir, dominated the wooded area near the camp. A thick ground covering of small plants and sprawling bristly bushes grew below the trees. Marta drew in the fresh woodland scents while she and the others gathered brush to add to their twigs.

When they finished building their new shelter, it was similar to their last one but large enough to house all five of them. Because twigs and branches were more readily available here, most of the lean-tos were large enough for people to sit inside.

"Let the waiting begin," said Carl with a laugh.

Marta turned to him. "The waiting, shall it be overlong?"

"Registration here shall take some time," he said to her great disappointment.

The second morning in Oranienbaum, Carl disappeared without a word. After the midday meal, Hans challenged Frau Doenhof to a game of rocks, and Marta and Frau Binz were able to take a walk. Marta had been dreading this moment, when they would be alone together, but she knew it had to come.

Not far from their shelter, Frau Binz asked, "How did he die? My husband. Did he . . . drown?" Her eyes watered.

"No, he didn't drown. After your ship left the port, I watched Herr Binz rescuing people who were headed to the dungeon. He was a brave man, and he died with the knowledge that his son was safe."

Frau Binz's eyes softened. "What happened?"

"Hans and I were hidden in a wooden barrel. He found us there and then prevented our discovery by drawing attention to himself. Just as he was about to round the corner and escape, a soldier shot him."

Frau Binz looked like someone had stabbed her and Marta involuntarily reached out to help steady her. "He died in the street?"

"Yes," said Marta. She wished she could soften the truth for Frau Binz, but she did not know how. "He died saving others, including Hans and me."

Frau Binz nodded, her tears flowing freely. "I'm not surprised. He always managed to help . . . no matter how dire the circumstances. Perhaps that's why . . . I held out hope . . . for so long." She grabbed Marta's arm and linked it with hers, leaning heavily on Marta for support.

When Frau Binz had recovered enough to use her voice, she said, "Please call me Gretta. I'll call you Marta. We're family now."

Marta blinked back her tears. "That is the nicest thing that I have heard since my father died." She looked away. The lean-to in front of her had a pair of ragged pants hanging over the top of it. The one next to it had a completely flat roof, open on three sides with a thick branch holding it up. The bottom end of the branch was dug deeply into the ground.

"Frau Binz," called a cheery voice.

"Frau Kassel," said Gretta with obvious joy. The two women embraced. "Frau Ebel, this is Frau Kassel." Marta gave the woman a nod of greeting.

Frau Kassel smiled. "It is good to make your acquaintance."

Almost immediately, Frau Binz and Frau Kassel launched into a conversation about all that had happened to them in the last few days. Although they tried to include Marta, she felt like an intruder. "Would you mind if I walk a little farther and then meet you at the shelter before long, Gretta?"

Gretta agreed. She and her friend moved off together, already in deep conversation. Marta walked for several minutes, wandering aimlessly among the immigrants and their shelters—one looked like a square table and another still had leaves on its branches. Each person seemed to have made do with whatever they could find to survive.

When Marta tried to retrace her steps, she became aware of how similar each shelter was to the other, and how similar it was to hers. She knew she was lost when she found herself at the far end of the camp. Turning around to find her way again, she came face-to-face with Sergey, a self-confident smile smugly set on his face.

"Again alone." His eyes brazenly traced the lines of her body. She could not run from him; she was already at the edge of the camp. She tried to move past him, but he stepped to the side and blocked her path. She wondered how he had come to Oranienbaum. He had not been on their ketch. It was small enough that she would have known. How she wished they had left him behind.

"You drop this?" He held a coin in his hand.

Sergey knew she couldn't possibly have that large a coin. Marta blushed at his presumption "No, that is not mine." She tried to move past him a second time.

"I believe it yours, or could be." His German seemed to have improved. "Your husband is again ill?"

She slipped to the side of him as she said, "He fares well," and walked quickly, almost running away from him along the edge of the camp. Her heart pounded, blending the noises around her into a cacophony of warnings against the soldier's evil intentions.

─◌

It had not been easy to slip away from Marta, but Carl congratulated himself on his stealth. He had walked since early morning, and now as the sun rose to its highest point, he was nearing the estate where he had had dealings before. He hoped the same dishonest estate manager was still in charge. With the owner dying a slow death and the owner's brother always away, the estate manager felt free to sell the dying man's belongings whenever the price was sufficient. Or at least he had in the past.

Although the estate had a fancy name that was almost unpro-
nounceable, the run-down buildings lacked the grandeur the name
implied. By Carl's standards, they were primitive—and must have
been even in their prime—more like a farmhouse and outbuild-
ings than an estate. The lilac bushes around the entrance and the
blue hyacinths along the path were the only claim it still had to
grandeur.

"Does your master fare any better?" asked Carl. The scent of
pine trees hung heavy on the air.

The estate manager smiled. "No, he is dying still."

"And his brother?" asked Carl.

"He travels the world, as always," said the man with a black-
toothed grin. The transaction went as smoothly as Carl had hoped.
Before long Carl handed a bag of money to the man and was given
a foot up to ride a dapple-gray gelding.

The manager's eyes sparkled as he held the money in his hand.
Carl knew he had been grossly overcharged, but if the man had not
been so greedy, he would not have been of service to Carl, both now
and in the past.

Once away from the farm, Carl moved with care, aware of everything around him—the blackbirds and gulls in the sky, the direction of the breeze in the deep green pine boughs, fluttering birch
leaves, and the scuffle of an unseen rodent hurrying away. Carl
rode the gelding for a while before returning the animal along with
additional gold coins taken from Quentin.

"I shall return for him," said Carl. "This shall pay for his care."

The man smiled and bobbed his head so many times that Carl
eventually turned from him. It would be midafternoon by the time
he returned to camp, and he would have to return with the same
stealth he had used when leaving. No one, especially the soldiers,
should be the wiser.

When he reached the outskirts of the immigrant camp and was
able to walk freely, he noticed a woman scurrying across the outer
edges. Her pace suggested distress. It looked like Marta.

Carl rushed to catch her, taking two long strides for each one of hers. When he touched her shoulder, she turned around suddenly as if to hit him. Her arm stopped in midflight and relief washed over her face. Instead of dropping to her sides, her arms reached around his neck and her body shook.

"What's this?" he asked. The back of his neck felt hot and yet her touch sent cold shivers down his back.

"I . . . Gretta and I walked through camp . . . then Frau Kassel . . . I went on . . . I became lost . . . and he was there . . . he is everywhere I turn. . . ." She took a deep breath. "You must think I am skittish, but truly I have seen him watch me everywhere."

Carl felt a fist of fury entering his heart. "Who was it, Marta? Who's been following you?"

"That soldier," she said. "That horrid Russian soldier."

Although it pained him to let her go, he gently moved her away and lowered his face level to hers, only a breath away. "Sergey. Is it Sergey who threatens you?"

"Yes, that is his name," she said.

Relief washed over Carl. If Sergey was ogling Marta, then he did not know what Carl was doing. He drew her back to him, too ashamed to let her see the expression on his face. She made him feel like a decent human being, worthy of love, but he knew better. He was used to looking out for himself and only himself. He had survived in the wilderness off and on for two years after leaving his mother, and had survived the ruthless, civilized world as an adult.

"That man is dangerous," said Carl. "Go nowhere alone. Do you understand?"

He could feel her nod into his chest. How he wished he were the man whom Marta needed. If he were a praying man, that's what he would pray for, a heart that would choose her over himself. But he was not a praying man—not anymore. He comforted Marta as best he could and eventually they returned to their lean-to together.

Marta had not felt so shaken and unprotected for a long time. With Carl so near and the facade of family around her, she had felt brave again, but one meeting with Sergey made her realize how dependent she was. She hated the hopelessness of that feeling. She crawled into the lean-to earlier than usual to sleep.

Marta ignored the depression that threatened to close in on her. No matter how she felt, she would need to stand on her own. Carl had told her repeatedly that he would leave, and still she played into his hands as if she believed he would stay. She would not give in to Sergey's stalking, her hope in Carl, or her own fears. If she wanted to go somewhere by herself, she would. No one would limit her freedom.

The next morning dawned warm and sunny. Marta felt the need to keep busy. She could not sit the whole day.

"I shall wash clothes this day," she announced after eating her porridge. If Sergey appeared, she would command him to scrub them for her. The idea made her smile.

Carl and Hans had finished eating and started playing the game of stones.

"Frau Doenhof," said Marta. "You must change so I can wash the disease from our garments."

The woman turned with an angry look, but Marta knew she had phrased her words well when Frau Doenhof responded, "It is due time for ye to speak with sense!"

"May I borrow your extra dress, Gretta?" Marta asked.

"Certainly. Take my washboard. And my last bar of lye soap."

"Thank you. I have a nightdress you can wear, and Frau Doenhof can wear hers. That way I can wash your clothes, too."

"And what are we to do while ye wander about with our raiment?" demanded Frau Doenhof.

"Perhaps we could become better acquainted," said Gretta.

"In the shelter," added Marta. Although Frau Doenhof acted completely put out, she helped Marta and Gretta stack their belongings at the front of their shelter so they could change without being seen. When the cool air hit Gretta, she began coughing.

"It shall do you good to rest inside," Marta said.

"Ye need not talk today," said Frau Doenhof. "There is time enough for that later."

"I am well," said Gretta. "It is only the sudden cold air."

Gretta's dress was too large for Marta, but she gathered the extra fabric and tied the apron tightly around her waist.

"And ye men—come not hither until we are dressed in proper raiment," yelled Frau Doenhof.

Carl and Hans looked up from the ground where they were playing.

"Wouldn't consider it," said Carl in a slow drawl. They continued playing. Hans gave a triumphant laugh when he succeeded in catching the first rock with the group of rocks in his hand.

"Hans, did you win?" Gretta's voice gave way to a throaty cough from deep within her chest.

Marta felt as if she had been kicked in the stomach. Gretta did not look merely run-down. She looked sick, much like the people Marta had nursed on the ship, most of whom had not recovered. Her breath caught in her throat. Unless something changed, Gretta might be taken from them again, permanently.

"It'll be just you and me this morning, Hans," said Carl as he picked up the last stones on the ground.

"Man-to-man."

"Most certainly. Why don't you practice with those rocks on your own for a while, while I take a rest? Then we'll play another game." Carl tried not to show that Marta's intent to leave the shelter by herself disturbed him. He had told her not to go anywhere without him. Still, she had chosen to do wash of all things, almost in direct defiance of what he had asked.

Hans set to work as Carl lay down and placed his hat forward, over his face. Carl closed his eyes. Marta would have to learn her own lessons the hard way. He would not volunteer to escort her. Of course, if she asked him, he would go. He had to get that woman out of his thoughts. His plan would go into effect tonight. Everything was set. Soon, Goralski would be sorry that he had ever swindled him.

Chapter Ten

As Marta tied the soiled clothing into her patchwork, the bundle felt heavier than she had anticipated. Hans had taken his rocks out, and yet she felt bumps under the patch that had been securely sewn back in place. She wondered if she should switch to a different blanket, one without the added weight of Carl's hidden treasures, such as the one Frau Doenhof had over her legs.

"Frau Doenhof," Marta called, interrupting a whispered conversation.

"What troubles ye now?"

Marta decided not to ask. "It is of no consequence."

She turned to Hans and Carl at the side of the shelter. "Have you other garments to clothe yourselves so I may wash the ones you wear now?"

"No. If you took these, I would have to walk around in the manner in which I was born," Carl said, his hat still covering his face.

"I have naught else to put on," said Hans.

Gretta called out to him. "What of your nightshirt, H—?" She started coughing hard.

"Ye are sick!" declared Frau Doenhof's muffled voice. "Now we shall all become ill. Heaven help us." The words were harsh, but her tone was soft, almost motherly. Marta looked toward the shelter. The woman was actually being kind to someone other than Hans. Frau Doenhof continued, "Ye have watched over others to the detriment of thyself. It is no wonder ye have taken ill."

When the coughing subsided, Gretta said in a strained voice, "I fare well."

"Ye shan't be well for long if ye keep on as ye have. Ye need rest and hot soup to warm thy bones. When did ye last eat a good meal?

And, mind ye, I speak not of the rubbish Frau Ebel boiled for us last eve."

Marta ignored Frau Doenhof's words and told Hans, "Put on your nightshirt so that I may wash your garments."

"It is crusted with mud."

"Then fetch it for me, and I shall wash it."

Hans started to enter the shelter, but Frau Doenhof stopped him. "Oh no. Ye remain where ye be. I'll give it to ye."

"It doesn't appear that I'll get my rest," said Carl, pushing his hat back. He stood and brushed off his coarse, homespun pants and jacket. "I'll go register us," he said.

"But we registered already," said Hans.

Marta saw Carl eyeing the bundle in her hands. "First, we registered to let Russia know we'd arrived. Then we had to register for passage to Oranienbaum. This time we'll be assigned a group to travel with. Before long, you'll be on your way to a new home."

"Hurrah!" shouted Hans, jumping up and down.

Carl motioned to the blanket in Marta's hands. "That patchwork is delicate. You do not plan to wash it, do you?"

Marta looked down at the material. "I shall not, if you do not wish it."

"I don't," he said.

Hans asked, "May I go with you to register? As the man of my family, should I not be the one to sign for my mother and me?"

Carl ruffled the child's hair. "You're absolutely right. Frau Binz, I'm taking Hans with me."

Carl turned to Marta. "The patchwork is much too delicate to be washed." Before she could reply, he left with Hans chattering beside him. Marta shook her head. How she longed to feel Hans's childlike excitement again.

Marta sighed and heaved the bundle of soiled clothing onto her back. Carl trusted her completely with all his secrets wrapped in an old blanket, but he did not tell her the true reason that he did not want the patchwork washed. If only she could feel confident that he cared about what was best for her.

"For shame," she scolded herself. "Do not lament what your life is to be." Complaining about her plight was beneath her, or at least it should be. She lifted her chin and headed toward the water.

Carl and Hans joined the mob waiting to be placed into groups. They moved from one area to another, but Carl recognized all the government agents who were working. "The lines are too long to register this morning," he said. "Let's play a game of pretend in its stead."

"How does one play that?" asked Hans, putting his hand into Carl's as they walked away from the crowd.

Carl was glad that Hans was too young to understand how things really worked. "If I weren't here," he said, "someone would have to take my place. He would have to be Frau Ebel's husband and your father. Let's see if we can find him."

Carl pointed to a man cooking his own food. "He seems like a nice gentleman. See what you think."

Hans ran over to the man. "Excuse me, Herr. I am Hans."

"Begone, ye vex me!" bellowed the man, throwing a stick at him. Hans ran back to Carl and grabbed him.

"A good father would never do that to you," said Carl. "We'll find someone else."

They talked to one man after another and walked between shelters most of the morning. Mentally, Carl crossed each candidate off his list. None of the eligible men had passed the test. If they liked children, they drank too much. If they liked children and did not overindulge in alcohol, then Carl disliked something about their looks. He would have to rethink his plan for Marta. Instead of finding a husband to protect her, he would have to resort to bribery to ensure her safe passage, because time was running out.

"Herr Ebel?" asked Hans. "Might we play a different game? I am weary of this one."

"I, also." Carl raised his arms to stretch his back. "Let's see how many soldiers we can count."

"My turn first," Hans said. "There is a soldier over there. That makes one."

—◌

Gretta's dark blue dress felt fancy to Marta after wearing her homespun brown one for so long. She passed scores of shelters, hundreds of uprooted lives, as she carried her load to the water's edge. Other women were already pounding and scrubbing their clothes on the rocks. She gave those nearest her a smile of greeting and then concentrated on her task. It felt good to be away from the shelter doing a valuable chore.

The women's voices flowed in and out of her mind like a summer breeze until she had almost finished. One woman said to another, "Fear not. Should you register as farmers, you can leave this place in days instead of weeks. We arrived yesterday, and already we're assigned to the Schulz group. Once we're given provisions, we shall depart for our new homes."

Marta's heart lifted. "Pardon me. Why must we declare that we are farmers?"

"So you do have a tongue." The woman laughed good-naturedly. "The Tsarina desires to have her steppes along the Volga farmed. That is where they send us."

The other woman piped in, "But methought we would live in the region of this great land where we choose to abide."

"No, your occupation shall be farmer, and you shall abide by way of the Volga, or you shall leave not this place."

Marta gathered her clean, wet clothing into her somewhat dirty patchwork. "I wish you both well on your journeys." The women thanked her, and Marta hurried back to the shelter. On her way, she noticed that many of the lean-tos were covered with clothing drying in the hot sun. Her mother would probably have disapproved of this public display—but no matter. Marta laid everything over their shelter.

She called to Gretta and Frau Doenhof. "Your garments shall be soon dry. With this sun, they should be ready for use before long."

"Shh. Gretta sleeps," whispered Frau Doenhof.

Marta prepared a meal of soup. She offered some to Frau

Doenhof, who opted for dry biscuits instead. Gretta continued sleeping. When Carl and Hans did not return, Marta ate her mid-day meal alone.

The patchwork was only damp from holding the wet clothing, so it was the first piece to dry. Marta picked it up, shook it, then folded it in half and then fourths. Her hands felt hard objects in various patches that she was certain had not been there on the ship. They felt like coins.

As she set the blanket on the gunny sack of seed, her hand brushed something hard on the side of the sack. Squatting down, she traced the object with her finger. It felt like a pistol! She backed up from the sack as if it were on fire. If Carl had purchased it for hunting, he would have left it in the open. Obviously, he was play-ing a dangerous game. No wonder he had protected that sack of grain so carefully on the journey.

By early afternoon, Carl and Hans returned to find Marta, alone, staring into the cold ashes of their fire pit.

"Are we registered?" she asked in a low, almost distant voice.

"To register takes time," Carl replied.

Her eyes did not stray from the gray ash. "What do you mean by that?"

"It's complicated," said Carl. "The process can take up to seven days."

She flinched as if he had hit her. "If you say your trade is as a farmer, you shall be let go to leave straightway." She turned her face to his and slowly looked up into his eyes. Carl was surprised at how tired she looked.

"I'll have to try that," he said, "right after we get something to eat."

Once they had each eaten a bowl of Marta's cold soup, Carl and Hans returned to the registration area. New officials, ones Carl did not recognize, had replaced the others.

"The crowd seems to have lessened," he told Hans, although it looked much the same as it did before. "Let's find ourselves a group so we can start this journey."

When his turn came, Carl said, "I'm Herr Ebel. I travel with my wife, my wife's sister, an aunt, and my son here, Hans."

"What is your trade?" demanded the strapping Russian in German.

"What occupation should I have to join a group?"

The man smiled. "We do not enforce any occupation."

"Of course not," said Carl, "but how can I best serve Russia?"

"If you are a farmer."

"Then I'm a farmer."

"We shall be good farmers and grow much food for Russia," added Hans.

"My desire is for more Germans like you," said the man. "Are you able to write?" Carl nodded, and the man continued, "Then mark your name here and write your occupation."

As Carl did so, he heard a man next to him say, "I am not a farmer, but a shoemaker. I would do a good business here. I shall not write farmer beside my name, for I am no farmer."

"Then ye shall abide here," said a gruff voice. "Next."

The official handed Carl a paper. "In three days, Herr Zweig's group shall depart by boat. I wish you a good voyage."

"Thank you," said Carl. He nodded toward the other man, who was beginning to become unruly. "What'll happen to him?"

"He shall abide here until he is ready to go."

"And if he's never ready?"

"We shall find a way to make him ready," said the man.

Carl leaned toward the German man. "After you're settled, you can sell your services to your fellow settlers. Don't let unimportant rules steal your dreams."

The man stared at Carl for a moment and then nodded. "I shall be a farmer. Where would you have me sign?"

The official patted Carl on the back. "Good man! Good Russian man."

Hans smiled. "I am a good Russian man also. When my father leaves, I shall be the head of the family."

The official laughed. "Da. A good little Russian man."

Hans frowned and stood taller.

Carl leaned over and whispered to the official. "Might we not enter his name as head of the family? It would make him feel more like a Russian man."

The official looked amused, especially when Carl placed a number of coins in his hand.

Carl winked. "Da?"

The man chuckled. "Da." He entered Hans's name on the official record. "Herr Hans, you are a Russian man, the protector of your family."

It was late afternoon by the time Carl and Hans returned to the lean-to. Frau Doenhof was in her clean clothing cooking the evening meal. Marta was repairing a torn hem on Gretta's blue dress. Gretta sat by the fire with a shawl over her everyday dress.

Hans did not wait for Carl but ran up to the women. "I am a Russian man now!"

Gretta hugged her son. "Of course you are."

"And we shall leave in three days."

Marta turned to Carl. "Can this be true?"

"I'm glad you told me about listing farmer as our occupation," said Carl, trying to appease any breach he may have caused with his earlier pretense of ignorance. "The process went quickly."

Marta smiled at him just as she used to smile when they were on the ship. "To which group have we been assigned?"

"Herr Zweig's."

Frau Doenhof looked up from her cooking. "The same Herr Zweig who was on the ship?"

"Yes, the widower."

Carl noticed Sergey out of the corner of his eye. The man was becoming bolder, eyeing their shelter openly from a distance. Carl shook his head. Sergey's notice was inconvenient today. He walked over to the soldier.

"Is it well with you?" Carl asked.

"Da, well, *Nyemtz*," said Sergey with a condescending smile.

Carl was angered by the derogatory term, but he smiled back.

The two men stared at each other for a moment before Sergey casually strolled away.

Carl returned to his companions. "I had to get rid of a pesky insect." Marta laughed, but the others continued talking about their upcoming adventure to their new home.

"Would you have a bowl of food?" she asked.

"Afterward." He had to act quickly before the man chose to return. The sack of grain was beneath the patchwork near the shelter's opening. Carl crawled inside. Unthreading the twine at the top, he removed what he needed and wove the twine back through the top. Then he unthreaded one of the patches on the blanket and removed several gold coins.

He glanced out of the shelter. Marta was giving Hans more soup. Now was the time. Trying not to draw attention to his movements, he slipped around the back side of the hut. The less the others knew, the better.

Marta's eyes followed Carl's figure as he wove in and out of the crowded city of sticks away from them. He walked nonchalantly, as if he had no cares and no destination, but she knew better. He slid into the distance without anyone except her noticing. Carl held more secrets than his patchwork.

"Would you like a third ladle?" Marta asked Hans, although her eyes continued to follow Carl.

"I've had only one," said Hans. "I need two more ladles of soup."

Marta looked down at him. "That's a lie, Hans. You've had two ladles. Would you like one more or no more?"

Hans gave her a charming smile. "I don't count very well. I'll take one more, please."

Before Marta could give him more soup, Gretta pulled him aside to speak to him. Marta assumed it was about his lie. She stirred the pot hard and fast. Hans was evidently learning much information from Carl, and some of it was not good.

Carl collected his horse from the estate manager. The day was warm. The sky was a brilliant blue.

"The beast shall serve you well," said the estate manager in Russian.

"I'm certain he shall," said Carl. He looked around the run-down establishment. "Do you suppose that your master has evening garments he would be willing to part with?"

"He might." The estate manager rubbed his hands together.

"I seek full evening raiment," repeated Carl. "I also seek garments like those upon your back."

"This raiment is of great worth to me," said the estate manager, with a wave of his hand.

"I understand," said Carl. He withdrew double the rubles the outfits were worth.

Once the transaction was completed, Carl immediately changed into the estate manager's old clothing and then left. Less than a verst from the main house, he encountered a peasant woman picking weeds from her garden.

"Good woman," said Carl. "I understand you have a room that you are willing to let for a price."

"I don't house beggars," said the woman, the lines on her face creasing deeper.

Carl smiled. He had stayed with her before. He went through the ritual of procuring the room, giving full assurance that her master would never find out about the extra money she received from the transaction. He entered by the back door and stored his immigrant clothing and evening dress in the room, making certain the window was unlatched. Then he left and rode hard toward St. Petersburg.

He did not keep track of time as he galloped through pine forests and skirted lakes in the eerie evening light. He thought only of the sweet triumph of revenge. After all the immigrants he had brought to Russia for Goralski, how could the man have turned on him? Carl grimaced. For the coin, of course.

His horse's galloping hooves seemed to echo the refrain, "For the coin. For the coin. For the coin. For the coin." Every man had his price, it seemed. Goralski had known from the start that Carl was a Jew. Carl's background hadn't been a problem, because he made the man a lot of money. But Goralski had waited until Carl delivered the largest group of immigrants of any recruiter. Only then had the man refused to pay him his fee and afterward had him deported like a common criminal.

A dark cloud passed before the sun, which hung like a pendant on the horizon. Carl urged his horse to go faster. Quentin's betrayal was even worse. He had thought to rid himself of Carl altogether, to kill him, and save the money it would cost to feed him on the return voyage. When Quentin tied Carl to his bunk, planning to toss him overboard after the ship was well out to sea, Carl learned that the Russian and the Englishman had been in the plot together. Goralski had paid Quentin to make whatever arrangements were necessary so that Carl would never enter Russia again. Goralski didn't care what Quentin did to Carl, as long as he never saw his face again. Carl wondered why he had trusted the Englishman.

Carl turned his mind back to the present plan. He had finally reached his destination. Stopping in the shadows of a dilapidated wooden shack, watching and listening for movement, he tied the horse's reins to a bush. Only after he was confident that he had not been observed or followed did he creep to the back door and knock. Two hard, three soft. A pause. Then three hard.

The door creaked open. A face centered by a large nose and sunken eyes appeared.

"What have you to offer me?" a rasping voice asked.

"The Goralski candelabrum."

The door opened wide enough for Carl to enter the windowless room lit only by a dying fire in the grate. After barring the door, the man moved to a chair behind a rickety table and motioned Carl to a bench across from him.

"The Goralski candelabrum, ye say." The man's stare was steady and seemed to take in everything, even in the dim light.

"The one given him by Tsarina Catherine for delivery of so many immigrants?"

"The same." Carl's stomach turned at the odors of fermented fruit and decayed scraps of meat that remained on the table, unfit even for dogs. He wished he had eaten a bowl of the soup Marta had offered him before beginning the night's activities.

The man rubbed his bony hands together. "Is it in your possession?"

Carl nodded.

"Let me see it."

"What will you give for it?"

The man pulled out a small bag from within his loose-hanging shirt and poured several gold coins on the table.

Carl was satisfied. It was about the same amount Goralski owed him. "Done."

"Done," the man said. "I must see it."

"I shall meet you tomorrow night," said Carl, "between here and the Goralski estate."

"Bring it to the fork in the side road—do ye know the one?—at full darkness."

Since the sun would not set until the night was halfway through, it would give Carl enough time to acquire the piece. He nodded. "Tomorrow after the sun has set."

Once their business was concluded, Carl could not leave the man's house quickly enough. He gulped in the fresh air trying to reverse the abuse his nose had sustained. After a hard ride back to where he intended to stay the night, he watered his horse and gave it a good rubdown before setting fresh feed in its box.

"You did very well tonight, *mon cheval*." Then Carl entered the back door to his room, ignoring the growls of his stomach.

The following morning, Carl remained in his peasant clothing and convinced his hostess to feed him porridge before he rode to Goralski's estate. The lovely mistress of the estate enjoyed riding in the fields at the edge of the property. Carl counted on Goralski's condescension toward his wife to keep her ignorant of his business dealings. She would not know that Carl no longer enjoyed her husband's favor. As he rounded a bend near the estate, he spotted a female rider coming toward him.

"Countess Goralski, what a pleasant surprise!"

"Why, Herr Mueller, you have come back from the German states again. Good day to you." It amused Carl that Countess Goralski tried to copy everything continental, because she had been schooled in England. "I hardly recognized you with your comely new beard," she continued. "It becomes you so well."

When they drew close enough, Carl kissed her gloved hand. "It has been far too long."

She smiled, blushing fashionably. "I insist that you come to the house to visit us. I am so bored. I trembled with joy at the sight of you, as shall my husband when he hears of your arrival."

"I regret that I cannot accept your gracious invitation. I'm on my way to an appointment." This was bad luck. He had thought that Goralski would be in Oranienbaum and not at his country estate. Having the man near would make his task more difficult. "Perhaps you will permit me to pay my respects this evening."

"That would be even better. I am giving a grand reception this evening, and now you are invited. I shall surprise Alexei with you. What an amusing diversion! It is even rumored that the Tsarina herself may grace us with her presence. Oh what a wonderful evening we shall have! Of course, you shall ask me to dance."

He bowed his head slightly. "I would be honored."

She prodded her horse. "Farewell then, until tonight."

Carl grinned. Things were working even better than he had planned. Her reception would be a collage of the French, English, and German aristocracy. Perfect. As soon as she was out of sight, Carl turned his horse around and returned to where he was staying to finish planning the night's events.

Marta tasted Frau Doenhof's stew. She had to admit that the woman was a far better cook than she was.

Frau Doenhof scolded, "Stop thy sulkiness. Ye should anticipate the morrow with joy. Few people gain the privilege to see a queen."

"What is that you speak of?" Marta was so distracted by the fact that Carl had not returned to the shelter the night before that she paid heed to little else. Perhaps something had happened to him.

"Tsarina Catherine, of course. Where hast thine head been that ye've missed the grandest tidings of the day?" Frau Doenhof harrumphed as Marta looked at her blankly. Frau Doenhof threw up her hands in disgust. "In the morn, wagons shall bear us to Catherine. She herself shall greet us. Should ye hearken more to the voices 'round ye, ye would know." Marta wanted to retaliate, but she bit her tongue.

Later that night, when Carl again did not return, Gretta asked, "Where is Herr Ebel?"

"He attends to his business," said Marta, acting unconcerned even though her heart ached at the idea of never seeing him again.

Hans piped in, "Fret not. I am the man of the family when Herr Ebel is gone."

Gretta tried to hold her son, but he shook away from her. "I am not a baby."

"No, you are not a baby," said Gretta. "You grow more like your father each day."

"Yesternight, I kept myself from sleep till past the setting of the sun at midnight," said Hans. "Since I am a man now, I shall remain awake throughout this night."

Marta stared at Hans. He had fallen asleep well before dark.

"Stop thy tales," said Frau Doenhof. "Ye'll obey whate'r thy mother commands."

Chilled by the evening air, Marta pulled the patchwork close to her, as if drawing Carl himself to her side. The quilt felt lighter, and squares in three different areas had rips in them. She would mend them on the morrow. Her hand sought the sack of grain. The hard object, the pistol, that she had felt the day before was no longer there. A shiver that had nothing to do with the cold ran up and down her spine.

—☙—

Carl changed to evening dress and mounted his horse again. Twice he almost turned back, scolding himself for his own arrogance, but victory was too close at hand. As his horse galloped through the trees, Carl's heart pounded. The exhilaration of risk heightened his senses. He could not deny himself the pleasure of facing Goralski in his own home.

He tied his horse to a tree in a thick grove of birch on the outside edges of the estate's treed gardens. Skirting the shadows, he slowly made his way up to the front entrance of Goralski's ostentatious home. Although the estate was coarse by continental standards, Carl knew that Goralski took great pride in trying to appear an English lord. The Goralskis lived too far north to have an English garden, but they had a maze of bushes and a small flowerbed that the countess tended like a child. In the center, well protected from the wind, was a rosebush that she had cared for and loved since her wedding day. On the other side of the garden stood ramshackle peasant huts.

With a deep breath, Carl walked through the double doors at the front of the house past the liveried servants standing guard on either side. Although they wore red jackets with brass buttons, they could not quite capture the air of disdain characteristic of continentals, especially under their Russian sheepskin hats. They were simply peasants dressed for the evening's festivities.

The countess talked gaily in the candlelit foyer with a group of elegantly gowned women. Carl noted once again that their clothing was more colorful and much lighter in weight than their English counterparts, since the Russians kept their houses exceedingly warm. Goralski stood by his wife's side. Carl stopped just inside the entrance to take in the layout, making note of any changes that had been made since the last time he was there. A large staircase rose in the center of the foyer and doors had been flung open to the ballroom on his right. Two hallways ran parallel to each other on either side of the foyer, where guests were being relieved of their wraps and greeted by the Goralskis. All in all, the layout appeared to be the same.

"You have come at last," called Countess Goralski. She waved at him. "I almost blundered and told Alexei about your arrival a number of times." She turned to her husband. "See whom I have invited. Are you not surprised?" His look of shock pleased Carl. He noticed several of Goralski's relations in the crowd, those who lived in his house and had met Carl during his previous visits.

Without waiting for her husband's reply, his wife turned to the women around her. "May I present Carl Mueller, Alexei's dear friend."

Goralski would not be able to renounce him publicly now without bringing shame to himself and his wife. If he dared to identify Carl as a Jew, Goralski would face possible death or imprisonment, and definitely disgrace, for hiring him and calling him "friend" in his own house.

Goralski recovered himself quickly and offered a stiff, "It has been a long time."

"Too long," said Carl. He greeted Goralski's relatives and then moved into the large ballroom, as others behind him were waiting to be received.

The evening was superb. Carl ate his fill of food and danced with Countess Goralski and several of her companions. She continued introducing him to everyone as Goralski's dear friend. Yet he knew that Goralski was watching him warily, and by the looks he was receiving from other gentlemen, he knew that the evening had suddenly become more dangerous.

Twice he tried to slip into another room, but immediately found himself followed. The evening was growing late, and he was running out of time.

"Has it made your heart merry this night to come to my reception?" asked Countess Goralski.

"While your arrangements are flawless, it is your presence that brings a smile to my countenance," said Carl. She laughed. Carl continued, "May I escort you to the refreshment table?"

"I should be delighted," she said. She laid her hand on his. "If the Tsarina is to appear, she should arrive soon."

"Then we shall listen for her possible arrival," he said. They strolled into the dining room, the only room with windows, where food was set out for the guests. Carl had chosen his time well. Only a servant was in the room. The candelabrum sat on a side table in front of a window left open to allow an unobstructed view of Countess Goralski's hedges. It contained candles, but they were not lit. If the countess had cared for the candelabrum, Carl would not consider taking it from her. He knew that she found it gaudy and ugly and only tolerated it because her husband took such pride in it.

"What can I get for you?" Carl asked.

"Let us not stand on propriety," she said. "You go to that side of the table, and I shall take this side."

Carl laughed. Once her head turned to the plate in her hand and the servant at the end of the room busied himself refilling a bowl, Carl crossed to the other side of the table. The candelabrum was within his reach. In a single movement, he tossed it out the open window into a thick bush and then filled his plate.

"What was that?" Carl asked.

"I thought I heard something, also," said his hostess. "Is it the Tsarina arriving?" Both hurried from the room before any of Goralski's men could follow them into the dining room.

"The Tsarina has not arrived," the countess said, visibly disappointed.

"My dear lady, I do not wish to see disappointment fill your face," said Carl. "Let us eat on the terrace, where we might keep watch for the royal carriage."

"An excellent thought," said the woman. They strolled through the back of the ballroom to the terrace as they nibbled on berries, mushrooms, small slices of poultry, and sweet rolls that were no larger than his thumb. The light from the nighttime summer sun cast eerie shadows on the grounds below.

"What lovely grounds you have," he said.

She looked pleased. "Thank you. While the sun abides in the sky so late, my roses flourish. Would you like to see them?"

"Very much, but I am loath to keep you from your other guests."

"I must attend them, but you may go see the roses and tour the remainder of our grounds if you wish."

Carl had been watching a man on the other side of the terrace who he knew had been sent to follow them. Carl pointed him out to Lady Goralski.

"I am a very selfish man. This gentleman has waited upon you with utmost patience, surely to ask you to dance. For his sake alone, I regret that I have dominated your attention." Carl kissed her hand and then waved to the man. "Come, my good man, our beautiful hostess shall stand up with you for the next dance." He bowed to her and nodded to the man.

"Borotov, I had not seen you," she said. "I should be happy to dance with you. Will you excuse us, Herr Mueller?"

"Only with a sense of great loss, as your beauty is the crowning blossom of this occasion." She blushed and waved to him as Borotov led her away. Carl set his plate down, and as soon as the couple were gone, he jumped over the rail and into the lengthening shadows to collect Goralski's treasure from the bushes. With as much speed as he was capable of mustering, he wove his way through the bushes, mounted his horse, and headed for the fork.

He rode hard in the white night, but when he neared the location where he was to exchange the candelabrum for coin, a sudden sense of looming danger overtook him. He glanced behind him, around him, listening. A reluctant darkness had finally fallen to mark the middle of the night. The wind sighed, and the trees whispered back. He urged his horse forward at a slow walk.

At the fork, the man with the crooked nose waited with lantern in hand. As he held up the light for Carl, a sneer crossed his face. Carl hesitated. He would not dismount.

"Have you the payment we agreed upon?"

The man held out a small sack.

"Show me its contents."

The man handed Carl the lantern and dumped gold pieces into his own hand. When Carl reached for them, the man pulled his hand away and poured them back into the sack.

"I would see the candelabrum first."

Carl handed the lantern back, reached into the bag hanging from his saddle, and pulled out the treasure. The jeweled piece glittered in the lamplight. The man handed Carl the gold, grabbed the candelabrum, and melted into the trees.

Left alone, Carl felt an urgency to escape. He turned his horse and it lurched to a gallop. For a while, he let the horse have its head, but then he had to follow through on his plan. He pulled on the reins and slowed the horse to a canter.

"There, there. Let's both of us calm ourselves." He retraced his path to a narrow lane where he guided his horse to a crumbled wall surrounding a small, deserted lodge. He dismounted and stooped behind a bush to pull out a stone. Only after he had set the sack inside the crevice and replaced the stone did his heart slow to its normal beat. Even if he was caught, which he did not intend to be, Goralski would never find the money he had been paid for the candelabrum. Just before he reentered the main road, he heard hoofbeats approaching from the direction of Goralski's estate. Without slowing down, they turned down the side road where he had exchanged the candelabrum for coins. At the fork in the road, his pursuers fanned out, as if searching for him.

Carl mounted his horse, pulled out the pistol, and raced in the opposite direction. The horse was panting hard. Carl's weight and the day's activities were almost too much for it.

Almost immediately, he heard the riders in the distance, behind him. A pistol shot rang out. Carl grunted in pain. His shoulder burned where it had been grazed. Urging his horse to go faster, Carl moved in and out of the trees.

Rounding a bend, his good arm caught on a branch, and the

pistol was yanked from his hand. He slid from the horse's back into a bush. The horse continued galloping at breakneck speed. Carl lay flat in the underbrush. The other horsemen dashed past.

When he could no longer hear them, he groped in the blackness for his pistol, but it was no use. The vegetation hid it from him like a grave hid a corpse.

Chapter Eleven

Carl did not know how long he waited in the bushes, straining his ears for the sound of his pursuers. Only when he was convinced that he was safe did he cautiously make his way across the wooded terrain toward the house where he would lodge. He was exhausted but did not let his fatigue govern his actions. By sheer force of will, he kept his legs moving forward. It was early morning when he reached the back of the peasant's house.

Once there, he waited behind a large bush until he was certain that no one was stirring. The shutters were unbarred in his room. Very slowly, he pulled himself across the sill, a task that would have been easy if his shoulder had been uninjured, and then gently set his feet on the coarse wooden planks of the floor. He listened. No one stirred in the house. Without a sound, he barred the shutters, staggered to the bed, and fell across it, sweat leaking from every pore in his skin and blood staining his shirt.

His predicament was not so bad, he told himself. He had certainly been in worse circumstances. Without another thought, he passed out.

⁓

Marta woke with heaviness on her spirit. Carl had not returned. He had been gone two nights now. Hans lay sprawled where Carl should have been. Depression seeped into her soul. Why had she ever let herself feel anything for him? She had known that the arrangement was temporary. She clenched her fists. He had been honest with her, but she had not been honest with herself.

Gretta coughed. After placing the patchwork over Gretta, Marta crawled out of their shelter to prepare for the day. Within moments, Hans followed her lead. As she busied herself with the fire, he picked up the bucket and went to get water. He looked so small.

By the time Marta turned back to the fire pit, Frau Doenhof had appeared with the cooking pot in her hand. "There is one law ye must keep in this household. I expect ye to do thy part of the chores, but henceforth, I will be the only cook."

Marta concentrated on starting the fire to keep a smile from escaping her lips. "I shall abide by your wishes."

"Good." Frau Doenhof took the pot to the side of the shelter where she kept her supplies. "Pour it in here, Hans," she said when the boy returned.

With the fire going and Frau Doenhof busy with their food, Marta sat back. She felt a seedling of joy sprout amid the heaviness of knowing that Carl was gone. She was going to make it. They all were.

Hans scraped his foot back and forth on the ground beside her.

"Hans, halt!" Marta said with a cough. "Or get behind the shelter where the dust shall not take away my breath."

Hans stood still. "Frau Ebel, shall my mother be well soon? Never before was she ill like this."

Marta leaned her head back to look at the morning sky. "Your mother has suffered many hardships, Hans. Her love for your father was great. Bearing the loss of a loved one weakens the body as well as the soul." Marta searched for a way to encourage him without lying. "Should you abide with her today, I feel certain you shall bring her cheer. After all, if a sad heart has the power to make one ill, then a happy heart shall help one feel better."

"I'll do that," said Hans. "I know how to make my mother smile."

During the morning meal, Gretta sat with them. Frau Doenhof fussed around her as if she were an infant who could do nothing for herself, and Hans refused to leave her side. He entertained her with funny stories about all the people he had seen since they left Lübeck. Gretta's eyes filled with delight. Because she did not have to respond, her coughing bothered her less and less.

By midmorning, Marta felt closer to the other three, like she was a part of a family. Hans, Gretta, Frau Doenhof, and Marta boarded the cart that would take them to see Tsarina Catherine. The carts, with their high sides, were not as crowded as the ones they had ridden when they first arrived, and Marta enjoyed seeing more of her new land. Although it had not rained since Marta had been there, the carts went through many muddy areas where insects swarmed. Strange birds with white chests called to one another, and she was surprised at the number of pine trees that were intermixed with birch on the wide, open terrain.

The carts stopped near a large dais. Marta and the others climbed down and walked to the adjoining field. They stood in the hot sun for some time before an entourage of carriages pulled into the field. The closed carriage in the middle looked magnificent, all in gold carved into thousands of ornate designs. Marta wished she could have been closer to the procession to better see the Tsarina's riches, but she and the others were toward the back of the group.

Marta rose on her toes and strained her eyes to glimpse their new monarch in her golden gown and many strands of jewels. Tsarina Catherine spoke in her native German tongue, but Marta could not make out the words before they were absorbed by the openness. When the woman stopped speaking, the people around Marta began repeating what sounded like an oath, swearing to be loyal Russian citizens.

Marta joined in with her neighbors, even though her words followed behind theirs. Frau Doenhof, standing next to her, moved her lips but did not utter a sound. Like Marta, she probably could not catch what was being said. Marta spoke louder to help her, until she noticed others doing the same thing as Frau Doenhof.

When the oath was finished, Marta knew she had become a Russian. She felt proud to be a citizen of such a large and generous country. As she waited for the Tsarina and her many subjects to leave and then rode back to their twig shelters, Marta enjoyed her new sense of belonging.

As Frau Doenhof and Gretta prepared their food, Marta said,

"Our oath to Russia makes us true Russians. It gives one reason for joy, does it not?"

"What oath?" Frau Doenhof slammed her spoon into the pot. "I swore no oath."

Marta's eyebrows drew together. "Of course you did."

"I moved my lips, but said not a word," said Frau Doenhof proudly. "I reserve my right to leave if I do not like this place."

Gretta laughed. "The Russians suffer not anyone to leave. It has cost them overmuch to bring you here. Have you not wondered why the soldiers abide nearby? They keep with our groups, not to protect us from nomadic tribes, but to halt any attempt at escape."

"Why should anyone want to leave?" Marta asked, but she received no answer.

―ᴄ

After a few hours of sleep, Carl felt ready to finish what he had started. He cleaned his wound, changed back into his immigrant clothes, paid the peasant an extra stipend in case he needed to return, and was on his way. His first stop was the estate where he had purchased the horse. The animal had run all the way back to its stable and was safely in its stall.

"The beast threw me to the ground," said Carl, much to the estate manager's enjoyment. He paid the man more coins. "I can't bother with him now. I'll return in a few days, if I think he is worth my time. Take care of him for me."

The man agreed, and Carl left. In the woods surrounding the farm, Carl dug a hole, placed his Russian clothing and bloody evening wear in it, and then rolled a rock over the top of it. With luck, he would never need them again. Finally, he made his way to where he had stashed his coins in the wall. He took out the sack and kissed it.

"That should teach Goralski a lesson."

―ᴄ

In preparation for the next leg of their journey, Marta mended clothing, stored food, and repaired the rips that Carl had left in the patchwork. It was hard to believe that they would finally travel to St. Petersburg and then on to the land, her land, the home of her future. She was excited to see St. Petersburg, having heard of its grandeur from Carl and other immigrants.

"Frau Ebel," said Hans. "I will go to the water to cool myself."

"No, Hans. Not without Frau Doenhof or me." She stirred the pot once for Frau Doenhof. Out of the corner of her eye, she saw Sergey watching her from behind a neighboring shelter.

"My mother said I might go," he said.

"I do not believe that," said Marta. "She has not stirred from her sleep since the morn." She saw Sergey looking again and shot him a look of defiance, and then turned her back on him.

She lowered her voice. "Hans, it is wrong to tell untruths. Your father was ever a truthful man."

"Herr Ebel is not always truthful. Untruths help us with the Russians."

"No, Hans, untruths never help in the end. Become a man like your good father. To speak truth is ever the better choice." Marta hoped the child was pondering her words as he began playing with his rocks.

—☙—

Taking back roads and roundabout routes, Carl entered the servant's entrance of Sascha Ivanov's house before the midday meal. No one noticed. He walked by his friend's case of swords and knives, stopping to examine a small one with an ivory handle that seemed out of place among the many larger blades.

He had not made it past the dining room, though, when a deep voice said, "I thought you might drop by for a visit." Sascha escorted him into the library, and once concealed from the eyes of others, they clasped hands warmly.

"Goralski and his cronies now treat me as a comrade," said

Sascha. "He even invited me to his reception last evening, but unfortunately I had a previous engagement. I wonder what could have placed me so high in his esteem." He poured Carl some vodka.

"From what I hear, you betrayed me, and then I got even with you." Carl took the drink and sat in one of the chairs he had used during friendlier times. Sascha was one of the few men in any country that Carl trusted with his life. He was growing tired of games with his enemies. It felt good to be in the house of a friend.

They did not talk for a while. Carl thought back over their relationship. The two men had been through a lot in the years since they had met, when Carl stopped two men from beating and robbing Sascha in France. At the time, a youthful Carl had been looking for a fight, and the villains had simply provided the opportunity. From that act of kindness, he had found a friendship worth more than anything he owned. His only regret at leaving Russia for good would be not being able to see Sascha again.

Sascha poured his own drink. "It wasn't wise to steal the candelabrum. Word travels fast. Goralski says that it was worth a great deal of money. Be careful, my friend. You have become the hunted."

"Let them hunt. I'm an elusive prey, much of it thanks to your help." Carl set down his glass and measured out a third of the coins from the bag tucked into his waist. "I pay my debts."

"You owe me nothing," said Sascha.

"Not yet," said Carl.

As Carl was leaving, he saw Sascha nod toward him, as if directing someone to follow, but Carl saw no one. He shook his head. Would he now be suspicious of everyone? Sascha had always done well by him. He had to relax and keep to his plan.

⁓

Although they did not need fresh water so late in the day, Marta went to fetch some, wanting to keep busy so as not to dwell too much on either the past or the future. She waved to the woman who had prayed for Hans to find his mother. The air was cool, refreshing. She was growing used to the large black birds around their camp that berated the settlers for invading their territory. She ignored their scolding now.

As she turned back toward the shelter, she saw Sergey towering over Gretta, Frau Doenhof, and Hans. Without concern for the water she spilled, Marta rushed forward.

"What is your business here?" she demanded, tempted to toss the remaining water at Sergey's back before he turned.

"Where could be your husband now, Frau?" he asked in a cool, disdainful voice.

"That is no concern of yours," Marta replied. Frau Doenhof's eyes grew big, and Gretta began to cough. Marta moved past Sergey, ignoring the trembling of her legs, and handed Gretta a scoop of water.

"It is my concern," he said. "Two nights your husband has not lodged here. He try to escape, no?"

"Yes, he has," said Marta. Frau Doenhof gasped.

"To go to homeland, it is a crime. Come with me." Sergey reached for her arm, but Marta shook him off. She handed the bucket to Hans and turned to Sergey with her hands on her hips.

"As you have not ceased your watch over us, you must know the truth of the matter. Why do you pretend otherwise? Herr Ebel has escaped my sharp tongue. If you look, you shall find that he abides nearby, hidden like a mouse. Tell him that I am happy to be rid of him. The farther away from me he abides, the better!"

Sergey looked shocked at her outburst, as if he had not expected anyone to stand up to him, especially this young woman. "Come with me."

"No." Marta let her chin rise in an ultimate act of defiance. "I do not follow you nor any man." Her words caught in her throat. She felt as if she could not breathe. She blinked quickly. Were her eyes deceiving her?

Carl stepped from behind a neighboring shelter. He had heard enough. He moved toward Sergey in full sight of the group.

"You attempt to take my wife from me again?" he asked in a

lighthearted voice. In the moment that Sergey turned, Marta flew into Carl's arms. She was sobbing, actually crying, her tears intermingling with the dust on his vest as she held him tightly. Carl kept one hand around her waist, but left the other hand at his side so he would appear more nonchalant than he felt. Marta's nearness, the sweetness of her emotion was causing his insides to jump around like a dancing gypsy troupe.

"You," said Sergey. "Where are you these two days past?"

"You're not the only one to watch my wife from a distance," he said, looking the man directly in the eye. "She's a spirited one. Ofttimes a man must leave for his wife to appreciate him when he's near."

As if in spite of himself, Sergey smiled. "We are much alike."

Carl gave him a slow nod. "You've taught me not to assume that you are not nearby, even when I don't see you. Perhaps 'tis time you gave me the same courtesy." Sergey's smile grew, and Carl knew he had chosen the right words. He continued, "I take orders from no one, especially not a woman."

"You tame her well," Sergey said.

"Now, if you'll excuse me, my wife must learn another lesson."

Sergey laughed as he moved away, repeating, "Good man."

Carl's free hand encircled Marta.

"Where have you been?" demanded Frau Doenhof as Hans ran to Carl's side.

"I had to prepare for a trip," he said, "as Marta probably told you." He gently pushed Marta away from him and picked Hans up with his good arm. "You were quite the little man while I was detained."

"I missed you," said Hans. He buried his head into Carl's chest.

With Hans on his hip, Carl gingerly placed his other arm around Marta's shoulders. For the first time, he questioned whether he should reconsider his plans, wondered if he could really become head of this little family.

That evening after dinner, Marta was cleaning up when Hans walked up beside her. "Frau Ebel, did you not tell an untruth today?"

Marta grimaced as she recalled her words to Sergey. Carl's dishonest ways were beginning to affect her, as well as the child. "Yes, I did, Hans. It was wrong of me. Please forgive me."

Hans hesitated. "Sometimes, is it better to speak untruth?"

Marta's heart sank. "No, Hans. We dare not bear false witness. In its stead, it is better to keep silent. Shall you and I start anew?"

Hans smiled. "You would be a good woman like my mother, and I shall be like my father."

Marta stooped to his eye level. "Yes, Hans." She hugged him. "Now be off to your bed."

When Marta woke on the dawn of their departure day, she closed her eyes and listened to Carl's steady breathing on the other side of Frau Doenhof. He really had returned. Inhaling the crisp morning air, she crawled out of the shelter. She could not help feeling a tremor of excitement. Today they would leave their shanty village and travel to their new homes and land. That's what she was excited about, she told herself, not willing to admit the true source of her joy.

After the others had risen, Marta tied their belongings into their blankets.

"You must wait on this one for a time," said Carl, pointing to the patchwork. "I'd like to repair a few rips."

"I have done so already," she said with a smile.

"There are new rips," he said. She felt her smile slowly fade. He was removing the last of his secrets from her wedding gift.

"I understand," she said. As Frau Doenhof cleaned the campsite and Hans doted on his mother, Marta finished packing all but what would go in her patchwork. When Carl rolled out of the shanty, he seemed to favor his left side. For a few moments, he stood next to Marta, as quiet now as he had been about his adventures of the previous three days, though Frau Doenhof had tried to bully the information out of him. With a deep breath, he motioned for Marta to follow him and led her to the side of the shelter.

He handed her their papers. "I think it best that you and the others board the boat first."

His eyes were serious. She took the papers from him. He was saying good-bye. She would never see him again.

"I thank you." She did not know what else to say. How could she express desolation in words? She opened her arms, and he crushed her to himself. Just as quickly, he released her, and though she stood unmoving, she felt as if she were staggering backward over a precipice.

"Are your plans worth the risk?" she asked with what remained of her voice.

"I would put you in too much danger if I remained," he said.

"I should be willing to accept that risk." Her voice was quiet. "As would the others." She cleared her throat. She had to say it now, while she still had the opportunity. "I would even be willing to give up my land if . . . what I mean to say . . . the others would not miss me." Afraid of the rejection she knew was coming, Marta could not look into his eyes.

It was Carl's turn to clear his throat. "I've thought all night about ways we could change our lot, but 'tis no good. If you knew the man I am, truly knew what I've done, and how I've lived. . . . I prefer you to remember me as you know me now. I don't want to dim the light in your eyes, that lovely glow that greets me as if I were someone who deserved your love. I'm not certain I'd want to live in a world where I thought you despised me; and Marta, you would despise me if you knew how truly despicable I am. Of that, I'm completely certain."

She was losing him, and she knew it, but what else could she expect? He had warned her. She had not counted on falling in love with him.

"Should I not have the right to protest this plan?" she asked.

"I've never been heroic, and today I take the coward's way again."

"We leave today!" shouted Hans as he rushed between Carl and Marta and into Carl's arms. Marta blinked back her regret and forced herself to focus on the day, which had suddenly become dreary. She watched Hans swing from Carl's arm. One last time,

Hans would be able to act like a boy instead of the man of the family.

When everything was packed, Carl said, "I'll meet you on the boat. I have some things to take care of." He turned and walked away.

"Herr Ebel," called Hans, running after him. Carl knelt down. Marta watched the two speak to each other in low tones. With a rough swipe through the boy's tousled hair, Carl handed him a sack that fit into the boy's hand. Then he walked away without looking back.

"Slovenly man. Will he not help us bear these burdens?" demanded Frau Doenhof.

"He has other business," said Marta. She turned to Gretta. "Let me bear that for you."

"That is just like a man," Frau Doenhof mumbled. "Ever away when there is work to be done. Hans help me with this." Hans did not meet Marta's eyes as he helped Frau Doenhof pick up her belongings.

Gretta slid an arm around Marta's waist. "Is everything in readiness?"

Marta finished tying up her patchwork and took a deep breath. "Yes. Yes, 'tis time to leave." She did not look back at the shelter where they had lived, a place she would always remember as having been close enough to touch Carl, though she never had. Her heart ached, but she was glad to be doing something. A portion of her life was over. She would concentrate on carrying their belongings, forcing her body to obey her, instead of giving in to her tears. She would look ahead. She would not look back. Ever.

After a few steps, Marta took Gretta's remaining sack. "You shall need a hand free to help Hans." Gretta's weakened condition threatened to delay their departure. Marta would not let this happen. She was now in charge, and she would make certain that they, all four of them, made it to their new home. Heaven help the person who tried to stop them.

Chapter Twelve

Marta took a deep breath and handed the papers to the official overseeing the boarding. She concentrated on keeping her hands from shaking.

"Where is your husband?" asked the man in fluent German.

Another official came over and glanced at the papers. "He is aboard already. Let them pass." As the first official folded the papers and handed them back to Marta, the second man gave her a friendly wink. Marta looked down.

She knew he was lying, and she was reluctant to board under false pretenses. She opened her mouth to protest, but Frau Doenhof pushed her forward.

"But . . . I . . . my husband is not . . ." was all that Marta could get out before the official turned to the next group.

"Get thee to the boat," said Frau Doenhof.

One step. Two steps. Keep walking, Marta told her feet. She wondered whether Carl would meet her if she ran back into the crowd of immigrants. She did not want to leave Oranienbaum under these terms—under the guise of a half lie and without Carl. She tried to turn once more to right the misunderstanding, but those behind pushed her forward. Marta knew that Carl was not on the boat. Only his money—or his glib tongue—had preceded them. She was better off alone, she repeated over and over to herself. Carl's lying had affected her again, and she hated that.

"Shall we seek out a place to rest with our things?" Gretta asked once they were on board.

"Could be Herr Ebel has prepared a place," Frau Doenhof said. Hans stared up at Marta gravely and shook his head. He tugged on her sleeve to get her to stoop to his level.

"I am the man of the family now," he said. He handed Marta the bag that she had seen Carl give him. Inside, she found a small fortune, an amount likely equal to all the groschen and pfennigs that Russia had paid them for their daily food since they had boarded the ship in Lübeck.

The coins were heavy in her hand. Carl had also given Frau Doenhof money to purchase food for them. She wondered if he had been making up the difference with his own coin. A small tear formed in one eye, and she quickly blinked it away. He knew they could not live on what Russia had paid them. With this money, they had much more coin than those around them.

Hans stood in front of her until she said in a quiet voice, "Thank you." She quickly slid the money into her bundle and away from prying eyes. Hans nodded and returned to his mother's side. His face looked so much older than it had this morning.

Herr Zweig and another man, who appeared to be a clergyman, walked over to their small group. "Welcome Frau Ebel, Hans, Frau Doenhof. This is a good day."

"'Tis a very good day, Herr, to abide among friends," said Frau Doenhof.

"Yes, we are reunited with friends for this final part of our journey," he said. "And who might this be?" he asked, smiling at Gretta.

"Frau Binz," said Marta. She turned to Gretta. "Herr Zweig is the leader of our group."

Herr Zweig bowed slightly. "Honored. And I would like you to meet Herr Jaeger, who shall pastor our new settlement."

After they exchanged greetings, Herr Jaeger was called over to talk with another gathering of settlers. He excused himself. Marta watched as he gently pushed his way between others to reach those who had hailed him.

Herr Zweig cleared his throat and addressed Marta. "I never offered you thanks for—" His voiced cracked, and he cleared his throat again.

"You owe me no thanks," said Marta. "It was my desire to help your wife." They watched the crowded docks for a short time. Then very gently, she added, "Would that I could have helped her more."

Hans stepped between them. "Herr Zweig, 'tis true? Shall we travel the whole way by boat?"

Herr Zweig laughed. "Most of it, lad."

Marta's heart sank. "I'm weary of the water. Had we been assigned the overland route, I should be more contented."

"I have learned to look forward only," Herr Zweig said. "Our vessel should carry us to our new homes before summer's end. By land . . . we should reach not our settlement until spring."

"Truly then, 'tis best to travel by water," said Marta, but her heart was not in her words. She still disliked boat travel. It reminded her of Carl. The vessel rocked.

"Shall we store our things below deck?" asked Frau Doenhof.

"No. No," Herr Zweig said. "Before long, this vessel shall bear us to St. Petersburg. Keep your belongings near."

"Very well." Frau Doenhof set down her things and started arranging everyone's sacks for Gretta to rest on. Herr Zweig left to greet other passengers.

Marta scanned the dock area for a last glimpse of Carl. She knew he was there, watching, waiting, making certain they were safely on their way. She only hoped that giving him her father's name was as great a help to him as his protection over their small company had been to her. With one last inspection of the dock area, she turned and looked toward the eastern horizon. Although she did not have a mother, father, or husband, she did have two other women and a child who were now her family. She must keep her eyes focused on the east. Looking forward.

⌐○

Carl let his eyes wash over Marta's form one last time. A lump caught in his throat. Saying good-bye to her and Hans had been more difficult than he had anticipated, but it was over now. Things were as they should be. At least all the bribes he had paid the sailors were working in Marta's favor.

"God of Abraham," he prayed silently. "If You are real, then You watched over my people in the wilderness. Would You watch over Marta and Hans? They're dear to me. Do for them what I cannot."

Enough of that. He had not felt this wretched since the day he left his mother's house, never to return, as if she were dead to him. That's why it was good that Marta and he had parted company. She made him weak, caused him to remember things that he had buried as a lad, made him question his very soul.

He watched until the ketch moved out into open water on its course away from him. He turned, blending into the crowd to stay out of sight, in case Sergey was patrolling the area.

Today, timing would be of the essence. As the afternoon soldiers changed shifts with the evening replacements, Carl slipped out of camp. He was surprised that it had been so easy. He had not seen Sergey even once—not on rounds, not harassing women, nothing. Perhaps he was sick. He sighed. Sergey's absence bothered Carl as much his presence.

—⁂—

Marta managed to find a spot near the rail to watch as they entered the wide mouth of the Neva River. Guarding the city from the vantage point of a small island stood a large fortress. Inside the walls, a tower with an enormous golden spire rose into the sky. Across from the fortress and downriver, a grand three-story building with hundreds of windows dominated the shoreline. Marta felt certain it was the Winter Palace that Carl had described to her during one of their shipboard walks. "Russia must be a great country," she thought, proud that it was her new home.

Soon Marta, Gretta, Hans, and Frau Doenhof climbed onto the dock in St. Petersburg and were carried along with the crowd onshore. They were herded into groups and given provisions for the journey, including a sheepskin cloak for the Russian winter. Marta shivered just thinking about the kind of weather that would require such a heavy piece of clothing.

"Can you believe it?" a fellow traveler grumbled. "They have decreased our allowance by three groschen! How are we to survive?"

Gretta answered gently, "We must put our trust in the Lord, as before."

After such long waits in Kronstadt and Oranienbaum, Marta was amazed at how quickly they were given additional supplies and sent aboard the ketches that would carry them toward their final destination.

As they passed through the city into the open river, once again Marta found a spot by the rail away from the others and stared down into the churning water. Carl had always preferred watching the water to enjoying the glorious beauty of the skies above them. The pain and sadness she was feeling compelled her to identify with the churning. Perhaps the scars he hid also kept his eyes there.

"No, enough," she told herself. She must put Carl out of her mind and look only ahead. How far they had come already! Yet their journey was only beginning. Marta tried to pray.

"I thank Thee, Lord God of heaven, for Your bountiful provision. I beseech Thee for a safe journey."

The words did not seem correct. Marta was no longer satisfied with a God who only watched from above. She needed a friend, a companion, someone bigger who could protect her in a future that loomed out of her control and caused her heart to groan with anxiety. She would never have breathed a word of her fears to any living soul, because she did not want to be identified as a heathen; but heaven help her, she had unanswered questions, as Carl did. Even as the thought alarmed her, she reminded herself that she was a Reformer. He was not. How could they be questioning the same things? Regardless, these questions had been with her since before the priest had fed and warmed her, since before a Jew had set her life back on course.

She felt a prickle on the back of her neck and looked around. What she saw horrified her. Sergey was aboard the ketch. All other thoughts disappeared. It had grown late. She was alone amid a crowd of strangers. He was pushing people aside. She pushed away from the rail and hurried in search of Frau Doenhof, Gretta, or anyone who could help protect her.

—⌒—

Carl reentered Sascha Ivanov's house through the open library doors and changed into the clothing that his friend had provided. Those looking for him would be expecting a man dressed in either the immigrant clothing that Quentin had seen or the evening dress he had worn to Goralski's house.

"Farewell, my friend," said Sascha. When Carl took his friend's hand, he knew that this was the last time he would ever see him.

"May we meet again," responded Carl, and then he slipped away from the house. He looked back at his friend, and once again, saw Sascha nod in his direction, as if giving his position away to someone. Carl stopped and watched. No one left the house. Nothing stirred. He made his way to the harbor.

When he was certain that all was as it should be, he hurried to the far end of the docks. Blending into the crowd, he easily found the ship on which Ivanov's servant had secured passage for him.

He patted the small bundle of coins in his pouch and thought with satisfaction of the others he had sewn into his clothing and shoes. It should be plenty for the journey, even if the captain took three months to cross the Baltic. He even had enough to set himself up modestly until he could find another means for earning a living.

Once aboard the ship, he greeted the captain and prepared to go below deck. Immediately, he heard the clomping of soldiers' feet. An inspection? He looked at the captain. Had he reported his dealings with Ivanov to others? The man's face gave away nothing.

Carl casually dropped his belongings behind a coil of rope and moved to the other side of the deck. He reached into his shirt for the identification papers he had purchased in the German states.

As the soldiers came on deck, Carl tried to appear nonchalant, but it was only an act. He was aware of those around him and what they were doing—the sailors pretending to work but watching the action, other passengers nervously taking their papers out of their sacks, the captain standing motionless on deck. Carl had been through similar inspections many times.

The officer directed his soldiers to herd the male passengers into a spot where he could see them in the dimming evening light. At first, his eyes passed over Carl, but then they traveled back and rested on him. Under the soldier's scrutiny, Carl stood steady. He looked the man directly in the eye and nodded.

"Check their papers," the soldier commanded.

A younger soldier approached a man several feet away from Carl. He examined the documents carefully and then moved to the man beside Carl. "Do we have a recruiting agent named Flegel?" the inspector asked another soldier, who held a paper that Carl assumed to be a list.

A triumphant smile formed on his lips. "No."

Flegel tried to run but was caught without a fight.

The officer bellowed, "As you can see, no immigrant shall get past us. Vows of allegiance to the Tsarina are sacred and shall be kept." Flegel was half escorted, half dragged off the ship.

The young soldier took Carl's papers.

"Stoltz?" the young soldier asked. Carl hoped his friend from Lübeck had not changed his mind and decided to return with immigrants one last time. He had paid him enough for his papers and help on the rowboat.

"He's on the list," the other said.

Carl took back his papers. The inspection was almost over when another man boarded. Carl recognized him at once. Quentin said something quietly to the soldier in charge, who nodded. They were baiting him, playing cat-and-mouse, as if Carl had a remote chance of not being recognized.

As Quentin wandered around the ship, Carl casually surveyed his options. Quentin picked up Carl's sack and emptied it on the deck. Carl could not run. Too many men. He could not fight. Too many weapons. He took a step back to the rail.

"What's this?" Quentin asked, using the tip of his sword to hold up a sack of some of his own jewels. Carl wished he had given all those incriminating jewels to Marta as he had first planned. "As I recall, this was stolen by a man named Mueller, a Jewish traitor to the Russian empire." As his finger moved to point Carl out to the soldiers, Carl made his decision.

He catapulted over the rail and dropped into the frigid water. Its iciness shot through him like a million knives, but he swam underwater until he was well away from the ship and hidden by other vessels in the busy harbor. The cold seeped into his body, numbing him. The coins that he had sewn into his clothing weighed him down. He did not know how much longer he could hold his breath. He had to come up for air. The cold was paralyzing his movements. He had to get out of the water—and soon.

—⟨⟩

Marta flung herself between Frau Doenhof and Herr Zweig. She knew she was being rude and interrupting their polite conversation, but they were her only hope.

"What's this?" demanded Frau Doenhof.

"Why it's Frau Ebel," said Herr Zweig, who looked delighted to see her.

"I—I—" Marta could not think quickly enough. Sergey was drawing closer.

"Honestly!" said Frau Doenhof, but she put an arm around Marta's waist.

—⟨⟩

Carl heard a faint voice in the distance. *"Où? Où suis-je?"* His body shivered violently. A voice answered, but it was speaking Russian. Then the first voice spoke again. *"Où suis-je?"* Suddenly, he realized that it was his own voice. He was reverting to the language of his youth. He felt the deep coldness of being alone and exposed to the elements, the same biting cold he had endured as a young man before he'd made a better life for himself. He struggled to open his eyes. He was in a small rowboat.

A bearded man sat beside him. "Do you speak Russian?"

"Da."

The man smiled. "Good. Good. It was fortunate that I was able to pull you from the water in time. I am a good fisherman, am I not? Perhaps to you, I am the best of fishermen? Do you not think so, my fine fish?"

"Indeed," answered Carl.

"A few more moments and you would have been only bait. You're not the biggest fish I have pulled from the water, but you're certainly the most prized," said the man as he rowed.

Carl tried to sit up to determine where they were. Was he far enough away from Quentin? Would others be watching for him?

The fisherman continued, "I said to myself, 'You are a lucky man.' Some days I get no fish at all. Today, I do well. Some days, I do not meet another human. Today, I meet you. This is a very good day, not just for you, but for me also." He kept up his chatter as Carl regained his bearings. The man was rowing toward a distant dock, farther away than those used for the larger ships. There was a good chance that Carl had swum far enough for his rescue to go undetected. If only he could feel his hands and feet, he could enjoy the triumph of his escape. The man had tucked a large fur blanket around him, but he still shivered.

"We're almost to port. The sea was good to us. We'll have plenty of fish to sell and more than enough to eat. I'll even give you some to take home. You live in St. Petersburg, no? It's a good place to live. It's cold in winter, but in summer, we have sunshine day and night."

"It's a beautiful city," said Carl between shivers.

Carl ducked almost completely under the fur as the rowboat pulled into a small, hidden inlet. From the sounds around them, no one seemed particularly interested in the small boat. The clipped march of a few soldiers sounded close, but they continued on.

He heard the man tie up his boat and yell, "Come. See my catch!"

Something was wrong. The icy water had made Carl's mind sluggish. He suddenly realized that the man had asked him nothing. Most fishermen would have questioned him about how he had fallen into the bay. Only a man who already had the answer would have failed to ask.

Carl tried to move, to escape, as the man continued talking. "Come. See my catch!" He laughed. "I have caught a rare and elusive Mueller fish."

Chapter Thirteen

Marta peered around Frau Doenhof. No one. She looked in the other direction. No one approached from beyond Herr Zweig either. Marta willed her pounding heart to slow down, as if she could release her fears on command, but her heartbeat continued at its own pace, and she could not fully catch her breath. She knew that Sergey was somewhere, stalking her, waiting for his opportunity.

"'Tis a fine evening," announced Herr Zweig.

"A very fine evening," said Marta in a voice that fooled no one. Frau Doenhof's arm gave her a gentle squeeze before releasing her.

"What troubles you?" asked Herr Zweig. He leaned forward slightly, his red hair framing the concerned lines on his face.

She was embarrassed to tell him about Sergey's advances, but she could not think of another answer. Marta looked to Frau Doenhof. The movement of wind across the deck ruffled the woman's stray hair as she stared in the direction from which Marta had come, seemingly looking beyond the coarse splinters of their ketch. Marta turned to Herr Zweig and shrugged.

He beamed. "I know that which shall bring joy to your fair face. Where is your husband? His presence brings light to your eyes even when your lips refuse to smile."

Marta's mouth went dry, and a tickle irritated her throat. She coughed.

Frau Doenhof's voice sounded like welcome thunder after a long drought. "How can ye expect her to know where that man abides, what with us packed in like leaves of cabbage?"

"'Tis true, but I have talent to find lost things," Herr Zweig said.

"Tell me where last you saw him, and I shall find him straightway. Then I shall have done you a service."

Sergey's voice cut in. "Where did you see last Herr Ebel?" His tone was smooth but laced with a thread of danger. Marta quickly turned toward him. She had not heard the clipped sound of his boots on the wooden deck as he had drawn near. He positioned himself in front of her.

She took a deep breath and raised her chin. If this would be her last stand, then she would go out fighting.

"My husband is not of your concern," she said.

"You wrong, Frau," said Sergey. "Your husband is very my concern." Sergey grabbed Marta's arms with his large hands.

"Now, now," said Herr Zweig. "Let us keep the peace. There is no need for anger."

Sergey's closeness repulsed Marta. She tore herself from his grip.

"Herr Sergey," continued Herr Zweig, "your only interest in Herr Ebel is that he is on this boat. Your husband abides on this boat, does he not, Frau Ebel? Your word is enough for us."

Marta knew that she could borrow no more time for Carl or herself. She was a woman unprotected and alone, but whatever happened, she vowed that she would not let this self-important soldier bully her. Marta took a deep breath.

"They quarreled," said Frau Doenhof. This time, Marta placed her arm around Frau Doenhof's waist and was surprised to find that the woman, beneath her tough exterior, was trembling.

In a clear voice, Marta said, "I've not seen Herr Ebel since Oranienbaum."

Sergey looked surprised, as if he had expected neither the truth nor the strength that she was now revealing. "Oranienbaum?" he repeated.

Marta gave a curt nod.

"You find him," said Sergey in a low voice filled with menace. "Or trouble shall be yours." In spite of Marta's new resolve, her legs felt weak. Sergey hovered over her as if he expected tears or pleas of mercy, but when Marta continued to stare at him coolly, he turned and left.

A light shower began to spit from a lone cloud that hovered above the boat. Marta raised her face to its coolness and enjoyed the tingling sensation on her hot skin. She would not live her life reacting to others. Let Sergey do his worst. She would persevere. Just as quickly as the cloud had come upon them, it left, taking its momentary refreshment with it.

Marta turned to Herr Zweig. "We are now but three women and a boy. What must be our course?"

"Your course?" repeated Herr Zweig, as if he were still trying to absorb her words and the turn of events.

"We shall not be given land now," she stated. All her work, all her trust in Carl had destroyed the very thing she wanted most. Now she would never be mistress of her own world. In spite of her disappointment, she stood up straighter. Even without the land, she would find a way to survive.

"Hans is the man of your household," said Herr Zweig.

"He is only six, hardly a man," said Frau Doenhof. "But take no thought of us. We shall care for ourselves."

Marta nodded. Yes, they would make it through whatever was cast upon them.

"Ye still need the protection of a man to get your land and supplies," said Herr Zweig. "Hans is not a man in stature, but in the eyes of Russia, he is your protector."

"What?" exclaimed both women.

"I had in mind to bring it up to Herr Ebel. I thought 'twas an oversight." Herr Zweig took out a handkerchief and wiped the sweat from his forehead. "Hans is registered as the man of your family, not Herr Ebel."

"How can thy words be truth?" asked Frau Doenhof.

The beginning of a smile formed on Marta's lips. "Then we shall have our land. We are as we were before."

"True. True." Herr Zweig turned to Frau Doenhof, who still looked dumbfounded. "I know not how this came to be, but your family is registered under Hans's name. Still, ye are but three women with a small boy. For your own protection, ye should all remarry."

Marta hid her disdain of Herr Zweig's words by turning away from the well-intentioned man. Another husband was a thought she would not entertain. Carl had kept his word. She let her heart soar in the knowledge that he had looked out for her interests to the very end.

—☙

Before the glib fisherman could draw an audience with another jubilant remark, Carl pulled aside the moth-eaten blanket that covered him. "I'm no *dummkopf*. For whom do you work?"

The man gave Carl a smile that showed three rotten teeth. "We are made of the same fabric."

"You work for Goralski?" asked Carl.

"Not that cold-water eel."

"Then who? Ivanov?" When the man did not answer, Carl swore under his breath. His friend Sascha was playing a double game, but was it to Carl's benefit or demise? "I am Ivanov's prisoner?"

The fisherman spoke in a voice too low for those on the dock to hear. "*Prisoner* is a harsh word. Ye'll not find a better man than Ivanov anywhere. If not for him, ye'd be drowned."

Carl watched the man's eyes. "And am I better off now?"

The man took Carl's blanket from him. "No need to see this ripped." He folded it and laid it aside. "Ivanov gave ye the opportunity to escape on your own, but ye failed."

Carl took a long, slow breath of air. "What's next?"

The man continued, "Turn ye over to Goralski's men, of course. It is the best plan."

Best for whom? thought Carl, but out loud he asked, "Why turn me over at all? I came with an immigrant group—"

"Herr Zweig's. I know. I followed ye and your beautiful woman, have followed ye ever since ye gave my lord a generous gift." He pulled Carl roughly to his feet.

Carl was still cold and numb from the water, but he shivered more from the new danger he faced than from the wind penetrating his wet clothing. "Why not put me back into that immigrant group? They cannot have ventured far. I'll just disappear."

The sailor laughed. "'Tis too late for that. Goralski knows Ivanov has found you." He motioned to the soldiers.

Four rough hands yanked Carl from the boat and hauled him onto the land. The sailor followed close behind. Carl could not stop shivering as the fisherman spoke in a low voice to the men. He had to escape this new danger. Ignoring the chill, Carl took a step back, away from the group. He turned and began running blindly, but within a few strides, a cursing soldier caught him and threw him to the ground. His body was still so numb that he barely felt any pain as he hit the dirt and the soldiers took turns kicking him.

"Ye Jewish dog," said one with an especially violent blow to Carl's ribs. Just as Carl felt he might pass out, the men stopped kicking him. He lay still, unable to move on his own. His hands were jerked up and a rough rope was tied around them. He heard the soldiers laughing and then felt the rope being pulled. Colors and sounds blurred as he tasted his own blood and smelled the earth beneath him. They were dragging him through the street. He heard his clothes ripping, and then felt the sting of his skin being scraped away. He tried to roll his exposed flesh away from the street, only to have more clothing rip and another area of skin scrape against the ground. He could not get his feet to obey his command, could not rise to walk behind the soldiers. By the time he was thrown into the lower quarters of what he assumed was Goralski's city house in Oranienbaum, he felt more dead than alive.

—⚬—

As their craft progressed up the Neva River, through an enormous lake, and then into another river, Marta and her companions settled into a routine. Frau Doenhof took charge of Hans in the morning and prepared the food for every meal. Marta remained with Gretta until their midday meal, after which both Gretta and Frau Doenhof rested. In the afternoon, Marta and Hans played games and tried to catch fish. The ketch carrying the immigrants to the Volga territories felt even smaller than its physically cramped quarters, especially in the corner where Marta and her companions slept and Gretta spent her days. There was no room to walk around because everyone lived on deck, with the hot sun beating down on them during the day and the damp air chilling them through the night.

Although Herr Zweig's prediction of their arrival before winter seemed reasonable, Marta wondered about the timing when, for several days, they scarcely traveled at all. What with stopping for supplies, burying those who died, and waiting on their captain's many errands at various ports, Marta preferred the Baltic captain who sailed backward at night. At least his treachery was predictable. Slowly, the glow of Carl's last deed faded, and Marta was once again left with a void in her heart.

"Are ye not well?" Gretta asked Marta one morning.

Marta shrugged. "I should ask that of you."

"My problems are physical, on the outside. I think yours are inside."

"We have both lost husbands." Marta smoothed the heavy patchwork over Gretta's legs. The material itself must be heavy, thought Marta, for when Carl took out all his treasures and left, the patchwork did not seem to lighten.

"Yes, we have. Some days I miss Herr Binz so much that it aches here," said Gretta, holding her midsection.

"You were wed to a very good man," said Marta. "Carl, on the other hand, is a scoundrel. Still, my mind dwells much on his welfare. Did he escape? Does he abide safe in Lübeck? Deep in my soul, I desire to do something for him, but my prayers fall to the ground. Would that they might fly straight to God, like yours."

"Even though I prayed for Herr Binz, and he died?"

Marta stared at Gretta. Had she given up hope?

"Do not look at me in such a manner. I have not lost my faith. I meant merely that we are not always given what is in our prayers. I do not understand why Friedrich died, but I know that my Lord is with me, sustaining me, even though the pain of loss nearly tears me apart."

Marta grabbed Gretta's hands between hers. "I understand the pain of grief. If I could but experience your faith. You and Herr Binz seemed to have a calm, a peace, that the rest of us do not have. It is as if you have a direct line to God, like a Russian noble who can freely approach the Tsarina's throne and have a word with her. You are a Reformer, as am I, but your faith is different."

Gretta studied Marta's face. "I enjoy God's peace because His Spirit lives within me. The Holy Spirit abides with all who believe on God's Son."

"Then why do I not feel this peace?"

"Jesus raps at your heart's door. Have ye the will to let Him abide with ye?"

"I do not know what you mean. I believe in Jesus, as do all Reformers."

"Are ye willing to let Him order thy life, willing to follow Him wherever He leads ye, even if it means giving up your plans?"

"Such as a husband and family? Even my land?"

"Even that. He must be the sole ruler of your heart, and ye must commit to love Him above all else." Gretta fell into a fit of coughing and sat up to take a drink of water. Marta supported her back. Gretta continued, "Through His Son, Jesus, God invites ye into a relationship more intimate than the sacrament of marriage, but He requires thine answer."

Marta struggled with what she was hearing. "What shall happen if I tell Him that I accept His invitation?"

In a low voice, Gretta continued, "Ye shall become a new woman. He shall come to stay with ye, and ye shall never be alone or unprotected again." Gretta lay back and closed her eyes.

Marta wondered. Could she love Jesus that way . . . give Him everything? She had been forced to become independent, in control—at least as much as a woman could be. What changes would this decision bring to her world? Could she trust anyone, even God, so utterly that she would relinquish all control of her life?

Gretta's words echoed in her mind, "Ye shall never be alone or unprotected again." How wonderful it would be to release her feelings of loneliness and the fears that had become second nature to her. She heaved a sigh, and without an audible word, a prayer emanated from deep within her soul. "Yes, please. I accept."

Nothing happened. Her breathing remained steady. Gretta slept. The noises around her did not change, and yet, slowly, Marta began to feel a little more rested, as if the barrel of fear confining her were breaking apart and she was finally breathing the fresh air of peace. Nothing had changed, and yet Marta felt a sense of belonging, as if she were a kitten releasing her first purr of contentment from deep inside. Her eyes began to water. Tears slid down her cheeks. She did not try to stop them.

Hans called, "Frau Ebel, I caught a fish!"

"And clean it I must, if it's to be eaten," said Frau Doenhof, lumbering up behind him.

"I shall help you," said Hans.

"I expect ye shall," said Frau Doenhof. "And be more the bother that ye did." She stared at Marta. "What ails ye?"

"Nothing," said Marta, and for the first time in a long time, she meant it.

—☙—

Carl was unable to count the number of days he remained in the darkness. He passed in and out of consciousness as he lay on the filthy hay, recovering from the injuries he had received at the hands of the soldiers. Except for the jailor who came once a day with bread and water, Carl saw and heard no one.

One morning, he awoke realizing that he was alive and would recover. He struggled to his feet and shuffled around the dank cell as far as the leg shackles that chained him to the wall would permit.

From that point forward, he tried to keep his muscles moving whenever he was awake, for he wanted to be tired enough to sleep instead of being kept awake by the scrambling rats and slithering reptiles. He also wanted to be prepared for any possible opportunity of escape. Keeping himself active was difficult, because without light, his rising and sleeping melted into one long, dark night.

During his exercises, Marta's smile would visit him, more often than he liked. Still, her memory calmed his heart and offered hope, even though nothing changed day after day, except the length of his beard and the gauntness of the flesh on his bones. When he was not thinking about Marta, his mind drifted almost involuntarily to thoughts about God and the stories about the people of Israel that his mother told him. Thoughts of his mother led to thoughts of Marta's Jesus, who had started all the trouble between Carl and his mother. Then anger would well up in him against his father. He would forcibly turn his mind back to Marta and something she had said or done, which would bring a smile to his face.

In the middle of at least his hundredth vision of her, the sound of soldiers' boots startled him. The door of his cell was unexpectedly unlocked, interrupting the silence, and though it should have been welcome, the sound irritated his ears.

"Step forward, you filthy cur," said a soldier.

Carl cleared his throat. "For what cause do you so honor me?"

"Goralski has ordered your presence." The man unlocked Carl's chains from the wall and yanked him forward through darkened corridors. Carl stumbled as the chains around his wrists and ankles clanked. His eyes did not have time to adjust before he was pushed into the brilliance of daylight. He squinted and then dropped his head.

He was in an enormous room where blindingly bright gold accents ornamented the walls and ceiling. He heard voices that slowly became two shadows and then men. Near a massive fireplace stood Goralski and Ivanov in a conspiratorially close conversation, as if neither heard the clanking chains that brought Carl to them.

Seeing his image in a mirror shocked him. He hardly recognized the gaunt, bearded man with ratted hair protruding in all directions. The tatters that had been his clothing did a poor job of hiding the filth of neglect on his skin. He turned from the image to count the number of soldiers behind him and survey the large windows that lined the walls. He might be able to work his hands free, but the leg irons posed more of a problem. He glanced at the three soldiers again. One of them had to have the key to his shackles.

"Always searching for a way of escape, eh?" said Ivanov. Both men were looking at him now.

"Without friends, one has only one's own resources," said Carl.

"Jew," said Goralski distastefully.

"A Jew you hired," said Carl.

Goralski stalked across the room and slapped Carl's face. He tasted the salty warmth of his own blood seeping from the cracked dryness of his lips.

"He should be put to death," said Ivanov.

"He deserves something worse than death," said Goralski, turning red in the face. "You shall pay for entering my country house."

Carl gave a slow smile that he knew would infuriate Goralski, a smile that said, "Despite my decrepit condition, I have the better end of the bargain."

Goralski hit him again. "Where have you hidden my money? You could not have already spent the full price of my candelabrum. You had too small an amount on your person." He shook as he tried unsuccessfully to control his anger. Carl was tempted to spit in his face, to emphasize his disdain.

"We dare not kill him here. Too many witnesses." Ivanov took a small pastry from a silver tray, sat down, and leaned back in a brocade chair. "Your country estate is close. Can we count on your people to be loyal?"

"We can," growled Goralski.

"I have the perfect vehicle. It's a closed wagon of sorts, a box, with no windows and only one door that can be barred from the outside."

"How soon can you deliver it?" asked Goralski.

"How soon do you require it?" replied Ivanov with a cruel smile.

Goralski strolled around Carl like a fat peacock that had just unfurled its feathers. Then Carl felt a heavy blow on his head and everything went black.

Chapter Fourteen

Carl could feel himself jouncing up and down, but try as he might, he could not determine where he was. He lifted an arm to rub his hand across his pounding forehead, but it would not move where he wanted. The sound of a chain rattled into his consciousness. Goralski had hit him. His hands were chained together. His feet were chained. Opening his eyes, he found himself sprawled on a rumbling, hard wooden floor surrounded by windowless walls. There were no seats or benches, only one door, and he guessed it was probably locked from the outside.

The faint light seeping between the boards was enough for him to surmise that his moving prison was a completely empty chamber except for something dark and lumpy in one of the corners. He scooted over to it. A cloth sack. Painstakingly, he untied the bundle. His stomach ached with hunger. Perhaps someone had done him a kindness by leaving a crust of bread.

He felt inside the sack and drew out the contents: knife, map, small bag of coins, bread, and—he could not believe his eyes—a key. He savagely bit into the loaf, relishing its scent and sweetness, and then took another bite before he had swallowed the first.

Although weak, Carl forced the heavy key into the keyhole that would release his chain's metal claws. The air that swept over his wrists and ankles let him know he was free. Placing the key in his waist, he stuffed another hunk of bread into his mouth. Half the loaf had already disappeared into his stomach.

He picked up the ivory-handled knife. It looked like the one he had admired at Ivanov's home, another assurance that Sascha was a true friend. The man had been playing a dangerous double game to try to save him. Carl almost wished he were a praying man so he could ask for blessings on this friend who had been so true to him.

Carl did not know how long he had been unconscious. He had to act quickly to protect himself and Sascha. If Ivanov had supplied the wagon and items in the sack, he would have made other provisions for Carl, as well. Carl began to test the walls and floorboards. He found one board on the floor, a large, square one, that was loose and could be pried up easily with the knife.

He raised it. A shaft of dim light filled the carriage. He easily removed the two boards on either side of the first, and looked down through the opening, holding on tightly so as not to be bounced out. The ground beneath rushed past as the horses pulled the closed wagon closer and closer to Goralski's estate and Carl's appointed death.

He stuck his head through the hole and watched the dizzying pace of hooves. A team of at least two horses pulled the carriage and two others kept pace on either side, one right beside the door. There was no one behind the carriage.

He knew he could not jump yet. He had to be patient and wait until the horses slowed. After attempting to read the map and being unable to see in the darkness, he wrapped it with the coins and knife in the sack and tied the fabric to his waist. He was ready. Through the hole, he dropped the chains that had held his hands. He waited. No one seemed to notice. Next he dropped the leg irons and waited. Again, no one noticed.

The thrill of the unknown, the excitement of life, coursed through Carl's veins as he felt the carriage slowing, apparently for a turn in the road. The moment before the turn was made and the horses resumed their steady pace, he dropped through the floorboards and landed hard on the cold ground, curling up in a tight ball and remaining still until the soldiers and closed wagon had completely rounded the bend and traveled out of sight.

As soon as the road was clear, Carl scrambled into the foliage on the side of the road. Untying his belongings from the pack, he studied the map. Sascha had made a mark on it to show

Goralski's estate. There was a line south and east from there that went through a number of small Russian towns until it finally ended at a town by the river Tversta. He would probably have to remain there for the winter before following Ivanov's drawing of a boat and its line that followed the Volga River. Near a curve in the river, the line broke off and headed west, overland toward the Don River, following it to the Black Sea. Apparently Sascha thought the safest way out of Russia was to the south. He noticed that his route would intersect with that taken by Marta's immigrant group. Carl felt his heart lighten. He would follow the line until he reached them. Then he would be hidden from all as an immigrant. Eventually, he would be able to head west beyond Goralski's reach.

Staying in the shelter of the woods, he made his way back to where he had dropped the chains. He collected them, brushed their impressions from the dirt, and hid them under a sprawling pine bush.

He considered what to do next. If he was near Goralski's estate, then it meant that he was near the place where he had buried his clothing. After determining his approximate location, he found the buried clothes and dug them up. The evening outfit was covered with insects and dried blood from where he had been shot. His peasant outfit was dirty, but wearable. He changed out of his tattered garments and buried them with the evening outfit.

Going to a nearby stream, he washed the dried blood from his face and hair and then proceeded to trim his hair and beard with the knife. Goralski's men would be searching for a scruffy Jew, not a Russian peasant. Carl knew he should fear for his life, but he could not suppress a grin. He loved the challenge, loved fighting the odds, enjoyed the thrill of living one more day.

When he had finished his grooming, he made his way to the estate where his horse was stabled. He hid behind a tree, watching. When he was convinced that no one was looking for him, he sauntered up to the estate manager.

"I trust you have cared well for my animal," he said.

"I treat all animals well," said the estate manager. "You have been long absent."

"Verily, I almost did not return for the animal." Carl looked around. "I will allow the beast one more trial. If he returns to you again, he shall be yours."

"I understand," said the man.

"I leave for a fortnight hunt. What provisions can you supply?" Carl held up a handful of coins.

By the time Carl left, he had only half the coins that Sascha had supplied him, but he was fully provisioned for his trip, from food and a gun to a winter coat that would also work as a bedroll.

He took out the map and examined it more closely. It would take him months to follow the immigrant trail by land. He hoped he would reach Herr Zweig's group before arriving at Torzhok, for he knew that by then winter would be heavy upon him. One man could make better time than a large group of immigrants. He smiled. A simple drawing of a woman beside Torzhok convinced him that Sascha's plan was indeed to lead him to rejoin Herr Zweig's immigrant group—and Marta. After he was out of sight of the estate, he turned his horse southward. Several big, wet snowflakes, probably the first of the season, drifted lazily down in front of him.

—☙—

On the boat deck, Marta fluffed the hay that Gretta would rest on. "I sometimes feel anger toward God because of Carl, though I know I should not. What of that?"

"You have only to speak your thoughts to God," said Gretta.

"'Twould not be respectful to say, 'God, my anger burns at Thee, because Carl left me,'" Marta said.

"Why would you not be honest with God? He is privy to your innermost thoughts."

"I shall try." Marta helped Gretta lie back down. The smell of fresh hay made the area feel cozy instead of tightly cramped.

"Talk to Him as you talk to me," said Gretta. Marta nodded, but she knew she would have to think further about what Gretta had just told her. Her world was changing, and not just on the outside, and Marta enjoyed every moment she spent with Gretta learning more about God.

In the evenings when Herr Zweig or Herr Jaeger read from the Bible, she was always at their feet, eager to catch every gem that fell from their lips. A new sense of joy seeped into her soul. Even the sight of Sergey watching her did not upset her as before. She memorized a line from Psalm 8 that said, "O LORD our Lord, how excellent is Thy name in all the earth!" Some days, she repeated it over and over. She felt like a meandering river, taking new and undiscovered turns each day and becoming closer and closer to God, just as their vessel took one curve after another, passing town after town, drawing them closer and closer to their new homes. At a city called Novgorod, the sailors forced those who were sick to disembark. They would have to stay in Novgorod for the winter. Marta was grateful that Gretta's health had improved enough for her to continue with them.

A day later, Hans began to shout, "We shall depart the boat! We shall walk on land! Hurrah!"

Marta and Gretta smiled. Hans was not more than a few steps from them. Marta thought he yelled the news more from wishful thinking than facts. Snowflakes began falling.

"The world is always brightest where ye abide not," said Frau Doenhof. "Before long ye shall wish ye were back on the ketch. Stop thy noise, Hans."

Hans gave her a winning smile and stopped talking, but he could not keep from bouncing between the women and gazing over the railing to see how close the boat was to its destination. Hans's announcement came true quicker than Marta expected.

Shortly after the midday meal, the boat docked near a small clump of wooden hovels, shacks that looked as if they provided the barest cover from the elements.

"Your mother shall need you to lend support," Marta told Hans. "Are you strong enough to help her?"

He nodded, and true to his word, Hans gently helped Gretta rise and walk alongside him. The four of them slowly left the ketch and stepped onto dry land together. Marta noticed that the carts waiting for them beyond the dock were better equipped to haul hay than people. Although riding in a cart was not something she would enjoy, Marta was thrilled to once again have her feet on solid ground, even if that ground would soon disappear beneath the snow.

"Women and children in the wagons," bellowed a voice. The men, apparently, had to walk.

The town, if Marta could call it that, consisted of poorly made shelters that looked more likely to fall down than to remain standing in a strong wind.

Frau Doenhof said under her breath, "Are these examples of a Russian house? I shall not abide in such a place."

"Shall the wagons carry us to our house?" asked Hans.

Herr Zweig answered from behind them. "No. No. It seems we need to travel overland for a while. Then we shall ride another ketch down the Volga."

"Why did this one not take us there?" asked Hans. Herr Zweig shrugged and wiped a snowflake from his arm.

Marta approached the last wagon, which was nothing more than a cart's heavy wooden bed with sides fashioned from twigs tied together with twine. At least it was supported on four thick, sturdy wheels. She stowed her belongings in it and then added Frau Doenhof's and Gretta's loads to hers. After pulling Hans up, Marta helped Gretta from above and Frau Doenhof helped her from below. Together, they were able to get her into the wagon and place her winter wear over her. The short walk from the boat had set Gretta to coughing, but her spirits, like her son's, were high.

"Imagine, Hans!" Gretta said. "One more leg of our journey is finished. Before long, we'll be in our new home."

Marta helped Frau Doenhof climb up, and they sat together on their belongings. The odors and closeness of those packed around her made Marta wish she could leave the wagon and move ahead at her own pace. Fortunately, the snow looked like it was lessening. A hand touched her elbow.

"Frau Ebel," said Herr Zweig, standing beside the wagon. "Would ye care to walk with me for a spell so that I may have a word with ye?"

She wanted to yell, "Yes!" in exuberance at this answer to an unspoken prayer, but only said, "With pleasure, Herr Zweig," in a voice that would not raise anyone's suspicion. She had been longing to walk, to stretch her legs. She turned to Frau Doenhof, who was sitting shoulder to shoulder with her. "I shall walk for a time."

"Ye shall lose thy place," said Frau Doenhof.

"I understand, but I must be free of this cart." Marta jumped down to the snowy ground.

Once she joined him, Herr Zweig said nothing, and Marta did not urge his confidences. The wagons rumbled around the edge of the town, just far enough away that Marta could not make a good study of the place or its inhabitants. However, as the snow's misty cover lifted, her overall impression of the town was one of disorganization and squalor.

She and Herr Zweig hung back to let the wagons roll farther ahead of them. Marta listened to a bird calling to its mate and noted the scents of unfamiliar plants and trees that suffused their fragrances over the landscape after the light snow. The forest was thicker here than near St. Petersburg, with more types of trees growing closer together. The dense forest around her felt both safe and confining as the carts traveled down the rustic path, each set of wheels rolling along a rut in the earth. With this first snow, the ground had not yet become soaked with the moisture that would eventually turn it to mud. Marta smiled. This road would lead her to her future. She was going home. She felt a stirring in her heart and could not help but thank God for bringing her to Russia.

In the midst of her wandering thoughts, Herr Zweig said, "I am a practical man."

"You speak truly," said Marta.

"There is no need for many words when few are enough." He

dropped his hands to his sides. "Many hardships befall us all, some of our doing and some not."

Marta thought of Frau Zweig and Herr Binz. "Verily."

"It is prudent to turn a bad situation to the good, whenever it is in our power." He did not seem to need her words as he sorted out his thoughts. Herr Zweig crossed his arms and then uncrossed them. "The families around us are the fortunate ones. They have one another for solace. I mean to say that we should take stock of our situations and make the best of them."

Marta nodded in agreement, and he looked at her hopefully. Herr Zweig seemed tense, expectant, almost uncertain of what he would say next. They continued walking for a few moments in silence.

Herr Zweig continued when he saw that she did not object. "I lack a wife. Ye lack a husband. We could marry tonight and continue together as a family in this new land."

Marta stopped. "Herr Zweig, my husband is not here, but he lives. I am yet a married woman."

He stumbled over his words. "There has been some gossip . . . I have heard that perhaps . . . without your knowledge of it . . . one of the soldiers suggested to me that perhaps your marriage was not . . . I know ye thought 'twas . . . but this happens to beautiful young women . . . a man shall say ye be wed, but the ceremony was not legitimate." He continued without taking a breath, "Ye have been good to me. I would return the favor and give ye my name."

Marta was horrified. "My husband abandoned me, but we were wed. I care not what others say. I pray you know that I must keep my vow, though my husband does not keep his."

"Of course. Of course," he said, trying to bluster his way out of the situation. "'Tis only that I thought to render ye a service . . . I am so greatly indebted to ye."

Marta extended her hand to him. "Your proposal honors me. I shall pray that you find another woman not tied to vows, one who may enjoy your kindness."

"Of course," he said with a fleeting touch to her hand. He crossed his arms and then dropped them to his sides, as if uncertain of their purpose. "I see that the other men need my aid. If ye would excuse me . . ." Marta nodded, and Herr Zweig rushed off. She did not hurry to catch up with the wagons. They were a ship's length from her, but close enough.

The day had already taken a troubling turn. Herr Zweig's proposal opened a fresh wound. She was embarrassed at what others were saying about her. How she wished she had family to defend her name. She grieved anew for her parents and siblings, and oh how she ached for Carl.

"Oh Lord, how shall I live with a broken heart? I have not the power to take even one more step forward." She stopped, squatted, and held her head in her hands.

As the woodland sounds and smells surrounded her, Marta felt God refreshing her spirit. She stood up, brushed leaves and twigs from her skirts, and resumed walking. God seemed to speak to her as she walked, pointing out the majesty and strength of the birch, pine, spruce, and fir trees and the sureness of the dirt path beneath her feet. He assured her that her life would progress in that way from then on, with God as her foundation amid the dangers and hurts surrounding her.

Although the carts slowly pulled ahead of her, a little farther each step, Marta was not concerned. She silently poured out the secrets of her heart, voicing all her confusion and complaints. She let the sounds of rustling leaves, occasional birdcalls, and the cool scents of spicy spruce and damp soil envelop her and give her new strength.

After her time of contemplation and prayer, Marta realized that the carts must have turned around a bend because they were no longer in sight, and she could not hear their creaking sounds. The sky was darkening, and in the distance, she heard the howl of a wolf. She hurried forward until she heard Hans calling to her, "Frau Ebel! Make haste!" In her hurry, she turned a corner at the edge of a forest and almost bumped into Sergey.

"Are you lost, Frau?" The coldness in his eyes made her shiver. "Like thine husband is lost." He said *husband* with so much disdain that Marta no longer wondered who had started the gossip about her marriage.

"I am not lost. I but tarry to enjoy the beauty of the Russian forest." She hastened ahead of him, running to catch up to the others.

Hans helped her to climb over the side of the wagon.

"None took thy place," said Frau Doenhof in her gruffest voice.

Marta gave her a warm hug. Although Frau Doenhof did not return the gesture, Marta knew that the woman must have fought off others to hold her space.

"For what reason have the wagons stopped?" asked Marta. "Is something amiss?" She peered ahead.

"A cart in the lead lost a wheel and overturned," said Frau Doenhof in a low voice.

Gretta continued, "We hear ill tidings that Herr Pfeiffer is caught beneath it."

Subdued by the tragedy, the travelers made their first campsite there, constantly sending up prayers for the man until at last they heard that he had died. They left late the next morning after a small funeral service for Herr Pfeiffer, the first of their group to die on this leg of the journey.

Days stretched into a fortnight, and Marta often donned the warm Russian cloak that she had been issued, especially as the leaves turned and tumbled in avalanches of color to the ground. Each day, she watched the others in her cart, yet came to know them but little. As the days grew shorter, the men began to squeeze into the wagons with the women, and slowly they became acquainted out of necessity.

Besides Marta, Gretta, and Frau Doenhof, there were nine others now in the cart. Herr and Frau Kessler were the oldest of the group. They had lost all seven of their sons to their German prince's wars. Herr Neussle was the quietest. A lanky man, he stared at the terrain or down at his hands most of the time. Marta wondered if he was afraid of what the future held or just trying to avoid talking to his wife. His wife's words were also few, usually berating or sharp. She was of small stature, and her furlike red hair gave her fits as she continually tried to keep it within the confines of her bonnet. Herr and Frau Schluter and their young son, Fritz, and their older daughters, Helga and Ute, kept to themselves near the front of the wagon. Herr Schluter appeared to be a strict man. One of the daughters, Ute, smiled shyly at Marta whenever she looked their way, but Helga's face remained stern. Their mother busied herself at all times, preparing for meals, sewing, or rearranging their bundles.

First snow, then rain, and then more snow made the travelers wet and cold most of the time. They moved forward a little less each day. To Marta's surprise, Gretta was rejuvenated by the cold. She no longer coughed, not even in the middle of snowstorms. Only her weakness remained.

"I have invited Herr Pfeiffer's widow, Nina, and her young daughter to join our cart. She is with child," said Gretta one morning.

As they readjusted their positions in the wagon, Frau Neussle said, "There is no room. Suffer not the woman to bear her bad luck to us."

"Trust ye not the Lord? The woman needs kindness," said Gretta. Marta was growing tired of Frau Neussle's constant complaints about their discomfort and would have taken pleasure in putting the woman in her place.

"She'll bring evil to us," said Frau Neussle with a shake of her gray hair. "Ye shall see that I speak the truth."

"She has survived, has she not? The Lord has a purpose for her yet," said Gretta evenly. Marta's anger softened with Gretta's insight.

"I pray you to remember," said Marta, "that the added warmth of extra bodies is ever welcome."

"That would be the only good she bears," muttered Frau Neussle as she moved to make room for the newcomers. From then on, Gretta and Nina spoke in low voices, a drone that was interrupted only by an occasional snore from Herr Kessler or a moan from his wife, who acted as if the weight of the world and all that was evil rested on her thin, bony shoulders.

When the sun broke through the clouds after several days of snow, Hans asked Frau Doenhof, "May we walk today?"

Frau Doenhof nodded as Fritz chimed in, "Me too. Me too."

"No," said his father sternly. Frau Doenhof and Hans jumped down from the slow moving wagon.

"Why may I not play with Hans?" Fritz whined, but he was quickly silenced. Marta watched Frau Doenhof and Hans moving in and out of the snow trying to catch animals and birds. She liked it when he was able to act like the child he was. He'd had such a difficult young life. Anna, Nina Pfeiffer's golden-haired little girl, sat quietly in the corner of the cart and gazed longingly at the passing landscape. Marta's heart ached for both children. How well she knew the pain of losing a parent.

"Frau Ebel," Anna said in a shy voice, "would you like to hear a story?"

"I would very much like to hear a story," Marta answered the four-year-old.

"This is one that my father used to tell me." Anna painted a story that not only whiled away the time, but also kept Fritz's attention and eventually drew Hans back into the wagon. Marta laughed and cried, but mostly she marveled that God had given so small a child an imagination that could keep Frau Neussle from complaining and Frau Kessler from groaning, even when their wagons were forced to stop over and over again.

When the story had come to an end, Herr Zweig approached them.

"What tidings bring ye?" asked Frau Doenhof.

Herr Zweig shook his head. "Another cart is stuck in a drift. No one is hurt, but it shall be hours before we can set it to course again."

"What next shall befall us?" Frau Doenhof asked.

Herr Zweig patted her hand awkwardly. "There is a town, called Torzhok, not many versts ahead, where we shall abide for the winter."

"And what of food?" Frau Doenhof asked in a lower voice. "Only two cabbages and a few crusts of bread remain."

"More supplies await us there," Herr Zweig replied.

By the next evening, two fortnights after they had left the ketch, they entered the outskirts of Torzhok, a small, ancient town on the river Tversta. When the immigrants arrived, they were taken to a small village on the outskirts of the town, a collection of wooden houses and huts that did not look much better than those in the first dilapidated town they had seen. Soldiers took small groups of people from the carts and prodded them toward the crude peasant dwellings.

"With me you come now," said Sergey to Marta. Frau Doenhof, Gretta, Marta, and Hans climbed down as quickly as they could in their wet clothing and lifted out their belongings, heavier because of their soaked condition. Sergey pushed them toward a crudely made shelter that looked as if it could not have more than one room. Marta wondered if he had chosen one of the worst shelters for them because she would not succumb to his advances. In response to Sergey's loud pounding, a Russian man opened the door.

Sergey said something in Russian and then repeated it in German. "Tsarina Catherine command you give food and share house with these people through winter."

The man stepped back, the small band of newcomers entered, and the door shut behind them. The one-room house was large, but not spacious enough for so many people, not to mention a horse and goat that were stabled off to one side. The smell of urine and ammonia inside the hut made Marta's stomach turn. She helped Hans and his mother remove their soaked coats, while the large Russian man and a young lad stared at them with angry eyes.

Chapter Fifteen

Leaves fluttered around Carl, but he did not hear their rustling as he galloped toward a nearby stream. Until now, he had survived even the direst of situations with ease through his own wit and cunning. Goralski's prison had been the closest he had ever come to death, and though he hated to admit it even to himself, the experience had unnerved him. He had not lived a good life—excitement and the promise of wealth always winning out over his better judgment. What if he had died? What would have followed? Oblivion? Or, as his mother promised, God's judgment? Instead of getting easier, the battle for his soul seemed to weigh more heavily on his mind. Perhaps the shock of discovering that he was not invincible had become the fissure through which so many thoughts that he had fought against now entered his mind. His thoughts seemed to gallop in pace with his steed. "I am the Lord thy God. No other gods. No other gods. No other gods."

His mother's last words from the day he left haunted him. "You may hasten to leave me, but you cannot flee God. No matter where you dwell or how great the distance between us, my prayers shall follow on your heels, and someday you shall be required to face the consequences of your choices. My hope is for you to turn to the Messiah before the days of your life have run their course."

A small branch hit Carl in the face. Enough thought. He had to concentrate now on following the path that Ivanov had set for him. He turned his horse into the stream, and they waded gingerly down its center until long past the hour of the midday meal. That would wash away their scent if Goralski chose to send the dogs after them. They left the stream where a large open meadow offered access to a rutted road leading south, and by the time the sun set that night, Carl had found an out-of-the way hunting lodge not far from St. Petersburg and begged for a space on the floor. His horse was lathered, and he was tired, but thanks to the estate manager's generosity, they both had a warm bed of hay and were even given a hearty meal the following morning.

"Wherefore do you make such haste, my friend?" asked the curious manager, studying the bruises on Carl's right wrist.

"It is the haste of anticipation," said Carl. He pulled down his sleeve and unfolded his map. "I carry news to my master's friends about a hunt."

He felt a twinge of regret. Why was it that every time he lied now, he knew he was lying? What had happened to the days of old when he had mixed lies and truth so easily that even he had difficulty telling which was which? Carl felt rested and took his time studying the map as he ate the warm bread that the manager supplied for him. He broke down the miles in his mind's eye. As the winter progressed, deepening snow would make the end of the journey difficult but not impossible.

He stood and gathered his things together. "I thank you for your hospitality. I shall remember to report your kindness to my master."

Carl rode west, looped around the hunting lodge in a large circle, and headed south.

"No one shall be able to follow us this day, shall they?" Carl asked his horse. "I shall have to find a name for you, seeing as how we'll be spending all of our time together. How do you favor Hansel?" The horse ignored him. "No? I believe that it suits you not. What of Petre?" They moved directly toward the first town on his map. Even if Goralski tracked him this far, he would not be able to catch him on the open roads.

By the time Carl had left the first two towns on the map behind him, snow was falling in large flakes. "If we manage to travel that far, I fear that we shall be forced to remain in Torzhok until spring. You shan't mind delaying our escape to civilization until the spring, shall you, Ivan?" The horse snorted. "You don't like that name, either. Would you consider a name like Strand?"

Carl longed to repay Quentin and Goralski for the bruises around his ankles and wrists, among other things. His fists tightened on the reigns. He would plot his revenge once he reached Torzhok.

⌐

Marta did not know what to do. She spoke only German. The peasant and his child spoke only Russian. Although the door was shut behind her, she could still feel the icy drafts from outside through cracks in the door. She longed for the warmth of the enormous, kilnlike stove built of square bricks that dominated the small room.

"It stinks," Hans whispered. Gretta shushed him.

Marta looked around her. The house was filthy, the wood floor was splintered, and yet, perhaps God had guided them to this particular home. She looked in the corner by the door. A small statue of a person in robes with a halo looked down on them. It reminded her of the icons in the Papist church in Lübeck, but they were of a different style.

Seeing where she was looking, the burly man raised his hand and touched his forehead, then his chest, and his shoulders. He had made the sign of a cross, but it was reversed.

"He is Russian Orthodox." Gretta made the sign of the cross the opposite way. The man spoke a word that Marta could not understand, and Gretta responded, "Jesus Christ." The man seemed to understand. Gretta leaned against the wall as if the conversation had been too much for her, as if her body was too weak to continue.

Frau Doenhof harrumphed. "Enough of this." She took a pot out of their belongings and handed it to Hans. "Go with that youngster there and fetch clean snow to melt." Hans took the pot and then, timidly, grasped the taller boy's hand. They left the cabin together.

Frau Doenhof turned to Marta. "Get ye away from the wall. Wipe up this wetness and prepare a place for us to sleep. I shall cook supper." Frau Doenhof grabbed a large cabbage out of her sack and showed it to the owner of the hut. "Da?" She walked past him to the fire.

The man gave a thin smile. "Da."

Marta took off her cloak and hung it on a peg by the door. She took a hard bristle brush that sat on a tablelike structure by the enormous kiln and began pushing the melted snow toward the door. Gretta remained against the wall, her eyes closed. When Marta had finished and placed the brush on the floor under her hanging cloak, she untied the blankets around their things and perused the room for a resting place for Gretta.

Near the open end of the oven sat a large wooden table and benches. The horse and a goat were stabled on the other side of the room, but there were no beds anywhere. Did the Russians sleep on the floor? The idea horrified Marta. With so many animals around, they could be trampled or pecked to death during the night. As if to prove her point, a chicken flew from the table, right into Frau Doenhof's hip.

"Ye shall be in my pot before long if ye carry on so," muttered Frau Doenhof.

Marta set the patchwork on the tablelike structure that rested against the side of the oven. The owner of the hut must have been watching her. He said something she could not understand and pointed to an area on top of the brick oven.

He climbed three steps on the back side and then pulled himself up. Marta handed him the patchwork. After spreading it out flat, he reached for the other blankets, and Marta handed them to him. With more unintelligible words, he climbed down and gestured for Marta to look at the sleeping area. She took a deep breath and climbed up.

"It's warm up here," said Marta. "Gretta, can you make it up?"

"I don't think so." Gretta had not moved.

A platform built into the rafters beside the stove adjoined the area where Marta knelt. She assumed that it supplied more sleeping and storage room, safe from the animals except for the chickens roosting on one side of it.

"What a clever design." Her patchwork and the blankets were still damp from the snow, so she spread the rest of them out to dry before returning to the others below. The bricks would hold the heat and keep the area above the stove and the platform next to it warm all night.

The owner had prepared a cover on the tablelike structure against the oven. He motioned for Gretta, who still leaned against the wall, to come. Then without another word, he left the house.

"He has made a place for you to rest," said Marta.

"My bones feel cold," said Gretta. "I doubt I can move."

"Here, I shall lend you aid." Marta reached for Gretta's arm and helped her to the table.

"You must remove your wet raiment." Marta helped her undress quickly and arrange herself beneath the covers before the boys or the man returned. Marta tied the wet clothing between studs near the bed to help them dry. Once hung, the clothing almost made a private room for Gretta, where she could rest next to the warm oven. Before long, the owner of the house returned.

"Thank you," said Marta.

"Da. Da." He pointed to himself. "Yuriy Vasilevich Potokov."

Marta nodded and tried to repeat his name. He laughed and said, "Yuriy."

"Marta Ebel." She pointed to Gretta. "Gretta Binz." The boys came in the door with smiles and rosy cheeks. She pointed. "Hans."

Yuriy nodded and directed their attention to his son. "Raczko." He looked over at Frau Doenhof, who was trying to manage the fire and make cabbage soup.

"Frau Doenhof." Marta was embarrassed that she could not introduce the woman by her full name. She did not know what it was.

When Frau Doenhof served the meal, Yuriy took out a bottle, poured a portion for each person, and then thinned the drink with water. "*Kwass*," he said, as he set a cup before Marta. From the odor, she could tell that the beverage was fermented. She drank it, but did not enjoy it.

After their meal and several awkward periods of silence, Yuriy gave Frau Doenhof and Marta the place above the oven to sleep while Hans, Yuriy, and Raczko took the platform in the rafters. Before they climbed to the rafters, though, Yuriy and Raczko knelt with their heads bowed and spoke softly together.

"He has lent us the best bed in his house," whispered Marta to Frau Doenhof. "We have been very fortunate in our placement. Yuriy is a very rich man." Marta turned onto her stomach, feeling the warmth of the oven beneath her.

Frau Doenhof looked around the one-room hut. "I call him not rich."

"He owns more animals than other peasants I've seen," whispered Marta. "We shall have goat's milk and eggs for the winter."

"The animals abide in his house," said Frau Doenhof. "He is but a coarse peasant."

Marta turned over and the odor of fresh horse droppings reached her nostrils. "If left outside away from the warmth of this oven, the animals would freeze to death. We are very fortunate."

When Frau Doenhof said no more, Marta pulled the patchwork up over her nose and soon fell asleep.

Yuriy left the next day to go hunting. Later, Hans and Raczko came in with beaming faces and a sack of turnips.

"Whence came these?" Marta asked.

Hans said, "A soldier was kind to Raczko and gave us food to give you. You know him, the one always watching you."

Marta didn't know whether to blush or get upset. "What nonsense. He gives food to all the immigrants."

Hans shrugged his shoulders. Frau Doenhof grabbed the sack, and the boys ran off to play. Marta was left alone to wonder what Sergey's gift meant.

By the time Yuriy returned with fresh meat three days later, Marta and the others had settled into a routine and had plenty of turnips, beets, cabbages, and potatoes. Hans and Raczko cleaned the animal droppings each morning and brought fresh snow into the house to be melted. They kept the fire stoked, tended the animals, and brought in food from outside. A couple of times, Marta asked Hans where he had gotten the money to buy provisions, but all he would tell her is, "I am the man of the family now. I shall provide." For a while, she thought he must be stealing, until one day she noticed him with the other small leather pouch that she had seen Carl carrying.

Every few days, Yuriy took the boys hunting in the forest or ice fishing on the river. Mostly they caught fish or downed hares and squirrels, but once they came home with a deer, and another time a wild boar. Together with the boys, Yuriy butchered the animals and stored the portions of extra meat in a lean-to shed on the side of the hut.

Frau Doenhof was constantly working at the oven, her face reddened from the heat as she made meals that everyone appreciated. She had even learned to brew *sbiten*, a beverage Yuriy made from honey and herbs to drink after his evening meals. His German guests drank it with their meals instead of the kwass. Marta was grateful not to have to cook. She preferred taking care of the house, or *izba*, as she discovered it was called. Keeping the floor clean was a challenge, but they had a good living situation. Still, Marta could not shake off a sense of restlessness and impending danger.

Gretta touched Marta's arm, causing her to startle.

"What ails ye so this morning?" Gretta asked.

Marta realized that she had been leaning on her handmade broom, daydreaming instead of sweeping.

"I ponder our situation. Each day we become more and more a true family."

"It is a good thing," said Gretta.

Frau Doenhof piped in, "Shall I have to scold ye like a mother in order to get ye to finish the floor?"

Marta continued sweeping and then led the horse outside, away from Frau Doenhof's terseness and the izba's acrid odors. She breathed the crisp, fresh air that carried the sound of Hans's and Raczko's laughter as they played in a snowbank.

Suddenly, Hans stamped his foot. "Da!"

"Nein," shouted Raczko, stamping his foot in turn. Marta laughed. Their Russian and German phrases were confused, but at least they had learned enough from each other to communicate.

That evening, after a hearty meal of stew, Gretta said, "Hans has learned from Raczko that he and Yuriy are believers in Jesus Christ, as we suspected. Raczko's mother died less than a full moon ago. He and his father prayed that God would send someone to help them. Yuriy knew not how to survive the winter raising a child, caring for animals, and dealing with his grief."

"But he is Russian Orthodox," said Marta.

"He worships the Father, Son, and Holy Spirit, just as we do. God used his religion to draw him into a personal relationship with Himself, just as He used Martin Luther's teachings to draw us," said Gretta. She cleared her throat. "I am well enough to sleep on top of the stove tonight."

Even Frau Doenhof seemed pleased. As Gretta started to mount the stairs, Frau Doenhof said, "I shall remain behind to see that ye fall not. Marta, ye help from above."

Gretta stepped down to let Marta go first. "I thank ye both for thy kindness."

⸎

The cheerful days faded into cold darkness as the winter grew fiercer.

"There is naught to do in here," complained Hans during an especially long snowstorm. "Why can we not leave the house?" Gretta looked at him sternly, and Hans apologized. "I am sorry for my complaint, Mother. I am grateful to God for our warm izba."

"Snow deep," said Raczko. "Danger." He translated what he said for his father.

"Da, da!" Yuriy used sign language to indicate that they could get lost in a blizzard like the one raging outside.

"I wish for wool," complained Frau Doenhof. "Then I should make blankets and warm garments for these boys who grow like saplings—and for us." With the meal already cooked, and nothing else to occupy her, she paced.

Marta watched Gretta and Yuriy attempt to use signs and exchange simple words. Yuriy put his arm around Hans's shoulders in an almost fatherly manner, and Marta caught herself staring before glancing away. They looked like one happy family, but that was not how it was supposed to be. Gretta and Hans would travel with her. She shivered, suddenly feeling that something was amiss. When Frau Doenhof climbed onto the platform above the stove to rest and the boys decided to braid the horse's tail, Marta took the opportunity to go off into a corner to pray for herself, for Carl, and for Yuriy's continued kindness—but not attachment—to them.

"Dearest Lord, why can I not purge this feeling of urgency from my mind? We all fare well. Is it Carl who courts danger? Please protect him, wherever he abides."

—◌⟩—

Carl rode on through the snow that encrusted his beard and clothing. He had given up trying to keep his face covered. The wind cut through his garments with impunity. The horse snorted, clomping wearily through the drifts. The poor beast was wearing down. Carl kept his eyes open for areas where he might find enough wild grass beneath the snow for his animal. As the storms and the days progressed, there was less and less feed to be found. At least they both had enough water. Carl grabbed a handful of snow from a low-hanging tree branch and stuck it in his mouth. Its icy coldness stung his lips and froze the inside of his body on its way down. He couldn't take time now to stop and melt enough for them to drink. After about an hour, he reined the horse to a halt. In the swooshing stillness, he heard the gurgling of a stream.

"This way, Midnight," he said. The horse nearly pulled the reins out of his hands. "Hold steady. That is not your name either." Carl dismounted near a stream that had a trickle of water still flowing. He picked up a boulder and dropped it, breaking the ice and forming a pool where the water could gather. "Drink." Obediently, the horse reached down to drink. Suddenly, the animal jerked its head up, its eyes growing large, and whinnied.

"What ails you, boy?" Carl asked. The horse backed away from the stream. At the edge of the woods, a lynx peered at them. Slowly, it crept forward on heavily padded feet. In one smooth movement, Carl slid his gun from his saddlebags and shot into the air. The cat bounded away, disappearing into the whiteness.

"I grieve to see you suffer, old boy." Carl patted the side of the horse's neck and led it back to the water. "We shall soon have to find a name you like. Would you consider Edward? That is a royal name from the islands." The horse snorted and shook its head.

—◌

As the snow deepened and the short days waned, Carl's horse tired more easily. Near the edge of a meadow, Carl had dismounted to give the beast a rest when he heard howling not far in the distance. Wolves! From the urgent, overlapping sounds, he could tell it was a large pack. He searched for a place to hide his horse and himself. If only he could light a fire, but everything was too wet. He tugged at the reins, guiding the animal toward a large thicket of bushes and trees. The howling grew eerily closer. The horse started to panic and lurched forward. Carl tore his gear from the horse's back, unfastened the halter, and slapped the animal hard on the backside.

"Begone, Snyek." The horse immediately took off running. Carl lost his balance and slid into a small gully, dropping his gun into a drift. A low growl sounded behind him. He lunged at the nearest tree and then scrambled up it, his feet sliding on the trunk. Once at the top, he looked in all directions, but he could not see where his horse had run. He hoped the animal had escaped. It deserved more for its faithfulness than death at the jaws of a pack of wolves.

All evening and through the night, Carl clung to the tree, snow covering him, his hands and feet nearly frozen. He had only his thoughts and memories to keep him company as the wolves leaped up at him, growled, and paced around the tree as if they were sentries. His numbed mind began to play tricks on him. First he was back in a French forest, collecting wild berries and nuts. Then he was peacefully in his mother's house, memorizing the words of God. "Honour thy father and thy mother." "Thou shall not steal . . . bear false witness . . . covet . . ." Carl felt himself slipping under the heavy weight of condemnation. He jerked himself awake. He must stay alert. Once again, he was alone, staring death in the face. Perhaps he was growing old, but the challenges of life were no longer as exciting as they used to be. He still expected to win, to beat the odds, but the edge had been taken off. It was Marta. She had ruined him. She had accepted what she knew of him and had included him in her life. And having belonged, it was hard for him to return to the man he had been.

On the second day, when he felt as if he were attached to the branches, almost unable to let go, the wolves disappeared as quickly as they had come. He waited until he was certain they were gone and then lowered himself to the ground, his mind as numb as his body. The storm had ended. Not much was left of his belongings, but he salvaged the little that he could and was glad that a small strip of hardtack had been hidden from the animals' voracious jaws.

He calculated that he must be getting close to Torzhok. He could see the signs of a snow-covered river ahead. As he trudged through snowdrifts, his mind wandered. Why had he come back to Russia? He might have fared well in Lübeck. What would he do once he reached civilization again? Of course, even a Russian winter was better than the torturous death Goralski had planned for him, but what an extensive journey Sascha had mapped out! He wondered if such a drastic change of plans had been necessary. Goralski certainly would not send his men this far to find Carl.

The cushioned silence of the white terrain slipped away as the muffled sound of a horse's whinny reached his ears. Snyek? Carl started toward the sound. His horse had found its way back to him.

He felt a smile form on his lips, and his heart lightened. He had let his mind sink into the desperation of loss. He moved forward. Things would turn out well as they always did.

He headed toward the sound of the whinny. Within moments, two horses, both with riders, appeared in the distance. Carl crouched down where he was in the snow, but it was too late. The men had seen him. Neither waved an arm in a friendly salute.

⸻

Marta woke to silence. It troubled her until she realized that the storm was over. As she went about her chores, she caught Gretta watching her intently.

"Do not fret," she said. "Take a walk and talk to the Lord about your troubles."

Marta folded her apron. "Gretta, what do you see as your future?"

"I know not," she said. "The future is not ours to know. The apostle Paul found a way to be content wherever he was."

"But you would not be content to remain here in Torzhok, would you?" asked Marta.

Gretta gave Marta a sad smile. "I shall try to be content wherever God leads."

"I realize that you shall likely wed again in order to survive on this wild frontier, but you shall marry a good German man, shall you not?"

"I know not what God shall require of me," Gretta said. "Now go, and take your walk, and try not to foretell the future. Leave it in God's hands."

Marta put on her cloak and tied a wool cloth around her neck before slipping outside. "I would like my friend to abide with me," she told God the moment she was out. She breathed carefully through her scarf to allow the air to warm up so it would not turn to ice in her lungs. The clouds above and the wind catching her clothes foretold another storm.

Pacing around the perimeter of the hut, Marta prayed, "I have need of peace, Lord. Why is it so hard a thing for me to trust You? I have not the power to purge Carl from my heart. Now it appears that Gretta and Hans may stay with Yuriy. Everyone I love is taken from me. I do not understand it. I tire of the struggle. Please, Lord, take over my life again, even if You take Gretta and Hans from me, even if I must go on alone. Help me, Lord. Abide with me, please. Let me not go from Your path." Only when the cold had seeped beneath her wraps and threatened to numb her, did she return to the izba.

Marta hung her cloak and joined Frau Doenhof by the oven. "Do you need help with the meal?"

They heard a pounding on the door. Yuriy rose to answer it, but those outside flung it open, allowing the frigid air to enter with them. Sergey came in first. Two other Russian soldiers followed, dragging the body of another man. The figure was coated with snow and blood.

Sergey directed his eyes at Marta. "Your husband." The strangers dropped the figure to the floor. "He found by the patrol."

"Carl?" It was a whisper and yet a scream. Marta's heart leaped and then sank in the same moment. Immediately, she was at his side, prying off his coat and hat to warm his freezing body. She did not know when Sergey and his henchmen left. She saw no one but Carl.

"You shall be well," she said to him over and over. "You abide among friends." Frau Doenhof started some water to boil. Gretta and Yuriy removed Carl's boots and rubbed his feet, while the boys worked on his hands.

Carl had a glazed look on his face. "Is that you?" he whispered to Marta. *"Ou mon ange guardien?"* His eyes closed.

Marta leaned forward. "Look at me, Carl. It is Marta. You have come home."

Yuriy and Raczko helped Marta carry Carl to the tablelike structure where Gretta had spent her first nights. They removed his soaked clothing, and Yuriy dressed him in his own extra set of clothes. At first, Marta refused to leave his side, but then they took turns tending him, keeping him warm, and giving him liquids.

Carl woke to the smell of cabbage soup. He felt warm, but he could not discern where he was.

"He has awakened!"

"Hans?" asked Carl.

Hans leaned over him. "You rested for four days! So weary you must have been!"

"I was," said Carl. "How did I come here?"

Marta, Frau Doenhof, and Gretta crowded around him. The last he remembered, soldiers were beating him. He tried to move, but his muscles ached and his fingers and toes tingled with what he knew was probably frostbite.

Marta put a hand on his chest. "Stay still."

"We are a family again," he said.

Her face grew into its prettiest smile. "Are we a family?"

Frau Doenhof scowled. "We shall see if having ye back be a good or bad turn of events, Herr Mueller."

"Herr Ebel," Carl reminded her.

Frau Doenhof harrumphed. "I have to start supper." She turned and left.

Gretta motioned to a man and a young boy, who came over to Carl. "These are our hosts, Herr Yuriy and Raczko. We cannot pronounce their surname." Carl greeted them in Russian, and their eyes lit up. As they conversed, Carl watched Marta. Physically, she looked the same, perhaps a bit thinner, but something was different about her.

Marta caught Carl watching her, and her heart soared. He could not stay away. He had said they were a family again.

I thank You, God! Thank You! Thank You! her heart sang while she took care of the animals, helped Frau Doenhof, and most importantly sat by Carl's side as he drifted in and out of sleep.

When he fell into another sound sleep, she could no longer control her nervous energy. She had to walk, to get out of the house, before she exploded with happiness. She was in love, and her husband apparently returned her feelings. He had given up his plans of revenge to follow her, to find her, to make his life with her. Of course, he had not said so much in words, but why else would he have traveled all this distance?

"I shall visit the Pfeiffers," Marta called to the others.

"Take ye this to them," said Frau Doenhof, wrapping bread in a cloth. Marta donned her coat, took the bread, and left for Nina and Anna's hut. She felt as if she were truly the most blessed of all women. A man loved her so much that he had braved the cold Russian winter to find her. She was angered at his wounds and the way that he had been dragged to her door, but it was probably Sergey's punishment to Carl for escaping. Marta knocked on the door.

Nina opened it. "Welcome!"

"Thank you," said Marta as she handed her the bread. "How fare you this day?"

"The baby shall come soon," said Nina.

Anna jumped into Marta's arms. "Frau Ebel! I thought of two new stories to tell thee."

"Then I must hear them." Marta nodded to the elderly Russian couple, but they only scowled at her.

"Your situation has not improved, I see," said Marta.

Nina shook her head no. "The good is that I do not understand what the woman yells at me. Her screaming is high and loud, though, and assaults my ears."

"She has not hit you?" asked Marta.

"No," said Nina. "She fears the soldiers too much for that." Nina looked tired. "I wish the baby would come." She patted her belly. "My Ludwig's last gift to me."

"How may I assist you?" asked Marta. At Nina's direction, Marta cut cabbage while Anna told her new stories, jumping around and knocking their fresh loaf of black bread to the ground.

"Anna, what have you done?" her mother scolded. "Pick that up for Frau Ebel."

"'Twas an accident," said Marta. Anna handed the loaf to her with an apology and climbed to her bed over the oven, trying to hold back the tears.

"I know not what to do with her," Nina admitted. "What has changed my sweet little girl?"

"These conditions. And without her father. The difficulties are great for you both," Marta said. "Perhaps she should come visit us and play with Hans during the day so she would have something to look forward to, and you could rest."

A look of relief passed over Nina's face. "'Twould be wonderful." In a voice that sounded more cautious, Nina asked, "'Tis true that Herr Ebel has returned?"

"Yes." Marta bundled up to go home. "He has long tried to reach us." She waved to Anna. "I shall call for you tomorrow."

The child's face broke into a smile. "I shall be ready as soon as I wake."

Marta laughed. "I shall not come so early. I shall see you after the midday meal."

On her walk home, she could not keep the skip out of her step. How did women hold in the joy that filled them at the sight of their husbands? Carl was home. He was really home. He had followed her because his love for her was greater than his desire for money. Marta laughed out loud.

Chapter Sixteen

Marta slid through the open door as quickly as possible to keep the cold from invading the izba. "Anna sends her love." She stopped.

In the middle of the room stood Sergey and two strangers. Yuriy and Carl stood before the men with Hans and Raczko on either side. All the men were speaking in Russian at once. Frau Doenhof and Gretta looked small, pressed against the wall by the oven.

Marta hurried to Carl and put her arm around his waist. "You must not stand. You're too ill." He looked pale, as if he might fall over at any moment, and yet he did not let her nudge him toward his bed. He casually draped an arm around her shoulders, but she could feel the heaviness with which he leaned on her.

Suddenly, Hans spoke, using the Russian he had learned. The only word Marta recognized was Ebel. Sergey shot a glance at her. The men said something and then moved toward the door. Sergey followed, slamming it behind him.

Carl squeezed her shoulders and then removed his arm. "Good man, Hans! You saved my life!" He took a step toward the platform where he had slept for days.

Marta helped him toward it. "What business did they have with you?" He looked as if he was concentrating on reaching the platform, so she waited to pursue the question.

Gretta hurried to her son. "Hans, what said you?" She spoke in a low voice. "Did you speak the truth?"

"Sometimes one must tell an untruth to save a friend." Hans avoided Marta's eyes.

"Though we may want to help those we love, an untruth is never acceptable," said Gretta slowly.

Hans averted his eyes. "Did I tell you that Raczko's going to teach me how to make a bear out of snow today?"

Gretta sighed audibly. "You shall go nowhere presently. You shall tarry to think about the wrong you have done. Would it please God? Would it have pleased your father?"

"My father helped people. He would have helped Herr Ebel."

"Yes, he would have tried to help, but your father would not have done it with an untruth. You are to sit and think about what you have done."

Hans stomped to a bench and sat down heavily. Gretta joined him and the two spoke in low voices.

Once Carl was able to lean against his table-bed, Marta continued, "Who were the men with Sergey?"

Carl sighed. "Those strangers were soldiers from Oranienbaum. They followed me. They intended to take me back as prisoner."

"Why would they do such a thing?" Marta pulled back the covers for Carl to lie down. "What did Hans say to make them leave?"

A slow smile formed on Carl's lips. "He said that I was his father and that I wed you on the ship after his mother died. When we quarrel, I leave the family, but I always return. The boy is a genius. He told the same tale we used when I came back to the camp in Oranienbaum. It caused Sergey to doubt. He believes I have followed you all the while."

She wanted to ask, "And did you not?" but instead, she asked, "Why would these soldiers desire to return you to Oranienbaum?" She almost did not want to know, did not want the truth to infect and eat away at her happiness.

Carl leaned against the table-bed. "I suppose I owe you that much." He lowered his voice. "A man named Goralski hired me to bring immigrants to Russia. He knew that I was a Jew and chose to hire me anyway, because I was a good recruiter. We both earned money for each immigrant I delivered safely."

"I do not like it when you speak of people as cargo," said Marta, but she did not shy away from hearing the remainder of his story.

Carl lay down, and focused his thoughts on his immediate

surroundings to keep from becoming distracted by Marta's beautiful, changing face. It always amazed him that Russian peasants still lived in conditions like those in the sixteenth century. Marta waited for him to continue.

"As I said, I was good at what I did," he said, "but Goralski became greedy. When I transported an especially large group, he kept the money he owed me and refused to pay me, because I was a Jew. As I have told you, being a Jew is a crime in Russia. No Russian is allowed to give money or land to Jews. He got a ship's captain to go along with his scheme, and I barely escaped with my life."

Marta pulled the blanket over him, and he settled into its warmth.

"We met shortly after that, did we not?" she asked.

Carl shifted his weight beneath the covers and smiled at her. "Yes, we did. You helped me reenter Russia so I could take back my money from Quentin and Goralski. Unfortunately, they caught me before I could leave the country."

Marta's face grew ashen. "Then how did you come to Torzhok?"

"I had a choice. I could escape to Torzhok and rejoin Herr Zweig's immigrant group or be executed. Ivanov, the friend who helped me escape, knew the route your group had taken. I caught up with you here, although I tried to reach you sooner, before the snow fell too deeply. It was luck that the patrol for your immigrant group came upon me when they did. Better fortune than I thought. I had become disoriented, and Goralski's men followed closer behind me than I anticipated."

The smell of burning wood from the oven stung Marta's nostrils. Luck? His return to her was not an answer to prayer, but the result of luck and the plans of a friend? Carl's words had been said easily, as if they had not just wrenched her heart from her body and squeezed all the blood from it. She shook her head. The heaviness of disappointment leaned on her more than Carl's weight had. He had not come back for her. He would not remain with her.

"And your plans?" she asked.

"First I must regain my strength." His hand moved to his face. "Then . . . I know not."

"Another of your many lies." She could tell that the ordeal had wearied him, but she was not ready to let him rest. "You shall leave again, shall you not?"

Carl turned away from her. "I shall."

"When it is convenient for you."

"Possibly in the spring." His voice grew weaker.

"So, we must welcome you each time you appear and play a part in your schemes whenever it serves your purpose." She felt like screaming but remained standing quietly before him.

Carl turned his face to her. He reached out a hand and laid it on her arm, a gentle touch that made her even more aware of her love for this man. "My life is complicated."

She pulled away from him as if he were a burning ember. "And filled with untruths."

"You have been good to me, better than I expected." Carl's eyes shut. "There is little I can give you for your help now. I have some money saved, but I doubt that money is what you desire from me."

"I do not want your things. I want the truth."

"Very well," he said. "If truth means so much to you, then from this moment forward, no matter how much it hurts you or me, I shall tell you the truth. I give you my word."

"Marta, come. I have need of thine help," called Frau Doenhof as she tried to lift a heavy pot from the oven. Marta turned and hurried to Frau Doenhof's side, more to escape Carl than to aid her friend. In spite of all that Carl had done to her, Marta longed to turn back time and erase the words spoken between them.

She helped Frau Doenhof set the pot on the table. "Stir this." Marta took the spoon. This routine was her life. She had not minded the monotony before Carl's return, but now, from deep inside, she knew what she wanted from life. She took a quick glance at Carl. He looked helpless in his makeshift bed. She sighed, releasing a bit of her anger. No matter what his faults, she wanted to love Carl and be loved by him, her husband. Could he ever feel about her the way she felt about him?

Frau Doenhof cleared her throat and spoke in a quiet voice. "My husband was an evil man, but I loved him."

Marta glanced at Frau Doenhof, startled at the seriousness in her voice. She was looking down at the table in front of her, holding a knife, her hand poised over a small wedge of meat.

Marta stirred the contents of the pot. "You need not tell me of him."

Frau Doenhof sliced the meat many times before she finally said, "Let me speak before I lose the courage to speak. For too long, I liked not the sight of thee, because it put me in mind of the people who stood by and watched while I suffered. Marta, I have done you a great wrong."

Marta stopped stirring. Frau Doenhof pointed the knife toward her. "In Lübeck, I was terrified. My life, as bad as it was before, prepared me not for the terror I knew when the soldiers shoved me into that cart. My life was over. Then all of a sudden, Herr Binz appeared. He untied my hands and led me to freedom."

"Yes, I saw him release you," said Marta. "Hans and I were hidden in a barrel."

"The taste of freedom after almost certain death . . . I would have done anything to keep it . . . anything." Slowly she turned back to the food and placed the knife beside it. "I met Herr Mueller soon after. He had connections, said he had the means to get me to Russia if I feigned to be his sister. You must understand that I owed him a debt."

Marta stopped stirring and touched Frau Doenhof's arm. "I do understand."

"No, you cannot," said Frau Doenhof. "Hear me out." She cut the meat savagely with the knife. "Once on the ship, Herr Mueller asked me to stand up at thy wedding. It was a small price to pay, and so I did. I doubted my choice when the ship's first mate, and not the captain, came forward to make ye wed."

"You are mistaken." Marta's hands felt empty. She picked up the spoon again and began to stir the pot's contents with strong, unhurried strokes.

"Perhaps," said Frau Doenhof. This time she turned to Marta. "But in the end, it mattered not. For the ceremony was not performed. You passed out before ye be wed, and because of my debt to Herr Mueller, I said it had been performed when you asked me."

"No." Marta's voice was no more than a whisper.

"Listen not to that scoundrel. He would have paid the man to make a pretense of the ceremony had you not collapsed. Think of me however you must, but fall not into his trap. He is not thy true husband."

Later, after Carl had rested, he felt that Marta had distanced herself from him. It was as if her body was there, but her mind was somewhere else completely. All evening she wandered around in her haze, almost oblivious to his presence, and he found that he missed her attention.

The next day, when Anna came over, Hans, Anna, and Raczko built a stick village on the floor. When they had rebuilt it for the third time, Raczko's pet rabbit knocked it over.

Anna stood up and stomped her foot. "Raczko, make it stop." When neither boy paid her any mind, she continued, "Hans, tell him what I said."

Carl hid a smile. What an unusual family. Surprisingly, the children's noises and the chaos all around refreshed him. Frau Binz cleaned. Frau Doenhof and Marta whispered near the hearth, a quiet argument. He wondered at the strange turn of their relationship from the time he had left them. They appeared more like relations than strangers who had been thrown together.

He leaned against the brick wall of the stove. He felt safe here. He could keep up the facade of being married until spring. By then, he would have formed another plan of escape, although this time, it would be harder to convince Sergey that he and Marta were simply having domestic problems. He rubbed his arm. The Russian soldiers had forced him to walk and then dragged him through the storm behind their horses. If it had not been for the snow cushioning him, he was certain that he would not have made it alive to Torzhok. Still, he was thankful that the soldiers found him before Goralski's men could catch him. They would have killed him immediately.

Frau Doenhof glared at him. He glanced at Marta, but she was putting on her cloak and harnessing the horse.

"Where do you go?" he asked.

"Out." She would not meet his eyes.

Marta had no intention of listening to any more of Frau Doenhof's accusations. They weren't true. They couldn't be. She led the horse through the door. The wind had stopped blowing, but the air was cold. She could not tell whether she or the horse was happier about being in the fresh air. She led the animal away from the house, forcing it to walk through the low drifts out toward the edge of the village.

The sting of the cold made her feel somehow more alive. Out of the corner of her eye, she saw Sergey walking toward her. She quickly turned the horse around to lead it back to the house, realizing only then how far she had come. She moved to the other side of the animal, placing it between herself and Sergey.

"Fräulein Ebel," said Sergey in greeting.

"Frau Ebel." How Marta wished that she had the authority to tell him to move on.

"Fräulein Ebel, confused my mind is," said Sergey.

She did not stop, but moved in front of the horse to lead it through a higher drift.

"I has knowledge," continued Sergey, "of man name of Carl Mueller who stolen a property of value. It belong to man of great power in Oranienbaum. He angry and want Mueller dead. Know you this Carl Mueller? Is he not the man who calls himself your husband?"

Marta refused to answer.

He moved closer. "Say you that he is innocent?"

Marta wanted to make him go away, but all she could say was, "I must take the horse back inside."

Sergey followed. "Mueller must be punish for crimes. Herr Ebel, if that be his name, must abide with immigrant group. Which is he?" He walked faster to keep up with her. "You should not yourself be with this criminal man. You good woman. You need have good man who make good life for you."

Marta noticed a tinge of kindness in his voice. She slowed down a little, but when she did not respond, his tone changed.

"I would see captain's log for your ship. Perhaps your marriage line is not on this record. Perhaps you not be wed at all."

Marta bristled as she hurriedly opened the door and led the horse inside. Everything looked normal. Frau Doenhof was busy over the fire, Gretta's head was bowed, probably in prayer, at the table, and Anna, Hans, and Raczko sat around the tablelike structure listening to Carl tell a story, alternately in German and Russian. That was what he was best at—telling stories.

Sergey stepped inside behind her and pointed to Carl. "Should you prove not to be wed, I shall myself give you over to guards." He moved closer to Marta.

Carl motioned for the children to move to the side. "Is there a problem?" He stood. Even in his weakened condition, Marta sensed the dangerous nature of his words. In spite of her confusion, his willingness to protect her warmed her heart.

"No," said Sergey. "Not of yet." Sergey stamped his boots on the floor, small clumps of snow falling to the wood, before he stalked outside and slammed the door behind him.

"What did he mean by that?" asked Carl.

Marta motioned for Carl to join her by the door. "Are we truly married?"

A mask crept over Carl's face, and Marta knew the answer. She saw a flicker of emotion that told her how much he wanted to say what she wanted to hear and then a second flicker as if he were battling against the promise he had spoken to her a short while before. She closed her eyes. Her heart that had floated amid the clouds at his return was now seared with his betrayal.

"I did it for you," said Carl softly. "We both knew I would be gone. I couldn't force you to live a life with no reward."

She opened her eyes slowly. "So you have laid me open to scorn."

"No. I've kept you pure. You can wed for love and—"

"I have done so already, though I knew it not at the time."

The emptiness that Carl saw in Marta's eyes made him want to reach back in time and change everything. This was the very hollowness of spirit from which he had wanted to protect her. "I'll make it up to you."

"My welfare is no longer your concern," she said. He winced at her coldness. He watched her move to Frau Doenhof's side. She did not look his way again.

"Shall you finish the story now?" called Hans. Carl turned back to the children. He tried to conclude the tale with the same flair, but the children moved off to play something else before it was complete.

Just then, the door flew open. The older man from the Pfeiffers' hut shouted urgently in Russian. Carl and Yuriy hurried over to him.

After a few exchanges, Carl translated. "Anna's mother is having her baby." He dropped his voice so Anna did not hear him continue, "It doesn't look good."

Marta reached for her cloak, but Gretta stopped her. "Do you know how to deliver a baby?"

Marta shook her head no. She looked frightened to Carl.

"You stay here and take care of Anna and Hans," said Gretta. "I shall go."

Yuriy reached for his coat and spoke.

Carl translated. "He says he'll go with you, Gretta. He helped deliver Raczko."

Gretta turned to Yuriy. "I would appreciate your help." Carl knew that Yuriy could not understand her words, but it looked as if he understood her meaning. The two left.

Marta looked drained. "Children, please hunt for eggs," she said. While they searched the izba, Marta helped Frau Doenhof with the cooking. As uncomfortable as their relationship had become, Carl had no intention of allowing Marta to cut him out of her life before he was ready to leave. He did not know what he was feeling, not being practiced in these sorts of matters, but he did know that he did not like the way she was treating him.

He sat down on the bench beside the table where the women were working, trying to think of some way to get Marta to talk to him again. "Would you please explain to me Martin Luther's arguments against the Papists?" He could tell that Marta did not want to talk to him, but that she felt obligated.

"Martin Luther believed that people do not need someone to go to God for them. Jesus our Lord already did that," she began. Surprisingly, he found her words interesting. She did not try to convince him, she gave him only what he had asked.

When Yuriy returned with a blank face and slumped shoulders, Carl translated his words for the women. "Anna has a new sister."

"I have a sister!" cried Anna.

Frau Doenhof spoke up. "Is that all the news?"

Carl continued, "Gretta has taken the infant to a woman who has recently had a child for nursing."

Marta and Frau Doenhof looked at each other. Nina had not survived.

Carl put his hand on Yuriy's shoulder. "You have done your best."

"It was not good enough." He took a bottle of spirits from a shelf near the oven and drank deeply.

Carl could tell that Marta was trying to hold back tears as she said, "Anna, dear, would you like to tell us some of your stories?"

The little girl climbed on Marta's lap, and Marta held her close as she began her tale. Carl watched her with the child. She said that she had married for love. Had she really fallen in love with him? He must have misunderstood her words. Women like Marta, as beautiful on the inside as on the outside, did not fall for scoundrels like him. Perhaps the way she was treating him was the way it should be. Instead of trying to make her change, he would plan to leave at the earliest opportunity. The sooner he was out of her life, the better for both of them.

Chapter Seventeen

Hans moved next to Marta, lifting her arm and placing it around his shoulders, just as her youngest brother, Wilhelm, used to do. "When shall my mother come home?"

"I know not," said Marta. "She still cares for Anna's sister. Perhaps we can go outside again this day. A frolic in the snow might relieve your mind for a time."

Hans smiled, but it was not one of his sweet smiles. It reminded Marta of Carl's smile, when things were going his way. How she wished she did not compare everything to Carl as if he were the center of her world.

"I feel shame, Lord, that I let Carl draw my attention away from You. Please forgive me," Marta prayed silently as she helped the children into their coats and scarves. Once outside, the boys and Anna hurried over to climb the highest drift they could find. Frau Doenhof had continued cooking, but since the news of Nina's death, she had hardly left Anna's side.

Hans and Raczko held Anna's hands. "Now go this way," she commanded. They obeyed. She continued, "Now to the tree."

Frau Doenhof came outside and tossed dirty water out of a bucket. "I shall watch them if ye like."

"I am content," said Marta. "You have been working too hard."

"I mind it not," she said. "Ye may find this hard to believe, but I love children."

"I can tell," said Marta.

Frau Doenhof turned to go back inside before stopping to say, "Ye know it be thine own fault that thine heart breaketh."

Marta looked at her friend, surprised. "I think not. I was not the one who lied." Even the mention of her situation hurt.

"When ye expect more than life can offer, ye set thyself up for pain." Frau Doenhof set the bucket on her hip.

"I suppose it is better to cloister thy soul and allow no person close," retorted Marta.

For a moment, Frau Doenhof looked as if she had been slapped, but she quickly regained her usual tight composure. "I know not all things. But I have some wisdom. Send in the children when ye tire of them." She turned from Marta and went back into the house.

Marta rubbed her forehead. Frau Doenhof was right. She had made Carl into a prince of sorts, her prince, even though she knew he was a scoundrel. She had allowed herself to dream, and now she was paying the consequences.

Anna screamed. "Get me out now!" Marta looked up. She saw Hans and Raczko but no Anna.

"Anna, where are you?" Marta yelled.

Hans and Raczko began to laugh as Marta moved through the deep snow as quickly as she could. "Anna!"

"She is here," said Hans. "Cry baby! Maybe if you were not so bossy, we would help you out of the snowdrift."

"You get me out now!" Anna's muffled voice sounded as if she were trying not to cry.

Raczko reached out his hand. "Here. Good girl." Marta saw him begin to pull the child out. "Pretty girl. No cry."

"Give me your other hand," said Hans. Together they pulled her to the harder snow where they could stand without falling through.

Raczko picked her up as she began to bawl. "You cry. Cry is fine." Marta stopped where she was. She felt tears beginning to cascade down her own face. She was tired of losing people in her life. Raczko continued to comfort Anna. "Cry it away. You cry. You be fine." Marta began to sob.

"Now we have two criers," said Hans. "She is well, Frau Ebel. Anna is not hurt." They brought Anna to Marta, and the two clung to each other, sobbing. The boys left them alone and before long were throwing snowballs at each other.

When the tears had almost stopped, Anna said, "My mama has gone away."

Marta nodded. "I know."

"Daddy is gone, too," said Anna. "I know not how to care for a baby."

"Frau Doenhof and I do," said Marta. "We shall help you care for your sister." Anna nodded, but then started wailing again.

Marta cupped the child's face in her hands. "What troubles you now?"

In a small, staccato voice punctuated with sobs, Anna asked, "Who . . . shall . . . care . . . for . . . me?" A snowball whizzed by them.

Marta hugged her. "Frau Doenhof and I shall. You and your baby sister shall both be our family."

That night, Anna cried herself to sleep. Her little shoulders heaved with sobs so powerful that the child could barely catch her breath. Marta cried silently with her and cuddled her tenderly.

The next morning, as if repenting for his deeds the day before, Hans tried to cheer Anna by setting her on the goat's back and giving her a ride around the izba. "Make way for Tsarina Anna."

Anna laughed. The goat walked proudly for a moment and then without notice, it jerked from Hans's grasp, twisted, and butted him. Anna fell off. Raczko rolled on the floor with laughter, unable to catch his breath. Before long, all three of them were laughing, and even Marta smiled.

After a few days, Gretta arrived home with the new baby, whom Nina had named Elisabeth after her mother.

"You are home," yelled Hans, running to meet Gretta. Marta took the baby from her, and Hans gave his mother an exuberant hug. Anna stood on tiptoes to catch a glimpse of the child wrapped in swaddling. Marta stooped down and moved the blanket aside so Anna could see. "Anna, here is your new sister."

"Hello, baby Elisabeth," said Anna in a soft voice. Gingerly, she touched the baby's tiny fingers, first clasped tight and then unfurling like a rosebud. Elisabeth cooed, and Anna grinned up at Marta. "She likes me."

"Yes, she does, and you shall be a wonderful big sister." Marta found herself smiling for a second time in just a few short days. She was going to be fine.

Yuriy drew up a bench for them. Then he pulled out a package that had been carefully wrapped in cloth.

"Raczko," he said. Yuriy showed them something made of canvas and hung it by ropes from the izba's rafters. It was a cradle.

Frau Doenhof's eyes glimmered as she held out her hands for the child. Marta gave Elisabeth to her and took a step back to view the scene before her. They were like a family, all of them—except Carl. He stood off by himself, away from the warmth.

⁓

Carl was glad to escape his confinement and go hunting with Yuriy. Being in the same room with Marta made him uncomfortable. Their easy friendship had deteriorated into estrangement. And her hollow eyes. They reminded him of his mother's.

He had always resented his aristocratic father for abusing and belittling his mother. He had fed, clothed, and educated Carl, but made it clear that both Carl and his mother were anathema to him—until the end. Carl spat into the snow as if he were spitting on his father's grave. He readjusted his fur hat.

Marta's words of the other day kept ringing in his ears, the same words that he had shouted at his father the last time he saw him. "My welfare is no longer your concern." It pained him to realize that Marta had seen in him what he had not noticed in himself— his deceit, selfishness, and total disregard for the feelings of others. He had become like his father.

That afternoon when he and Yuriy returned, Marta was sitting at the rough-hewn table with Sergey and Goralski's two soldiers towering over her. Gretta must have been out caring for other families' needs, as she often was. Frau Doenhof gave him a warning look. Herr Zweig and Herr Jaeger stood next to her. Marta's eyes blazed with a defiant rage that Carl had never seen before. The soldiers immediately moved toward Carl, swords drawn.

"What is your business here?" Yuriy dropped a hare on the table.

"Herr Mueller is under arrest." Sergey did not face him as he spoke but kept his eyes on Marta.

"My name is Ebel. What is the charge against me?" demanded Carl in Russian.

"You are charged with thievery and posing as a false member of this immigrant group." Sergey slowly turned to face Carl. "We shall carry out your death sentence immediately." A malicious light flickered in his eyes. Although Marta did not understand Russian, Carl could tell that she recognized the danger.

"Take leave of us and never trouble my family again," she said.

Sergey leaned toward Marta threateningly with his gun pointed at her. "I is soldier Russian, made in power by Tsarina Catherine. Persons who heed me not shall I punish with strength. Make proof to me that husband and immigrant is same man, not bad man Russia official seek. Or prepare to watch, for he die."

"Now, now. Frau Ebel means no disrespect," said Herr Zweig. "I can assure you that Herr Ebel sailed with us from Lübeck, so he is a fellow immigrant. I have known him by no other name. As for the marriage, no records are available in this wilderness. Why do ye not let Herr Jaeger wed them a second time? It shall not undo the first marriage, but shall provide you and your assiduous soldiers the proof they need."

Carl watched Marta's face. She revealed nothing of what she was thinking.

"I shall not wed my wife again for your satisfaction." Carl was confronted by the tip of a sword at his stomach. He took a step back.

"But should I perform another ceremony," said Herr Jaeger, "these men shall have the proof they need." He turned to the soldiers. "There is no need for you to kill this man. Heaven knows there has been enough death among the settlers."

Herr Zweig added, "Tsarina Catherine needs men on the frontier."

Frau Doenhof moved to Carl's side and placed a comforting hand on his arm. "Herr Zweig has found the solution. Marta, ye must wed thine husband again. Otherwise, he shall be murdered on our doorstep."

Frau Doenhof could not have shocked Carl more if she had punched him in the stomach—she who knew his dishonest and selfish nature. Marta walked up to Carl, and he tried not to show the desperation he felt. Whether he lived or died rested in the hands of a woman whom he had used and betrayed since the moment he met her. He looked to the soldiers. There would be no escape. He could taste death, his death, and he was not ready to see his father again, if indeed there was an afterlife. His mother's words of warning that he would never be able to flee God haunted him again. Was God so persistent that He had followed Carl even into this wilderness?

"Release him," said Marta. "If we are to wed again, then I would have a word with my husband." Carl breathed his relief and had never enjoyed the feel of air entering and leaving his lungs so much as he did at that moment. He translated her words for the Russians, and Yuriy pleaded Carl's case before the strangers. Carl was glad that Yuriy was present. The soldiers listened to him and sheathed their swords. Without Yuriy's help, he doubted if Sergey would have allowed a ceremony to take place. Marta took Carl's hand in hers and moved to the corner farthest from where everyone stood. Her hand was so small compared to his, and yet in it he felt strength mixed with tenderness.

The gentleness of her touch left him when she released his hand and said, "We must wed if you wish to live." He shook his head no, giving her one last means of escape from him. She continued, "Be you so repulsed at the thought of taking me as your wife that you would embrace your own death?"

"No, but I won't subject you—"

She waved her hand to silence him. "My offer is not without

requirements. First, we shall allow everyone to believe we are truly wed, even our closest friends, but we shall continue as in the past." Carl stared at the ground. He could handle that.

"Agreed," he said.

"You shall accept Anna and Elisabeth as your own daughters and act as protector for Gretta, Hans, and Frau Doenhof, even though, legally, Hans is our protector."

It wouldn't be for long. "Agreed."

"Third, you shall remain with us, no matter where we settle, until we have claimed our land and house and have stored enough food for the winter."

"That could be a year from now."

"Or more," said Marta. Carl gave a slow nod, and Marta continued, "And finally, when you leave, you shall not stay in Russia to seek your revenge. You shall take your leave and depart Russia by the shortest possible route."

"What I do is my business."

"These are my conditions." Marta stood firm. "You shall come and go as you please no longer. Should you not return to stay with me for life, then return ne'er again."

Carl rubbed his neck. If he agreed, his enemies would win. He would have to give up his plans to pay them back for what they had done to him. He regretted giving her his word never to lie to her again.

"I accept, but only because I have no choice."

"Nor do I," said Marta.

Carl could not help but smile, for the situation amused him. "Mutual helplessness," he said. "It is not the best foundation for a marriage."

"Mutual need is better than unfounded dreams," said Marta. "Leastwise, now we both know where we stand." Her words cut Carl's heart, but he wasn't sure why.

"I give you my word," said Carl.

"I expect you to keep it."

Carl shivered slightly at Marta's coldness and his narrow escape from his own execution. They returned to the group, Carl purposely displaying a confident smile.

"My wife and I have agreed to wed anew." He shrugged. "A wife can change a husband's mind even when no one else can."

Marta closed her eyes for a moment, as though praying, before looking up. "Herr Jaeger, if you please, we should like to be wed . . . again. Frau Doenhof, will you stand up with me?"

Carl spoke to Yuriy in Russian. The man nodded and stood next to Carl. Sergey stood tall without a single emotion passing his face, but his eyes smoldered with repressed anger. Carl wondered if there had ever been such a ragtag ceremony as theirs, and yet it took place with none of the dramatics that had plagued the moments before it.

After the vows were spoken, Sergey muttered in Russian, "She save your filthy neck, for this time now."

Carl smiled broadly, as if Sergey had congratulated him. "Most men marry their lovely brides only once. I am fortunate to marry mine twice. Thank you, sir, for making it possible. I applaud your diligence in fulfilling your duties and shall not keep you from them any longer." He stepped in front of Marta, as if he were forming a barrier between her and Sergey. He switched to German, so that Marta would understand what he said next. Bowing slightly toward Sergey in exaggerated deference, he said, "You do your duty, sir, and I assure you, I shall do mine."

In spite of her resolution not to feel anything, Marta thrilled at the tone that announced Carl's protection over her to everyone in the room. She immediately quenched the feeling. No, Carl and she had a business arrangement, nothing more.

After all the men but Carl and Yuriy had left, the children went back to playing, and Frau Doenhof resumed her cooking. Marta picked up Elisabeth and looked into her innocent eyes, feeling as small and helpless as the newborn child.

"So does this mean that we have a truce?" asked Carl quietly.

Marta sighed. "It means that we shall act as if we both desired this union so that we shall not worry our friends. Our marriage is now one of convenience to both of us. We are the only ones who shall ever know."

"Then I shall play the same part that I have since we first met, only this time, we are in it together—both sharing in the intrigue." He tried to get Marta to smile, but she turned away.

When Frau Doenhof took Elisabeth from her, Marta began to clean the izba, but in her thoughts she prayed, "Dear Jesus, I know Thou hath forgiven me of so much—more than the offenses that Carl has placed before my heart. But each time his betrayal comes to mind, I grow angry. Help me to forgive him truly in my heart. Please remind me of Thy forgiveness each time the anger arises in my soul. Should I forgive him now, perhaps he shall one day be able to accept Thy forgiveness and gain eternal salvation. Help me, Lord."

Marta had not quite finished cleaning the entire dwelling when Gretta returned.

"Mama!" cried Hans. "Where have you been? Herr and Frau Ebel were wed again, but this time I saw it."

Gretta looked at Carl and Marta in surprise. "I come from the Donner family. They have all fallen ill." Her face looked flushed.

Frau Doenhof harrumphed. "Ye should be taking care of thyself, not traipsing all over the village caring for others." She helped Gretta remove her wraps. "Thou art hot with the fever. Hans, fill the bucket with snow. We must cool thy mother's head." The words were said evenly, but Frau Doenhof's eyes betrayed her concern.

—☙—

The next morning, Marta wiped her brow with her arm as she washed Elisabeth's swaddling clothes. It seemed that no sooner had she changed the little one than she would make another mess and Marta would have to change her again. With Gretta sick, there was more work and fewer hands. Marta sighed.

Carl walked up behind her. "A baby in the house adds many unpleasant chores."

"Do you offer to help then? You may take over the wash, if you like."

"No, thank you. I shall continue to hunt and fish and leave the wash to your excellent skills." He hesitated and then lowered his voice. "Hear you that the old Volkers have died of the fever? And the Kunz baby?"

Marta's heart ached. "There is not a house in the village that has not tasted the fury of this sickness."

"At least no one in this hut except Gretta has caught it. We can be grateful for that."

"I suppose we should be grateful, but what about Gretta? We cannot let her die. Hans needs her." Marta picked up Elisabeth and swayed from side to side, rocking her.

"Only Hans?"

It infuriated Marta that he had discerned her deeper meaning. Yes, she needed Gretta just as much as Hans did. She still had so much to learn about God and His ways. Gretta was a woman who could teach her.

As Gretta's health continued to deteriorate, Marta spent more and more time by her side. Snow began to fall again, small flakes at first, and then larger, until it became hard to tell when one snowstorm stopped and another began. Then one day, the sun rose higher in the sky and the icicles hanging from the roof began to drip. The children ventured outside to play under Frau Doenhof's stern eye.

"It shall be good for Elisabeth to have fresh air," Frau Doenhof told Marta, as she carried the baby out with her. Carl and Yuriy had gone hunting earlier that day, which left Marta and Gretta alone, a pleasure that Marta had not had for what felt like far too long.

Gretta sat up on the table-bed, and Marta brought her hot soup. "You know that Carl and I were wed again."

"Yes, he shall make a good husband, eventually. I feel certain." Her statement surprised Marta. She was about to ask Gretta what made her so sure, when Gretta coughed, a deep raspy bark that took her breath away for a few seconds. She continued, "Herr Ebel shall make a good father for my Hans."

"You shall be well, I am sure. Hans needs you too much. We all do. How could I go on without your wisdom and strength to guide me?"

Gretta took Marta's hands gently in hers. "Do you not now confuse me with God? Is your faith still so small that you lean not on Him? You must be strong. I shall die, and you and Frau Doenhof shall have three children to depend on you. I have already spoken to her about it."

"Gretta, how can you speak with such calm? Are you not the least angry with God? Do you want to die and leave Hans alone?"

Tears formed in Gretta's eyes as they looked deeply into Marta's. "Do you think it is easy for me to accept this, to struggle for every breath and to know that I shall die and leave my only son? Yes, I feel anger. I am overcome with grief that I shall not live to raise my son. But I still love and trust God. I know that He shall watch over Hans as He watches over you and me."

Gretta began to cough again, and for the first time, Marta noticed blood on the cloth she held to her mouth.

—❦—

Carl and Yuriy checked their traps and found three large hares. "We shall eat well tonight, da?" Yuriy patted Carl on the back.

As Carl was checking the last trap, he heard heavy steps behind him. "Nothing in this one."

Instead of hearing Yuriy's answer, Carl felt pushed from behind. Knocked off balance, he fell to the ground. Immediately, he rolled to the side, expecting a second blow. The attack did not come, and Carl heard a whinny. He looked up. A horse took a step forward. It was thick haired, ragged and thin, but appeared healthy.

"Snyek! Is that you?" The horse whinnied again. Carl looked more closely. "It is you. I chose a good name for you. Snyek. Snow." He stood up and hurried to the animal's side, patting its neck as he leaned his face against it. "How did you ever survive?"

"What have we caught here?" asked Yuriy coming out from behind a grove of trees.

"This is Snyek, the horse that carried me from St. Petersburg. Is there room in your izba?"

"For such a faithful friend, we shall make room." He patted the horse.

"Thank you." Carl liked this kind Russian. He was different from those he had dealt with before. His religion involved more than the rote traditions Carl had observed with some other men. Yuriy's beliefs seemed to spill over into his life.

As they walked home leading Snyek, Yuriy asked, "Carl, my friend, why do you not sleep beside your wife?"

"Ours is a business agreement."

Yuriy laughed. "Perhaps it began as an agreement, but as you lay ill, she stayed by your side night and day. Now she gives you the best portion of food. That is love, not business."

"You are mistaken, my friend. We married for practical reasons."

"Perhaps that is why she hides her love behind a mask of strength," he said matter-of-factly. "You are a fortunate man in your choice of wife, if you care to be."

Carl wondered at Yuriy's words. Could Marta still love him, after all he had done? Snyek had found him, had accepted him as master, even after he had suffered through a most difficult winter alone. Could Marta possibly have forgiven him? Could she truly love a scoundrel such as he?

He rubbed Snyek's velvet nose. "Welcome home, faithful friend."

⁓

Marta shivered. The weather had turned cold again as first one and then another blizzard swept in from the north. The odor in the izba had become worse since Carl had brought home another horse. After two weeks of pounding, frigid winds whistling through the cracks in the walls, everyone's nerves were raw, especially hers. She tried to talk to Gretta, but the woman's eyes remained closed, and she didn't seem to hear. Marta talked anyway, because she felt the need.

"Hans shall do well, Gretta. It makes my heart glad that you have already talked to him and said your good-byes. Worry not about Hans. I shall love and care for him as my own, no matter what comes to pass. You . . . have been as dear to me as my own mother, like the sister I never had. I shall miss you."

Anna screamed. "Pull not my hair!"

"Enough!" said Marta, standing. "Do not disturb Frau Binz with that noise." She looked to Carl, and he motioned Hans to his side. Carl was the only one who seemed to be able to calm or discipline Hans now.

Frau Doenhof took Anna and held her until she stopped crying. When she was calm, Anna traced the scar on Frau Doenhof's face with her fingers. "What is this?" she asked.

Frau Doenhof spoke gently. "It is a scar from a deep hurt long ago."

Yuriy took over at Gretta's bedside, gently rubbing her cold hands and speaking to her in Russian.

Frau Doenhof's mood changed suddenly, and she scolded Yuriy. "She understands you not, as you understand me not."

"I understand you," said Yuriy in a low voice. Frau Doenhof blushed, set Anna down, and hurried back to the fire.

Marta helped Anna place a cool cloth on Gretta's feverish face. Yuriy's kindness had made Gretta's last few weeks a little gentler, a little more bearable. Gretta had said so herself in one of her lucid moments.

Raczko watched from a distance. "Like Mama. Just so, Papa cared for Mama."

"He is a good man," Frau Doenhof offered, and Raczko went to her side.

"You, too, shall stay not with us?" he asked in his best German.

"I cannot. My place is with my friends," said Frau Doenhof. "I gave Frau Binz my word."

Marta looked from Frau Doenhof to Raczko and then to Yuriy.

She had been so focused on her own problems that she had missed what was happening around her. She now realized that Yuriy was interested in Frau Doenhof and Raczko had become attached to her. Raczko retreated to the corner and started brushing the new horse. He wiped his eyes with a sleeve and faced the wall.

Two days later, the storms had passed, and Gretta was dead. She expired during the night. In the morning, Yuriy pointed to the gentle smile on Gretta's face. In broken German, he said, "Like my Tanya. With God."

Marta started to tense up, to try to hold back her tears as she had always done before in the face of death. Then she remembered Gretta's words, "He shall come to stay with ye, and ye shall never be alone or unprotected again." She had to remember that Jesus was with her. Her soul cried out for her Lord, and she let the tears fall. Carl's hand touched her shoulder.

"I'm sorry," he said. She turned to him, sobbing, then remembered herself and pulled away. She must be strong. Have faith. Trust the Lord. There was no one else she could trust. Carl's arms came around her again and she lost her resolve, sobbing into his chest.

When Marta's tears subsided, she noticed that Hans did not cry. He simply stared at his mother's still form until Raczko put an arm around his shoulders and led him outside to play. Marta worried for Hans. He kept his feelings to himself, too much like she used to do.

"We'll have to start a fire so we can bury her," Carl told her gently. "The ground is still frozen too hard for a proper burial. We'll have to bury her in deep snow until the grave is ready."

Carl and Herr Zweig started a fire in the snow with Yuriy's help. The men brought wood and created a bonfire that lasted days until they were able to melt a patch of snow and thaw a piece of land. Marta and Hans went out together to check on the progress of the grave many times as the men finally started to dig. Hand in hand they walked to the hole that grew in size each time they visited it. It seemed like a poor place to lay such a good woman to rest.

When the hole was large enough and deep enough, Frau Doenhof climbed through the drifts to get Herr Jaeger, who said a prayer over Gretta's body. As the men shoveled the dirt back in place, Frau Doenhof took the girls inside, but Marta and Hans remained. When Herr Zweig, Carl, and Yuriy were done, they left the two orphans to their silent vigil of grief.

"I cannot bear to leave her here," said Hans.

"I cannot either," said Marta. And so they remained, watching the newly turned ground in a cold wind that could not numb them any more than the sight before them had. Neither could move from the spot, paralyzed by the horror and loss they felt, until Carl returned and placed his arms around Marta's waist and Hans's shoulders and gently drew them back into the izba.

Yuriy spoke to them, and Carl translated. "The ground has been consecrated. Although you could not tell, Gretta is buried next to Yuriy's dear wife." Marta felt herself exhale as if she had been holding her breath for days.

After Gretta's funeral, winter started to release its hold on the land. The snowpack softened. Creaking, groaning sounds echoed off the Tversta River as the ice began to break. Herr Zweig broke the monotony of their routine by visiting them at least once a day, often at mealtimes.

Carl teased Frau Doenhof. "You have found the way into Herr Zweig's heart, through his appetite."

"Harrumph!" Frau Doenhof said, lifting a pot of venison stew out of the oven. "I should not take a man who wanted me only for my cooking."

"And what of Yuriy?" Carl continued. "He has stayed in the house much more of late. It seems he can't take his eyes off of you."

She jabbed a bucket into his stomach. "Make thyself useful and fetch me a pail of snow."

That night, as Marta cleaned up after supper, she noticed Frau Doenhof and Herr Zweig talking quietly. Frau Doenhof's face was slightly flushed.

Marta finished scraping the last dish and turned to Carl. "Look how she smiles, and she looks younger than I have ever seen her."

"She's not too many years older than you. That's what admiration does for a woman."

"Admiration? Then I must look to be about two hundred." Marta moved away from Carl to the other side of the room. She did not know why she had been so curt with him. Still, she was a little jealous of the attention Yuriy and Herr Zweig paid to Frau Doenhof. If only Carl—but she would not allow her thoughts to go there. Frau Doenhof had a brusque nature, but she was growing softer in her manners the more she was admired.

One day, Herr Zweig came with the news they had been waiting to hear. "We have been ordered to pack our things and be ready to depart for the settlement tomorrow."

Carl's face clouded. "The river has not yet thawed."

"We shall not travel by boat. Our course is overland by wagon until we reach the Volga."

"But there is still a forearm's length of snow on the ground," Frau Doenhof protested.

"We shall attach runners to our wagons, and the Russian army shall lend us animals to pull the sledges."

As much as Marta dreaded a boat ride, she was not anxious to travel over snow either. A wagon could easily tip over on a slippery hill.

She recalled Herr Pfeiffer's tragic death. "Why are we traveling overland and not by river?" she asked.

Herr Zweig smiled wryly. "They want to rid themselves of us as soon as possible. I have heard, too, that they have not enough ketches to send one here. We shall board a vessel at the Volga."

That day, Yuriy hardly left Frau Doenhof's side. Marta even caught Frau Doenhof smiling and laughing at something Yuriy said, but the next morning, she looked no worse for having to leave him behind.

Carl wanted to take Snyek with him, but he decided that the poor beast had suffered enough. "I'm glad we finally settled on a name for you," he said. "Yuriy is a kind man. He'll take good care of you." Carl hugged the horse's neck. "Thank you for everything, Snyek." The horse whinnied its farewell.

Leaving Torzhok was harder than Marta had thought it would be. For the last time, she walked to the small mound of snow that had drifted over her friend's grave. Yuriy and Carl followed her. Yuriy touched her arm and spoke softly. Carl translated.

"He says that he shall see to it that flowers are planted on the graves, both for his wife, Tanya, and for Gretta. He shall take good care of the land."

Marta turned to Yuriy. "You are a good man. *Bol'shoe spasibo.*"

Raczko and Yuriy helped them put their final belongings in the already crowded wagon.

"Good-bye! *Das Vedanya,*" Hans called to Raczko over and over again. Marta was glad that his spirits were so high, but still she worried. Since the day Gretta died, Hans had not cried or mentioned his mother at all. "Farewell! *Das Vedanya,*" he called once more.

As Torzhok disappeared from sight, Hans beat his fist repeatedly against the side of the wagon, harder and harder.

"Halt," said Carl. The child was silent for the rest of the day. Anna and Frau Doenhof were brooding, too. Marta held Elisabeth for a short time, the only time she could wrestle her away from Frau Doenhof. Three children. Such a responsibility! Marta closed her eyes and listened to the swooshing of the large flat wooden blades over the icy ground. They were as large and cumbersome as the wheels had been, but they worked well on the snow-covered terrain.

Carl rubbed her arm. "We'll fare well. You shall see." The sledge hit a bump and the vehicle flew in the air. Carl grabbed Hans and Anna to keep them from falling out.

"We move too fast," said Frau Doenhof. "Tell them to slow their pace, or we shall all meet our deaths."

Marta silently agreed.

"We won't overturn," Carl laughed. "Not while I'm in charge of this household." Marta watched him guarding the children as they sped through a rough turn. In spite of everything she knew about him, she believed that Carl was right. As long as he was with them, everything and everyone would fare well.

Chapter Eighteen

Carl gritted his teeth. How much was a man expected to bear? Yuriy and he had hunted enough to give both their families extra meat for the upcoming months, a treat. He thought he had provided well for his family, but the day-to-day constant care amid shoulder-to-shoulder humanity was wearing his patience. Carl knew he was a selfish man, but he had no idea how selfish until now. If it were not for the presence of soldiers to make him keep his promise, he would have left the group a few days after departing from Torzhok.

Their sledge bumped up and down, jangling his brains, and the passengers chattered and complained without giving him a moment's rest for his thoughts. Worst of all was Herbert, a man who had been assigned to ride with them at the last minute. As Carl glanced his way, Herbert took advantage of the opportunity to speak.

"It is so beautiful a day for a ride in the countryside!"

"Beautiful? You don't see the angry clouds above our heads?" Carl challenged him.

Herbert looked up, as if he had never seen the sky before. "Oh yes, 'tis a fine day indeed."

Hans said, "The cold wind blows even to my bones."

"Ah, but the wind refreshes the soul," said Herbert.

Carl rolled his eyes. Nothing ever bothered Herbert. If it snowed, he said that it was good for the trees. If wild animals got into the food at night, Herbert was grateful he could help them make it through the winter. Carl wondered if the man was right in the head.

He looked over at Marta. While holding Elisabeth, she alternated between comforting Anna and keeping Hans from standing up and flying out of the wagon. Frau Doenhof dozed beside her. Carl did not know how Marta kept going, never raising her voice and always doing whatever tasks were necessary. She caught him looking at her and gave a brief smile. Things between them had improved, but sometimes just being near her made him feel guilty. A hiccupping cry started from within the blanket in Marta's arms, rousing Frau Doenhof.

"Elisabeth needs to be fed," Marta said. Carl took Elisabeth from her and passed her to a woman who was leaning against the boards behind him. The woman handed her own infant to Carl, who quickly transferred the squirming bundle to Frau Doenhof.

"Thank you again, Frau Kreigle, for nursing Elisabeth," Marta said. "Without your help, it is unlikely that she would survive on the small amounts of millet porridge we are able to feed her."

"I'm happy to help."

Frau Doenhof was making silly faces and cooing at the Kreigle baby. "What a fine lad you are," she said in a high-pitched voice. The woman actually appeared as if she meant it.

Carl had had enough. "I shall walk for a time." Hans's hopeful eyes shone in his direction. Carl would have preferred asking Marta to join him, but he said, "Come along, Hans." Marta's face broke into another smile, and he added, "When Anna takes her nap, you can join us too."

"I shall watch Anna," said Frau Doenhof. "Get thee hence and stretch thy legs."

Marta's face lit up, and Carl knew that she was just as relieved as he was to escape the wagon. In spite of their differences of opinion on things, sometimes they seemed more alike than different.

The next time the sledge slowed down, the three climbed down and then waited for the rest of the sledges to pass so they could walk in the ruts the runners had made. Marta's legs felt much better once she was standing on the snowy ground.

"Herr Ebel, look at me," cried Hans. He ran back and forth between the drifts, falling into the deepest ones.

"Where does he find such energy?" asked Marta.

Carl chuckled. "He's a boy. I remember myself at his age. The world was an enormous place, and I couldn't wait to explore it."

"And what did you explore?" asked Marta.

"Mostly my father's castle." Carl gave Marta a grin.

"You speak in jest, do you not?"

He shook his head and then raised his shoulders.

"Are you a prince or some other such high nobility?"

"My father was a duke. The castle was small, but it was filled with swords, spiders, and secret passages."

"Secret passages?" asked Marta. "Now you exaggerate."

"One passage connected my father's bedchamber to the back stairs. Another led from the main hall to the music room. I must have found ten different passages." Carl picked up a handful of snow and formed it into a ball.

Marta stood dumbfounded for a minute. "Did not anyone object as you popped in and out of walls?" she asked.

"They probably would have, had they seen me. I was an embarrassment to my father, so no one took much notice of me. They were too busy with my father's two younger children."

Marta wondered what Carl's father might have had against him, but she thought it wiser not to ask. "What of your mother? Surely she tried to keep you in hand?"

"She did, but it didn't always work. Besides, she wasn't with me most of the time." Carl threw the snowball at Hans, who squealed in delight and began making a snowball larger than he could hold to throw back at Carl.

Marta intended to duck when Hans threw his snowball, but it landed before coming near them. "I grew up with four brothers in a house of three rooms. It was ever filled with noises and clashes, so much that it muddled my thoughts, but in between our quarrels, we laughed often. My father saw to it." Marta was trying not to show how completely taken she was with Carl's disclosure. She had suspected that he was a class above her, but she never dreamed that he was from the French ruling class. Though she tried to stay calm, her insides were screaming, "I have wed a nobleman!"

Carl ran after Hans to rub his face in the snow. They were laughing and getting wetter by the minute. Marta could not help but think what a good father he would make for Hans . . . if only.

"Take care that you do not wet yourself through. It is so hard to get warm," she shouted after them. Carl motioned that he had heard her and proceeded to roll in the snow. When he stood up, he was covered in white. Hans copied him, and Marta threw up her hands in exasperation, but she couldn't help laughing to herself.

Before long, the two tired of the game and walked back alongside Marta.

"You had four brothers?" exclaimed Hans while Marta tried to brush him off.

Marta raised her eyebrows. "I did."

"Where are they now?" asked Hans.

Marta choked a little. "I know not. Our prince took each of them when they turned twelve to fight in his wars."

"I will be a soldier," said Hans.

"And you would make a good one," said Carl. The words struck Marta in the chest with a sharp pain.

"No," said Marta. "You abide in Russia so that you shall not be forced to fight a prince's battles. That is what was promised us. No German shall have to serve in the armies of Russia. My brothers were taken away, kidnapped, and we n'er heard of them again. I watched my mother die a bit each time one of her sons was taken. You do not understand what you wish for."

"He speaks of a boy's dream to be a champion, not the reality of war," said Carl. "Let him dream. He is safe here with us."

Marta nodded. Carl caressed her shoulder to reassure her. She watched Hans pull a large stick out of the snow. "Look," exclaimed Hans, holding up his prize. All Marta saw was an icy branch, but Carl said, "That will make a good walking stick."

Just then, Sergey appeared on horseback, riding back from the front of the line of wagons. "I what know you do. Again to escape, you run."

Under his breath, Carl murmured, "*Quel stupide*! Such a fool!"

Marta tried to stifle a smile. Hans grabbed both of their hands.

"You not escape from me this time now," yelled Sergey. He did not have full control of his animal. Instead of pulling his horse to a stop, he kept moving forward as if he did not know the danger he posed to them.

Carl immediately stepped in front of Marta and pushed Hans to her side. "You have caught us. You are too intelligent for us."

Sergey leered at them, but he began to rein in his horse. "My eyes they closely watch you always. Forget not this." The sledge in front of them stopped, causing Sergey's horse to rear. He fell into the snow.

Hans began to laugh. Marta tried to hush Hans and hide her own smile as Sergey got up.

"What has happened now to stop the sledges?" asked Carl, biting his lips to hide a smile, but Marta could detect the lightness of his words. "Why don't you both climb back into the sledge, and I'll discover what is amiss."

They passed Sergey and hurried forward. Marta's stomach tightened, though she tried to hold in her mind the comical image of Sergey lying in the snow. Every time they stopped during daylight hours, it meant that something bad had happened.

As soon as Marta and Hans were safely in the sledge, Carl joined the line of men trying to free a large, awkward sled runner from where it was stuck in a drift.

"At least the sledge did not slide down the hill like that wagon two days past," said Herbert.

"Every happenstance has not a good side to it, Herbert," said another man. "Keep thy foolish merriment to thyself." He bent over to dig. Carl found it amusing that Herbert's cheerfulness annoyed some of the others, too.

"Day after day it is the same. The sleds stop and we dig," grumbled another man. "How many days shall pass till we arrive by way of the river?" No one answered. They continued digging.

The problem did not seem serious to Carl. It was not life threatening, and he was in no hurry. He still had a long time left in his

agreement with Marta, whether they reached their destination today or not.

Herbert said, "It is good that we have begun our journey early,
despite these small bothers. Perchance we shall make the settlement in time for spring planting."

That night, after they had set up camp and eaten, Marta joined
Carl for a walk when he mentioned that he had to rid himself of the
crowd for a while.

Marta felt the same way. "It shall be pleasant when we reach our
home at the settlement. Perhaps we shall build some secret passages
in it," she teased. "Truly, were you not frightened abiding alone in
those cold, dark passages?"

"I wasn't alone. I had company aplenty with the spiders and
mice."

Marta shivered.

"Verily, the passages behind the castle walls were my secret, soli-
tary domain. I was *le roi*, the king. No one looked down on me
there. Behind the walls of the castle, I could go anywhere and find
out anything I wanted to know . . . and some things I wish I did not
know."

"I regret that my words reawaken bad memories."

"You have a right to know, since now you are my legal wife." He
took a deep breath. "I overheard the servants as they talked about
me and my parents. That's how I learned that my father had married my mother, but when he learned that she was a Jewess, he had
the marriage annulled. Unfortunately for my mother, I had already
been conceived. So, besides being a Jew, the annulment made me
illegitimate, the illegitimate son of a duke." He said it easily, as if he
were talking about the weather.

Marta continued walking at a steady pace. Carl was nobility, but
he had more reasons to be looked down upon and ignored than
Marta had ever imagined.

"Lord," she prayed silently, "heal those hurts that he tries to
hide. Heal that small boy inside who still wants to be noticed by his
father. Be his true Father."

The next day was like all the rest. By afternoon, another sledge became stuck and the men gathered to free it. Anna and Elisabeth rested peacefully in Frau Doenhof's lap. Marta watched Frau Doenhof stroking Anna's golden hair and gazing at her as if the child were a priceless treasure.

"You care for them so well," said Marta.

Frau Doenhof gave her a ghost of a smile. "No better than ye do Hans."

The men continued to work until they freed the sled runner, whereupon they all climbed back into the sledges and continued on their way. The extra movement of men getting back inside woke Anna and Elisabeth. Anna looked as if she was going to cry.

"Anna, have you a story to tell us?" Marta asked.

"No," said Anna. "My head hurts."

Frau Doenhof felt her head. "No fever."

"I cannot tell a story now," Anna insisted.

"Then I shall tell one," said Hans. "There was a castle where a girl lived."

"You're telling it wrong," said Anna.

"And in another castle lived a boy who liked to wear a crown," continued Hans.

"You tell it wrong!" said Anna.

"Then you tell it," he said. He tapped the walking stick that was always with him now.

"I shall." Anna took a deep breath. "First, you have to begin a story right. The German states have great storytellers. My father said that they always start a good story with: Once upon a time . . ."

Marta observed the forest around them, thick with hardwoods, wild cherry, and alder. She only half listened to Anna's story. She had heard it many times before. It was one of the child's favorites. She ruffled Hans's hair to thank him for distracting Anna. He shook off her hand. He was enjoying the story. Carl and Marta sat beside each other without talking as Anna's tale went on and on and on.

The moment she was done, Hans stood up. "Can we walk now?"

Carl shook his head no.

"Why n—?" He stopped and pointed ahead through a clearing in the dense forest. "What sight is that?"

"There is nothing there," said Anna, straining to see.

"Sit down," said Marta.

"It is the river," said Hans. "I see the river." Marta's and Carl's eyes met. The river? Were they really near enough to see the Volga River? Carl stood, supported by those around him.

"It is the river," said Carl. "We're almost there!" An enormous cheer went up from their sledge, and everyone in it began singing, unable to contain their exuberance. Carl grabbed Marta's hand and squeezed it. Marta's heart leaped. She wished the moment would never end.

Chapter Nineteen

The cart creaked beneath them as Hans asked for the twentieth time, "Have we arrived?"

Marta rubbed his back. "The river seems nearer than it truly is." The wagons had to skirt some marshy areas on the way to the river, which slowed them down considerably.

"You said that yesterday." He sat up as high as he could, trying to see the water in the distance. "We need not spend another night in the woods. We shall reach the river today, shall we not?"

"It's over the next rise," said Carl. Marta hoped he was telling the truth. Soon after they had spotted the river, the sledges began to hit spots where the snow had almost completely melted. Before the day was out, they had had to make camp, remove the runners, and replace them with thick, large wheels. The following morning they had continued their journey, but the wheels repeatedly became wedged in the soggy ground, and they had to stop more often than before. Marta wondered if they could have reached the river more quickly by walking.

Frau Doenhof strained forward, holding Elisabeth and keeping an arm around Anna. Marta did not feel the sense of urgency that the others seemed to feel. Honestly, she was dreading another ketch ride, no matter how exciting everyone kept assuring her it would be. As the wagons moved over the rise, they came upon a large, swollen river, the famous, spiderlike Volga, which stretched its multitudinous legs randomly over the face of the Russian landscape.

"We have reached it," Frau Neussle yelled, startling Elisabeth and making her cry.

"At last, we shall leave the wagons!" cried Frau Kessler. Laughter and voices rose from the wagons, as if the river marked the end of their travels. Marta did not pretend to share their joy. A feeling of foreboding loomed over her, though what she dreaded with such intensity she could not put into words.

"But ice still is upon it," said Hans.

A ketch rested in the middle of the river, apparently frozen in place during the winter, now a crippled reminder of the winter's brutal force. Its hull had been crushed, and the remaining pieces bobbed as if still anchored in place. Marta's heart felt tight in her chest. Their ketch floated amid chunks of ice skipping in the water's current.

Hans continued, "Cannot another way be found? The ice shall sink the ketch."

"Those ice pieces are much smaller than Frau Doenhof's stew pot," Carl assured him, but he touched Marta's arm as if to encourage her, as well. "I shall inquire about the method we must use to go aboard." Marta watched Carl leave their wagon and follow the line of men hurrying forward.

Carl found himself next to Herbert as he moved toward the officials standing near a crude group of huts.

"Good day to thee, Carl," said Herbert.

"Good day?" said Carl teasingly. "How can it possibly be a good day? This cold air makes it a terrible day for boat travel."

Herbert smiled. "On the contrary, this is a perfect day. Can thee not smell the freshness in the air? It invigorates the soul."

"And the ice chunks in the river?" asked Carl.

"Shall force the captain to attend to his job," said Herbert. "A captain must remain alert at all times. Besides that, I have not seen a chunk larger than my hat."

Herr Kessler caught up to them. "I just heard from a soldier that many boats were frozen in the Volga over the winter. Some were ruined."

"They must have hauled immigrants until the last moment," said Carl. "Perhaps that's why there is a shortage of boats now."

Herr Zweig joined them. Carl asked, "How long until we board?"

"Fortunately for us," said Herr Zweig, "we are a nuisance to the

Russians. They wish to rid themselves of us as much as we wish to reach the settlement."

"With our dream finally near, I do envy thee, Carl," Herbert said. Carl was surprised at Herbert's hint that something in life might not be perfect.

Herr Zweig cleared his throat. "Yes, he is blessed with the most beautiful women in this group and three healthy children. What more could a man want?" He turned his attention to another conversation going on beside him.

Herbert lowered his voice so that only Carl could hear him. "I consider thee fortunate, because thou hast the knowledge to escape and return whenever thou chooseth. If I tried, I should end a corpse like Herr Schmidt."

"Herr Schmidt? Didn't he die of the fever in Torzhok?"

Herbert nodded. "That is the story told. I dwelt in a peasant's hut with him. Our hosts were worse than dogs, and Herr Schmidt had had enough. He got cabin fever. The truth is that he tried to escape and was shot down like a rabbit in cold blood."

Carl put a hand on the man's shoulders, and they turned away from the group to discourage others from listening. "I am a happily married man. I shall not leave my family. But I tell you, if I were prone to do so, I might welcome a companion who had given no prior indication of discontent, a companion who is sly and quick."

Herbert smiled. "But as thou sayest, thou shall not leave, and I shall not leave. We shall grow old and fat together with Herr Zweig."

"What say ye?" asked Herr Zweig.

"We but comment on your fine appetite," Carl offered.

"Yes, I do know a good cook when I find one," he said, patting his round stomach. "Oh, there is the man who appears to know what we are to do. Carl, speak to him."

Carl stepped forward and began to address the administrator in Russian, but his mind was contemplating the words just spoken. Herbert was putting on a front just as he was. The man was clever. He appeared motivated. But could he be trusted? If so, Carl would welcome him.

By the time Carl returned to Marta's side, she was extremely worried. "They shall not take us in those rowboats until the pieces of ice are smaller than the cabbage in Frau Doenhof's pot, shall they? What if we should capsize?"

"We choose not our course," said Carl. "We are at the mercy of the Russians." As Marta retrieved their bowls from her supplies, he poured himself a cup of hot sbiten, the drink that Yuriy had taught Frau Doenhof to make. "Tomorrow, midmorning, we shall begin boarding." Carl took a sip of the Russian honey and herb brew, which he had developed a taste for on previous trips to Russia. However, unlike the Russians, he usually enjoyed his during meals. He preferred it to the kwass that the Russians drank with meals.

Frau Doenhof dished out the stew she had prepared. "A boat will be no worse than to be trapped here and killed by wolves."

"Are there wolves here?" asked Hans, wide-eyed. His hand tightened around his walking stick.

"Yes," said Carl, "but they are kind. Before arriving in Torzhok, a pack of wolves watched over me for two days. You can rest easy about them." The group finished their meal with few words, all lost in their own thoughts.

Finally Carl said, "Hans, space will be tight on our ship." His eyes rested on the boy's stick. "You will need to leave it for another." When Hans made no response, Carl and the women set up a makeshift camp and put the children down to sleep.

"Carl, do not tell untruths to Hans." Marta sighed. "He must understand the dangers of the steppes, whether from wolves or other evils."

"He need not know all at once. Not before sleep."

The next morning, when it was Marta's turn to get into the rowboat, she could do so only by sheer force of will.

"You look like a deposed princess facing her execution," whispered Carl as she sat down. Marta wondered if he had seen such a thing. Anna and Hans were on either side of him, and Frau Doenhof sat beside Marta, holding Elisabeth.

The sailors rowed out into the river, amid the floating chunks of ice. The chilly vapors reached up and touched Marta, threatening her with the river's frigidity and power. She held up her chin and tried not to listen to each groan of the boat and the dull clunking of the ice against its sides. She felt as if her journey had come full circle. She had left the German states in a rowboat that kept her barely above the icy fingers of death. Now she would begin the last leg of her journey, and she was again facing the uncertainty of a rowboat. She thought of the Binzes and how much had been lost. She hoped that she and the other settlers would reach their homes soon, for she was losing sight of her dream.

"That one heads right for us," said Hans. Marta looked where he pointed. A large, jagged crust of ice bounced on the river, turbulent with spring runoff. It was the size of Frau Doenhof's stew pot, and it was coming fast. Marta's breath caught in her throat. The sailors didn't see it. They were focused on rowing. Marta touched Carl's hand. He was already watching.

"I do not know how to swim," said Marta in a shaky voice. Carl looked around and picked up the walking stick that Hans had managed to sneak into the boat. He thrust it toward the ice chunk and jousted the obstruction away from the side of the boat.

A sailor noticed and yelled something in Russian. Two oars joined Carl in guiding the ice chunk past the boat.

"Well done, Hans," said Carl. Hans sat up straighter in his seat and kept his eyes on the water.

"There's one," said Hans. Marta looked, but it posed no threat. Hans continued, "And there. And there."

He looked at Marta, a proud smile dancing on his face. Forcing a smile to her mouth, Marta nodded at his excitement, but the constant reminder of their danger made her stomach churn.

When their small craft came alongside the ketch that would carry them down the river to Saratov, Marta wondered how they would ever climb aboard without falling into the river. Carl climbed the rope ladder behind Hans and then Marta, using his body as a barrier in case they should slip. They both made it on deck without incident. Carl quickly climbed down and tied Elisabeth to his body. Then he helped Anna and Frau Doenhof in the same way he had helped the others. Before he boarded, Carl aided several other women and children onto the ketch.

Watching him, Marta felt proud of his courage and kindness. She could do little more than lean on the rail, trying to regain the strength and courage she knew she would need to complete this voyage. She wondered why the final portion of her journey was not bringing more excitement. That's when she saw Herbert, who was the first to climb the rope ladder from another rowboat. He stepped out of the small boat to climb up, but his foot slipped, and he fell into the water. He looked panicked and went under, appearing again on the surface three boat lengths from them.

"Help him!" yelled Marta. Everyone on the edge of the boat began to yell.

"He shan't make it. The water's too cold," said Carl casually.

"Can you not help him?" asked Marta.

Carl chuckled. Immediately, Herbert seemed to get a grip on his panic, and he swam with powerful strokes back to the ketch, dodging ice chunks along the way. Carl helped to pull him up, and Marta placed her patchwork around his broad shoulders.

"What had you thought to do?" asked Carl in an amused voice. Marta gave him a scalding look.

"Everything must be tested." Herbert laughed, but his face changed immediately when soldiers approached them. He now gave the impression that he was half dead and scared out of his wits. Marta shook her head and turned away. Instead of the overly positive man she had thought him to be, Herbert had proven himself a liar just like Carl.

For Carl, the days on the boat were unendurable, day after day, nothing but the river and the forests along its banks, sometimes with cliffs on one side and flatlands on the other; other times with flatlands on both sides. In some places, the Volga was so wide he could not see the shore at all. Every so often, they would pass a city, village, or settlement, but none of the sights in this primitive country could compare with the views he remembered from the Loire or the Seine in his native France. Time and again, the captain stopped at settlements for supplies and repairs while the passengers had to wait on the ketch. Carl suspected that, like their sea captain, the river vessel captain was a greedy man who prolonged the journey in order to sell more food to the passengers. Carl's only relief from boredom was the time he spent with Marta, Hans, and Herbert, who was becoming a friend.

"Herr Ebel," yelled Hans, though they were only a step apart. "I caught a fish so big that we can feed everyone on the ship."

"Hans," said Marta. "Do not exaggerate."

"Fish stories are meant to be exaggerated," said Carl with a laugh.

"If you refuse to help," said Marta, "then say nothing."

Carl took the fishing pole from Hans as Marta took the boy a few steps to a bucket of water to clean his fish. Carl sat down and tossed out the line himself. As the ketch drifted slowly downstream, he watched a barge being hauled upstream by towrope, a sight seen more often now that the ice had melted and the river had begun to slow to its normal, lazy pace. A few tattered boys tugged at the rope, anchoring their bare feet on the rocky shore.

"It is a great day," said Herbert, sitting down beside him.

Not for those poor souls pulling the barge, Carl thought. He turned to Herbert. "Do you intend to take another swim?" Herbert smiled but did not comment.

In a low voice, Herbert said, "When we reach Saratov, I beg you to cause a distraction."

Carl nodded but said, "Do not be foolish."

"I merely test the waters."

"I thought you did that already." Carl chuckled at his own joke.

Herbert smiled, then stood and stretched. "Now I must find a widow who is looking for an extra mouth to feed." He pushed his way between two other families to move away.

Marta returned and sat down next to Carl. She had Elisabeth in her arms. "Is he well?"

"Who? Herbert?" Carl nodded. "How do you fare?"

Marta sighed. "The time seems overlong when we travel by boat."

Carl pulled in his line and wrapped the string around the pole. "And so it is. Where's Hans?"

"I left him with the small Linden girl," she said. "They play near the large coils of rope on the other side of the ketch. Should you stand up, you may see them. Frau Doenhof waits nearby."

"Good." They both looked out into the open river. Carl continued, "This puts me in mind of our time on the ship that bore us to Russia."

"So much time has passed. So much has happened." Marta leaned to the side to accommodate another woman's movements and held Elisabeth closer. "Someday, Hans shall ask about you. I should like to know what to tell him. Tell me of your life, some fact that I know not."

"Like what?"

"I know not. . . . What was your mother like?"

"She was much like you," he said. "Kind, generous. Life for her was like this river in early spring, filled with ice chunks, but she traversed it without complaint. My father gave her a small house on the far end of his land. I lived with her but spent most of my time in the castle."

"It was there that you learned so many languages," she said.

"Here, let me hold her," Carl said, taking Elisabeth.

"I thank you." Marta smiled at him. Perhaps Gretta was right. He might turn out to be a good husband after all. Carl returned her smile, just before Elisabeth spit up on his jacket.

Sergey's boot bumped into Carl's back. "Where plan you go now?"

"We at this moment make plans to escape the boat. We shall walk on water to the shore and then fly with the birds to freedom," said Carl, handing Marta the baby and wiping his jacket.

Sergey's eyes flared. "No disrespect show to soldier of Tsarina." He hit Carl's head with his hand. "My eyes you watch." Carl did not bother to look at him.

"You should not taunt him," said Marta.

"Then what should I do for my pleasure?" he asked.

A commotion drew Marta's attention to the other side of the ketch. People were moving, and then suddenly Hans was in front of her.

"Frau Ebel, come quickly." His face was pale, and his eyes large, dilated. "She hit her head. Her blood spurts out. Help her, Frau Ebel. Please help her!" He pulled her hand. Carl took Elisabeth from Marta, and she moved as quickly as she could through the crowd to where the children had been playing.

By the time Marta reached Hans's friend, there was nothing she could do. The girl's parents were crying over her unmoving body. Blood stained the ropes and their clothes as if it were a dye with a life of its own. Marta watched, but as if in a dream. Her emotions had been overworked on this journey and she felt only numbness at the horror of witnessing another death.

Frau Doenhof was telling the parents between sobs, "She but climbed on the coiled ropes to play. Her foot caught. She fell and hit her head on the chains. I could not stop the flow of blood. I tried. I wanted to go back just moments and say, 'Take ye care, children.' But I could not go back. I could not stop the blood." Frau Doenhof looked older, weighed down with unspeakable sorrow. Herr Zweig's hand rested on her shoulder, and she grasped it as if it were a lifeline to the living.

"No," said Hans beside Marta in a half whisper. "I did not mean to kill her too."

"Speak no such nonsense." Marta picked him up and pushed her way back through the crowd. "You killed no one."

"Yes, I did," he said. "I taught her how to climb there. And I forgot to tell her to watch out for the loose rope."

"'Twas not your fault that she tripped."

"It is like my mama and papa." He suddenly looked at Marta with horror. "Stay away from me," he said, pushing her away. "Or you might die, too."

Marta grabbed him, forcing him to stay in her arms. "None died because of you, Hans. People just die sometimes."

His protests became unintelligible and ended in a jumble of sobs. Marta held him close to her and let him cry. She knew these tears were a long time in coming. At first, his body was tense. Gradually, he relaxed, until finally he clung to her as if he would never let her go.

Carl found them. "I gave Elisabeth to Frau Doenhof. The child seemed to give her comfort. Anna also sits at her side."

"When shall we go ashore to bury—?" Marta asked quietly.

Carl shook his head. "We're headed there now."

When the boat pulled near shore, a group of men left in a row-boat with shovels. Carl was with them. Before long, they had dug a deep hole. The girl's family came next, along with Herr Jaeger to say a few prayers over the child's body while the others watched from the ketch. Marta stood by the boat's rail, holding Hans, much the same way they had stood before Gretta's grave.

"The ground has not been consecrated," said Frau Neussle. "This is truly a god-forsaken land."

Marta tightened her grip on Hans's hand. "Don't listen. Your friend is with God now." She had thought she was strong enough to handle almost anything, but now she felt weak and for the first time, she understood why her mother had given up, had stopped fighting. Marta could no longer fight for her own life, but she had to fight for Hans, and she knew that her help could come only from above. She took a deep breath and continued, "Hans, you are not the one in charge of whether I live or die; God is. You do know that, do you not?"

"I hope you live," he said quietly.

"As do I," said Marta. "And I hope you live, as well." She squeezed him to her side as if she might protect him from whatever might come.

Marta glanced upstream. Some days she could see both shores, but today, the Volga was so broad that she could not see the other bank. It looked like an enormous sea. She forced herself to stand by the ketch's rail and watch Herr Jaeger say a prayer over the child in the distance. She did not know what words he used, but could see him trying to comfort the grieving parents, who sobbed uncontrollably. The mother's wails carried over the water and pierced Marta's heart.

Marta felt lightheaded when she watched the small body of Katarina Linden being lowered into the dark hole. Leaving such a small child in a cold grave was almost unbearable. After the men shoveled the dirt back into place, the family erected a rude cross made out of branches. Then Herr Jaeger and Carl slowly coaxed them back into the rowboat.

When Carl returned, he looked grim and tired.

"Such a cold, thankless grave," Marta said.

"I don't know much about your God," said Carl, "but if I understand correctly, don't you believe that Katarina is with Him now and not feeling the coldness?"

Marta felt her spirit settling. She had let her mind worry about so many things since Gretta's death that she had forgotten who was in control of their lives. She had told Hans the same thing, and yet perhaps it was she who needed to hear it. Marta turned to Carl. For all his talk about not believing in God, she felt a twinge of hope that perhaps, just perhaps, God was also drawing him closer.

"I believe that," said Hans. "And my mama's there. And my papa. Maybe they can take care of Katarina until her family comes."

"That is a good idea," said Marta.

From then on, Hans had a more settled look in his eyes. Still, Marta did not feel completely at peace until many days later when their boat finally docked at Saratov after three more stops to bury others. The town was a coarse, dreary mass of dilapidated buildings and huts that looked as if it held several thousand people.

"Hans, stay with me," said Marta on the morning when they prepared to leave the ship.

"I am a Russian man, not a baby," said Hans.

Marta took a second look at him. Perhaps he was embarrassed about his reaction to Katarina's death. Although Marta felt that they had just come through an enormous pass in their relationship, the boy probably needed some time to regain his self-respect.

"I do not consider you a baby," said Marta. "But we must stay together when we depart the boat. It is a large village, and we do not know it."

"I shall meet you at the end of the dock."

"No, I think we must stay together."

"May I just catch up with Herr Ebel?" he asked, heading for the dock. She was surprised that Carl would have disembarked without her.

She nodded her head. "So be it." The moment Hans was out of sight, Carl came up behind her.

"Where's Hans?" he asked.

"He sought to join you on the dock," she said. "We must find him." She held Anna's hand and took a step forward.

Carl held her arm. "He knew where I was. I spoke to him moments before he talked with you. We shall not go after him."

"But—" Marta began.

"If Hans does not face consequences for his actions, then he shall not learn," said Carl. Marta felt trapped. She did not know how to raise children, especially a boy who lied as often as Hans did. She did not know what was expected of her or what she should do. Frau Doenhof stood stoically by Carl's side, with Elisabeth in her arms. She evidently agreed with his decision.

Marta sighed. Although she remained with Carl, she peered in all directions as they left the ship. Hans! She wanted to call out his name, but did not. Where was he? There were so many people in Saratov compared to the other towns they had visited.

"Keep him safe, Lord," she prayed and held tightly to Anna's hand.

Chapter Twenty

Saratov was even worse than Carl had expected. It was a town coated in a muddy spring thaw, hardly more than a settlement. They walked down the road from the dock, following those who had left the boat before them. Their shoes grew heavier with mud as they went, and Carl noticed Marta's eyes scanning the crowd, no doubt searching for Hans.

"He'll find us when he's ready," Carl assured her. "He's been given a lot of hardships to work through. He may need time to understand the changes in his world." Although his words sounded confident, Carl was growing a little concerned himself. He had not expected this from the child.

"I promised Gretta that I would watch over him," said Marta. "He is but a child. We must find him."

"Stand aside," said a large soldier, forcing Marta, Frau Doenhof, and Anna out of his way and into a mud puddle. Carl bit his tongue. Once the soldier had passed, they returned to drier ground.

"Where are we bound?" Frau Doenhof asked.

"I don't know," said Carl. They met with the rest of their group at what might have been a shed for animals. It smelled of recent use, but at least the ground was dry, and it was large enough for everyone. It was a three-sided structure that would keep the weather from attacking them from above.

"Herr Zweig told us to wait here," said a stern-faced man whom Carl didn't know by name.

Herbert sidled up to Carl. "Can we not do something while we wait?"

Carl knew that Herbert was asking him to create a distraction. "We have been confined for too long," Carl called out. "While the women take a moment's rest, let's have the men and children play a game."

"Yes, a game," cried Herbert before anyone could express disapproval. "The children shall catch the men. No running. You may only walk, and each child must touch the arm, hand, or back of every man in our group before he gets away." He gave them the boundaries and then shouted, "Go!"

Everyone laughed as the children began to pull their fathers and friends into the game. An older woman began a favorite German song, and the other women joined in. Carl saw Marta smile and begin to sing. He led Anna to the center of the group. Why his heart felt so full at that moment, he had no idea.

Out of the corner of his eye, he saw Herbert disappear behind the shed. He laughed out loud. Anna touched him and then hurried to touch the arm of Herr Kessler. Carl could have told Herbert that now was not the time for escape. The settlement had too many soldiers, unkempt men full of their own importance, but Herbert was smart. He would find that out for himself, and unless Carl missed his guess, he would return on his own before long.

Marta watched the game with delight. The men made it fun by trying to escape from the children's touch. It was good for them all to move around after months of overland and boat travel. She loved being in a city, a real city. It was filthy, but there were wooden shops lining the mud-filled lanes, and hundreds and hundreds of huts in all directions, izbas both smaller and larger than Yuriy's. She tried to imagine their new village in a few years. She hoped it would be bustling like Saratov, but more organized and attractive, like a proper German town.

Marta was glad when she saw Herr Zweig returning. It looked as if the children's exuberance was wearing out the men. As Herr Zweig approached from a distance down the crowded street, the children went back to their mothers and grandmothers, and the men gathered to meet him.

"I fear something is amiss," said Frau Doenhof, handing Elisabeth to Marta. "He never scowls in such a way as that." She joined Herr

Zweig. Marta could see that the man was huffing, and his face was flushed. Frau Doenhof and Herr Zweig spoke in low tones until he reached the crowd. Then he raised his voice.

"The Russians have lied to us. Again!" he shouted.

"What trouble now?" a man with frowning eyebrows asked.

"We shall have no wagons to carry us to the settlement, only wood, wheels, shafts, and axles. We shall have to build our own."

The men groaned. "What of our seed? Shall we be able to plant our crops?"

"We shall have wheat, rye, barley, and vegetable seeds, but the planting season shall be almost past once we reach our homes."

"And livestock? We shall have our animals, shan't we?"

"We can hope and pray that we shall. They were vague about how much livestock is available to us. We shall cross the river to Pokrovsk to collect our animals, but we shall receive one more allotment of money to purchase what we need."

"Is our settlement on this side of the river or the other?" asked a man of slight build.

"It is downriver on the opposite shore, the Wiesenseite," said Herr Zweig.

"Then why did they not send us to Pokrovsk?" demanded another man.

"Perhaps due to some confusion, I know not," Herr Zweig replied. "We must cross the river again to reach our settlement."

Marta cringed. Not another boat.

"Then we should not put our wagons together until we have been taken downriver," said Carl. "I suppose we can buy our supplies here."

Herr Zweig nodded. "Yes, at exorbitant prices." He hesitated. "And we have no accommodations. We shall have to find shelter as best we can under this roof in the open air, for as long as we are in Saratov."

"I shall leave this deceitful country at the soonest possible moment," grumbled one man.

"Now, now," said Herbert, appearing as if from nowhere. "That is no way to talk. Our pilgrimage is nearly over. In just a few days, we shall see fulfilled the promise we left our homes to find."

A few people calmed down. Others grumbled among themselves until Carl put a stop to the complaining by encouraging action. "Since we have no choice, Herr Zweig, show us where to collect the bits and pieces of our future."

The crowd broke into family groups to plan for meals and sleeping arrangements, while the men set off to procure the supplies they had been promised.

When Hans had not returned by the midday meal, and Carl had finished hauling his fourth load of goods to their makeshift shelter, Marta said, "Please, Carl, I must find Hans. I fear he has met with some ill fate."

"I'll find him," Carl replied. He turned to leave. "You stay here and guard our goods."

"But Hans is more important than all the goods in the world. I, also, shall search."

Carl walked back to Marta and stood close, his velvet-brown eyes penetrating hers. "In this town filled with soldiers, you are the most valuable of all. Do not go anywhere without me. Stay here with the others."

Marta felt a thrill rising at his words. *Perhaps*—

But she did not let her mind go in that direction. She looked down and concentrated on Elisabeth, who was sleeping between a large bag of winter wheat and a bag of hard beans.

Carl placed a hand on Marta's arm. "Fret not. I shall find him."

"Perhaps we should report his disappearance to Sergey. Then the soldiers could help us search for him."

"Say nary a word of Hans to that viper." Carl turned and left. Marta began praying even harder for Hans and for Carl to find him as she started to go about the task of organizing their supplies.

Frau Doenhof and Anna returned from doing the wash with a group of other women just as Elisabeth woke up. Holding the baby in her arms, Frau Doenhof moved from one barrel or crate to the next, taking stock of what she would have to work with during the coming winter. Marta moved aside a large roll of canvas to look inside the bag of wheat seed that they had brought all the way from Lübeck. Devoid of Carl's secrets, its value had risen in Marta's estimation. She smiled.

"See who I found," said Carl when he returned. Hans was by his side, looking younger than ever.

Marta felt like shouting at the boy and hugging him at the same time, but she gave a curt nod, balancing the two emotions. The child had a large black eye and a rip in the sleeve of his shirt.

"So, you decided to come home." Her maternal side won out, and she opened her arms to him. Hans pushed her away, and Marta felt a twinge of heartbreak.

"I am hungry," he said.

"Then you should have been here for the midday meal," said Frau Doenhof. Hans's face fell. Marta was glad when she saw Anna sidle up to him and give him the crusts of bread that she had saved. After eating, he rested against the bags of seed. Marta let him be, not knowing what else to do. For the rest of the day, she saw Carl only when he dropped off seeds, supplies, or provisions. One load included some tools—a rake, a sickle, hatchets, and an auger. How they would carry so much, she did not know.

Soon a gaunt-faced woman came up to Marta, surveying the goods Carl had accumulated. "How is it that you have twice as much as the rest of us?"

"Do we? If so, perhaps the merchants favor my husband because he speaks Russian," said Marta. "He must be able to get good prices."

"I knew it," said the woman. "They even cheat us of the pittance we were given."

After the woman left, Marta could no longer take Hans's sullen disposition. "You know that your mother would have been very unhappy with your untruthfulness. Why did you not stay with us, and how did you get that blackened eye? You have fought with someone. You disappoint me greatly."

"I disappoint you?" he exclaimed.

"Yes, there is no excuse for your behavior."

The child's eyes welled up with tears, and his mouth quivered. "You are not my mother, and you know nothing." He turned his head away from Marta. She stared at him, but he did not turn his face back to her. Once again, she felt as if she were letting Gretta down, but she did not know what to do to fix their predicament.

Over the next few days, Frau Doenhof kept Anna occupied and the rest of the group well fed with her delicious cooking, and Marta dealt with a sullen, almost unresponsive Hans and a cranky Elisabeth, who must have been growing, because she was always hungry. Carl seemed continually busy, even after his own work was done.

"Herr Ebel, would you help me negotiate for a cow?" asked one man.

"Herr Ebel, tell them that they have charged me double for my seed," demanded another.

It was only in the evenings, when the children had fallen asleep and Frau Doenhof had left for an evening walk, usually under Herr Zweig's protection, that Marta was able to have Carl all to herself.

"Every day we remain here is a day that we lose for sowing," said Carl. Their blanket was spread on the hard ground, and the children were sleeping in front of them.

"So you have become a farmer," said Marta.

"I have done many things in my life," said Carl with a smile. "This season I am a farmer."

"You were once a nobleman."

"The illegitimate son of a nobleman, then a scholar, then a man who learned to survive by whatever means he could, then an agent, then . . ."

"A husband and a father."

He squeezed her elbow and leaned back against a barrel. "I am a man who needs challenges."

"You certainly have them now." Marta pulled the patchwork over her legs. It felt lighter. "The challenge of surviving in Saratov seems to agree with you."

"It gives me great pleasure when I can convince a shop owner to charge someone the right price instead of three times what an item is worth. I enjoy the challenge to provide for you and the children when it seems we're at the end of our resources. I even take delight in the little intrigues in the lives of those around us," he said.

"What intrigues?" asked Marta.

Carl looked around him to make sure no one was listening and then lowered his voice. "Herbert plans to escape our group and head back to the German states."

"What? Why?" asked Marta.

"Shh," said Carl. "Speak in a whisper. His actions amuse me. He is extremely resourceful. He just might succeed."

Marta shook her head. "He has so much to lose."

"Or gain," said Carl. "It matters how one views it."

"The German states stole everything from me," Marta said, then quickly changed the subject. "You spoke of intrigues. What else goes on that I know not of?"

"You know about Frau Doenhof, do you not?"

"Frau Doenhof is not involved in any intrigues," said Marta. She stared at Carl. "Is she?"

He laughed. Frau Doenhof, as if on cue, turned the corner and entered the shed. She sat down between them.

"Always thou keepest me from my wife," said Carl. "And after all the good I have done for thee."

"Work ye thy charms on someone else," she said. "They persuade me not."

"Then perhaps we should speak of Herr Zweig and his charms," teased Carl.

"Watch thy tongue, or ye shan't eat on the morrow," she said, but her voice was not as harsh as Marta would have expected.

Marta felt a laugh rise to her lips, but in the distance, she caught sight of Sergey leaning against a building, watching them. Her mirth drained from her.

"That scoundrel," said Frau Doenhof, following the line of Marta's gaze. "He is the one who brought trouble upon our Hans."

"What?" asked Marta and Carl together.

"Hans told an untruth to ye and ran ahead, but he tarried at the dock's end, as he promised," said Frau Doenhof. "That vermin Sergey took 'im and handed 'im over to a group of street boys who would not let him go. They were hid away when Carl rescued Hans."

"How came you to know this?" Marta asked.

"Herr Zweig heard of it," said Frau Doenhof.

Marta felt her heart plummet. "I have little knowledge of how to raise a young boy, and less wisdom." She turned to Carl. He was returning Sergey's stare, but even with Carl looking directly at him, Sergey continued watching them with blatant disregard for their privacy.

"The lesson was good for him," said Carl, "and no harm was done."

Marta disagreed. A wedge had grown between Hans and her. She knew not whether their relationship could ever be mended.

The next morning, Marta took Hans into a far corner of the shed, where they could talk without others hearing. He held his mouth tightly shut, as if determined not to speak.

"Hans," Marta began, "I now know the truth. It sorrows me that I did not allow you to tell us of your plight. Please forgive me." The boy's lips softened. Tears squeezed from his eyes and dripped slowly down his face. Then his body began to shake, and he started crying in earnest.

"My sweet boy." Marta wrapped her arms around him.

Muffled against her, he said, "My heart feared so. I feared I should die and never come back."

"You are home and safe with us now." She sat him on her lap, reminiscent of when she had held him in the church at the news of his father's death. They had grown from mere acquaintances into family. "My heart, too, trembled with fear."

He looked up at her. "What did you fear?"

"I feared that I had lost you forever, and I could not bear it."

Hans wiped his eyes with his fists. "I am sorry I lied. And I am sorry I said what I said before."

"What?"

"I do want you to be my new mother."

Marta's heart filled nearly to bursting. "I can think of nothing that would give me greater pleasure than to be your mother."

That night, Carl was ready to move on. His family members had settled down on the floor for the night near their pile of provisions. Frau Doenhof and the girls were already asleep amid the stacks.

"If we don't leave soon," Carl whispered to Marta, "Saratov shall have all our money."

"You have done well with what we had. I do not know what we . . . what I would have done without you. Your knowledge of Russian has helped."

"It's not the Russian, it's—" Carl stopped himself.

Marta studied him and then said, "Whatever it is, I thank you."

"These Russians! They steal the people blind and force them into debt. How are the settlers supposed to live with the pittance that shall be left after these vultures get through with them? Almost everything the Russian government promised has been a lie. People have suffered, frozen, starved, and died—all for a lie! It shames me to think that I coerced people to leave their homes . . . made them sign a contract, just to get them here to Russia so that I could collect my fee."

Hans sat up. "The Krautfressers are like you, Herr Ebel."

"Speak not that word, Hans. It is unkind," said Marta.

"The Russians are not like me," said Carl. "I do not rob the poor, people who have barely enough to take them through the winter."

"But you speak untruths," said Hans, "as do they."

Carl's heart sank. "It's different. My words don't hurt anyone. I say what I have to say to stay alive."

"But you said you were my father," said Hans. "That kept no one alive."

Carl thought, *Oh yes it did*, but he knew he could never explain it to the boy without revealing how many had wanted Carl dead, and why. So he said, "You're right. I was wrong, and I apologize."

Hans nodded and lay back down. "I apologize, too." He yawned.

"I want to tell the truth always. My mother begged me not to deceive others. And it makes my second mother sad when I tell untruths." Carl glanced at Marta, whose face creased in a smile at Hans's words.

"Well, Hans, you are wise," said Carl. "And my wife doesn't like me to tell untruths either. So we have settled it. You and I must stop telling untruths. And if we do tell them, then we must remind each other to stop. So be it?"

"So be it," said Hans's soft voice before the heavy breathing of his slumber took over.

The following morning, Herr Zweig informed everyone, "Our group shall join with another group, and we shall depart for the settlement together."

Together, the two groups consisted of about forty people. The men worked collectively to load all of their new belongings on the barges that would take them across to Pokrovsk. At one point during the loading, Marta saw a man coming down the street who was dressed more like a German than a Russian. He looked thin, almost gaunt. He waved his arms as he moved toward them.

He shouted in German, "Brothers from my homeland! Brothers from my homeland!" As some in the group started to look toward him, Sergey and others from the Russian guard stopped the man, but Marta heard him say, "It was lies. All lies!"

"What goes on?" asked Hans. "What calls he to us?"

No one answered, but Marta was certain that the others suspected what she did. More disappointments awaited them. Still, they allowed themselves to be prodded like cattle to the boats.

Frau Doenhof and the children had already entered the vessel when Marta held back. "I cannot travel in another boat."

"This is the last time you need travel over water," Carl assured her. "We arrive next upon the eastern shore. Soon you shall receive your land."

The sound of his words lifted Marta's spirits, and his hand on the small of her back renewed strength to her limbs. "My own land."

"I know something that might distract ye from thy fear of the river," said Frau Doenhof as Marta sat down beside her.

"Frau Doenhof, I—" Marta began.

"Enough of that name," Frau Doenhof said tersely. "We are family. Call me Olga. That is my given name."

"Olga."

"What should I call you?" asked Carl.

"Olga. The name Doenhof belongs to another time and another man. Now I shall be Olga. As for my distraction—"

"Olga, nothing you tell me could have the power to remove my fear of this beast of a river."

"Herr Zweig and I are to be wed."

Marta's breath caught in her throat.

"Look not upon me with such amazement," said Olga in a severe voice.

Marta began to laugh. "Do not be cross with me. I did not expect such good tidings. Oh, my dear Olga, I rejoice with you."

Olga's apparent chagrin turned to a smile. "My thanks to ye."

"When shall we have the ceremony?" asked Marta.

"Before we leave for the settlement. Would you stand up with me as a witness?"

"Of course. It would give me great pleasure." Marta's emotions deteriorated from excitement for Olga to disappointment for herself. "I shall miss you."

Olga harrumphed. "We shall be neighbors." She squeezed Marta's hand. Olga was not like Marta's mother, as Marta had first thought. Olga was a survivor, a woman who had borne more than most, but who still had the strength to take her life and re-create it when hard times came upon her. Marta had a lot to learn from her friend.

To her relief, Marta sensed her future beginning the moment their ship reached the shore. As they left the ketch behind them, Hans held tightly to her hand, Olga held on to Elisabeth and Anna, and the men carried their belongings. The boat had drifted south of the town, so the men had to walk to Pokrovsk to collect their promised livestock. While the women and children waited, Marta and Olga talked of the wedding and their hopes for the future. Then Anna started telling everyone a story about their new village.

As she listened, Marta stood with her back to the river and watched the wild grasses swaying in the breeze on the rolling steppes. Ahead of her lay her providence. A surge of excitement swelled to giddiness within her. She had finally come home. Marta could not yet see the settlement, for it was in the far distance, at least a day's ride away, but she was close enough to know that her journey—its struggles, friendships, joys, and heartbreaks—was almost at an end.

Chapter Twenty-one

Carl and the other men collected their livestock without incident. The Russians' smiling greetings while calling the settlers "Nyemtzy" angered him, but he chose to ignore the insults. It gave him some satisfaction to join the other men in calling the Russians "Dummkopfs" with equal cordiality.

Together, the men drove their livestock around the swampy areas along the shore, back to where the women and children waited. The native Kalmuch ponies were especially troublesome. They had not been trained like the horses in St. Petersburg or those on the western half of the continent.

When they reached the women, Carl's hands drew into fists at his side. Sergey was watching Marta again. The man would not leave her alone. Carl wished he had the power to send that officer, and the eight others from the Russian guard, away for good. Instead, he moved between the soldiers and Marta, blocking Sergey's view.

It had taken most of the day to unload their belongings, collect and secure their animals, and set up a campsite. Carl felt exhausted. "You were a good help to me this day, Hans, but it's time you stopped fooling everyone. You cannot be as young as you appear. You must be at least fifteen, and I'm certain you have worked with animals your entire life." Hans grinned at the compliment.

Marta stood next to their new Kalmuch ponies. "They are a handsome pair." She nodded in the direction of their two cows. "Soon we should have milk."

Carl was glad that he had been able to purchase both a male and a female of each. "It will not be long," he agreed. Both of the females, pony and cow, were pregnant.

He wished he had more energy to build their wagon tonight, but that would have to wait until the morrow. He looked across the river to the opposite bank, the Bergeseite, where hills led upward to a distant treeline. He surveyed the shore for good landing areas. Deep ravines cut into the steep cliffs downstream. He would have to plan his landing well when the time was right. What a contrast between the two banks. On their side of the river, he could see nothing but silvery grasses, blowing in the wind like ocean waves, and a few stunted trees in low areas.

Marta turned to him, her stray hair dancing softly around her beautiful face. "We are almost home."

That night before the group settled down to sleep on the hard ground, everyone stood to watch Herr Zweig and Olga marry. Marta could not believe how much younger Olga looked with the bridal glow of hope shining in her face.

"Dear God," Marta prayed, "bless my friend. Grant her the joy that she deserves. And help me to feel happy for her."

Marta took a deep breath. From the beginning, she had assumed that Olga would make her life miserable, and now she had, not by her presence but her forthcoming absence. For now, Carl was holding Elisabeth, and Anna and Hans were behaving. Somehow, she would find a way to cope alone with all three children.

Just after the wedding, when the Zweigs left for their own area, Anna began to cry, "I want my mother. I want my mother!"

Marta looked at Carl and then back at the child. "Anna—" she began, but did not know what else to say. Anna had not cried for her mother since Torzhok. What had brought this on?

Carl picked her up. "Perhaps it's the change in our family that has set her off." As if following her sister's lead, Elisabeth also began crying.

"Not you too, child," said Marta, trying to comfort her and feeling completely at a loss for what to do.

Olga appeared out of the darkness. "Shush, what mean ye by all this noise?"

"We have it under control," said Marta. "You go on back."

Olga harrumphed, and then turned to Anna. "Would ye like to sleep with me, dear?"

"Yes." The girl released a ragged breath that ended in a hiccup and reached for Olga's hand.

"No," said Marta. "Not tonight. This is your wedding night."

Olga waved her hand as if to ward off a pesky insect. "The child shall be asleep in moments."

Marta shifted Elisabeth to her other shoulder, trying to calm her, but the child's wails increased.

"What of Elisabeth?" Anna asked. "She wants to come, too." Another hiccup.

"Elisabeth could not sleep without her big sister, now could she?" asked Olga, holding out her arms for the baby.

Marta protested, "But Herr Zweig shall not want—"

"Yes, he shall," said Olga. "Herr Zweig knows how I love these two. 'Twas he that sent me to fetch them." As soon as Elisabeth was in Olga's arms, she stopped crying. "Come with me, girls." Olga grabbed Anna's hand, and they faded into the darkness.

Marta sat on the ground, confused and heartsick about the breakup of her family, and yet a small part of her felt relieved. Hans sat beside her and cocked his head to see her face. Then he draped his small arm around her shoulders.

"I shall stay with thee," he said. She turned and folded him in her arms with a soft kiss.

"So shall I," said Carl, positioning himself on the other side of Marta. "Shall I have a kiss too?" Hans began to laugh, and so did Marta.

"You both smell like ponies," she said, pushing them away. Hans smiled, as if she had given him a compliment. Carl shrugged.

"I'll guard the animals tonight," he said. "Sleep well, my family." He stood and disappeared into the darkness. Marta knew that Carl stood sentry not only to guard the animals but also to protect Hans and her. How she loved having him around. Loved? Yes, loved. She watched the stars glimmering in the night sky. Though they floated in a sea of darkness, they still twinkled with joy, just like her.

"Where must I sleep?" asked Hans, interrupting her thoughts.

Marta laid out the patchwork. Hans curled up in it and fell asleep before he even had time to say his evening prayers. Marta picked up another blanket and walked in the direction that Carl had gone, picking her way through sleeping immigrants. Before long she found him.

"What's this?" he asked.

"You must not catch cold."

"Thank you." He placed the blanket over his shoulders. "Is Hans already asleep?"

"Yes." Marta sat on the ground beside him, watching their animals against a background of shooting stars.

"I'm glad Olga took the girls," he said. "I suspected they would miss her, and she them. It was only a matter of time."

"Verily?"

"Yes, but I didn't expect it to be this soon, not on her wedding night." He paused. "Should the Zweigs wish to raise Anna and Elisabeth, would you be in favor of it?"

"Do you think that is their desire?" Marta looked at him and found herself mesmerized by the darkness of his eyes.

"I do," he said.

She pulled her gaze from him. "I would miss them terribly, but honestly, I should be relieved. I did not know how relieved I would feel until Olga took them with her."

"Good," said Carl. "I think Elisabeth and Anna have already accepted Frau Zweig as their substitute mother. You shall still see them. It shall be like you're their favored aunt."

Marta smiled at the thought. She, who had no siblings left, could still be an aunt. *I give You thanks, Lord*, she said in her heart. To Carl she said, "I must return to Hans. He fell asleep almost before his head touched the blanket, but one never knows when children shall wake. I would not want him to be alone or frightened."

Carl gave her arm a squeeze. "May your dreams be pleasant."

Keeping a watchful eye out for Sergey, Marta hurried back to the shelter and fell asleep next to Hans. In the morning, Olga's departure from the household became reality for all of them as Marta dished out the porridge. Though she had done her best, it was lumpy and tasted as unappetizing as it looked.

Hans whispered something to Carl, who answered quietly, "No, Hans. You shall eat it now, or you shall not help me with the animals. Frau Ebel does not need your complaints after she worked hard to cook our morning meal." After they had finished the meal and their belongings were repacked, the men began building the wagons, and Marta went directly to Olga.

"Frau Ebel," called Anna, rushing into her arms as if she had not seen her in days. Marta gave the girl a warm hug.

"Olga," said Marta. "I need your help. Please tell me your cooking secrets."

Olga laughed, a hearty, prolonged chuckle. "That's right. I've tasted thy cooking." She seemed to force the smile from her face. "I regret that my marriage causes hardship for you. To teach you to cook is the least I can do."

They spent the morning going over cooking methods to use and various roots and herbs to add to different foods to enhance their flavors. Marta did not mention the girls, and neither did Olga. They had arrived at the decision without words.

When the time came for the midday meal, Hans looked as if he might complain. But one look from Carl and the words froze on his lips. Marta smiled as she spooned out the stew she had made with Olga's assistance. Hans reluctantly took up his spoon and scooped a small amount of broth into his mouth. The grimace he wore quickly turned to a smile as he thrust his spoon back into his bowl for more. Carl's reaction to the improvement was not quite so obvious, but Marta knew from the slight nod of his head that he too appreciated Olga's lessons.

It took the men two days to get everyone's wagons in working order. On the morning of the third day, they tried to hook their Kalmuch ponies to the wagons. Immediately, some of them bucked and reared. A few kicked until they damaged the wagons they were meant to pull. The men spent a few more hours repairing the damage before they could start for the settlement. Finally, a few men skilled with horses were able to calm all the ponies. Once that task was completed, the immigrant group set out toward their settlement with much singing and pleasant conversation. As the wagons progressed, Marta and her companions watched the horizon. Everyone wanted to be the first to espy the new town.

"I wonder what appearance our house shall have," said Hans. "I hope it is like Raczko's."

By early afternoon, the lead soldier commanded, "*Stoj!*" The wagons halted.

"Why do we stop?" asked Hans.

"Perhaps to let the animals rest." Marta was surprised when the soldiers told them to unload their possessions.

"What meaneth this?" a man shouted. "Where are the houses we were promised?"

"Carpenters shall come," a soldier said.

"Where are we to live until then?"

"You'll have to make do as best you can." The soldier rode a safe distance from the angry crowd. The other officials followed and held their firearms at the ready.

More lies. Marta realized that they would be at the mercy of the wind, sun, rain, and wild animals unless they could build a shelter soon. Except for a few trees near a small river that ran nearby, there was nothing but grassland for as far as they could see. How would they build homes without wood?

The men formed a group to discuss what they would do. Carl was tired by the time he came back to where Marta and Hans waited by their possessions.

"What has been decided?" she asked. He wished she could have been with him to help calm all the bickering and fighting among the disappointed immigrants as they met hour after hour to discuss their situation.

"Tonight and for many nights, we'll sleep in our wagon, since there are just the three of us," he said.

Hans said, "But Anna told me she gets to sleep on the ground under their wagon."

"That is Herr Zweig's choice," said Carl. "Tomorrow, we'll help the women start to dig *zemlyanky*, our homes underground, and pens for our animals. It shall be easier to dig them like caves in the banks of the river or along steeper hillsides. Otherwise we shall have to dig them as a pit in the ground, which would take longer. On the day that follows, we shall begin to clear the fields. Our first priority has to be the fields. Otherwise, we have no hope of bringing in a harvest this year."

Marta looked incredulous. "Dig? You mean we are to live in holes in the ground?"

"For the time being. You said you wanted land. Well now you shall have your land above you, around you, and beneath your feet. It's much more than you ever dreamed, is it not?" He grinned. "From now on, my dear wife, take care what you wish for."

Marta started to laugh, as if the ridiculousness of their situation could no longer be expressed by mere words. Hans joined in. Still chuckling, they started moving their things around in the wagon to prepare places to sleep. Carl decided that they should keep everything they could inside the wagon, so that wild animals would have no reason to bother them. They arranged one edge of the wagon for Marta to guard and the opposite side for Carl.

"Hans," said Carl. "You can lie at the center of the wagon, far from where anything can bother you."

As he was falling asleep, Carl could hear the gurgling of a freshwater spring and the flow of the river—a tributary of the Volga. Tomorrow he would find a site a bit away from the river to start building, perhaps with a steep rise in the land, if he could find one. It would look more like a root cellar than a home, but it would get them through this first winter until they could build decent homes. In his mind, he started planning how he could build an underground home and still keep the rain out.

The following morning, Marta made hot porridge that was much tastier and less lumpy than her first day's. Carl made a point to thank her, and Hans followed his example.

Carl brushed his hands on his legs and stood up. "Now we begin to dig our house."

"But why can we not have one on top of the ground?" asked
Hans.

"We shall someday," said Marta, "but we do not have the lumber
we need to do it."

"Who wants one aboveground when you can have one underneath?" asked Carl. "It shall be an adventure for us." Hans smiled
at him. Carl was glad. He did not want to have to endure the boy's
complaints. They would only remind him of his own.

Taking their possessions along in the wagon, they searched for
a place to build in the thigh-high grassland. Others had already
begun to excavate. The Zweigs were digging on the steep edge of a
dry gully not far from the river.

"So we shall not have to go far for water," explained Herr
Zweig.

"Not me," said Carl. "I prefer higher ground."

"See? We face our home to the south, so we shall get the sun's
warmth longer. We shall have a fine house," said Herr Zweig proudly.

Carl and Marta selected a spot of land convenient to a gurgling
stream, but not close enough to be worried by it. The rise was sufficient, but they would still have to dig down. Hans hurried off
to mark the surface outline of the house he wanted to build. Carl
leaned toward Marta and caught the fragrance of her hair sweet-
ened by the grass-scented wind.

"The house must be large enough to hold the three of us, with
room for cooking and sleeping," he said. "We shall dig another pit
attached to ours for the animals. I doubt that Russian carpenters
shall ever come into this wilderness. We'll start with the cave and
plan to build a real house next summer."

Carl took a sickle and started clearing the tall grass. Hans ran to
them. "That is how big I want it." He pointed to the markers he had
put up. "I have seen a castle that was bigger, but I think a house like
that shall do for us."

Carl laughed. "Hans, even you and I couldn't finish a house that
size before winter. We shall be fortunate to have a cave half the size
of Yuriy's izba."

The three of them took turns digging a large open pit through the thick sod and heavy chestnut-colored soil.

"We'll have to go deep," said Carl.

Marta nodded, but he could tell that she was wondering how they would cover the hole to keep out the rain and snow. "Don't fret," he assured her. "We shall make a good, strong roof."

"Nothing daunts you," she said, "does it?"

"Life is a challenge, if you view it right."

"I shall remember that." Marta looked over their ground. During the summer and part of the fall, their animals would survive in the open, but when the snow came, they would have to be taken inside. It would be so nice to have a second room or cave, she thought with a smile. Then the animals would be protected from the cold and benefit from the heat of their hearth without roaming through her orderly house. Yes, building two adjoining caves, one for them and one for the animals for the winter months, would work fine this first year.

Marta dug the entire day as Carl, who was dragging branches from a grove near the river and cutting them to size, explained to Hans that he would have to watch the animals and prepare their feed. "Do you see all this wild grass?"

Hans nodded.

Carl continued, "Make bundles of it and tie them together with long strands of grass. Make as many grass bundles as you can every single day. When our home is finished, we'll store your bundles in the second pit so that our animals shall have enough food for the winter. We shall need as many as you can make."

"I can do that," said Hans.

"It may be a while before we can call this pit a home," said Marta. "I must start a vegetable garden at once. Then when that is underway, I shall dig on until the house is finished."

Carl told her that before the men could start plowing, they would have to search the groves to find wood strong enough to make plow handles. Only then could they build their plows from the parts they had received. Carl and the other men began their search.

The sun was warm and bright. Marta felt grateful that they had
made it to their land in time for planting season. Between breaking
the sod, planting the vegetable seeds bought at Saratov, and then
digging and fixing food and looking out for Hans, Marta welcomed
the reprieve of shutting her eyes to sleep. Each night, they bedded
down in their wagon, not bothering to make canvas tents as so
many others had. Even as Marta slept, she dreamed of the rough
ground and the insects that she battled daily. The night went by so
fast that it felt as if she had just closed her eyes when the sun rose
on a new day.

She did not complain, though. She knew Carl's work was just as
difficult as hers. The following day as she fought with a particularly
stubborn mass of roots, Carl came up from behind her.

"I now have my own *sokha*," he said, displaying his plow proudly.
"Now I am truly a farmer." His eyes crinkled in laughter.

That afternoon, Carl tried to plow with his Kalmuch ponies,
but he made little headway. The ground was so hard that he, Herr
Zweig, and a few other men had to combine their horses and oxen
just to break through the stringy sod. Marta could only shake her
head at the news. No matter where they turned, they met challenge
after challenge.

Once the garden was in and the men were busy plowing, Marta
began to feel guilty for not offering to take Anna and Elisabeth
back from Olga. One day, after Carl had left to work in the field,
she took Hans, and they went for a short visit to where Olga was
digging her home. Hans and Anna ran off together.

"I must continue to dig our home," said Marta, "but I thought
we should discuss the girls."

Olga did not mince words. "Let them stay with us. They are like
my own now."

Marta hugged her. "I would not be a very good aunt to them if I
did not leave them in the care of the best mother they could have."

Olga hugged her back, tears brimming in her eyes. "I give you
my thanks. I feared I should have to give them up."

After arriving back at the hole that would soon be their home,

Marta spent the day digging while Hans watched the animals, tied bundles of grass for them, and carried dirt away. The sun burned Marta's skin. Her back ached. In the back of her mind, she worried about the intensity of the sun and the dry winds from the south that beat on them and their plants without mercy. As she worked, she began to pray for those around her and their land. By the end of the day, she felt peace, knowing that she was building her future with her own hands.

Carl returned at dusk looking as filthy as she felt. "After we planted the wheat, rye, and barley, we divided the farming parcels, an equal share for each man. I'll show you yours at first light."

Marta could hardly sleep that night, though her body was exhausted. In the morning, after a quick bite of breakfast, Carl took Marta's and Hans's hands in his and walked over the rise to fields that seemed to go on forever. "You're standing on your land."

Marta squeezed his hand as a sense of pride flowed through her. She was home. She was finally home.

"We own all of this?" asked Hans, shielding his eyes from the sun to view the distant horizon.

Carl laughed and swung him onto his shoulders. "No, not all of it. You'd never be able to work all of this alone."

For several days, the men worked out in the fields, the children took care of whatever livestock were not needed for the day, and the women dug their homes. It was lonely work. Marta missed Olga's and Carl's companionship. Yet, day by day, their pit grew to the size it needed to be. From that point, Carl would go to the fields in the morning, but after the midday meal, he stayed with Marta to help her build a roof with limbs and twigs that he pulled from the trees along the river. Once the structure was in place, Marta and Carl stood back and looked at it. The center rose higher than the ends, and the lower eaves were only inches from the ground. They had been fortunate to build their zemlyanky into a slight rise.

Marta said, "It seems a good house, but this roof cannot keep out the rain. Even if it could, the rain and snow might puddle in front of the house and then flow inside and flood our home."

"Then we shall prepare the house to keep out the rain," Carl said. She looked at him oddly but followed his lead. He mixed mud and dry grass together and then plastered the mixture over the limbs and twigs that made up the roof. Marta's neck and back ached each night from working with the heavy materials.

When that was completed, Carl said, "I must return to the fields, but the roof is almost complete. The last step shall be to cover this with another layer of mud, and then with boughs and brush."

"Whence came your knowledge to do this?" asked Marta.

Carl laughed. "In my father's house, I had a tutor who would not be approved in most households. He had traveled with gypsies and nomadic tribes before he returned to civilization. From him, I learned languages, etiquette, and survival skills. He kept me quiet and busy, which was all my father wanted. As a result, I received, let us say, a more interesting education than most of the French nobility."

Marta shyly said, "Perhaps God used him to prepare you for this day."

He smiled. "While you finish our home, I'll work out a drainage plan."

From that moment forward, Carl spent every spare moment designing a drainage system for their house. Because they had built into a rise, he was able to direct water away from the pit's opening by digging a drainage ditch. He dug an enormous hole at their entrance and filled it with many large rocks that he and Hans hauled from the fields. Then he placed wood from a crate over the rocks for them to walk on. Carl surveyed his work and noticed Marta studying his design with a questioning look.

"When it rains, the water shall immediately rush down into our home and flood us out unless it has somewhere else to go," he explained. "Now it shall drain away from us, toward that low area near the creek, after Hans and I dig the ditch the rest of the way."

Marta still said nothing.

"Are you troubled?"

Marta looked at their home with its small doorway positioned several handbreadths above the ditch. "You are so clever!"

Carl couldn't help smiling. "If you think that I am clever, wait for the time when we shall have a pig to butcher. Once butchered, we shall take its bladder, dry it out, and stretch it to make a window." He looked around their handiwork. "It appears we are about ready to move in."

"Oh no," said Marta, "not until we fasten canvas to the ceiling." Carl laughed at her. "What good shall canvas do?"

"It shall keep insects and crumbles of soil out of our food," she said. Carl obliged her. He spent time working out how best to attach the canvas that they had purchased in Saratov. He was glad that the structure was tall enough for Marta. He would not be there for long and so did not mind bending slightly to enter it. Once Carl had a plan, he and Hans pulled more trees from downriver to hold the canvas in place. Marta seemed pleased once her ceiling was secured. Carl did not much care about the canvas, but he was grateful that the cave was cool after working in the sun's incessant heat.

During the next several weeks, Marta, Carl, and Hans worked together all day and often into the night to prepare their home and land for the winter. In the morning they rose at dawn, and at night they were so tired that it seemed to Carl that he closed his eyes and awoke, without ever actually sleeping.

He lay in the stillness listening to Marta's and Hans's breathing on the other side of the room, and bent his arms under his head. He could not help but worry that they had planted their grain crops too late, and that the small vegetable gardens would never produce enough food in time for winter. Even the sunflowers did not seem to be as tall as they should have been at this time of the season, even though Marta and Hans carried water to them from the stream nearby.

The sun had been unrelenting, and the season was extremely dry. Mice were everywhere, eating crops, eating supplies—sometimes he thought he heard their scratching feet even in his dreams. How long would it take, he wondered, to fill a larder with food? He might have to stay for another whole year. He marveled that the feelings of frustration that he had lived with for so long did not envelop him now. Some days, as he surveyed their land and the crops waving in the breeze, he almost acknowledged that a hand far more powerful than his must have fashioned it all. What was that verse? "In the beginning God created the heaven and the earth." Sometimes he wondered why he refused to believe in God, and then the image of his father would rise in his mind, and he would close his thoughts to all that was eternal.

On a day when Carl did not need the horses, Marta and Hans drove their wagon to the banks of the small river. From ragged, wild trees, they picked poor quality apples, plums, and pears to dry.

"We shall also need a great amount of fuel for the winter," Marta said, piling some branches and a dried pad of manure in the wagon. Fortunately, the groves along the river would provide enough firewood for their group. By the time Carl returned for supper, they had the beginnings of a small pile of winter fuel.

"I shall dig a place to store that as soon as I have opportunity," he said. Marta thought about what a wonderful man she had married. It seemed to her that he could do anything. Gretta's words had come true. Carl did make a good husband—and a good father for Hans. If only he could see it. If only he would give up his quest for adventure, or whatever it was he sought after—or ran from.

Every free moment that either of them had, they worked on digging a second pit beside their house for the animals and a third for food storage. Both pits were much smaller than their home and were connected to them by a three-foot thick wall that had one opening. Digging both rooms at once made their progress slow.

Marta collected stiff stalks of grass and reeds and made a broom. As she swept, she told herself, "I will not have a filthy house, even if the floor is made of dirt."

Inside, the house was dark as nighttime. The men had to bend over when standing, but the zemlyanky was home. She was glad that Carl had thought to buy so many candles in Saratov. Who would have guessed how much they would need them?

Carl hurried in from the field. "A storm blows our way. It looks to be a bad one. Lightning has started a grass fire. No one's field has been struck yet, but we must direct the animals inside."

"In here?" asked Hans.

"They shall have to rest here until we finish the cave next to ours," said Carl. "The sky is black. I fear we shall have hail. If the hail's big enough, it might hurt the animals." Marta, Carl, and Hans had just brought in the last of the animals when the massive cloud began releasing its burden.

From their entrance, they looked up to watch the rain falling in torrents. "At least this shall put out any lightning fires," said Hans.

Marta felt her sunburned face. It stung, but she silently thanked God that He had given them good weather for building and sowing, and that she was in her own home with her own husband and child.

Though water rushed at them, it stopped at Carl's drain and then was immediately diverted to the lower ground through the ditch. Marta listened to the water tumbling over the rocks and beating against their makeshift roof.

"Do you think that Anna fares well?" asked Hans. "She trembles at storms." Marta noticed that his voice quivered.

"I sometimes tremble, too," said Carl. He draped his arm around the child.

The storm beat them with rain so violently that Marta was reminded of the night she and Hans had sat in the church together. In her mind's eye, she saw the lines of the good priest's face. Then the storm ended as quickly as it had come.

Marta, Carl, and Hans slowly left their shelter, leading their animals behind them. The drain had worked. It had kept them safe. Not far from them stood a bedraggled Olga, sobbing Anna, soaked Elisabeth, and red-faced Herr Zweig.

"We have lost everything but our animals and what we were able to bear," Herr Zweig said. He pulled his Bible from underneath his coat. "The rest was dragged away by the river."

Chapter Twenty-two

A rainbow appeared in the sky as Marta rushed forward, Hans and Carl on either side of her, mud clinging to their shoes.

"My poor dears," exclaimed Marta, taking Elisabeth from Olga. The drenched six-month-old's clothing immediately soaked Marta's homespun brown dress. "Let's get inside where you can dry off."

Anna was crying but struggling to hold back her tears when Hans grabbed her arm and said, "Why do you cry now?"

"The water scared me," said Anna.

Carl placed a hand on Herr Zweig's shoulder as they moved toward the house. "What has befallen?"

Anna blurted, "The river came into our house and tried to carry me away." Olga nodded, and Marta could feel the horror her friends must have felt, though Olga's face showed nothing. Marta was certain that beneath the tough exterior, Olga was trembling.

Marta led the others down into their house. "It is good you came to us."

Carl added, "You shall stay with us until you've built a new home. And I won't hear any words of refusal."

Herr Zweig's eyes were moist. "I thank you." As he set his few remaining possessions down, he said, "I did not know what was about to take place. The river looked so peaceful. I should have followed your lead and built on higher land."

Carl hooked their door wide open to let in as much light as he could. "The bank was too close to the river for my comfort."

"I wish I had listened to you," said Herr Zweig. He looked at Olga, concerned lines tracing his face.

"It feels good and warm in here, Mama Olga," said Anna. Marta smiled. She waited for her eyes to adjust to the darkness.

Carl lit one of the candles that he had purchased in Saratov. "We'll have to check the fields for damage." He looked at Hans. "Why don't you come with us." Hans tried to hide the smile of self-importance spreading across his face.

"'Twould be best to do so right away," said Herr Zweig. He turned to Olga. "Would that be acceptable to you, my love?"

"Yes, we shall fare well here," she said. "Get ye hence."

After the men left, Olga and Anna changed out of their wet clothes, and Marta hung the garments on their wagon where the sun was once again beating the earth with its rays. In the distance, Marta saw Hans trailing the men as they assessed the flash flood's damage to their crops. By the time Marta returned to the zemlyanky, Olga had changed into a borrowed set of nightclothes and was preparing food, and Elisabeth had shed her blanket and was sitting upright, wearing nothing at all. Anna, dressed in Hans's nightshirt, sat beside her.

"It is good to have you home again," Marta said. "Oh! When did Elisabeth start sitting on her own?"

Olga stopped and looked at the child. "Why, just at this moment." They shared a smile.

"Hello," called a voice from the outside. Olga continued cooking, apparently unconcerned with her appearance. Herbert popped his head in the doorway. "My things were washed away. Would ye have room for one more? I have my animals with me."

"Of course," said Marta. "Carl is in the fields with Herr Zweig."

"Then I shall join them there." He tipped his hat to them and then left. Marta was glad that the water had done its worst while the weather was still warm enough to rebuild.

"He seems a friendly man," said Olga.

"Yes," said Marta, deciding not to express her reservations about him.

Another call came from above.

"Did the river destroy your things, also?" asked Marta when a man appeared at the door. Marta recognized him as Herr Krauss. His family was part of the new group that had joined theirs.

"We have not suffered as much as others," explained Herr Krauss, "but our things are in water to our knees. May we leave our dry belongings here as we try to salvage some of the rest?"

"Of course," said Marta. "And you and your family may stay with us until you find new shelter. 'Twill be crowded, but warm."

"I thank you, Frau Ebel," said Frau Krauss, and they left their belongings in the room. Marta looked around their small, one-room zemlyanky. It would be close inside, but they should be able to fit everyone.

Later, after Olga had changed back into her dried clothing, Marta confided to her, "I know I should feel more sadness at your losses, but I am so grateful that you have come to us again."

Olga was busy preparing food, but she gave Marta a small smile for the kind words.

Leaving to fetch more water, Olga turned back in the doorway. "It pleases me that all is well between ye and thine husband. Good things can come from bad situations."

Marta stood staring at the doorway long after Olga left. She and Carl had fooled even Olga. She felt guilty, but more than that she felt hollow. No one knew.

The first night with others in the house was potentially awkward, but Carl solved their problem. "The women shall sleep together over there, and the men shall sleep here."

Although only a small area of about a pan's length would separate the men from the women, Marta mouthed, "Thank you," to him, and he gave her a wink.

The displaced families spent the entire next day trying to recover what they could from their homes and the river. Marta had her hands full caring for the children, including the four-year-old Krauss twins. Though her home was spacious compared to others, it was not big enough for four families to live in without them constantly getting in one another's way. On the second night, Carl, Herbert, Herr Krauss, and Herr Zweig slept out under the summer sky so they could fully stretch their limbs. Inside, the women were glad for the extra room.

The following morning, Herbert and the Krausses found land where they wanted to rebuild. They had recovered enough of their sodden belongings to continue on their own. Only the Zweigs remained with the Ebels.

"I regret to trouble ye for so long a time," said Olga.

"Say not a word of that," said Marta. "I am grateful for every day that you abide here. We work well together, and I enjoy your company."

"Over and over, I point to good sites for our new home, but Herr Zweig finds fault with each one. To nearly lose all of us filled him with more fear than he wills to confess. He knows we will be safe here." Olga quickly wiped a tear from her face.

"And you do more than your share of the work," said Marta. "The potatoes, watermelon, herbs . . . all do well. There shall be more than enough for both our families for the winter. Fret not. Herr Zweig shall provide a good home for you."

"I hope that shall be so." Olga turned away.

That evening, Olga sent Marta out to call in the men for supper. Marta loved that time of day, when the work was nearly over, and the day was cooling down. Hans ran up to her.

"Is it the time to eat?" he asked.

"It shall be after you call the men and wash your face and hands. You have so much dirt on you today that I can barely see who you are," said Marta.

Hans ran back to Carl and Herr Zweig. "Supper!" He turned and hurried back to Marta. "I shall be washed before you arrive home!" He ran ahead of her.

Herr Zweig hurried past her almost as fast as Hans. Marta waited for Carl as he finished his work and picked up his tools. She took a couple of the smaller implements from him, and they walked back toward their home together in a companionable silence.

Marta stole a sideways look at Carl's face and found him doing the same to her. They both smiled.

"The weather is beautiful this evening," said Marta.

"You are beautiful," he said. Marta breathed in the scents of the fields and treasured Carl's words in her heart. Carl took the tools from her and leaned them against their wagon before following her into the house.

After dinner, Herr Zweig picked up his Bible and read to them, as he had every night since the flood. "This is from Ephesians six. 'Children, obey your parents in the Lord: for this is right. . . .'"

Carl had to work hard to keep from snorting. Why should he have obeyed his despicable father? Marta's God required too much.

Herr Zweig's voice droned on, "And, ye fathers, provoke not your children to wrath: but bring them up in the nurture and admonition of the Lord. . . ."

Carl nodded. He wished his father had heard those words. Yes, that was exactly what his father had needed to hear. Maybe not everything in the Gentile Bible was nonsense. Carl leaned forward and listened to the rest of the reading.

The next day, the sun was again warm and bright. Marta and Olga went out to weed the garden and give the children a chance to run and play. Elisabeth was tied to Olga's back and was soon lulled to sleep by the movement.

To distract herself from going over Carl's compliment about her beauty again and again, Marta asked, "Are you happy in your new life?"

"Herr Zweig is kind." Olga pulled a large weed. "My first husband was a cruel man."

"How long were you wed?" Marta watched a rabbit scamper away.

"Long enough for him to have murdered my children," she said in a quiet voice.

Marta felt the air catch in her throat. "He killed your children? How terrible."

Olga sighed. "I speak not of it to others, but ye are as a sister to me, so I shall tell it to ye. My husband would drink overmuch and then beat me. He beat every one of my precious babies from my body—all four of them—before they had a chance to live. When I tried to flee his wrath, he gave me this." She pointed to the scar on her cheek. "Though it fills me with shame, I felt gladness when he killed himself with drink."

"I hope your future holds only good things, Olga." Marta meant it with everything in her, and she sent up a prayer to that effect. "Perhaps God will grant you more children."

"Perhaps. I already have two beautiful girls, more than I hoped. But I thank ye for thy kind words." She wiped her hands on a cloth. "Now we must attend to our work. Ye must learn how to truly cook for thine husband."

After they had finished working in the fields, Carl paced behind Herr Zweig as he surveyed a piece of property on the other side of the settlement from Carl and Marta's home. "You're going to have to settle for something, Zweig. This is prime property, even better than my own homestead."

Herr Zweig held his chin. "Hmm. It seems good, but it is not as close to water as our old place."

"That convenience cost you your home." Carl picked up a rock and tossed it into the distance.

"Very well. This shall do. We can begin to dig on the morrow."

"We still have three hours of daylight," Carl said. He handed Herr Zweig one of the tools he had brought with him. "We shall begin now."

Herr Zweig paused, studying Carl before putting his own shovel in the ground and beginning to dig. A few hours later, when the men began their journey back to their home, Carl noted that Herr Zweig was walking tall, his posture no longer slouched and unsure. Herr Zweig would recover.

That night, as was his custom, Herr Zweig read aloud from the Bible. "Blessed are the pure in heart: for they shall see God. . . ."

If that's true, then it's hopeless, thought Carl. *I'll never see God.* He noticed that Marta, especially, seemed to like hearing the readings as she and Olga held the children or mended clothing by candle-light. His mother would have liked Marta.

Herr Zweig continued, "Blessed are they which are persecuted for righteousness' sake: for theirs is the kingdom of heaven."

Carl rubbed his chin. He had to respect some of the things he was hearing. He did like the idea of a God who seemed fair, even though this God required much. Carl had heard many religious arguments, but he had not paid attention to the Bible itself, except for memorizing its verses as a boy. He leaned forward and listened once again.

While the Zweigs settled the children for the night, Carl invited Marta to step outside with him. Marta seemed to welcome the chance to leave the confines of their zemlyanky. Caressed by moonlight, she stood near enough for him to feel the warmth of her body.

"The air smells so fresh and good in the open. I can smell the wheat, and the grasses," Marta said. She leaned against him, and then seemed to remember herself and stood straight.

Carl held his arms stiff at his sides to keep from embracing her with all the passion racing through him. He had to force his mind to focus on other thoughts. Finally, he said, "Olga outdid herself on the stew tonight."

Marta seemed delighted. "I made the stew."

"You did?"

"Do not be surprised," she said, laughing. "Olga teaches me many things."

"Then I should not mind if they stay here a bit longer."

The crisis had passed, but Carl knew he would have to do something soon. Marta had become much more than a friend. To keep his word, and his sanity, the arrangements would have to be changed.

For the next few weeks, while Carl and Herr Zweig worked the fields, Marta and Hans helped Olga and Anna dig the Zweig home. Carl planned to complete the adjoining cave for his and Marta's animals after the Zweigs had moved to their new zemlyanky. He felt bad that he could not help with the digging until after the evening meal. With watching the children, tending the gardens, making the meals, and digging, the women had so much work to do already.

The Zweig home was not as big as the Ebel home, but it was just as nice after Carl and Herr Zweig put a drainage system into place, completed the roof, and hung canvas to catch stray bits of dirt that fell from the ceiling.

Marta had looked sad when it was completed. As Herr Zweig read to them for the last time before moving to his new home, Carl's mind wandered. He would miss the company of the Zweigs, and yet he wanted to have his family to himself for the little time that remained. He already knew that he would regret leaving Marta most of all, and found himself wondering what it would be like to truly be her husband for life. She looked up, catching him watching her, and gave him a small smile. He wondered if Marta would miss him.

No more of that, he reminded himself. He turned his mind from Marta to the reading.

Herr Zweig was speaking some words of Jesus. "Think not that I am come to destroy the law, or the prophets: I am not come to destroy, but to fulfil. For verily I say unto you, Till heaven and earth pass, one jot or one tittle shall in no wise pass from the law, till all be fulfilled." Carl wrinkled his brow. It sounded like Jesus was talking about Jewish Law. Carl leaned forward and listened. It was as if God Himself were speaking directly to him about his heritage and the fulfillment of the Jewish Law. By the time the Zweigs left, Carl's mind was filled with many new ideas about Marta's Jesus and His teachings.

The house felt empty to Marta once the Zweigs had moved out, especially after Carl and Herr Zweig left with a group of the men for a half-fortnight trip to Pokrovsk, which the Germans now called Kosakenstadt. Under heavy guard, they went to buy the final provisions they would need for the winter. Marta was grateful that Sergey had gone with the men. She had not seen much of him since they had arrived, but she did not like the idea of Carl being far away with Sergey still close. While Carl was gone, she spent most of the time digging out the animals' cave and a drainage trench for it.

Having Hans around was a comfort. Still, Carl's absence made the days drag for Marta. In the back of her mind, she kept wondering if this was what it would be like when—if—Carl decided to leave. They may not have had a real marriage, but they had settled into a friendship that she thoroughly enjoyed.

When Carl returned, Marta told no one about how her heart leaped at the sight of him or how she could not stop smiling when she was around him. She continued in her daily routine of caring for Hans, cleaning, washing, tending the garden, and putting up food for the long winter ahead.

"We were told that lumber shall be delivered to our settlement in the spring," said Carl. "I hope it's the truth."

"As do I," said Marta.

Carl had brought the necessary ingredients, and she and Olga got together to make cheese, pickles, and many other foods that would be welcome during their long winter. The chores that she had hated at home along the Rhein, like making soap, she now did with pleasure. As she laid the soap cakes out to dry, she laughed at the young filly and the calf that pranced about their land. While she worked, she thought about the new area they were digging in their home, working a little each night to extend their cave. Soon there would be a small pantry, and in the animals' cave there would be a trough for the ponies and a roosting place for the new chickens that Carl had brought back with him. There was so much to do merely to survive the winter that the days were passing quickly. Marta reflected on all she had—a home, a husband, a son, friends, land, and especially the Lord. Life could not be much better than it was at that moment.

Carl ate the last bite of another of Marta's delectable meals, blessing Olga in his thoughts. He had actually missed his wife's cooking during the trip. Then Hans asked a question that threatened to sour his stomach.

"Shall the Kirghiz attack us like they did the other settlers?"

"No," said Carl. "We are too far away and too well protected." He did not want to get into a discussion of the tribe and the rumors that he had heard. Marta did not need to know the horrific details of how the nomadic tribe had raided settlements, caught babies repeatedly on their spears until they died, carried off women and children as slaves, and destroyed everything they couldn't carry with them.

"I heard that they attacked a settlement and killed most of the people," said Marta. "How can we protect ourselves?"

"First," said Carl, "with that fine door that I made for you, the Kirghiz would not be able to enter this home. If ever you see horsemen in the distance, get inside with Hans and bolt the door."

Hans said, "They could dig through the roof."

"We plastered a very thick layer of mud over the top of this house," said Carl. "They count on surprise and speed. They shall not stop to dig. The German settlers in the villages that were attacked lived in homes above the ground. We are much safer this way."

Marta laughed. "And we thought 'twould have been better to have the houses we were promised."

Carl smiled, relieved that the discussion appeared to be over.

When the harvest began, Marta and Hans accompanied Carl to the fields. They worked together day after day to bring in the grain. In the evenings, Carl took long walks to the stream by himself, but Marta didn't mind.

One morning, when the harvest was complete, Marta stirred a pot of millet porridge over the fire. Hans was still asleep. She watched Carl as he ducked to come in from tending the animals. His hair was windblown, and she admired his silhouette against the daylight peaking through their doorway. The days were growing shorter, and she noticed that Carl had been brooding a lot. She tried to remember when it had started. Was it when the Zweigs moved out? Could it be that he missed their company? She stirred the porridge. Then it struck her. It was Olga's cooking he missed. It had to be that!

As if Carl could read her mind, he came over and gently touched her shoulder. "You are a good student, and Olga is a good teacher. The meals you cook for us are delicious."

Marta thrilled at his compliment and his touch. Such mixed-up emotions she felt. It was as if they truly were becoming a family—Carl, Hans, and her. But that would all change if Carl left . . . and she would have to let him go as she had promised. If only he would choose to stay.

He smelled the wildflowers she had woven into her hair. "You remind me more and more of my mother."

Marta liked what she heard. "You must miss her. How did she die?"

Carl sat down hard. "She's not dead, at least as far as I know. But she's dead to me."

Marta stopped stirring. "What do you mean by that?"

Carl stood up and began pacing. "'Twas my father—and that deathbed wish of his. For years, he ignored her and then suddenly she spent every day at his bedside. When it was over, I had lost them both—him to death, and her to—" He stopped and looked at Marta as if he had just remembered she was there. "I shall go awaken Hans."

Marta pulled the porridge off the fire just before it burned. *I have a mother-in-law*, she thought to herself. *Somewhere in the west, I have a relative.* The thought warmed her.

The autumn breeze blew around Carl as he and Hans fished the river. The house was finished. The crop was in. They had enough food to survive the winter and they had enough seed for next year's planting. He had kept his side of the bargain.

Marta, with all her soft womanly ways, was too much for him. If he stayed cooped up with her all winter, he doubted that he could keep his promise to be married to her in name only. He watched Hans pull in a fish.

When the time comes, he'll be ready, Carl thought. Winter would set in soon. They had had good weather later into the fall than was normal, so the harvest had been better than expected. In Saratov, he had heard of other farmers whose crop had been burned by the sun's heat. They had been extremely fortunate in their location. They were probably one of the only settlements this year that would not have to rely on Russian kindness to survive the winter.

"I have it!" Hans pulled the fish onshore. It flopped around in the grass, trying to flip itself back into the stream. "No, you shall not escape." Hans crawled on the ground, trying to catch the fish. He grabbed it, but it kept sliding out of his hands. When he finally caught it, he took a stone and hit it over the head as Carl had taught him. "There. Now we have enough for supper." He grinned at Carl, satisfaction beaming from his face. Carl felt his heart skip a beat.

That night, Marta watched Hans carefully. He seemed out of sorts at supper, but would not tolerate her mothering.

"I am too big for that," he said. "I am a Russian man." Marta was about to draw Carl's attention to Hans's flushed face, but he seemed preoccupied. Was he brooding about his parents again? Or was it all the work he had left to do? Rain had pelted their roof for hours, but Marta could no longer hear it. Carl's work would have to wait until the soil dried.

"His mind is so full of his work—to prepare the soil for next season and store seed, and so much more," she thought. "I must disturb him not."

When she helped Hans prepare for bed that night, he felt almost feverish, but his eyes were bright. "Did you see how big my fish was?"

"Yes, I did."

"'Twas the best tasting fish we have ever eaten, was it not?"

"Yes, it was." Did she dare put her hand to his forehead again? "Let us pray and sleep now. You may speak more of your fish on the morrow." A mouse scurried out from the hay and across the room.

She prayed with Hans and for him, and then joined Carl on the other side of the room in the candlelight. "You seem to fret over something."

"Fret? No, my mind is filled with many things. Has Sergey bothered you lately?"

Marta laughed and shook her head no. "I have not seen him almost since we arrived." A question had been burning in her for days, ever since Carl's outburst. "Would it displease you should I ask you a question?"

He looked at her strangely, eyebrows creased. "You don't usually feel the need to ask my permission."

"I hope you'll not think that I pry needlessly into your private affairs, but I should like to know what fate befell your mother."

Carl's face darkened. "You couldn't possibly understand."

"I have the willingness to try." She stood before him. He studied her eyes, searching them for something. Could it be acceptance? "Whatever you tell me, I shall try with all my might to understand," she said.

He shifted in his seat and then stared at the table as he spoke. "When my father lay on his deathbed, he begged to see both my mother and me. I refused. I was told that he had experienced a great religious conversion. I supposed that he wanted our forgiveness. My mother went to him and soon forgave him. Then she betrayed me, our Jewish people, and all that we had stood for through those years of humiliation." He looked warily at Marta, and then continued, "She yielded to that man's wishes and joined the very group that had rejected her for her whole life." He hesitated again, and then spit out his words with resentment. "She became one of Martin Luther's Reformers. She became a Christian."

Marta wanted to hold him, to tell him that she loved him, that God loved him, and that everything would soon be good for him. Instead, she stood still and silently prayed for wisdom. Quietly she said, "But, Carl, do you not know that Jesus is the Jewish Messiah?"

He stiffened. "I did not expect you to understand."

Enough had been said. She went to the fire and poured him a cup of hot sbiten. "The wind whistles." She set the cup before him. "Do you think another storm approaches?"

"The scent of snow was in the air today."

Marta continued standing beside him, as his wife, his help-mate, his friend in so many ways. Yet now she felt distance growing between them. He was like a boat attached to a line in her hand, floating downstream away from her. She wanted to pull the boat upstream, to bring it close to her, and to climb inside. But she did not know how. "Carl, I do not know why such a battle rages within your soul."

"There is no battle," he said.

"What I mean to say is that I regret the pain you feel because of your mother." He seemed to have retreated into himself and did not respond. She shivered. The wind could not make it through the thick walls, but she suddenly felt cold. "I shall go to bed now."

Carl startled, almost indiscernibly. "No, tarry. Bring me the patchwork."

She did. Deftly, he opened the last three squares. They held gold coins and a few jewels.

"What are these?" she asked.

"I want you to know," he said, "that we are not indebted to the merchants in Saratov or Kosakenstadt, because I had money stored away in your patchwork, a third of the money that my commissioner Goralski owed me. I hid it in here when we were in Oranienbaum."

"No wonder its weight was so great," she said. "Is that the reason we could buy so much more than the others in our group? It had naught to do with your skill with the language."

"My secret and now yours," he said. "I also used some of the money to bribe the merchant thieves in Saratov so that our companions would not have to bear so much debt."

"You are a good and kind man," said Marta softly, her eyes beginning to sting with tears.

Carl placed the coins and jewels from two of the squares in the hiding place where they stored their other money. He replaced the rest of the money in the last patchwork square.

"Good night then," she said. "And I thank you that you have

trusted me with your secrets." She had a terrible urge to lean forward and give him a kiss, but she stopped herself, as if suddenly shy around this man who was her husband. Instead, she took her blanket and rolled herself into it on her bed of wild grasses.

As she drifted off to sleep, she shook off her foolish thoughts of the drifting boat. Carl and she had quarreled, but then he had trusted her with his deepest secrets. They trusted each other as a man and wife should, and every day they grew closer. Had she not seen it many times in his eyes, and in the way his muscles twitched, as if he desired to hold her? Could he know how much she wanted the same? Their relationship was no longer a business arrangement. Carl loved her as she loved him, and she felt sure that he wished to stay. She wondered when he would tell her. Marta could not stop the singing in her heart. If only Carl could know the joy she had found in Jesus. Then, she was certain, they would have a real marriage. She prayed for him, and then fell asleep with a smile on her lips.

Marta startled awake. It was the middle of the night. She had to check on Hans. Something was wrong. She groped her way out of bed to where Hans was sleeping and reached out to touch him. She felt nothing but wild grass. He must have rolled. She felt all around. Perhaps he had wakened and asked to sleep with Carl.

She moved to where Carl slept. The house seemed unusually quiet. She stopped and listened. No movements. No breathing. Nothing. No sound from outside or inside. Suddenly, she started to panic. Was she the only one in the house?

"Carl," she called quietly. When he didn't answer, she tried again, louder this time. "Carl." She lit a taper from the banked embers of the fire. In the dim light, she could see that Carl's bed was empty. The patchwork that she had given back to him to use as a cover was gone. Suddenly, a burning realization flowed from her head to her stomach. He had left her again.

But where was Hans? "Hans," she called out, searching frantically. The cave's door was not bolted. She opened it and peered into the night. Even if he had had to relieve himself, he would not have gone far.

"Carl? Hans?" she called, but heard only the wail of wind gusting through the tall grasses and the icy whisper of snow pummeling the ground. Marta shut the door. She could not let herself dwell on the empty hole that Carl had burned into her with this final betrayal. He had left her and taken her precious boy with him. She pulled off her nightclothes and hurriedly began to dress. She did not bother combing her hair as she pulled on her heavy sheepskin cloak. No matter what it took, she would find that scoundrel and get Hans back.

Chapter Twenty-three

Carl whistled, and Herbert crawled out of his cave into the moonlight. The rain had stopped, but more clouds threatened.

"Only bring what you can carry," said Carl. Herbert held up one item, a bundle of provisions wrapped in a blanket.

Without another word, they skirted the edge of the settlement. When they passed an area within view of Carl and Marta's home, Carl forced himself not to look. His words to her about his parents had seemed weak even to him. He had refused to believe in God because of his own hurts as a child. He shook his head. Was so much in his life based on a child's perspective? He felt himself changing toward Marta, Hans, and perhaps even toward God. It made him feel uncomfortable, out of control. Was he ready to change? Did he want to change? He refused to answer these questions, though they tried to force their way to the surface of his consciousness.

He was glad for a companion, anything or anyone to distract him from the wincing ache in his heart. Herbert touched his arm and dropped to the ground. Carl followed, breaking brittle stalks of wild grass with his weight. Waving their farewell to autumn, the frosted, armlike grasses hid the men as a Russian sentry passed within a stone's throw. It disgusted Carl that these Russians patrolled to keep the immigrants from leaving, and yet they would probably retreat to Saratov or look the other way if raiders attacked the settlement.

After the sentry had gone and the two men were once again moving away from the settlement, Herbert asked, "What hast thou planned?"

"The raft I have been building in the evenings is now complete. I've hidden it in the rushes downstream a few versts from the settlement." Carl gazed at a lone star peeking through the heavy clouds. He hoped the weather would hold until they could cross the river.

Herbert grabbed Carl's arm. "Do you expect us to sail all the way down the Volga on a raft?"

"No, just across it. I've rejected the plan to sail downriver. The men who are after me shall expect me to choose that route. I shall have to travel back to civilization on foot."

"I enjoy a good walk. It is a commendable plan." Herbert sniffed the air. "The sky holds the scent of snow." As if on cue, the wind carried a few flakes past their faces. By the time they were halfway to the raft, a swirl of falling snow surrounded them, as if trying to dissuade them from their purpose.

"If we had waited another month, we probably could have walked across the Volga," said Carl.

"But so could the soldiers," said Herbert. They trudged forward, the snow cutting their cheeks with its icy sharpness. "They shan't be able to track us in this."

By the time they found the raft bobbing violently in the usually sluggish little river that emptied into the Volga, the wind had increased, and snowflakes pelted water and land alike. In the rushes, Carl found the two oars that he had made. The men dropped their sacks onto the raft and clambered aboard.

"Is this a worthy craft?" asked Herbert, looking out over the rough water.

"We shall discover that in time," said Carl with a smile.

Herbert laughed. "What an adventure this ride shall be."

As they untied the rope, Carl thought he heard someone calling his name. In spite of his resolve, he looked in the direction of his former house, but the thick snow veiled his view. Perhaps his guilt was finding a voice. They pushed off from the edge.

At first, the small river's strength surprised Carl, but soon the two men worked as a team to row the platform downstream and into the lazy Volga. Though the surface of the river was relatively calm, the flow was surprisingly strong and relentless, jolting the craft chaotically.

The men let the current carry them downstream as they rowed at a diagonal, following the river's curve and using its force to propel them toward the opposite bank.

"We have traveled over halfway across," shouted Herbert.

"Always the optimist." Carl could not see anything ahead of them, even with the added light from the falling snow. They had begun a perilous journey. Still, he enjoyed feeling the thrill of battle against the river's icy touch. Carl could understand struggles like this. The river wanted to kill them. They wanted to survive. Everything was straightforward. It was a question of life and death, not love and responsibility. Still he thought of Marta, Hans, and his mother's God, and his heart roiled like the river.

Their raft caught a shoal, and they were hurled forward. Carl positioned his oar to try to control the raft, but it was too late. It rammed into a boulder hidden just beneath the surface. The end of the raft flipped into the air.

"Hold fast!" Carl tried to grab onto the wood, but his hands slipped, and he sank into the Volga with all his possessions. Water flooded his mouth and nose as he tried to catch his breath. The slow but relentless current pulled him deeper. In the midst of his panic, he saw his gentle mother's face calling to him, begging him to forgive his enemies as she had forgiven his father. He struggled out of his thick fur coat and tried to propel himself to the surface. He felt the weight of his legs. They kicked, but something heavy had attached itself to his boot. He reached down and yanked off the patchwork that held his belongings. Fighting the icy water that pummeled him in all directions, he tried to move upward, but was suddenly unsure which way was up. He gave a mighty kick. Instead of his head breaking the water's surface, he hit something hard. It sounded like wood. Even in his muddled state, he realized that he was underneath the raft and out of air!

"I'm not ready to die," his mind screamed as the darkness threatened to overtake him. Suddenly a realization seeped into his semiconsciousness. Only the power that had parted the Red Sea for his people could save him now.

"God, help me," he cried, his mouth filling with water. "Please."

⟋ℰ⟍

Marta darted through the wild grasses around her, knocking them down like villains that were holding her son hostage. "Hans! Hans!" She knew that she probably should have wakened others and reported her errant husband to the officials, but she would not betray Carl even now.

Most of the night, she searched for Hans, moving farther and farther from the settlement. As she prayed, she found herself edging toward the river. The snow had blanketed the entire landscape, making indistinguishable mounds all over the area.

As she scanned the sea of whiteness before her, she saw something dark protruding from a berm—a shoe. "Hans?" She hurried to it. "Please, God, let him be alive." She brushed the icy shroud of snow from the mound. It was Hans! She felt for a heartbeat. He was alive. She removed her cloak and wrapped him in it. With strength that she didn't know she possessed, she carried him back to their zemlyanky.

Once there, she began her vigil. Hans lay, unmoving, eyes shut, barely breathing. His fever threatened to burn still hotter. She kept a cloth soaked in melted snow on his brow, repeatedly changing it with a new one, and tried to warm the rest of his body with blankets.

"Hans, awaken," begged Marta through parched lips. Hans groaned. Beads of sweat covered his face.

She had so many questions, and no one to ask. She felt so helpless, so alone . . . no, not entirely alone. She recalled Gretta's words. "Ye shall never be alone or unprotected again."

"Lord," she said, "I know not why Carl left Hans in the open, but should Hans die, I believe that I shall not find forgiveness and mercy in my heart for Carl." Even as she said it, she felt God urging her to forgive Carl. She argued, "But I have forgiven him so much already. How much more must I forgive? How much more?"

"How much have I forgiven you?" Her spirit heard, but she ignored it. Hans needed her attention now.

As the storm raged outside, Marta battled Hans's fever and her emotions. Once his body warmed, it grew as hot as his forehead. Every couple of hours, she would crawl out of the cave and fill a bucket with more snow so she could wipe down Hans's face and body, trying to keep him alive. Only once did she leave to feed the animals and bring them into the adjoining cave. The winter had begun. Their survival was in her hands. She stopped. No, their survival was in God's hands.

After cooking a small pot of soup and trying to slide some of the broth down Hans's throat, she kept a vigil by his side. She prayed for his healing, but it felt to her that her prayers lodged in the cave's thick walls, never penetrating its roof. Perhaps her prayers reached heaven, but she felt that her connection with God had been lost. She sighed.

Nights and days passed, but time made little difference to Marta. Wretchedness had displaced joy; hopelessness had supplanted faith. She longed for the comfort she had felt during Herr Zweig's Bible readings when her family surrounded her.

"Where are You, Lord?" she prayed. "I need You."

As if in answer, a verse from Scripture came to mind. "And grieve not the holy Spirit of God, whereby ye are sealed unto the day of redemption. Let all bitterness, and wrath, and anger, and clamour, and evil speaking, be put away from you, with all malice: And be ye kind one to another, tenderhearted, forgiving one another, even as God for Christ's sake hath forgiven you."

In her heart of hearts, Marta knew she would have to forgive Carl. "I cannot do it." She wearily leaned her head against the wall near where Hans slept. She heard footsteps outside her door.

"Carl?" she called, but her throat felt dry. She checked to be certain that Hans was still breathing and then hurried to the door.

Olga entered, snow covering her clothing and the shawl over her head. "What has taken place here?"

Marta looked down at herself. She had not combed her hair or changed out of her clothes since she had found Hans.

"Hans," was all she could say.

Olga set down her bundle, and Marta stared at it in horror. It was Carl's pack, with the patchwork tied around his things. It was wet and muddy, but it was his.

"I shall tend to Hans. Ye rest," Olga said.

Marta nodded, but instead of resting, she knelt down and touched the patchwork.

Olga put an arm on her shoulder. "Herr Zweig went out to hunt meat by way of the Volga and found it downriver early this morning."

Marta emptied the patchwork of its wet contents. Carl's extra shirt. His comb. A day's supply of food. His knife. Tears welled in her eyes. The only thing worse than knowing that Carl had left her was knowing that he had left the world, that there was no possible chance of ever seeing him again.

Why? Why, Lord, did You take him from me? I need him alive. Now there is no hope that he shall return to me. And I shall never have the chance to forgive him, thought Marta. She was not certain how she made it from the door to where she slept. Memories of her times with Carl, both good and bad, flashed through her mind as feelings of tenderness and anger waged war in her soul. *Why was he so foolish to cross the Volga in a storm? Why did he not at least wait until spring? Why did God let this happen?* Somewhere amid her pain, she fell into a dreamless sleep.

When she opened her eyes, she felt as if she had not slept at all.

"I have placed food for ye on the table," said Olga. Marta took the time to comb her hair and pull it back into place. She went to the table and tried to eat, but even Olga's excellent cooking could not entice her. She felt as if she had died, and yet she still lived. Carl was dead, and Hans was dying. What was left for her?

"I am," she heard a voice say deep in her spirit. "Am I not enough?"

She shook it off. "How does Hans fare?" she asked Olga.

"Not good. But every breath is a sigh of hope."

Marta went to his side. All color had left his cheeks. His breathing continued ragged and shallow. "If you need to return to the children, I can tend to Hans."

"Now, now," said Olga in her gruffest voice, clearing her throat once. "Herr Zweig chose to watch the children so that he did not have to bear the bad tidings of Carl to you. I shall abide with ye a bit longer."

"I thank God that you have come." Marta wrung out a cloth and dipped it in cold water.

Hours later, when Marta went outside to collect more snow, she was surprised to find Herr Zweig sliding down into her entryway.

"Where are the children?" asked Marta, but he pushed past her, yelling.

"Olga! Olga! Come! Make haste!"

Marta followed him inside.

Olga looked up. "What is the trouble now?"

"Elisabeth." His eyes were wild with the same look they had held the day that his wife died on the ship in the Baltic. Marta clutched her chest. Not more bad tidings. She could take no more.

"What of Elisabeth?" asked Olga. "Tell me of her at once."

"I cannot wake her. Her breaths barely come. She must be about to die. Our baby girl is about to die!"

— ဢ —

Carl felt himself drawn down, darkness pulling him deeper and deeper. His world went black, and then he startled awake. It was nearly morning. He was on solid ground. What had happened?

He looked at Herbert sleeping beside him. Herbert must have saved him. Then he remembered the two strong arms that had pulled him onto the raft. All Herbert had said was, "I thought I had lost thee. I prayed. I have not prayed for many a day."

Then somehow they had managed to make it to shore. The memory of the previous night haunted him, not only because he had almost died, but also because he had asked for God's help and in the next moment, Herbert's hands had found him. Carl had not even caught a cold, although he had nothing to keep him warm. Why would God, whom he had denied most of his life, help him? Could he trust this heavenly Father in a way that he could not trust his earthly father? Carl shivered, regretting that he and Herbert had lost all of their possessions in the river. He would need a warm coat—they both would—to survive. He was glad the weather had warmed a little, but he would have to find a coat soon.

Carl heard movement from the direction of a nearby encampment of nomads. He shook Herbert, holding a hand over his mouth to keep him quiet. Silently, they prepared to follow the procession of the Khirgiz tribe they had spotted two days before. Carl's stomach growled. If only they had not lost all their food to the river!

The nomads, who had already done so much evil, had obviously pillaged a village recently, for they were heavily laden with extra ponies and wrapped bundles. As the warriors passed through the snow, not even their horses' hooves made a sound. Carl and Herbert had been following them since shortly after they had arrived on the western shore. Although they were across the river from Marta's settlement, it unnerved Carl to think how close this menace was to Marta and Hans.

After several hours, Carl nodded to Herbert, indicating that he wanted him to go farther to his right. Herbert immediately complied. Carl had no idea how he had managed to find a companion as skilled and even-keeled as Herbert. First the river, and now this. They faced an even more ominous danger as they moved in closer to this group of warriors.

The last man in the procession had let three of the ponies fall behind the day before. Carl had not taken them then, but even last night when the group made camp, they did not go searching for the ponies, which seemed odd to Carl. It was almost as if the men had collected so much plunder that they were not concerned about losing a few stray animals. Now the ponies were a good two versts behind and beginning to veer in another direction. If this tribe no

longer wanted them, then Carl did. By midday, it was obvious that
the warriors had no intention of searching for the beasts. Carl and
Herbert slowly fell behind and then made their way back to the
heavily laden beasts. When they caught up with the animals, the
ponies were digging beneath the snow to feed on the tall grasses,
which were bent over by the weight of the snow.

"Easy boy," said Herbert, as if taking stray animals were his
trade. Before long, they each had a pony. The bags hanging from
the animals' sides were filled with furs, blankets, and food! They
each grabbed some hardtack and dried fruit, and then wrapped
themselves in fur, tying it on with strips of blankets.

Once settled, they began riding carefully in the opposite direction of the warriors. The snow was only a forearm's length deep in
most places. To their surprise, no one followed. That made Carl
wary. Why had the nomads let the ponies get away?

"We are extremely fortunate," said Herbert later that evening as
they made a small fortress of snow as a shield from the wind. "It is
as if God's hand is with us, ever since the river."

"Perhaps the warriors were in too much haste to find the beasts,"
said Carl, but a warning sounded in the back of his mind.

As they settled down to sleep, Carl valiantly fought off images of
Marta and then Hans.

"He's so young," Carl scolded himself. "How could you lay so
great a burden on his small shoulders? Your father abandoned you,
and now you've deserted a boy who is more your son than you ever
were to your father." He hoped that Hans would not use him as an
excuse to keep from living a good life. Carl sat up. *Is that what I've
done?* he wondered. It was true. He had used his father as an excuse
to turn away from God, the God of his childhood, Israel's God.
Through his own pride, he had allowed his father to rob him of his
heritage.

Carl leaned against a tree, breathing the fir-scented air as darkness slid over them. Countless stars salted the heavens, making mil-
lions of diamond-like sparkles on the snow. They reminded him of
God's promise to Abraham, to make his descendants as numerous

as the stars. He remembered his mother repeating that promise. He could almost hear his childhood reply, "I am one of them, Mama. And so are you."

Another voice forced itself on his memory, Herr Zweig reading his Bible. "Your father Abraham rejoiced to see my day: and he saw *it,* and was glad." Then he heard, "Jesus said unto them, 'Verily, verily, I say unto you, Before Abraham was, I am.'"

"I Am," God's name revealed to Moses. It had angered Carl to think that Jesus called Himself God. Marta had defended Him, saying that Jesus was God in human flesh, come to earth to sacrifice His life to pay for all the sins of the world. To pay for everything Carl had done. Could such a thing be possible? The words of Isaiah stated that God was Israel's Redeemer. The Shema, the watchword of Israel, came back to him. "Hear, O Israel: The LORD our God *is* one LORD."

If God is one, then how could He have a Son? He remembered asking that same question as a youth when he read the prophecy of Agur, son of Jakeh, in one of the proverbs of Israel. "Who hath ascended up into heaven, or descended? who hath gathered the wind in his fists? who hath bound the waters in a garment? who hath established all the ends of the earth? what *is* his name, and what *is* his son's name, if thou canst tell?" The words still puzzled him.

Herbert stirred. "What ails thee? Canst thou not sleep?"

"My thoughts won't allow sleep to come." To escape his thoughts, Carl asked Herbert, "For what cause do you choose to leave Russia?"

"When I came to this country, I left my parents, my siblings, and the young woman I loved, all for the promise of wealth and adventure. I was a fool. Now I return home."

"We're all fools."

"Why didst thou choose to leave?" asked Herbert.

"I don't belong here," said Carl. "I was a Jew among Reformers."

If Herbert was surprised by Carl's revelation, he hid it well. "Thou art a fellow immigrant. That is all that matters."

Carl gave him a strange look. What was it with these immigrants and their ability to accept him? He had not found such acceptance anywhere.

Herbert continued, "Are you a Jew by birth or religion?"

"My mother was a Jew."

"Your nationality is Jewish. But what of your faith? That is the question you must answer. I have not followed God well, but I have in mind to change. To almost lose my life in the river makes me reconsider how I have lived. I am not a good man, and the weight of my sins feels like a heavy burden laid across my back." Herbert settled back down to sleep.

Carl, too, felt like he carried a huge weight on his shoulders. He had never thought of what he had done as sin. As he lay awake, his mind traced over the years. Money, success, revenge, and his pride had always been paramount. "Thou shalt have no other gods before me." He remembered reciting the Ten Commandments as a child, and he reviewed them now, one by one, recalling the countless times he had disobeyed God. For the first time in his life, he realized that God was holy, and that he, Carl, was a sinner. He shuddered to think of what would happen to him if God gave him what he deserved. He covered his face with his hands and begged silently from the depths of his soul, "God, have mercy on me."

How weary Carl felt, weary of always fighting, of always trying to get the upper hand, of forever being alone. Words of Jesus that had haunted him from the first time he heard them came back to him now. "Come unto me, all ye that labour and are heavy laden, and I will give you rest." Carl's heart stirred. These were the words of the Jewish Messiah. Oh how he wanted to believe they were true! He needed that rest.

"Carl," he heard in his heart. He turned over. "Carl," he heard again. He started to cover his ears, and then remembered the story of Samuel. Could God be calling Carl as He called Samuel? "Carl, listen to Me," he heard deep inside.

"I'm listening," he silently spoke to the inner voice that would not leave him alone.

"You shall not take vengeance. Vengeance is Mine."

Carl recognized the words from his early study of the Law and Prophets. In the starlit sky, he imagined he saw the faces of Goralski, of Quentin, of his father. He felt his anger beginning to surge, but he suppressed it. He released a profound sigh. "I shall no longer seek my revenge. I give my enemies to You," he said in his heart, and a huge weight began to lift from him. Suddenly, the words of the prophets filled his mind, more verses his mother had made him memorize when he was a child and then after them, verses he had heard from the Reformers.

"But with everlasting kindness I will have mercy on thee, saith the LORD thy Redeemer."

Could he dare to believe that God loved him enough to forgive all he had done wrong?

"But he was wounded for our transgressions, he was bruised for our iniquities." According to Herr Jaeger these words were written by the Jewish prophet Isaiah. But who did Isaiah mean? Who was wounded? Carl remembered the nightly Bible readings when the Zweigs stayed with the Ebels. He recalled the words, the miracles, the life, the death, and the resurrection of Jesus. It could be no one else. Carl sat up. *Truly Jesus is the Messiah, God the Son!*

Carl wanted to stand up and shout, but he stopped himself. He wasn't sure if it was a scent, a sound, or just his intuition, but he could feel the air changing, charged with danger. A distant thought broke through and exploded in his mind. What if there were two parties of Khirgiz warriors? The first group had let the ponies wander because they knew the second group would eventually pick them up on their way. Someone had told him, perhaps Herr Zweig, that these warriors often traveled that way.

Herbert's eyes opened and shifted from side to side as if he too were sensing the danger. He sat up. A Khirgiz warrior jumped out in front of them. Carl and Herbert rose at the same time. Another warrior jumped from behind and a third moved in from the side. Only three. Carl was relieved.

Carl drew up his hand to defend himself from the first attacker.

He landed a blow to the man's face. Carl was fighting for his life, getting hit, rolling in the snow, and charging forward.

Herbert ducked out of the way of a stick and Carl took a blow in the ribs. He bumped into Herbert and stumbled, just missing a deadly strike to his heart from one of the warriors. Carl took a hit on his side, then wheeled into his attacker with a powerful punch. He tripped a man about to beat Herbert on the head and ducked to miss a blow aimed at him. Carl smiled. He no longer feared death, because he now belonged to God.

Suddenly from behind, Carl felt a warrior hovering over him. He reeled to face him just as the giant bore down on him.

Chapter Twenty-four

Olga took off her apron and set down her spoon. "I shall leave ye now. I know ye understand I must leave."

Marta nodded, although she did not think either of the Zweigs saw her.

"Left ye our girls alone?" asked Olga. Marta tilted Hans's fevered head and very slowly dripped a few drops of broth into his mouth.

"No, of course not," said Herr Zweig. His voice faded behind the closed door. "Our neighbor . . ." Hans coughed up the spoonful, spilling it on his covers.

Marta looked around the empty room. She would need to latch the door as soon as she collected another bucketful of snow. She left Hans's side to get the bucket. The door opened. Because she was expecting one of the Zweigs, her mind took a moment to comprehend who stood before her, yet she immediately found it hard to breathe, and the room felt as if it were closing in on her. Sergey stood in the doorway, his frame outlined by the whiteness of the snow until he shut the door behind him.

"Frau Ebel," he said in a low voice. He stepped forward. "Your husband is again away?"

She had to think fast. "It was good of you to come, under the circumstances," she said. Her words stopped him. She could tell that he had not expected her to be calm. She had to get to the stick she used to stir the fire. Where was it?

"I expect not welcome," he said.

There it was by the oven. "Friends are always welcome." Marta took a small step toward the oven as if shifting her weight.

"I desire not friendship only," he said with a nervous laugh. "I would better care for you than husband who is not good. I show love at you, and leave ye not alone."

"He is still my husband, good or bad," she said, hoping her voice would remain steady. He moved toward her. She continued quickly, forcing her voice to remain low, "It surprises me that you entered under our roof, when death is so close to our door." She took another small step toward the oven.

Sergey stopped. "What trick is this of you?"

As if on cue, Hans's breathing grew audibly ragged again. Her fear of losing Hans far outweighed her fear of Sergey. Marta dropped the bucket and hurried to Hans's side. She would continue fighting death with the same vehemence she would fight Sergey if he came any closer.

"I need snow," said Marta, letting panic rise in her voice, "to bring down his fever." Hans's face felt terribly hot to her touch. She heard the door slam behind her and breathed a sigh of relief. Quickly, she rushed to the door to bolt it, but before she could, it opened again. Sergey stood with a bucket of snow. He handed it to her and then took a step back.

"When snow you need, set bucket out of door," he said in a gruff voice. He closed the door behind him. Marta's eyes grew large. Sergey, the man she had feared the most, was helping her. She took the snow and immediately put some in her cloth to wipe across Hans's forehead and body. She had to get his fever to break. All night, Sergey provided snow for Marta. Although she did not understand the kindness Sergey was bestowing on her, she thanked God for His provision. Each time she took in a new bucket of snow, she wondered about Sergey. Did he truly care for her as he seemed to be telling her? Beneath his rough exterior, was Sergey truly a good man?

As the sun began to rise, Marta dozed. It was only then that the reality of her new life closed in on her. She had lost Carl. She was losing Hans. The day she had dreamed about so long ago was about to dawn—she would be a single woman landowner in Russia—and yet this was not what she wanted. Her heart was shredded by her love for what had been her new family. Why had God taken them away? No, she realized, God was all she had left. She ached for His comfort. Why had she pushed Him away when she needed Him most?

"I feel so wretched, Lord. Please forgive me," she whispered. "You have forgiven me of so many sins, and yet when You asked me to forgive Carl, I refused. And now it is too late. I know not how I could have forgiven him for all the heartache he brought upon me, but because You asked me to forgive, I would have tried. Please help me, Lord, to be close to You again."

The door opened, and Sergey appeared again. Marta struggled to her feet to thank him, but this time he did not bring snow. He dragged in Carl, holding him by the scruff of his neck.

A shrill sound escaped Marta's lips. Was she dreaming? "Carl? You are alive!"

"Get husband to work do for you," Sergey said.

Marta took a step forward, but she could not think. Was she hallucinating? Carl was dead. How could he be here? The room felt as if it were moving beneath her. She could not catch her breath.

Carl lunged forward to break Marta's fall. He held her limp body in his arms, cursing himself for handling everything wrong.

"Next you try escape," said Sergey, "I kill you." He looked at Marta. "You deserve not such good woman." He slammed the door behind him.

Carl gently lowered Marta onto her wild grass bed. As he looked at her, trying to decide the best way to explain the last few days, he heard the sound of Hans's raspy breathing. What had happened while he was gone? He hurried to the child's side and felt his head. Hans was burning with fever.

Marta moaned.

"All shall be well," he said more to himself than Marta.

"Are you a ghost?" she asked, holding her head.

"No. I've come home," he said.

Marta gave a bitter laugh. All her resolve to forgive him flew from her heart. "You and your lies. For months I begged God to urge you to stay with us." She closed her eyes.

"How came Hans to be so ill?"

"He must have followed you. I found him covered with snow. Herr Mueller, you have robbed us for the last time. You stole his affection and then abandoned him. Now it shall cost him his life, and you shall have taken from me the only family I had left. We no longer need your deceitfulness or your help. Go away and never return."

Carl knew he deserved her words, but things had changed. He no longer wanted to leave her—ever. Somehow, he had to make her understand.

"You're tired," he said. Although Carl had not rested in far too long, he felt more alive than he had since he left. "Rest quietly. I shall see to Hans."

"Do not command me," said Marta, her eyes flashing. "You have not the right. The day Olga brought your things to me, the ones Herr Zweig found along the river, that was the day Carl Ebel died."

Carl had never heard such bitterness from Marta. This latest damage to their relationship might not be repairable, but this time it really mattered to him. He closed his eyes. He had to win her back. It might take years, but they would become the family that he knew they could be—they must be.

"What do you want from me?" he asked in a low voice.

"I want you to do what you do best. I want you to leave." She rubbed her forehead. She was so tired. She should not be having this conversation now. She was shaken, weak, and so very tired. "I told you that should you leave me again, you must never come back. You promised. You have lied to me yet again. You have no place in my household."

"That was only part of my promise," said Carl. Hans's ragged breathing concerned him. "Marta, I regret that I cannot do as you bid me. First, I shall care for Hans, and then I shall convince you, somehow, that you cannot rid yourself of me."

She moved to the door and draped her cloak around her shoulders. "Of course you shan't leave now. Not in winter. I don't wish your death from the cold. Come spring, though, you shall do as you have always done." She opened the door. "Hans is near death and so is Elisabeth. If you remain to tend to Hans, then I shall say farewell to my niece."

"I'll be here," said Carl. The door slammed shut.

Carl tried to pull his thoughts together. He could not think of Marta. He had to save Hans, and then he would do what he could for Elisabeth. Carl searched his memory, trying desperately to remember what his mother had done for his childhood fevers. He seemed to recall herbs and poultices, onions and garlic. He didn't remember most of the names or what the plants looked like, but he remembered the odors. He remembered how she had had him make poultices every day for his dying father. Yes, that was it. If only he could find the right ingredients. "Please, God of Abraham, guide me to them," he prayed as he started rifling through Marta's stores.

Marta knocked on Olga's door, and it was opened quickly.

"Marta! What—?" Olga said with alarm. "Hans has not—"

"My husband has returned from the dead," said Marta. "Sergey caught him and brought him home. He is tending to Hans."

"Good heavens," exclaimed Herr Zweig. "Here, sit thee down. Elisabeth rests quietly now. I shall care for the animals, both ours and yours. Ye can have a woman's talk." He left quickly, before Marta could thank him.

Both women sat at the Zweigs' rough table. Marta leaned forward, her head in her hands.

"I know not what to do," she said.

"To open thine house is not the difficulty," said Olga. "To open thine heart after pain, that takes true courage."

"I thought I could forgive him. When I thought he was dead, I desired the chance to forgive him, but once I saw him . . ." She sat up straight. "I shall not . . . I cannot open my heart to him again," she said. She dropped her arm to the table, suddenly remembering why she had come. "How fares Elisabeth?"

"She has a cold. Nothing more. My husband panicked." Olga

brought Marta a steaming cup of broth. "Drink this. Thou art tired and have not cared for thine own needs."

Tears began to stream down Marta's face as she took her first sip. The liquid warmed her from the inside.

Olga continued, "It relieved me that Elisabeth's illness is not serious. Herr Zweig told me that he would dig her grave and mark it with a beautiful carved stone, if it came to that. He is a loving husband. I dug all four graves for my children. With every shovelful of dirt, I hated my first husband more, but my hate hurt him not. In his stead, my hate hurt me."

Olga stood up and moved around, avoiding Marta's eyes. Clutching her hands in front of her, Olga took a deep breath and turned to look Marta in the eyes. Olga's eyes brimmed with tears and her words sounded choked and forced. "Marta, I clung to my bitterness as if 'twere my right. I found not God's peace, for I refused to forgive. Now Herr Zweig shows me God's love. His example shamed me, and I asked for God's help to forgive Ian for the pain he brought to me and our children. Now I am free, and I have joy. Marta, let not bitterness steal thy joy."

"I feel too weary to think," said Marta. She stood. "I must return to Hans."

Olga caught her arm. "No. First ye must rest." She led her to a mat, and Marta did not protest. Although her mind was swirling, within moments she was asleep.

It was evening by the time Marta awoke. Olga made her eat, and then Herr Zweig escorted her home. They did not speak, but his awkward pat on her arm just before she descended to her home told her of his concern. It was almost like having one of her brothers back.

Marta took a deep breath and entered the house. It smelled of strange odors. Carl was working over Hans, laying something on his chest. Hans was coughing, and she could hear loose rattling in his chest instead of the dry hacking of before.

"Does he breathe easier?" asked Marta. She forgot that she had promised herself never to speak to Carl again.

"He is not well yet," said Carl, "but he has improved."

Marta looked at Carl. His eyelids were heavy.

"I have rested," she said. "Go lay yourself down. I shall tend to Hans."

"First we must talk." Carl yawned.

"My only concern now is Hans," said Marta. "'Twould be best to save your words and sleep." Carl stared at her for a moment and then went to lie down. Marta released a breath that she did not know she was holding. She was not ready to talk. She prayed, "Forgive me, Lord. Help me."

Hans's eyes partially opened and then closed. "Water?" he said in a gravel-filled voice.

Marta quickly gave him a drink. He tossed and turned, and then settled into sleep. She touched his forehead. His fever had broken. Tears rose to her eyes. Hans was going to live.

All night, she was wide awake with thoughts that fought for control of her mind. Could she ever forgive someone who had hurt her and Hans so much? She nodded. Yes, she would. She had to. God had forgiven her. She must forgive Carl. But what mischief did he plan this time? Was he lying? How could she ever trust him? How could she live through it should he leave her again?

By morning, she was exhausted. The moment Carl got up, she said, "I need to leave . . . to find brushwood."

He nodded, though she knew her excuse did not fool him. He spread the frayed patchwork on the table and fingered the symbol in the center square. "My father's family crest," he said. Marta slipped into her sheepskin cloak as Carl continued, "My father gave this to my mother before he died, after she forgave him of his cruelty to her. My mother slipped it in with my belongings on the day I left."

Marta was tempted to wait and hear more of what Carl had to say, but she hurried out the door. She needed time to think. Heading away from the settlement, she walked and walked, unsure of where she was going until she ended up near the banks of the river. She stood, listening for God's voice in her heart, yet hearing nothing.

"Help me," she prayed again. "Lord, if You would have me trust him yet again, You must show me how. Help me to forgive him for good and all."

"Frau Ebel," said a deep voice near her ear.

Marta startled and took a step backward. It was Sergey. "Hello."

"Good day." He smiled.

"I thank you for your kindness to Hans." Marta gave him a brief smile.

"I do not for Hans," he said. "I do for you. You good woman."

She smiled. "I thank you for your words. It is good of you to stay out all night to help us."

Sergey took another step forward. "Why you keep man who love you not?" His words seemed to mimic her thoughts only moments before. "He no deserve you." Sergey came closer, and, looking into his hard eyes, Marta realized her mistake. This man was not her friend.

"He is my husband," said Marta. "I vowed to stand by him." She stepped back. "Sir, I must go."

She turned to leave, but he grabbed her arm and spun her toward him.

Sergey's eyes looked wild, almost desperate. "I man of great patience. Please say my time to wait it is over." Marta glanced around her. No one was near.

"I would to you love show. I would leave you not." Sergey clamped her to him with a single arm around her waist. "Have you, I must." Marta screamed as he tried to kiss her.

His face tightened in anger. "You keep him over me?" With his free hand, he pulled open her cloak.

Marta struggled as everything became clear to her. Suddenly, she knew what she wanted in her life. She wanted Carl and Hans. They were not perfect, but she wanted them more than she had wanted anything else in her life—and she wanted to get away from the madman who was clutching at her.

As the fabric of her dress began to tear, Marta heard Carl's deep voice say, "Release her." Sergey's hands immediately stopped, and

Marta wrenched herself away as she yanked her coat back into place.

"You have forget who authority is here," said Sergey, but his voice did not sound as certain as his words.

"You forget that she is my wife," said Carl. "That makes me the ultimate authority over her. Marta, go home." The strength of Carl's words should have comforted her, but she had never seen him look so angry. She knew that if she left without him, he would kill Sergey.

"I shall go home, husband," she said, "if you will accompany me." She would not have Sergey's blood on her hands, no matter how vile a person he was.

Silence.

"Carl. Please."

"Very well," said Carl. Marta breathed a sigh of relief.

"Stupid Germans you." Sergey pointed at Marta. "You, Frau, why you take liar and thief?" Then he stabbed his index finger toward Carl. "And you, fool man. After escape across Volga, you back here come. Nyemtzky. For woman? For fool stupid woman?"

Carl's fist made contact with Sergey's mouth. The man fell to the snow-covered ground with a thud. Blood splattered onto his clothing.

"If you ever touch or speak ill of my wife or child again," said Carl, "not even a woman's merciful heart shall turn my wrath from you."

Carl was glad that Sergey's next words were spoken in Russian so that Marta could not understand him. "You think you've won this battle, but you haven't. You'll rot out here, all of you. Your settlement shall disappear like others have before you. You'll die from the weather, or marauders, or your own fears. You've lost, Ebel. You've lost, and you don't even know it."

Carl took Marta's arm and the two of them left Sergey lying in the snow with Russian curses spewing from his mouth.

Marta's heart felt as if it had grown larger than it had ever been in her life. She looked sideways at Carl. "You were not captured? You returned to me of your own accord?"

"Yes." Carl cleared his throat. "Herbert killed a Khirgiz warrior who was about to murder me. When the man and his companions fell, we both knew that we had to go home. Herbert headed west, and I rode all night and then crossed the river this morning to get back to you and Hans. I couldn't get here fast enough. I wanted to be home with you, my beloved wife, more than I ever wanted anything else in my life."

Marta hoped that he was telling the truth. He had said the words she had always wanted to hear, but she did not know how to feel or what to believe.

Awkwardly trying to fill the time while she thought everything through, she said, "I thank you for your aid. You have rescued me many times since we first met." She took a sudden breath. "Oh no! If you are here with me, then Hans abides alone."

"Olga came over shortly after you left." Carl seemed a little embarrassed. "The moment she came, I knew I had to find you. I felt the Spirit of God urge me to make haste and run to your aid."

"God?"

Carl took Marta's hands. "Marta, I felt Him speak to me, the God of Abraham. And something else happened out on the river. I was given the desire to know Him . . . and His Son, the Messiah."

Marta's mouth opened, but no words escaped. There was too much to ask him, too many hopes that waited in the depths of her being, too much forgiveness pouring out of her heart.

"When I left," Carl said, "you and Hans came with me. Here." He touched his heart. "I realized that we would always be a family, whether we were together or not. When Herbert and I parted, he took with him a message of love and reconciliation for my mother, and I came to deliver my message to you in person. Marta, please forgive me for all I've done to hurt you. I love you."

Marta closed her eyes and took a deep breath. She remembered the first time she had seen Carl, a man of the world who had risked imprisonment to help her hide in a barrel. How much they had both changed. So much of what she had prayed for had come true. She would trust the Lord for the rest. She leaned into Carl.

He encircled her with his arms. "If I were to live my life without you, Marta, it would be a life only half lived. Will you be my wife, my true beloved, until death?"

Marta felt a glow rising to her cheeks. She nodded.

Carl's brown eyes seemed to penetrate Marta's heart. He lowered his face to hers, and their lips met for the first time. No matter what hardships might stand in the way, they would build a new life here—together, with the help of God—on the steppes of the Volga River.

⁓

Authors' note: Although the Kirghiz attacks on German settlers did not begin until 1771, references to the attacks have been included in this story in order to offer a more complete picture of the suffering the Volga Germans endured during the early years of their time in Russia.

Glossary

bol'shoe spasibo. Russian for "many thanks."

brötchen. German for "roll."

da. Russian for "yes."

dummkopf. Derogatory German word meaning "stupid" or "dummy."

izba. Russian for "house."

krautfresser. Derogatory word German immigrants called Russians, meaning "cabbage gobblers."

kwass. A fermented drink made from rye and barley over which the Russians poured warm water before drinking (also spelled "kvass").

mon cheval. French for "my horse."

mutter. German for "mother."

Nyemtzy. Derogatory term Russians called German colonists, meaning "stupid" or "dummy" (singular: Nyemtz).

ou mon ange guardien. French for "or my guardian angel."

Où? Où suis-je. French for "Where? Where am I?"

Quel stupide! French for "What a stupid one!"

Sascha. Russian name meaning "helper and defender of mankind."

sbiten. Russian-brewed drink made from honey and herbs.

snyek. Russian for "snow."

Stoj! Russian for "Halt!"

vater. German for "father."

verst. 0.6629 miles.

zemlyanky. Russian for "underground dwellings."

For Further Reading Concerning the Volga Germans in Russia

Bartholomew, Mary. *Sabina's Dream: A Story of a Girl with Volga-German Heritage.* Bisbee, AZ: Bandera, 1966.

Beratz, Gottlieb. *The German Colonies on the Lower Volga.* 1914, 1923. Reprint, Lincoln: AGSBR, 1991.

Casson, Lionel. *Illustrated History of Ships and Boats.* Garden City, NY: Doubleday, 1964.

Cross, Anthony. *By the Banks of the Neva.* Cambridge: Cambridge University Press, 1997.

————. *Russia Under Western Eyes 1517–1825.* London: Paul Eled Productions, 1971.

Giesinger, Adam. *From Catherine to Khrushchev.* Lincoln: AHSGR, 1974, 1981.

Honnef, Hans Peters Verlag. *Lübeck: Ansichten Aus Alter Zeit.* Rhein-Druckstöcke: Roland Myer, 1959.

Iroshnikov, Mikhail P., et al. *Before the Revolution.* New York: Abrams, 1991.

Keller, Conrad. *The German Colonies in South Russia.* Vol. 2. Translated by Anthony Becker. 2d ed. Lincoln: AHSGR, 1983.

Kloberdanz, Timothy J. *The Volga Germans in Old Russia and in Western North America: Their Changing Worldview.* Lincoln: AHSGR, 1979. First printing was in *Anthropological Quarterly* 48, no. 4 (1975).

Kock, Fred C. *The Volga Germans in Russia and the Americas from 1763 to the Present.* 3d printing. University Park, PA: Pennsylvania State University Press, 1978.

Landström, Björn. *The Ship: An Illustrated History.* Garden City, NY: Doubleday, 1961.

Roosevelt, Priscilla. *Life on the Russian Country Estate: A Social and Cultural History.* New Haven: Yale University Press, 1995.

Stumpp, Karl. *The German Russians.* Translated by Professor Joseph S. Height. Trostberg, Germany: A. Erdl KG, 1967.

Villiers, Marq de. *Down the Volga: A Journey Through Mother Russia in a Time of Troubles.* New York: Viking, 1991.

Walters, George J. *Wir Wollen Deutsche Bleiben: The Story of the Volga German.* Edited by Christopher Walters. Updated by Charles Walters. Kansas City, MO: Halcyon House, 1982, 1993.

Weigel, Lawrence A. *The Weigels Family History 1763 . . . 1996.* Self-published.

MAGAZINES AND JOURNALS

Giesinger, Adam. "Back to the Beginning: A Visit to the Volga Colonies in 1765," *Journal of AHSGR* 16, no. 4 (Winter 1993): 15–24.

Goral, Verna. "Before They Left Germany," *Journal of AHSGR* 14, no. 4 (Winter 1991): 5–10.

Janke, Leona Schmidt. "Eastward Migrations of Germans," *Journal of AHSGR* 16, no. 3. (Fall 1993): 9–12.

Jedig, Hugo. "The Germans in Russia During the First Fifty Years of the Soviet Regime." Translated by Nancy Bernhardt Holland. *Journal of AHSGR* 14, no. 4 (1991): 5–10.

PAMPHLETS

"Facts About Germany." Societäts-Verlag.

Weber, Frederick R. "German Russian Shanty." Circa 1890–1930, Historic Centennial Village. Greeley, CO.

WEB SITES

American Historical Society of Germans from Russia: www.ahsgr.org.

Cyndi's List: Germans from Russia: www.cyndislist.com/germ-russ.htm#History.

Germans from Russia Heritage Society: http://www.grhs.com.
The Germans from Russia: http://www.prairiepublic.org/features/
    GFR/index.htm.
The Volga Germans: A brief history: www.lhm.org/LID/lidhist
    .htm.